## SNOWBOUND

When the Sacramento heist turns sour, the three gunmen head for the Sierra Nevada mountains to the safe house they had set up for themselves in the small village of Hidden Valley. There is a storm approaching and the residents there are preparing for Christmas. None of them have any idea of the killers in their midst. Rebecca Hughes is too busy dealing with her faithless husband. John Tribucci and his wife Ann are getting ready for the birth of their first child. And all Zachary Cain wants to do is drink himself into forgetfulness over the death of his family. None of them are prepared for three desperate men who decide to pull the ultimate heist—and hold an entire town hostage!

## GAMES

Senator David Jackman needed to get away for the weekend, and he had just the spot in mind—the family island, a secluded spot off the coast of Maine. And he had just the person in mind to join him—his free-spirited mistress, Tracy. But once they arrive, nothing seems right. All the guns are missing from the house. They find a couple of dead animals, ritualistically slaughtered. Then their boat is stolen. Soon, suspicion turns to terror as David and Tracy are stalked by two deadly and possibly deranged adversaries. The Old Man had always told David that life is a game, but if that is the case, this could be the biggest game of all—and the final one!

# snowbound
·············
## games

### two mysteries by
# BILL PRONZINI
Introductions by Marcia Muller
and Robert J. Randisi

STARK
HOUSE

**Stark House Press • Eureka California**

SNOWBOUND / GAMES

Published by Stark House Press
2200 O Street
Eureka, CA 95501, USA
griffinskye@sbcglobal.net
www.starkhousepress.com

Distributed by SCB Distributors.

SNOWBOUND
Originally published by G. P. Putnam's Sons
and copyright © 1974 by Bill Pronzini
Reprinted by permission of the author.

GAMES
Originally published by G. P. Putnam's Sons
and copyright © 1976 by Bill Pronzini
Reprinted by permission of the author.

"A Biased Introduction" copyright © 2007 by Marcia Muller

"A Rose by Any Other Nameless" copyright © 2007 by Robert J. Randisi

ISBN-10: 1-933586-19-2
ISBN-13: 978-1-933586-19-9

Cover type set in Radiant Bold Extra Condensed. Text set in Figural and Dogma.
Cover design & book layout by Mark Shepard, shepardesign.home.comcast.net
Proofreading by Rick Ollerman

*The publisher would like to thank Bill Pronzini for all his help on this project.*

First Stark House Press Edition: November 2007

0 9 8 7 6 5 4 3 2 1

# CONTENTS

# A BIASED INTRODUCTION

by Marcia Muller

I am married to Bill Pronzini, so you probably assume I have a personal bias toward his work. This is true. However, when I first read the two novels contained in this volume, I was an aspiring writer with a lot of time on my hands to both read and write—a result of being totally unemployable. Bill Pronzini was merely a name to me, although I had heard tales of him through the leader of a writers' group I frequently attended: he'd begun writing young, selling his first short story at 22; at 27 he'd gotten the news of the sale of his first novel, THE STALKER, while on his way to Majorca, Spain, to which he and a friend had been lured by a European firm to write material of dubious repute. He sounded...interesting.

I'd read the first few books in his "Nameless Detective" series—the first in a book club edition without a dust jacket, so I didn't see the label the publisher had given the series, and wasn't even aware that the character had no name until I picked up a second book, one that did have a jacket. Now that, I thought, was real skill: to make the reader bond so thoroughly with a character that it didn't matter if he had a name.

Bill has always been the sort of writer to take risks. He's tried his hand at many different types of fiction—westerns, science fiction, and mainstream fiction—as well as series detective novels and stand-alone thrillers. He's also penned hundreds of short stories and essays, edited numerous anthologies, and written several nonfiction books, including a five-pound tome in collaboration with me, 1001 MIDNIGHTS. I weighed it once; you could use it as a doorstop.

But back to the beginning, to those days when I had more time for reading than I do now. A friend had recommended both SNOWBOUND and GAMES, and I read them back-to-back over the course of a weekend. The books had a profound affect on me. I came away with various impressions: of evil and heroism; of extreme and frightening isolation; of a flawed or damaged person's ability to triumph over seemingly impossible adversity and emerge stronger and/or redeemed. And for the rest of that weekend, I simply could not get warm; the icy chill of snow and fog that respectively permeates SNOWBOUND and GAMES had crept into my bones.

My impressions of these novels had faded over the past 31 years (I frequently can't remember either the titles or details of my own early work), and frankly, I was concerned that a rereading prepratory to writing this introduction would show that the books did not hold up over time—especially since Bill, like most good writers, has reservations about his early work. Much to my delight, I found them to be as good as they had been on that long-ago weekend—better, even, because I have grown as a writer myself and thus can appreciate things that had not caught my attention back then.

The closed environment of each book is impressive. SNOWBOUND takes place in a remote valley in the Sierra Nevada; when an avalanche closes off the one road out, the scene is set for terrifying events. GAMES is set on a private island far off the coast of Maine; when the only boat on the island disappears, two visitors are trapped, and the sinister games begin.

SNOWBOUND is told from the viewpoint of several of the small valley town's residents, as well as from the viewpoints of the criminals who arrive to hide at a safehouse on a nearby lake following a botched robbery. Evil emanates from the leader of this trio—enough to chill you even if the winter atmosphere doesn't. The residents are all flawed in one way or another and coping with personal demons. An outsider has rented a cabin there, looking for a refuge from his grief and guilt, only to earn the enmity of the townspeople who resent his standoffish ways. A wife is tormented by her husband's infidelities, but cannot quite summon the courage to leave him. Strange events have taken place recently, including someone breaking into the town's cafe and taking nothing, but spoiling produce and supplies by leaving the door open to the elements. And, as is typical of small towns, rumor is rife, and people are not exactly what they seem....

Enter the criminals, at first only waiting for the police interest in them to die down. But when the avalanche occurs and isolates the valley for an indefinite time, their leader devises an elaborate plan to take over the town and rob the citizens and businesses. When they put their plan into action, the mettle of each of the residents is tested as it never has been before; their true strengths and weaknesses are revealed, their lives forever changed—some for the better, others for the worse.

Unlike SNOWBOUND, GAMES is told from the viewpoint of one person: Senator David Jackman, a man who views life as a series of manipulative games, which he has learned to play exceedingly well. Jackman invites his mistress Tracy to accompany him for a romantic getaway on the private island where he spent happy summers as a child. But someone else is on the supposedly unoccupied island, and what originally seem to have been harmless pranks turn sinister once they find the boat they arrived in has gone missing. When the games become deadly, Jackman is forced to call upon strengths he never knew he possessed to stay alive, and he begins to question the tenets by which he has lived.

This volume is a particularly good pairing, because the two novels are completely different treatments of the theme of trial and redemption that appears frequently in Bill's work. They are also swiftly paced and peopled with characters you can care about and root for. I love them, as I love all of Bill's books (well, except for one western which I've consistently refused to read just to annoy him). I think you will, too.

PETALUMA, CA
MARCH, 14, 2007

# A ROSE BY ANY OTHER NAMELESS

by Bob Randisi

My heavy interest in reading mysteries began in the mid to late sixties. It's no coincidence, then, that Bill Pronzini's first short story was published in 1966. I started reading him back then, especially enjoying his private eye stories as they appeared in digests such as *Mike Shayne Mystery Magazine, Alfred Hitchcock's Mystery Magazine, Shell Scott Mystery Magazine* (which published his first story, "You Don't Know What It's Like."), etc. With each story I wondered when his first novel would come, and if it would feature his "Nameless" private eye? Then in 1971, there it was. THE STALKER was not a Nameless novel, but a riveting suspense novel that gave just a small hint as to what this man would soon do with his God given talent to tell stories.

The second novel, THE SNATCH, finally introduced Nameless to the novel reading public. (Those of us who read short stories had already met him.) Finally, a Nameless novel, and many more would follow. But the third book to follow was THE JADE FIGURINE, written as "Jack Foxx." I had already read the short story by the same name in AHMM in 1970, so I knew it was a Pronzini novel and grabbed it up.

In 1975, when I became a published author and joined the Mystery Writers of America, I met Bill Pronzini and told him of my intention to become a Pronzini "completist." He wished me luck. Little did I know he would soon outdistance me as I fought valiantly to keep up. Now, years later, his output is prodigious, and we are once again being treated to a couple of the early books, the suspense novels GAMES and SNOWBOUND.

Bill's ability to see-saw back and forth between first person, character driven P.I. novels and the third person, plot driven suspense novel is impressive. He gave a hint of it with his first three novels.

In 1975-76 three suspense novels in a row appeared from Bill—the aforementioned GAMES, SNOWBOUND, and also THE RUNNING OF THE BEASTS, written in collaboration with Barry N. Malzberg. All three novels could have been what in the business are called "breakout" books. They were all tautly written, deftly plotted, expertly conceived, and well reviewed. With the right kind of handling they might have become bestsellers, might have catapulted Bill Pronzini onto the bestsellers lists. They did not, through no fault of Bill Pronzini's. He had done his job, as he had and has always done. A writer's job—to entertain.

As a reader you may believe that it is the desire of every writer to become a best seller. You'd be wrong. It is the desire of every writer to entertain his or her readers. In this respect Bill succeeds every time out of the box. "Nameless" is now one of the longest running private eye series in history. And with books like 2006's THE CRIMES OF JORDAN WISE he is still writing suspense novels worthy of being best sellers. And after more than 40 years Bill Pronzini remains one of the finest entertainers in our business.

Writer, entertainer... a rose by any other.... And me, as a reader I'm still running, trying to keep up with the master. He keeps me entertained... but exhausted.

CLARKSVILLE, MO
JULY 2007

# snowbound

By Bill Pronzini

For BRUNI, who suffered too;
And for CLYDE TAYLOR, who had faith and several good ideas;
And for HENRY MORRISON, Agent 001

# Book One

Monday, December 17,
Through Saturday, December 22

> Whenever the door of hell opens,
> the voice you hear is your own.
>
> —Philip Wylie
> *Generation of Vipers*

# One

Mantled with a smooth sheen of snow, decorated with tinsel and giant plastic candy canes and strings of colored lights, the tiny mountain village looked both idyllic and vaguely fraudulent, like a movie set carefully erected for a remake of *White Christmas*. The dark, winter-afternoon sky was pregnant with more snow, and squares of amber shone warmly in most of the frame and false-fronted buildings; despite the energy crisis, the bulbs strung across Sierra Street burned in steady hues. On the steep valley slopes to the west, south and east, the red fir and lodgepole pine forests were shadowed, white-garbed, and as oddly unreal as the village itself.

A car with its headlamps on came down through the long, cliff-walled pass to the north—County Road 235-A, the only road presently open into or out of the valley—and passed the pine board sign reading: HIDDEN VALLEY • POPULATION 74 • ELEVATION 6,033. Just before Garvey's Shell, where the county road became Sierra Street, the car moved slowly beneath the spanning Christmas decorations, past the Valley Cafe and Hughes' Mercantile and the Valley Inn and Tribucci Bros. Sport Shop. When it reached the All Faiths Church, at the end of the three-block main street, it turned into the fronting lot and then swung around to the small cottage at the rear: the Reverend Peter Keyes, home from the larger town of Soda Grove, eight miles to the north, where he had relatives.

Diagonally across from the church—beyond the village proper, beyond Alpine Street and the house belonging to retired County Sheriff Lew Coopersmith—was a long, snow-carpeted meadow. In its center a boy and a girl were building a snowman, their breaths making puffs of vapor in the thin, chill air. Traditionally, they used sticks for ears and arms and a carrot for a nose and shiny black stones for vest buttons and eyes and to form a widely smiling mouth. Once they had finished, they stood back several paces and fashioned snowballs and threw them at the man-figure until they succeeded in knocking off its head.

Sierra Street continued on a steady incline for another one hundred and fifty yards and Y-branched then into two narrow roads. The left fork was Macklin Lake Road, which serpentined through the mountains for some fifteen miles and eventually emerged in another adjacent community known as Coldville; deep drifts made it impassable during the winter months. Three miles from the village was the tiny lake which gave the road its name, as well as a large hunting and fishing lodge—closed and deserted now, eight days before Christmas—that catered to spring and summer tourists and to seasonal sportsmen. The right fork, cleared by the town plow after each heavy snowfall, became Mule Deer Lake Road and led to a greater body of water two miles to the southwest, at the rearmost corner of the valley. Near this lake were several summer homes and cabins, as well as three year-round residences.

The third valley road was Lassen Drive. It began in the village, two blocks west of Sierra Street, extended in a gradual curve a mile and a half up the east slope, and then thinned out into a series of hiking paths and nature trails. Hidden Valley's largest home was located on Lassen Drive, a third of the way up the incline; nestled in thick pine, but with a clear view of the village and the southern and western slopes, it was a two-storied rustic with an alpine roof and a jutting, Swiss-style veranda. Matt Hughes, the mayor of Hidden Valley and the owner of Hughes' Mercantile, lived there with his wife, Rebecca.

Five hundred yards above was a small A-frame cabin, also nestled in pine, also with a clear view, also belonging to Matt Hughes. Neither the Hugheses nor any of the other residents of Hidden Valley knew much about the man who had leased the cabin late the previous summer—the man whose name was Zachary Cain. They had no idea where he had come from (other than it might have been San Francisco) or what he did for a living or why he had chosen to reside in this isolated valley high in the northwestern region of California's Sierra Nevada; he offered no information, he was totally reticent and unknowable. All they knew for certain was that he never left the valley, ventured into the village only to buy food and liquor, received a single piece of mail every month and that a cashier's check for three hundred dollars, drawn on a San Francisco bank, which he cashed at the Mercantile. Some said, because of the quantity of liquor he bought and apparently consumed each week, that he was an alcoholic recluse. Others believed he was an asocial and independently well-off eccentric. Still others thought he was in hiding, that maybe he was a fugitive of one type or another, and this had caused some consternation on the part of a small minority of residents; but when Lew Coopersmith, on the urging of Valley Café owner Frank McNeil, checked Cain's name and description through the offices of the county sheriff, he learned enough to be sure that Cain was not wanted by any law enforcement agency—and then dropped the matter, because it would have been an invasion of privacy to pursue it further. As a result, the villagers finally, if somewhat grudgingly, accepted Cain's presence among them and left him for the most part strictly alone.

Which was, of course, exactly the way he wanted it.

He sat now, as he often did, at the table by the cabin's front window, looking down on Hidden Valley. He was a big, dark man with thick-fingered hands that gave the impression of power and, curiously, gentleness. The same odd mixture was in the long, squarish cast of his face and had once been in his bar-browed gray eyes, but the eyes now were haunted, filled with emptiness, like old, old houses which had been abandoned by their owners. Brown-black hair grew thickly, almost furlike, on his scalp and arms and hands and fingers, giving him a faintly but not unpleasantly bearish appearance. The image was enhanced by the gray-flecked beard he had grown five months earlier for the simple reason that he no longer cared to continue the daily ritual of shaving. The waxy look of the skin pulled taut across his cheekbones and beneath his eyes added ten false years to his age of thirty-four.

The cabin had two rooms and a bath, with knotty pine walls and thick beams that crisscrossed the high, peaked ceiling. It was furnished spartanly: in the living room, a small stone fireplace, a settee with cushions upholstered in material the color of autumn leaves, a matching chair, a short waist-high pine breakfast counter behind which were cramped kitchen facilities; in the bedroom, visible through an open door on the far side of the room, an unmade bed and a dresser and a curve-backed wicker chair. There were no individual, homelike touches anywhere—no photographs or books or paintings or masculine embellishments of any kind; the cabin was still the same impersonal tourist and hunters' accommodation it had been when he leased it.

On the window table in front of Cain was a bottle of bonded bourbon, a glass containing three fingers of the liquor, a package of cigarettes, and an overflowing ashtray. The only times he moved were to lift the glass to his mouth or to refill it when it became empty or to light another cigarette. It was very quiet in the cabin, but he could hear the cold clean humming of the wind as it blew across the face of the slope, fluttering snow from the branches of the trees and tugging querulously at the weatherstripping around the glass. And he could hear, too, from time to time, the faint strains of the recorded Christmas carols which constantly emanated from the Mercantile's outside loudspeakers and which, owing to the thinness of the air, were sometimes audible even this far above the village.

As had happened before in the past two weeks, each of them brought forth memory fragments from the bright corners of his mind....

> Oh come all ye faith-ful, joy-ful and tri-um-phant,
> Oh come ye, oh co-o-me ye, to Be-e-eth—le-hem....

...Angie singing those words softly, sweetly, as they trimmed the tree the year before, smiling, that question-mark loop of gold hair hanging down over her left eye, her face slightly flushed from the hot-buttered rums they'd drunk earlier, and Lindy tugging at the hem of her dress, dancing up and down, saying, "Mommy, Mommy, let me put the angel on top, let me put the angel on top!"

and Steve hanging his stocking on the mantel, very intent, very careful, the top of his small tongue held catlike in the open space between his missing front teeth....

Si-i-ilent night. Ho-o-ly night,
All is calm, all is bright,
Round yon vir-r-gin, Mother and Child...

...Angie's voice again, softer, reverent, while all of them sat in the darkened living room and looked at the winking lights of the tree, the kids drowsy but refusing to give in because they wanted to wait up for Santa Claus, Angie's voice making the words into a lullaby that finally put them both to sleep, and he and Angie carrying them upstairs and putting them to bed and then tip-toeing downstairs again and setting out the presents, filling the stockings, and, when everything was arranged, going up to their own room and lying close, holding each other in the silent, holy night....

Cain got abruptly to his feet, shoving his chair back, and carried his glass away from the window. He stood unsteadily in the center of the room, look-ing at the fireplace, and it reminded him of the one in the house near San Francisco's Twin Peaks, the house that no longer was. He turned away and went across to the breakfast counter and around it into the kitchen area for a fresh package of cigarettes. Spasmodically, he tore off the cellophane and got one of the cylinders into his mouth and began patting the pockets of his Pendleton shirt. His matches were on the table. He went over there again, sat down, lit the cigarette, drained the bourbon from his glass; then he stared again into the valley, refusing to hear the faint carols now, concentrating on what he saw spread out before him.

White world, soft world, clean world; snow had a way of hiding the ugliness and disguising the tawdry trappings of humanity, of creating the kind of beau-ty a whore creates with makeup and the right kind of lighting. Here, in this idyllic, fanciful little valley, you could almost believe again in Christmas and God and Peace on Earth, Goodwill to Men; you could almost believe life had meaning and was worth living, and that there was hope and joy and justice in the world. But it was all illusion, it was all a lie. There was no God and there was no peace, and there was no justice; there was nothing to believe in, there was nothing left at all.

Cain picked up the bourbon bottle and poured himself another drink.


SACRAMENTO

The three of them went in for the ripoff at two thirty, exactly half an hour before the scheduled arrival of the armored car.

The place was called Greenfront—one of those cash-and-carry super-department stores where you can buy anything from groceries to complete

home furnishings—and it was located on the northern outskirts of Sacramento. A former employee had dropped word in the right places in L.A., eight
weeks before, that he was willing to sell a detailed package on the complex.
Kubion had picked up on it immediately; he was a planner, an organizer—
between jobs and looking for something ripe and solid—and on paper the job
looked pretty good. He gave the guy an initial finder's fee of five hundred, told
him there'd be another two thousand if a score developed, thought things over
for a while and figured a three-man team, and went to talk to Brodie. He'd
worked with Brodie before, and he was sharp and dependable and had a mul-
titude of talents, like being a good wheel man and having contacts that could
supply you with most anything short of a tank; Brodie was looking, too, and
said he liked the sound of it so far, count him in. They talked over who to get
for the third man. Both of them wanted Chadwick; but Chadwick was unavail-
able, and so were two others they tried, and finally they had to settle for Loxner. Loxner was big and bluff and slow-witted and knew how to take orders well
enough, but the thing about him, like the thing about a lot of strong arms in
the business, he was tough only when things were moving smoothly and he
was behind the gun. If there was any kind of fight, the word was he went to
mush inside and maybe you couldn't depend on him to do anything except
crap his shorts. Still, he'd been around a long time and had only taken one fall,
and that said something for him right there. So they talked to him, and he was
free and hungry, and that made the team complete.

That Monday the three of them had driven up to Sacramento to look things
over. A single surveillance of the afternoon ritual with the armored car, using
binoculars from a copse of trees to the rear, convinced them that the job was
not only workable, it was a goddamn wonder somebody hadn't ripped the
place off long before this. Kubion evolved a full-scale plan right away, but they
hadn't wanted to use it if there was an alternative method; the financing
would be heavy and would cut deeply into the take. They visited the store several times, individually and in pairs, and they camped in the trees for three
successive Monday afternoons. But they couldn't find another way to do it that
was as clean and sure as the original. They even considered hitting the
armored car instead, but that was a dangerous and by no means simple or
guaranteed proposition—particularly since the car operated strictly within
residential and business districts. And there wouldn't be any more money in
the store by doing it that way, since the car delivered each payload to one bank
or another after making a pickup.

For reasons known only to its management, the armored car company did-
n't necessarily use the same guards on the same run each Monday. And, con-
versely, their signal for admittance to Greenfront never varied: one long, two
short, one long on the bell beside the rear entrance door. These two facts, discovered during surveillance, convinced the three of them finally to take Greenfront according to Kubion's initial plan. With the method of operation settled,
they agreed to pool their slim cash reserves in order to eliminate outside
financing and an even larger slice off the top, and went to work setting it up.

Brodie knew something about photography and spent two days outside the company's offices in downtown Sacramento, taking unobtrusive color photographs of the guards and of the type of armored car used by the firm. When the pictures were developed and blown up, Kubion took the ones of the cars to a mechanic Brodie knew in San Francisco, and the mechanic thought it over and decided he could make a dummy, for around eight thousand, that would pass any but the closest inspection. Then Kubion went to L.A. with the photos of the guards, to a costumers again supplied by Brodie, and put out another two thousand on three duplicate guard uniforms, three sets of simple theatrical disguises, and six money sacks of the type utilized by the armored car concern. Brodie handled the weaponry, through a safe gunsmith in Sacramento; he bought three .38 caliber Colt New Police revolvers, the same model carried by the guards, and a Smith & Wesson Model 39 automatic, .38 caliber, as a backup. On each of the subsequent three Mondays, Brodie followed the car which serviced Greenfront—one stop each week, using different rented vehicles on each occasion, to avoid the possibility of detection; by this means, he learned that the stop just prior to Greenfront was a place called Saddleman's Supermarket, two miles from the department store complex.

The former Greenfront employee had supplied a detailed map of the office as part of his finder's package, and the three of them went over it several times to be sure they knew exactly what to expect once they were inside. The rear entrance, through which the armored car guards were admitted to the building, opened on a set of stairs. At the top was a second door, also kept locked, and beyond there was the office: windowed cubicle occupied by the store manager, six desks manned by the general staff. One door leading down into the store proper, to the far left as you entered from the rear. Safe in the same wall as that door, vault type, to which both the manager and the chief accountant had the combination. Thick plate-glass window beginning waist-high in the fronting wall, which looked down on the aisles and departments and checkout counters on the main floor. Seven employees, plus two armed uniformed security officers—one of those the one who came downstairs to admit the armored car personnel. Two other guns in the building, one each to two additional security cops stationed on the main floor. No alarm system of any kind.

There was no problem in any of that, no problem at all once they got inside. The only sweat was the dummy armored car. They would have to drive it to Greenfront, leave it in plain sight in front of the door for the estimated fifteen minutes it would take them to complete the job, and then drive it away again afterward; but that couldn't be helped, and the score was plenty large enough to warrant the risk.

With Greenfront being open twelve full hours on both Saturday and Sunday and with the armored car coming only once a week, they figured that between a hundred and a hundred and twenty thousand would be awaiting transfer on this Monday afternoon. There might have been more money in the safe the following Monday, Christmas Eve, but it wouldn't be a great deal more; and on Christmas Eve there was always a traffic problem—last-minute shoppers, the big rush—which meant increased police patrols. And according to the finder's package, Greenfront sometimes put on extra security guards just before Christmas. This Monday, then, was the best time for the hit.

Brodie found a garage for rent on a short-term lease, in an industrial area four blocks from Greenfront, and that minimized somewhat the risk with the dummy car; he wore one of the theatrical disguises while visiting the realtor and paid the deposit in cash. Also, as a final precaution, Loxner arranged for a safe place to ground, in an isolated section of the Sierra called Hidden Valley. It was there they figured to make the split and to spend a week or so letting things cool down before they separated.

The week before, Kubion and Brodie had driven up to this Hidden Valley and established residence—two San Francisco businessmen on a combination vacation and work conference, they said—so that they would not be complete strangers when they came back after the job; and when they came back, Loxner would keep out of sight: still two men, not three, to ensure further that none of the locals would tie them in with Greenfront. Brodie and Kubion returned to Sacramento on Friday, and the mechanic delivered the dummy car inside a storage van late Saturday night, directly to the rented garage. There had been nothing to do then but wait for Monday afternoon....

They left the garage at two twenty-five, with Brodie driving and Kubion beside him and Loxner in back. Each of them wore one of the disguises: false mustaches and sideburns and eyebrows, putty noses, cotton wadding to fatten cheeks and distort the shape of the mouth. They saw no police units in the four blocks to Greenfront. Fifty yards beyond the office entrance at the rear was the loading dock, with a couple of semis drawn up to it and warehouse-men pushing dollies back and forth on the ramp; none of the men glanced at the armored car as it pulled up and parked.

Brodie went around and opened the rear doors, and Loxner came out with the empty money sacks. The two of them stepped up to the door, while Kubion stood watching by the right rear fender. Loxner pressed the bell, one long and two short and one long, and they stood there under the dark afternoon sky, waiting for the security cop to come down.

It took him two minutes, twenty or thirty seconds longer than usual because they weren't expecting the armored car for another half hour. He opened the peephole in the door and stared out through the thick glass covering it and saw the car and the three uniformed men—everything exactly as it was sup-posed to be. Satisfied, he worked the locks and swung the door open and said, "You guys are pretty early, aren't you?"

"There's a fire over on Kingridge," Brodie told him. "Big warehouse right across the street from Saddleman's. They've got the streets blocked off, hoses and pumpers everywhere, and we can't get in. So the company told us we might as well go ahead with our other rounds."

"Fires in the middle of December," the guard said, and shook his head. "Well, everything's just about ready upstairs, but you might have to wait five or ten minutes."

"Sure, we expected that."

The guard stepped aside to let Brodie and Loxner enter. When they were past him, he turned and started to close the door—and Brodie's left hand slapped across his mouth, jerking his head back; the swiftly drawn revolver jabbed him sharply in the small of the back. Softly, Brodie said, "You make a funny move or say anything above a whisper when I take my hand away, and I'll kill you first thing. Believe it."

The guard stood motionless, his eyes wide and abruptly terrified; he had a wife and three kids, and he was no hero.

Kubion glanced out at the loading dock and saw that no one on the ramp was looking in his direction. The area was otherwise deserted. He drew his own gun and shut the door, leaving it unlocked. "All right," he said to the guard, "who opens the door up there? You or the other guy in the office?"

Brodie took his hand away, increasing the pressure of the Colt. The guard's throat worked three times before he found words, thickly hushed. "My partner. I tell him it's okay and he opens up."

"That better be right," Kubion said. "If it isn't, you're a dead man."

"It's right."

"Fine. Now when we go into the office, you keep your mouth shut. Don't do or say anything. We'll take it from there."

Convulsively, the guard nodded. Kubion pushed him over to the stairs, and they went up single file. At the top, the guard called out, "Okay, Ben," and there was the scrape of a key in the lock. The heavy steel-ribbed door opened, and the other security cop stood before them with his hands in plain sight. Kubion shoved the first one into the office, moving to one side so that Brodie and Loxner could enter, covering the startled second guard.

"Everybody just sit tight," Kubion said sharply. "No panic, no screams, no heroics."

"It's a holdup, my God!" somebody said, and one of the two women employees gasped—but the two guards just stood there staring at Kubion's gun. Brodie fanned immediately to the left and watched the rigid office staff sitting at their desks; none of them made further sounds. Loxner was at the open door to the manager's cubicle, eyes and gun on the fat, white-faced man who had gotten to his feet within.

For a long moment the office was a fixed tableau fashioned of fear and disbelief. Then Kubion—smiling, thinking that they were going to get it done well within their allotted fifteen minutes—gestured to the manager and said, "Come out here and open the safe. Quick, no arguments." Obediently, woodenly, the fat man stepped out of his cubicle and started across the office.

And that was when the whole thing went suddenly and completely sour....

# Two

It began to snow again just after Lew Coopersmith left his house and walked over to Sierra Street.

He pulled the collar of his mackinaw high on the back of his neck, moving more quickly under the thickening flakes. Like most residents of Hidden Valley, he did not particularly mind the snow, but then neither did he relish walking or driving in it, especially when the snowfall had been as heavy as it had this winter.

Lean and tall and durable, like the lodgepole pines on the valley's eastern slopes, he was sixty-six years old, felt forty-six, and surprised his wife, Ellen, every now and then by knocking on the door of her room just after bedtime and asking her if she felt like having a go. There were squint lines at the corners of his alert green eyes and faint creases paralleling a stubby nose, but his narrow face was otherwise unlined. His hair, covered now by a woolen cap, was a dusty gray and showed no signs of thinning. Only the liver spots on the backs of his hands and fingers hinted of his age.

For twenty-two years, up to his retirement four years before, he had served as county sheriff. Police work had been his entire life—he had been a highway patrolman in Truckee and Sacramento and then a county deputy for eleven years before finally being elected sheriff—but he had always looked forward with a kind of eagerness to what were euphemistically termed his Leisure Years. And yet retirement had developed into something of a hollow reward. Shortly after he finished his final term, he and Ellen had moved from the county seat to Hidden Valley—an area both of them had decided upon sometime earlier—and almost immediately he had felt a sense of impotence, of uselessness. He found himself constantly wondering how his former deputy and the new county sheriff, Ed Patterson, was handling things and took to driving over to the county seat periodically and stopping in to talk about this and that, strictly social, Ed, you understand. Even after four years, he still dropped in on Patterson now and then, as he had done when Frank McNeil and some of the others had gotten their backs up about Zachary Cain, the loner type who had moved into the valley the previous summer.

The trouble was, he didn't know what to do with himself. There was always plenty to do when you were an officer of the law, dozens of things to occupy your time, some excitement to life; but in Hidden Valley, what the hell was there? Reading and smoking your pipe in front of the fireplace and puttering in the basement workshop and watching television and bulling with the locals and the seasonal tourists at the Valley Inn and driving up to Soda Grove occasionally to take in a movie—weekend and evening pastimes, shallow pursuits void of significance or commitment. He felt severed from the ebb and flow of life, put out to pasture. Good Lord, sixty-six wasn't *old*, not when you felt forty-six and your mind was just as sharp as ever and you had always been a doer, a man involved, a man empowered. His retirement very definitely had been premature, but the decision could not be unmade and he would have to go on making the best of it, just as he had done for the past four years.

When he reached Sierra, Coopersmith turned right off Shasta Street and went into Tribucci Bros. Sport Shop. In season, the Tribuccis dispensed large quantities of bait, outdoor wear, licenses, and fishing and hunting accessories to visiting sportsmen; now, in winter, the bulk of their business was in winter sports equipment (on a limited local basis), as well as in tobacco products, newspapers, magazines, and paperback books.

The younger of the two brothers who operated the store, John Tribucci, was alone behind the counter at the far end. In his middle thirties, he had a strong, athletic body and shaggy black hair and warm brown eyes under slightly canted lids; he also had a ready smile and a large amount of infectious energy. When he wasn't tending the shop, he was usually skiing or ice skating or tramping around the woods in a pair of snowshoes or fly fishing for trout or, when he could find the time, backpacking into the higher wilderness elevations of the southern Sierra: Owens Lake and Mount Baxter and the John Muir Wilderness. In an age of electronic depersonalization and ecological apathy and teeming cities and developments which had begun to spread over the land like malignant fungi, Coopersmith thought that any man who took pains to maintain his own identity, who loved and thrived on nature in all her majesty, was worthy of admiration and respect; he accorded both to John Tribucci.

Coopersmith asked, after they had exchanged greetings, "How's Ann today, Johnny?"

"Fat and impatient, same as ever," Tribucci said, and grinned. His wife was eight and a half months pregnant with their first child—a major event in their lives after eleven years of nonconception. "Make you a bet she gives birth on Christmas Day."

"As much as you want a son for Christmas? No way." Coopersmith winked at him. "Give us a can of Raleigh and a couple packages of pipe cleaners, would you, Johnny?"

"Coming up." Tribucci took the items from the shelf behind the counter, dropped them into a plastic sack, and made change from the five Coopersmith handed him. He said then, "Snowing again, I see. If it keeps up like this, we're liable to have a slide to contend with."

"Think so?" Coopersmith asked, interested.

"Well, the last time we had this much snow—back in sixty-one—there was a small one that blocked part of the pass road; those cliffs will only hold so much before some section or other weakens and gives way. Took the county road crews four days to clear through, the longest we've ever been snowbound."

"Seems I recall, now that you mention it. Nice prospect."

"Inconvenient, all right, but there's nothing you can do to stop an avalanche if one decides to happen. With less snow, though, we should make it through okay."

"Ah, the joys of mountain living," Coopersmith said dryly. He picked up the plastic sack. "See you later, Johnny."

Tribucci laughed. *"Ciao.* Give my best to Ellen."

"Will do."

Coopersmith went out and walked farther north on Sierra, crossing Mooc Street. The snow, slanting down off the western slope on the cold wind, clung icily to his mackinaw and trousers. Except for two cars and a delivery van parked against the two-foot windrows along each curb, packed by the village's single snowplow, the street and sidewalks were empty. But he saw three customers inside the Mercantile as he passed: Webb Edwards, Hidden Valley's only physician—a quiet, elderly man given to wearing Western-style string ties; Sally Chilton, Edwards' part-time nurse; and Verne Mullins, another retiree in his sixties who had spent forty-five years with the Southern Pacific Railroad. The store was the largest in the village and supplied groceries and hardware items and drug sundries; it also housed the Hidden Valley Post Office. Holly wreaths and sprigs of mistletoe decorated both halves of the front doors, and a huge, flat cardboard Santa Claus and two cardboard reindeer had been erected in one of the long facing windows.

Between Lassen Drive and Eldorado Street, diagonally across from Garvey's Shell, the windows of the Valley Café cast scintillas of bright light into the dark afternoon. Within the glow, the flakes of falling snow were like particles of white glitter. Coopersmith paused under the jutting front eaves of the building, brushed his clothing and stamped clinging snow from his booted feet, and then pushed the door open and went inside.

The interior was a single elongated room, with yellow plastic-covered booths and vinyl-topped tables along the left wall and a long lunch counter fronted by plastic stools along the right. In the center of the wall above the counter was a huge, varnished, bark-rimmed plaque, cut from a giant sequoia, on which was lettered the menu in neat white printing. The glaring fluorescent tubes overhead gave the cafe a sterile, slightly self-conscious appearance.

None of the booths was occupied, and only two of the stools; sitting side by side midway along the counter were Greg Novak, a long-haired, brittle-featured youth in his early twenties who worked for Joe Garvey and who also operated the village snowplow, and Walt Halliday, owner of the Valley Inn—plump, mild-eyed, wearing black-rimmed glasses which gave him a falsely studious look. Behind the counter were Frank McNeil and his sixteen-year-old son, Larry; the youth, recruited to help out during Soda Grove High School's Christmas vacation, as he had been during each summer vacation the past few years, was washing dishes in a stainless-steel sink at the far end, and McNeil stood talking to Novak and Halliday. Dressed all in white, like a hospital orderly, the café owner was a ruddy complexioned man in his mid-forties, with a blunt face and bristle-cut red hair. In addition, he possessed a sordid sense of humor and a complaining attitude: Coopersmith did not much care for him. But his food was good, his coffee even better than Ellen's, and he was therefore tolerable for short periods of time.

The three men glanced up as Coopersmith entered and called out greetings. He lifted his hand in acknowledgment, slid onto a stool three away from Halliday. "Coffee, Frank," he said.

"Sure thing." McNeil drew a mug from the urn on the back counter, set it before Coopersmith, put a spoon beside it, and immediately went back to stand in front of Novak and Halliday.

"As I was saying," he said to them, "Christmas shopping is a pain in the ass."

"Well, I don't know about that," Halliday said. "I kind of get a hoot out of it. How come you're so down on Christmas, Frank?"

"It's all a bunch of commercialized bullshit, that's why."

"Listen to Scrooge here."

Novak said, "So what did you find for your wife in Soda Grove, Mr. Halliday?"

"One of those clock radios, the kind that comes on automatically like an alarm in the mornings and plays music instead of ringing a bell in your ear."

"Sounds like a nice gift."

"She'll like it, I think."

"You'd probably of done better to get the same thing I'm giving my old lady," McNeil said.

"What would that be?"

Without bothering to lower his voice in deference to the presence of his son, McNeil answered, "Well, I'll tell you. It's maybe six, seven inches long and what you call durable, guaranteed not to wear out if you treat it with care. You can use it any time of the year, and the old lady appreciates it more than anything else you can give her. And the best thing about it, it doesn't cost you a cent."

"That's what *you* think," Halliday said, smiling.

"Only one problem with a gift like that, though."

"What's that?"

"I ain't figured out how the hell I'm going to wrap it."

The three men burst out laughing, and Coopersmith sipped his coffee and wondered what had happened to the spirit of Christmas. When he had been young, Yuletide was a time of innocent joy and genuine religious feelings. Now it was as if Christmas had evolved, in no more than half a century, into a kind of wearisome though bearable space-age anachronism: people going through the motions because it was what was expected of them, worshiping mechanically and superficially if they worshiped at all, no longer caring, no longer seeming to understand what it was all about. And so there were dirty jokes and scatological remarks told in all manner of company, and everybody laughed and pretty much agreed that it was just a bunch of commercialized bullshit, can't wait until it's over for another year; it made you feel angry and sad and a little ashamed.

McNeil came down to stand in front of Coppersmith, still chuckling, his face red and damp in the too-warm air circulating through the café's suspended unit heater. "Need a warm-up, Lew?"

"No, I don't think so. Thanks."

McNeil leaned forward, eyes bright, eyes leering. "Say, Lew, you hear this one? I like to bust a gut laughing first time I heard it, and same goes for Greg and Walt there. There's this eight-year-old kid, see, and he wakes up about 2 A.M. Christmas morning. So he goes downstairs to see if Santa Claus has come yet, and sure as hell old Santa is there. But what he's doing, see—"

Coopersmith got abruptly to his feet, put a quarter on the counter, and went out wordlessly into the falling snow.

McNeil blinked after him for a moment and then turned to look imploringly at Novak and Halliday. He said, "Now what in Christ's name is the matter with *him?*"


SACRAMENTO


Somebody knocked on the door, the one connecting the office and the interior of the store below.

The fat manager stopped moving, his head turned toward Kubion; the tableau froze again, thick and strained with suddenly heightened tension. There was a second knock, and Kubion thought: If we don't open up, whoever it is is going to figure something's wrong. He gestured to Brodie, who was nearest the door.

The guard who had let them in downstairs said in a liquid whisper, "It's locked, I've got the key."

Brodie stopped, half turning, and Kubion said to the guard, "Get the hell over there, then; watch where you put your hands. When you get the door open, stand back out of the way."

The guard crossed the office, wetting his lips nervously, taking the key from the pocket of his trousers. Brodie stepped back three paces, up against the wall beyond the door. A third knock sounded, insistent now, and then ceased as the guard fitted his key into the lock. A moment later he pulled the door inward, stepping back away from it.

"What took you so long?" a voice said in mild reproof from the landing outside.

The guard shook his head, not speaking.

A shabbily-dressed, frightened-looking woman came first into the office, clutching a handbag in both hands; behind her was another uniformed security officer, one of the two normally stationed on the floor below. He was saying, "Caught this lady here shoplifting in Household Goods. She had—"

When he saw Kubion and Loxner and the guns they were holding, he frowned and stopped speaking. The guard who had opened the door said stupidly, "It's a holdup, Ray," and the floor cop reached automatically and just as stupidly for the gun holstered at his belt.

"Don't do it!" Kubion yelled at him, and Brodie came away from the wall, trying to get around the shabby woman, trying to keep the operation from blowing. But the guard had committed himself; he got the revolver clear and brought it up. The shabby woman began to scream. Brodie knocked her viciously out of the way, and the cop fired once at Loxner, hitting him in the left arm, making it jerk like a puppet's; then he swung the gun toward Brodie.

Kubion shot him in the throat.

Blood gouted from the wound, and he made a liquid dying sound and went stumbling backward into the fronting window; the barrel of his back-flung gun and the rear of his head struck the glass, webbing it with hairline cracks. The shabby woman sprawled against one of the desks, screaming like a loon. The manager was on his hands and knees crawling behind another of the desks, and the other employees had thrown themselves to the floor, hands over their heads, the two women moaning in terror. Like ash-gray sculptures, the two office guards stood motionless. The shrieks of the shabby woman and the echoes of the shots and the sudden startled shouts filtering up from the floor below filled the office with nightmarish sound.

There was no time for the money now, the whole thing was blown; they had no choice except to run. Brodie came over to the rear door immediately, went out onto the landing, but Loxner kept on standing by the cubicle with bright beads of sweat pimpling his face and his eyes glazed and staring at the dark-red stain spreading over his khaki uniform sleeve just below the elbow. Kubion shouted at him, "You stupid bastard, move it, move it!" Loxner's head pulled around, and he made a face like a kid about to cry; but he came shambling forward then, cradling his left arm against his chest. Kubion caught his shoulder and shoved him through the door.

"Stay the fuck in this office, all of you," he yelled. "We'll kill anybody that shows his face!" He backed out and slammed the door, turning, and Brodie and Loxner were already running on the stairs. Kubion pounded down after them. Brodie reached the lower door first and threw it open and the three of them burst outside. Two warehousemen and a truck driver were coming toward them from the loading dock. Brodie fired wide at them, and they reversed direction in a hurry, scattering. Loxner tried to drag open the armored car's front passenger door with his right hand still holding his gun; Kubion elbowed him viciously out of the way, opened the door, pulled him back and crowded him inside while Brodie ran around to the driver's side. There were half a dozen men in the vicinity of the dock now, but they hung back wisely, not attempting to interfere.

The dummy armored car started instantly, and Brodie released the clutch; the tires bit screamingly into the pavement. He took the far corner of the building in a controlled power skid, went through the parking lot at fifty and climbing. At the nearest exit a new Ford had just begun to turn into the lot from the street. Brodie swung the wheel hard right and the armored car's rear end slewed around and made contact with the Ford's left front fender, punching the machine out of the way, spinning it in a half circle. Fighting the wheel, Brodie slid the heavy car sideways again as a Volkswagen swerved to avoid collision. The armored car straightened and began pulling away, made another power skid left at the first intersection, and all the while Kubion sat hunched forward on the seat, saying, "Son of a bitch, son of a bitch, son of a bitch!" in a kind of savage litany.

# Three

Smiling with his usual charismatic boyishness, Matt Hughes handed the Reverend Peter Keyes his mail through the gated window of the Post Office enclosure.

"Yesterday's attendance in church was very good, Reverend," he said. "Your idea of moving the commencement time up to noon was a good one."

"I expect the fact that this is the Christmas season had more to do with the rise in attendance than the new hour," the Reverend Mr. Keyes said. He was a short, round, benign-featured man, reminiscent of a somewhat scaled-down and clean-shaven Santa Claus: an accurate physical reflection of the inner man and of his spiritual leanings. Hughes thought of him fondly as the antithesis of the fire-and-brimstone mountain preacher of legend and fact. "But in any event, it *was* gratifying. One can only hope this coming Sunday's attendance will be larger still, though I suppose one hundred percent of the able-bodied is too much to hope for."

"Maybe not, Reverend. I'll make a point to remind the good people of the valley as I see each of them this week."

"Thank you, Matthew," the Reverend Mr. Keyes said gravely. He was the only resident of Hidden Valley who called Hughes by his full given name. "Well, I've several things to attend to. I'll see you again tomorrow."

When the Reverend Mr. Keyes had gone, Hughes left the Post Office enclosure and came around the long counter set parallel to the Mercantile's rear wall. The store was empty now, except for his single full-time employee, matronly and white-haired Maude Fredericks, who was stacking canned goods in the grocery section which comprised the northern third of the wide, deep room. The old-fashioned potbellied stove set to the right of the counter glowed dull-red warmth through its isinglass door-window—putting that stove in three years ago had been a very wise idea, he thought; it gave the place a kind of country-general-store flavor that appealed to locals and tourists alike and the Christmas music added a different but no less pleasant warmth to the surroundings.

Hughes smiled complacently and went to stand by the cardboard Santa Claus in one of the front windows. Outside, the snow swirled and danced in gusts of wind like shifting patterns in a monochromatic kaleidoscope. Mountain winters had always fascinated him—the soft, fat, intricately shaped snowflakes, the trees bending under their heavy white coats, some whiskered with stalactitic icicles like strong old men braced against the winter wind; snow eddies such as those he was watching now, so capricious you felt like laughing in the same way you would at the antics of kittens. As a child, he had used to sit for hours, face pressed to window glass, absorbed in the white splendor without, and when his mother would come in and ask him what he found so intriguing, he would answer her the same way each time, a kind of game they had played: "Snow magic, Mom; snow magic."

At the age of thirty-two, he still retained the aura of that same perpetually enthusiastic little boy. The slope cornered tan mustache he had worn for two years added a certain maturity to his features—as did the vertical humor lines which extended downward from a Romanesque nose and, like a pair of calipers, partially encircled a wide, mobile mouth; but his bright blue eyes and the supple slimness of his body and the demonstrative way he used his hands when he talked were prominently indicative of bubbling and guileless youth.

Nonetheless, he was unquestionably Hidden Valley's wealthiest and most respected citizen. In addition to owning the Mercantile, which he had inherited from an uncle ten years before, and in addition to having served two successive terms as mayor, he owned a thousand acres of mountain land lucratively leased to a private hunting club, a portfolio of blue-chip stocks, and a high five-figure bank account. He was married to a woman considered by most everyone both intelligent and enviably attractive: an equally substantial form of wealth. If he had been an ambitious man, he might have left Hidden Valley for less secluded surroundings—might have entered successfully into the larger business world or perhaps even into politics. But he was not ambitious, and he derived a great deal of contentment from his position of importance in the valley. To enhance it, he offered unlimited credit to regular customers, maintained a "banking" service for the cashing of personal and business checks, could be counted upon for a loan in any emergency, and regularly contributed money to the All Faiths Church and to civic betterment projects. It was, he sometimes thought, a little like being the benevolent young monarch of a very small, very scenic, and very agreeable kingdom.

Behind him, now, the telephone began ringing distantly in his private office. Without turning from the window, he called, "Maude, would you get that, please?"

"I'm on my way, Matt," she answered. Her footsteps sounded on the wooden flooring, and after a moment the ringing ceased. The loudspeakers began to give out with "Deck the Halls." Maude's voice called above the music, "It's your wife."

Hughes sighed. "Okay, thanks."

He crossed the store and stepped behind the counter again. Small and neat, his office was nestled in the far right-hand corner adjoining the storeroom; it contained a pair of file cabinets, a glass-topped oak desk, and an old-fashioned, black-painted Wells-Fargo safe, bolted to the floor and wall, in which he kept his cash on hand. Entering, closing the door behind him, he cocked a hip against the edge of the desk and picked up the phone receiver and said, "Yes, Rebecca?"

"I just called to tell you we're out of coffee," his wife's voice said. "Would you bring a pound of drip grind home with you tonight?"

"I think you'd better come down and pick it up, dear. I won't be home after closing."

There was a brief silence; then Rebecca said, "Oh?"

"I have to go over to Coldville," he told her. "I was going to call you a little later to let you know."

"Why do you have to go to Coldville?"

"Neal Walker called and asked me to come. He wants to discuss some civic problem or other he's having."

"Mayor to mayor, is that it?"

"Yes."

"I see. And wives aren't allowed?"

"You'd be bored, dear, you know that."

"I suppose I would."

"I'll probably be late. Don't wait up."

"No, I won't," she said, and broke the connection.

Hughes replaced the receiver, sighed again, and then went around the desk and sat down in his leather armchair. He pyramided his fingers under his chin and sat that way for several minutes, lost in thought. Then, abruptly, he straightened, picked up the telephone again, and dialed a Soda Grove number.

A woman's soft young voice said, "Grange Electric, good afternoon."

"Hello, Peggy. Can you talk?"

"Yes. Is something the matter?"

"No, not a thing. I just wanted to talk to you."

"Well, you'll be seeing me in another three hours."

"I know that. I've been thinking about it all day."

She laughed softly. "What were you thinking?"

"You *know* what I was thinking."

"Yes, but tell me anyway."

"I'll tell you when I see you. I'll *show* you."

"Oh, yes, I can imagine you will."

Hughes moistened his lips, and his breathing was thick and rapid. "You know something?" he said. "This conversation is giving me an erection. I never thought a man could get an erection talking to a woman over the telephone."

The girl named Peggy laughed again. "Well, don't lose it, okay? I'll see both of you at six or a little after."

"At six," Hughes said. He waited until she had rung off and then reached out almost reluctantly to recradle the receiver for the second time. Using a handkerchief from the pocket of his gray wool slacks, he wiped away a thin sheen of perspiration which had formed on his forehead; then he stood up and went out again into the front of the store.

Over the loudspeakers, the Mormon Tabernacle Choir was singing about love and faith and the spirit of Christmas.


*SACRAMENTO*

When they were two blocks from Greenfront and he was certain they had no immediate pursuit, Brodie slowed the armored car to the legal speed limit.

Time was a precious commodity, but they couldn't buy any of it if they drew attention to themselves getting the dummy back to the rented garage.

The alley off which the garage was located had both its entrances on parallel industrial streets crowded with trucks and vans. Brodie made the turn onto the nearest of them without seeing any sign of a police car and drove a block and a half to where the alley mouth bisected the block to the left. Kubion, watching the street in a flatly unblinking stare, said, "It looks okay; nobody paying any attention" and Brodie nodded and made the swing into the narrow opening between two high, blank warehouse walls.

Midway through the block, the alley widened to the right to form a small parking area; it fronted a weathered brick structure which had been independently erected between the rear walls of two warehouses. One-half of the building had a sign on it that said BENSON SOLENOID, MANUFACTURER'S REP. The other half was the garage.

They had left the doors open, and the area was deserted; Brodie drove the armored car inside without slowing. Kubion was out of the passenger side before the car had come to a full stop, closing the two wooden halves of the doors, barring them with a two-by-four set into iron brackets. Turning, he began to strip off his guard uniform, the false mustache and sideburns and bulbous putty nose he had been wearing. Brodie and Loxner, out of the car now, were also shedding their uniforms and disguises—Loxner one-handed, his left arm hanging useless at his side and ribboned with blood. His eyes still had a glazed look, etched with pain, and they wouldn't meet either Kubion's or Brodie's; but he'd kept his mouth shut, and he was functioning all right.

Their regular clothing was in a locked storage box at the upper end of the garage, along with the suitcases in which they had planned to carry the money. Kubion unlocked the box and took out one of the cases. Into it they put the disguises, because they didn't want the cops discovering they had worn them, and the .38 automatic Kubion had had tucked into his belt under the uniform jacket; the uniforms, which were untraceable, were allowed to remain discarded on the oil-splattered floor.

Brodie and Kubion got immediately into slacks, shirts, winter coats; then they transferred the New Police Colts into their coat pockets. Loxner took off his undershirt and tore it into strips with his teeth and his right hand and bound the wound in his arm. He had difficulty getting into his own clothing, but neither Kubion nor Brodie went to help him. With Kubion carrying the suitcase, the two of them moved past the dummy car—it, too, was untraceable, and they had worn gloves from the moment it was delivered to make sure it stayed clean of prints—and crossed to the double doors.

Loxner joined them, struggling into his coat, as Brodie took the bar away and cracked one of the halves. The area was still deserted. Hands resting on their pocketed guns, Kubion and Brodie led the way out and over to where they could look both ways along the alley. Clear. In the distance there was the fluctuating wail of sirens, but the sounds were muted, growing fainter, moving elsewhere.

Slightly more than six minutes had passed since their arrival at the garage.

They went to the right, straight through the block to the next street over. Kubion's car was where he had parked it that morning, a hundred feet from the alley mouth. When they reached the car, Kubion unlocked the doors and put the suitcase on the floor in the back; then he went to the trunk, opened it, removed a folded blanket, closed it again. He gave the blanket to Loxner.

"Lie down on the rear seat with this over you," he said. "Cops will be looking for a car with three men in it, not two."

Loxner still wouldn't meet his eyes. He said, "Right," and stretched out on the seat under the blanket, holding his wounded arm like a woman holding a baby. Brodie took the wheel. Sitting beside him, Kubion opened the glove box and took out the California road map and Sacramento city street map stored within. He folded them open on his lap.

If the job had gone off as planned, they would have taken Interstate Highway 80 straight through to Truckee and then swung north on State Highway 89—the quickest approach to Hidden Valley. But because they were professionals, covering against just such a blown operation as this, they'd also worked out a more circuitous route to minimize the danger of spot checks by the Highway Patrol. There was an entrance to Interstate 80 not far from where they were now, and they could still use that all right; it was only twenty-five minutes since the abortive ripoff, and the cops would need more time than that to organize and set up effective road-blocks. As soon as they reached the Roseville turnoff, eight miles distant, they would cut north on State 65 to Marysville, pick up State 20 to Grass Valley, and then take State 49 through Downieville and Whitewater and, finally, Soda Grove. It would double their time on the road, making the trip to Hidden Valley a minimum of four hours, but it would also put them well clear of the police search and surveillance area.

It took Brodie seven minutes to get them out of the warehouse district, swinging wide of Greenfront, and onto the cloverleaf that fed Interstate 80 eastbound. They saw no police cars until they came out of the cloverleaf and merged with the flow of traffic, and then it was a highway patrol unit traveling westbound with red light and siren, exiting the freeway on the same cloverleaf—alerted but no longer an immediate threat. Kubion had had his gun out and hidden beneath the bottom folds of his coat, but now he slid it back into the pocket. He lit a cigarette and made sucking sounds on the filter, pulling smoke into his lungs.

Brodie accelerated to pass a slow-moving truck. "So far so good," he said, to break the tense silence.

"We're not out of it yet," Kubion said thinly.

"Don't I know it?"

"Hold your speed down, for Christ's sake."

"Take it easy, Earl. You don't have to tell me how to drive."

From the back seat Loxner said, "You got anything in the glove box for this arm? It hurts like hell, and it's still bleeding."

"No," Kubion said.

"The bullet went clean through, but Jesus, it hurts."

"Yeah."

"I never been shot before," Loxner said defensively. "That's why I maybe froze up a little back there. You get shot like that, for the first time, it shakes the crap out of you."

"Yeah, yeah, shut up about it."

"Fucking security cop, fucking cop," Loxner said, and lapsed into silence.

Brodie held the speedometer needle on sixty. "A hundred grand, maybe more, shot straight up the ass. And we're out better than ten on top of it. Now what the hell do we do for a stake?"

"We'll make a score somewhere," Kubion said.

"Sure—but where?"

"You leave that to me. I'll think of something. I'll think of something, all right."

# Four

The light began to go out of the somber afternoon sky at four o'clock, dimming rapidly behind a thick curtain of snow, turning the pines and fir trees into wraithlike silhouettes on the steep slopes of Hidden Valley. Distorted by the snowfall, the brightening village lights—the multihued Christmas bulbs strung across Sierra Street—were hazy aureoles that seemed somehow to lack warmth and comfort in the encroaching darkness. And the thin, sharp wind sang lonely and bitter, like something lost in the wilderness and resigned to its fate.

That's me, Rebecca Hughes thought as she sat listening to the wind in the big, empty Lassen Drive house: something lonely and bitter and lost and resigned. A dull candle sitting in the window, waiting for the return of the prodigal. Alas, poor Rebecca, I knew her well....

She reached out in the darkness and located her cigarettes on the coffee table. In the flame of her lighter, the six-foot Christmas tree across the living room looked bleak and forlorn—colored ornaments gleaming blackly, silver tinsel like opalescent worms hanging from the dark branches: a symbol of joy that was completely joyless in the shadowed room. The furnishings, too, seemed strange and unused, as if they were parts of a museum exhibit; she had picked out the decor herself when she and Matt were married seven years before—Pennsylvania Dutch with copper accessories—and she had loved it then, it represented home and happiness then. Now it was meaningless, like the tree, perhaps even like life itself.

Turning slightly to light her cigarette, Rebecca saw her reflection in the hoarfrosted window behind the couch. She paused, staring at herself in the flickering glow. A pretty face once, an animated face, with laughter in the gray eyes and a suggestion of passion in the soft mouth. But in this moment, with her chestnut-colored hair pulled back into a tight chignon at the back of her neck, the face looked severe and weary and deeply lined; in this moment, she was a twenty-eight-year-old woman who was forty years of age.

She moved her gaze from the window, snapping the lighter shut and putting the room in heavy darkness again, thinking: I wonder who she is this time? Not that it matters, but you can't help wondering. Probably not a valley resident; Matt has always been so very careful to preserve his saintly image here. Young, of course. Large breasts, of course, he always did like large breasts, mine never quite appeared to suit him. My God—how insanely ironic if that were the reason behind it all! I'm sorry, Rebecca, your tits are much too small, I'm going to have to find a mistress or two or twenty, you *do* understand, don't you? Yes, certainly I understand, dear; I couldn't possibly expect you to be faithful to me when my boobs are so small, I'm only sorry they didn't grow larger so we could have had a perfectly happy marriage.

Well what difference did it make, really, why he did it? He did it, that was all. Pathetically, in her eyes like a child who thinks he's being very clever with his mischief; yes, like a child: pleasant, good-hearted, pious, playing an adventurous game and not quite realizing the wrongness of it, not quite realizing his own hypocrisy. When she had found out about the waitress in Soda Grove six years ago and confronted him with the knowledge, he had broken down and cried, head against her bosom, saying, "I don't know why I did it, Becky, it just happened, and I'm sorry, forgive me, I love you," and she had forgiven him, and four months later it had happened again; it had been happening ever since.

This particular little affair had been going on for about a month now. It had started like all the others, with a transparent excuse for not coming home in the evening, and it had progressed like all the others: Matt returning after midnight two and three and four times a week, with perfume lingering on his body and long hairs on his clothes (blond this time), falling into bed exhausted. He had not touched her, of course, since it began; he never touched her, never wanted her, never had anything left for her in any way. It would be like this for a while yet, a few more weeks. Then he would tire of the new girl, or she would tire of him, and the cycle would begin anew: an apology for his neglect, a few less than ardent nights (*she* had always been passionate, that couldn't be the reason for the endless string of mistresses), expensive gifts, a period of attentiveness—and then, just when she would begin to think she had a husband again, he would call her to say that he would not be home until late....

She had not bothered to confront him again after the Soda Grove waitress. He would have told her the same thing he had that first time, and have begged her forgiveness, and have professed his love for her. And the terrible thing was, she knew he *did* love her in some way she could never understand and did not want to lose her. He would never, as a result, leave her for one of the girls with whom he slept. Things would have been so much easier if there had been that possibility, Rebecca often thought; the decision would have been taken out of her hands. But it would never happen, and she had simply been unable to take the initiative herself: Little Orphan Rebecca with no place to go, no particular skills, a little afraid of the big wide world beyond these mountains where she had been born and reared; who could not seem to stop believing in love-conquers-all and happy endings and other fairy tales. So she forgave him tacitly each time and remained with him—enduring, pretending. Withering.

She felt suddenly very cold, as if the wind had managed to get inside the warm house; gooseflesh formed on her bare upper arms, beneath the short sleeves of the blouse she wore. Standing, putting out her cigarette in the cloisonné table tray, she went out of the dark room to the stairs in the main hall. The bedroom she shared with Matt was at the front of the house, directly above the living room. It, too, seemed cold and dismal to Rebecca tonight—and the wide, antique-framed double bed was a kind of index of her melancholy.

She did not turn on the lights. She could see well enough in the dark: walking half-blind through life or half-blind through a familiar house, easy enough to do once you got used to it. Crossing to the walk-in closet, she took out a heavy wool pullover and slipped it over her head. Then she stood for a moment, arms folded across her breasts, hugging herself. What now? she thought. Back downstairs to sit smoking by the window? Television? Soft music? Loud music? Another book? How about a hot bath—or, more appropriately, a cold shower?

She wished she knew how to sublimate. That was what modern women did, wasn't it? They sublimated their frustrations, they developed hobbies or joined committees or became Fem Libbers or played bridge or painted pictures or wrote stories or took jobs or studied astrology or Far East religions—things like that. Well, that was fine for modern women, but what about old-fashioned members of the "weaker sex" like Rebecca Hughes? She wasn't a collector, and she hated card games, and she had no artistic talent of any kind, and the only jobs you could get in an area such as this were prosaic and totally unrewarding, offering no mental commitment whatsoever. There were no committees or clubs in Hidden Valley, you had to go to Soda Grove, and besides, she was neither a joiner nor a mixer, and if that wasn't enough, she was afraid to drive any distance in snow and ice. She had no interest in astrology or Far East religions or any of the other passions of the Aware Woman. It was not that she was apathetic or incapable of individualism; she had always possessed a genuine fondness for literature and read extensively and considered herself well informed and had opinions and believed in certain causes. She belonged to several book clubs and regularly utilized the services of the mobile county lending library when it came through twice a month; she read until her eyes ached and her mind refused to grasp the meaning of words and sentences. And how much reading could you do? Too much—and not enough.

The simple truth was that she did not know how to sublimate; she was not modern, and she was not by any means "liberated." She recalled clearly enough the time she had decided she *was*, two years previously, and her resolution to strike back at Matt in the most fitting manner: by doing exactly what he was doing, sauce for the goose as well as the gander. Why not? she'd thought then. Why couldn't she, too, find solace and fulfill her needs in someone else's bed?

And so she had called Rae Johnson, a girl in Reno whom she had gone to school with, a blackjack dealer in one of the casinos and a self-proclaimed free spirit, and Rae had said, Sure, come on over. Rebecca had told Matt she was going away on a visit for a short while, and he said he thought that was a fine idea, it would do her good—very eager to get rid of her because he was in the middle of one of his affairs then. She took the bus to Reno from Soda Grove, and Rae conducted her on a tour of all the clubs and introduced her to several male friends, sensing that Rebecca had come for a fling without anything having been said about it.

She had liked the man named Doug, she could no longer remember his last name, the moment she'd been introduced to him. Witty, charming, intelligent, easy to talk to, and when he had asked her up to his apartment for a drink, she consented readily enough; she had done a lot of drinking that night—something she seldom did because she was prone to violent and prolonged hang-overs—and the liquor and the flashing neon and the bright sophisticated con-versation had apparently dissolved all inhibitions, and she had needed des-perately to be loved, it had been a long time then as it was a long time now. They sat together on his sofa and drank vodka gimlets, and he kissed her, put his tongue in her mouth, stroked her breasts almost casually—and all at once the euphoria and the anticipation and the passion faded away, and she was completely sober; she was like slick silver ice inside. She broke the kiss, and he looked at her smiling and suggested they go into the bedroom, and she could see the outline of his penis, half-erect, her eyes on him there and nowhere else, and fright spiraled inside her, and she couldn't go through with it, she simply could not go through with it. She pushed away from him, flushed and ashamed, straightening her skirt and blouse, putting on her coat, not looking at him at all then; and even though he did not protest, was in fact nonchalant in his mild defeat, she had had the abased feeling that he was silently laugh-ing at her.

She left Reno the next morning, not explaining to Rae because Rae knew by looking at her what the trouble was, and came back to Hidden Valley filled with the sense of resignation. There had been no more flings....

Aimlessly Rebecca left the bedroom and went downstairs, along the hallway into the bright copper-tone kitchen at the rear of the house. Again, she did not turn on the lights. She rummaged through one of the pine cupboards over the drainboard, looking for the coffee, and then remembered she had used the last of it during the afternoon—that was why she had called Matt, for God's sake. No coffee then, and how about a nice hot cup of tea? Yes, fine, and it did not matter in the least that she hated the taste of the stuff.

She filled a kettle with icy tap water, set it on the stove, and went back to stand in front of the drainboard, waiting in the darkness for the water to heat. As she stood there, she found herself staring through the window over the sink, through the snowy dark and the ghostly pines at the faint haze of light in the cabin five hundred yards farther up the slope. Zachary Cain, reticent recluse, she thought. Never talks to anyone, seldom leaves the cabin. Accord-ing to Matt, he buys five or six bottles of whiskey a week, which means he sits up there and drinks alone, and I wonder why, I wonder who he is?

When the water finally began to boil, she made the cup of tea and laced it liberally with sugar and carried it into the living room. As she sat again on the couch, she continued to wonder about the man named Zachary Cain—who he was, why he drank so much, what his reason was for coming to a place like Hidden Valley. And, even though it didn't really matter, couldn't really matter, if he too were somehow lonely.

# Five

Lying not-quite-drunk in the darkened cabin bedroom, Cain felt a sense of acute loneliness that was for the first time disassociated from Angie and Lindy and Steve.

The day had been another of the bad ones, filled with painful memories of his family that deepened what was an already mordant despair. But with the coming of darkness, those were not the only memories which had plagued him. Inexplicably, he found himself thinking of things he had locked away in a corner of his mind for the past six months.

There was his work, his abandoned profession. He had been an architect—a good one, a dedicated craftsman—and he recalled how it had been and how you could lose yourself in mathematics and blueprints and sheer creativity, and the way you felt when you saw one of your designs taking shape in wood and glass and stone, standing complete, an entity you alone had conceived.

There were the friends with whom he had willfully severed all relations, by disappearing from San Francisco without word shortly after the accident: Don Collins, another senior employee of the architectural firm for which he had worked and his closest friend; Bert Rhymer, whom he had known since their collegiate days at Stanford; Barry Kells, Fred Gaines, Walt Yamaguchi. And all the easy confidences they had exchanged, the interests they had shared, the laughter they had known.

There were the simple pleasures and relaxations, the little things that rounded out and made complete a man's life: the look of San Francisco, the multi-faceted jewel of lights that was The City on a warm spring or summer night; drinking ice-chilled beer and fishing languidly for bass beneath the cotton-woods and willows on the narrow waterways of the San Joaquin Delta; sailing on the Bay on bright windy afternoons, venturing under the Golden Gate Bridge and out onto the Pacific beyond Land's End for a glimpse of San Francisco as the seafarers saw it; reading books and viewing old movies on television and listening to the immortal threads of sound woven long ago by Bix and Kid Ory and Satchmo and W. C. Handy. These, yes, and a dozen more.

The memories flooded his mind unbidden, unwanted, and he could not seem to consume enough alcohol to drive them back into that mental corner. The loneliness was born then, selfish pathos, and because he didn't want it and could not reconcile it, he was angry with himself and almost desperately uneasy. The normality of his past life was dead and buried—he too was dead, inside where it counted—and even at Christmas, even if miracles were possible and the effort was worth making, you could not resurrect the dead. But the loneliness persisted, creating a senseless paradox: hollow man who wants and needs to be alone, and is lonely.

Cain lay motionless on the bed, with his face turned toward the closed door—vaguely aware of the thin strip of light filtering in beneath it, aware that he had not shut off the lamps when he'd quit the front room a few minutes earlier. The hell with it, he thought. The hell with the lamps. He moved his head in a quadrant then and stared at the closet door opposite. Inside, the 30.06 Savage was propped against the back wall, fully loaded, where he'd put it when he first came to Hidden Valley. He could not get up and go over there tonight any more than he had been able to do it any of the other nights. He simply did not have the guts to kill himself, the fact of that was inescapable; he had found it out on the evening three days after the accident, when he had left the hotel room in downtown San Francisco, driven out to Oyster Point, got the rifle from the trunk and loaded it and put the muzzle into his mouth, finger stiff on the trigger, and sat there for thirty minutes that way, sweat drenching him, trying to pull that trigger and not being able to do it. It would always be as it had been on that night—but that did not stop him from thinking about it, the single shot that would end all the suffering and allow him the same oblivion which he had through his carelessness inflicted on Angie, on Lindy, on Steve....

"Christ!" Cain said aloud, and reached over to drag the bourbon bottle and an empty glass from the nightstand. He poured the glass half-full, drank all of it in two convulsive swallows, gagged, felt the liquor churning hot and acrid in his stomach.

Lonely. Lonely!

He swung his feet off the bed and went shakily into the bathroom and knelt in front of the toilet and vomited a half dozen times, painfully. When there was nothing left, he stood up and rinsed his mouth from the sink tap, washed his face and neck in the icy mountain water. Then he returned to the bed and sprawled out prone, breathing thickly.

Angie and the kids, gone, gone.

But not architecture, not San Francisco, not Don Collins and Bert Rhymer—not *me*....

Lonely.

No!

Lonely, lonely, lonely....

# Six

In the living room of his brother's Eldorado Street house, John Tribucci sat with his wife, Ann, and played that fine old prospective-parents game known as Choosing a Name for the Baby.

"I still think," Ann said, "that if it's a boy, he should be called John Junior." She was sitting uncomfortably, hugely, on the sofa, one hand resting on the swell of her abdomen; beneath the high elastic waist of the maternity dress she wore even her breasts seemed swollen to twice their normal size. Long-legged and normally slender, she had high cheekbones and rich-toned olive skin and straight, silky black hair parted in the middle—clear testimony to her part-Amerind heritage, her great-grandmother having been a full-blooded Miwoc. Pregnant or not, she was the most beautiful and the most sensual woman Tribucci had ever known.

He said, "One Johnny around the house is plenty. Besides, I refuse to be prematurely referred to as John Tribucci, *Senior.*"

Ann laughed. "Well, then, there's always your father's name."

"Mario? No way."

"Andrew is nice."

"Then we've got Ann and Andy, the Raggedy twins."

"I also like Joseph."

"Joey Tribucci sounds like a Prohibition bootlegger."

She made a face at him. "You come up with the most incredible objections. You're still holding out for Alexander, right?"

"What's wrong with Alexander?"

"It just doesn't sound very masculine to me."

"Alex is one of the most masculine names I can think of."

"Mmm. But there have still got to be better ones."

"I haven't heard any yet."

"Well—the last time you seemed to like Stephen."

"But you weren't exactly overjoyed with it, as I recall."

"It kind of grows on you. I like John Junior better, but I guess I'm willing to compromise—for now, anyway."

"All right, for now it's Stephen. On to girls' names, since the unlikely possibility does exist that I've fathered a female."

"You," Ann said, "can be a damned male chauvinist at times."

"Guilty as charged."

"And balls to you, love. Okay, you didn't like Suzanne or Toni or Francesca, and I don't like Pamela or Jill or Judith. But I've been thinking and I came up with three new ones, all of which are pretty and one of which even you are bound to like. The first is Hannah."

"Somebody's German maid," Tribucci said. Then, when she glared at him:

"Just kidding, it's not bad. What's the second?"

"Marika."

"Better, much better. Marika Tribucci. You know, that has a nice ring to it."

"I think so, too. In fact, it's my favorite. But the third is also sweet: Charlene."

Tribucci had been smiling and relaxed in Vince's old naugahyde easy chair; now the smile vanished, and his eyes turned dark and brooding. He got to his feet and walked across to one of the front windows and stood looking out into the darkness.

Behind him Ann said, "Johnny? What's the matter?"

He did not answer, did not turn. Charlene, he was thinking. Charlene Hammond. It had been a long while since he had thought of her and the night on the deserted beach near Santa Cruz. The incident had been in his mind often for the first few months after it happened; but that had been thirteen years ago, when he was serving the last of his four-year Army stint at Fort Ord, and time had dulled it finally and settled it into the dim recesses of his memory. Even so, it had only taken Ann's innocent suggestion just now to bring it all back in sharp, unwelcome focus.

He had met Charlene Hammond in late July of that year, on the boardwalk in Santa Cruz. She'd been blond, vivacious, ripe of body and suggestive in her mannerisms; not particularly bright, but at twenty-two and living on an Army base, you don't really care about a girl's intelligence quotient. They'd had a few dates—dances, shows, summer events—and when they'd known each other for three weeks, she let him make love to her in the back seat of her father's car. He saw her again two evenings later, and that was the night they went to the beach—because the car was awkward and because they were young and there was something exhilarating in the idea of screwing out in the open with the ocean close by and the clear, vast sky overhead. Charlene had chosen the spot, and he'd known she had been there before for the same purpose; she hadn't been a virgin for a long time.

They parked the car on a bluff and descended to a sheltered place under the cliff's overhang where they couldn't be seen from the road above. There they had spread out a blanket and opened cans of beer, made out a little, taking their time, letting the excitement build. Still, neither of them wanted to wait very long, and excitement builds rapidly on a warm, empty night with the sound of the surf murmuring and throbbing in your ears.

They were lying in a tight embrace on the blanket, she naked and he with just his pants and shoes on, when the two motorcycles came roaring down onto the beach.

Startled, they broke apart, and Charlene fumbled for her clothing and made the mistake of standing up to put it on. The moonlight had been bright, and as clearly as he could see the cycles approaching, the two riders could see him and Charlene and Charlene's nakedness. The bikes swerved toward them. He had an instant premonition of danger; he grabbed her arm, tried to pull her away in a run toward the bluff path. But the cycles swung in hard turns, cut them off, forced them back to the overhang.

He saw, as the bikes pulled up in front of them and stopped, that the two riders were young, in their late twenties or early thirties, dressed in black metal-studded denim and heavy boots, one bearded, the other wearing a gold hoop earring. Charlene was crying, terrified; she had most of her clothing on again, but it was much too late—he knew it had been too late from the moment they'd been seen. He tried to talk to the two cyclists, and it was useless; they were either very drunk or flying on drugs. The bearded one told him to move away from Charlene, and he said no, he wasn't going to do that, and the one wearing the earring dropped a hand to his boot and came up with a long, thin-bladed knife.

"Move now, boyfriend," the bearded one said, "or both of you going to get cut. And we don't want to cut nobody, really."

Charlene screamed, clinging to him. The bearded one grabbed her wrist, spun her to him and held her. Instinctively he started to move to help her, but the knife jabbed forward, darting, pushing him back against the dirt and rock of the bluff. Charlene's cries then were near hysterical.

"Soggy seconds for you, man," the bearded one said to the other. "Watch boyfriend here until I'm done." And turned to Charlene and slapped her several times and pulled her over to the blanket and threw her down on it; tore her clothes off again, dragged his own trousers down. She kept on shrieking, and he kept on hitting her, trying to force her legs apart to get himself inside her. The one with the knife divided his attention between them and Tribucci, giggling softly.

He stood it as long as he could, held at bay by the knife and by fear. And then he simply forgot about the knife and forgot about being afraid and waited until the earringed one's attention had drifted once more to the struggle on the blanket, pushed out from the bluff at that moment, and kicked him between the legs with all his strength. The earringed man screamed louder than Charlene, dropped the knife, and bent over double. He kicked him in the face, kicked him in the head once he was down, turned. The bearded one had released Charlene and was trying to stand, trying to pull his pants up from around his ankles. He ran toward him, shouting, "Run, Charlene, run!" and saw her fleeing half-naked toward the path, and reached the bearded one and kicked him three times in the head and upper body and then threw himself on top of the man and hit him with his fists, rolled his face in the sand, hit him and hit him and hit him and hit him—

And stopped suddenly, because he had become aware of the man's blood spattered warm over his hand and forearm. He struggled to his feet, gasping. The bearded cyclist did not move. He turned to look at the other one: not moving either. One or both of them might have been dead, but he did not care one way or the other then; he just did not care. He walked to where the surf frothed whitely over the sand, knelt and washed the blood off himself; then he found his shirt, put it on, and went slowly up the path to the road. Charlene and the car were gone. He walked along the road for a mile or so to where three teen-agers in a raked station wagon responded to his outthrust thumb and gave him a lift down the coast to Fort Ord. He had been very calm the entire time; reaction did not set in until he was in bed in his barracks.

When it did, he could not seem to stop trembling. He lay there the entire night trembling and thinking about what had happened on the beach and asking himself over and over why he had done what he had. He was not heroic or even particularly brave. He had no strong feelings for Charlene. The two riders very likely had had rape and nothing else on their minds. Why, then? Why?

He had had no answer that night, and he had none thirteen years later; he had done it, and that was all.

The next morning he had called Charlene, and she'd asked him briefly if he was all right and how he'd got away and for God's sake he hadn't called the police, had he? Because she didn't want to get involved; if the police came around to her house, her father would throw her out on the street. She did not thank him, and she did not tell him she was sorry for having left him maybe hurt or dying, for not having summoned help. He hadn't seen her or spoken to her again.

For a week he combed every local newspaper he could find, and there was no mention of anyone answering the description of the cyclists having been found dead on the beach or anywhere else near Santa Cruz. So he hadn't killed one or both of them, and that knowledge had taken away some of the haunting immediacy of the incident and he had been able to begin to forget; he'd told no one—not Ann, not Vince, not his parents—about that night, and he never would....

"...Johnny, what is it? What's come over you?"

Ann had gotten up and crossed to stand beside him, and she was tugging at the sleeve of his shirt. Tribucci blinked and pivoted to her, saw the concern in her eyes—and the dark recollection faded immediately. He smiled and kissed her. "Nothing," he said, "just one of those brooding spells a man gets from time to time. It's finished with, now."

"Well, I hope so."

He put his arm around her and walked her back to the sofa. "I didn't mean to upset you, honey; I'm sorry, I won't let it happen again."

"You had the oddest look on your face," she said. "What could you possibly have begun brooding about when we—"

And the door to the adjoining family room opened, and Vince appeared, sparing him. Heavier and three years older, Vince wore thick glasses owing to a mild case of myopic astigmatism and was just beginning to lose his hair; for the past hour he and his wife, Judy, had been watching television, or what passed for television on a winter night in the Sierra.

"Just saw an early weathercast from Sacramento," he said. "There's a heavy stormfront moving in from the west, coming right at us. We'll likely be hit with one and maybe two blizzards this week."

"Oh fine," Tribucci said. "Great. A few more heavy storms without a long letup, and we'll sure as hell have slides before the end of the winter."

"Yeah, and I'm afraid at least one of them is liable to be major."

"You two sound like prophets of doom," Ann said. "Where's your Christmas spirit? This is supposed to be the jolly season, you know."

"Ho-ho-ho," Vince said, and grinned. "You people decide on names for your offspring yet?"

"We sort of like Stephen if it's a boy."

"And if it's a girl?"

Tribucci looked at Ann. "Henrietta Lou," he said. She threw a sofa pillow at him.

# Seven

Earl Kubion had a savage, pulsing headache when Brodie finally brought them into Hidden Valley at twenty minutes past eight.

They had been on the road for more than five hours, fighting snow and ice from the time they reached Grass Valley, forced to stop in Nevada City to put on chains, forced to drive at a reduced speed over the treacherous state and county roads. And even though they hadn't encountered any roadblocks or spot checks, and the three highway patrol units and two local county cruisers they had seen had paid no attention to them, Kubion sat tense and watchful the entire time, waiting for something that had not happened. Waiting and listening to the monotonous swish of the windshield wipers; listening to the radio newscasts on the robbery: Sacramento police and the highway patrol were making a concentrated search for the three holdup men, one of whom was reportedly wounded in the left arm; the armored car hadn't been found yet; the one security cop was dead and the woman shoplifter had suffered a nervous breakdown; citizens warned to be on the lookout—the same bullshit over and over again.

Waiting and smelling the heavy odor of Loxner's blood from the back seat, nauseating in the warm confines of the car. Waiting and smoking two packs of cigarettes in short, quick inhalations. He felt now as if his nerves were humming like thin wires in a storm, as if he wanted to hit something, hurt somebody; headaches like this affected him the same way each time: making him irrational, poising him on the edge of pointless violence.

Kubion had lived by and with violence for half of his forty-two years, but it had always been rigidly controlled, resorted to only when unavoidably necessary—as in the case of the Greenfront floor cop—and then in a calm, detached way so that he never lost his grip, relied on intellect to bring him through the fight. When he wasn't working, there had been no thoughts of and no inclination toward force and savagery; only soft, big-assed black chicks (he had always had a thing for big-assed black chicks, screw what anybody thought) and the night life in New York and Miami Beach and L.A.

But a little more than a year ago the headaches had started. Any kind of tension brought them on, and any kind of irritation was liable to push him over the brink into impulsive and unreasoning violence. He had broken Tony Filippi's collarbone and fractured his skull with a gun butt after a job in San Diego last spring because Filippi had fouled up his end of it and almost cost them the score; he had seriously beaten one of his women in a Miami hotel three months later because she had tried to play cute-sex when he was laboring over a payroll ripoff—and had been barely able to buy his way out of a threatened assault charge; he had ruptured a kid parking attendant just two months ago in Anaheim because the kid had gotten snotty with him and he had just finished checking out a job which proved unworkable—that, too, costing him money to fix. When he was feeling right, Kubion looked back on these times with disgust and apprehension and promised himself he would never let it happen again; but then he would get uptight about something, and one of the headaches would come on, and all the control would fall away under the black burning pressure of the impulse.

He had gone to two doctors, one in Miami and one in L.A., and submitted to two thorough physical examinations. Neither of the doctors had found anything organically wrong with him. The first one said the headaches were probably caused by nerves and prescribed tranquilizers; Kubion tried them for a while, and they had seemed to be helping, he thought the problem was licked—until the headache in the Miami hotel and the beating he had given the woman there. The second one said severe headaches were sometimes a sign of mental disorder and suggested Kubion ought to consult a psychologist. He hadn't taken that advice; it was garbage for one thing, and he didn't trust shrinks for another. They were nothing but sharks with fancy degrees and fancy two-bit double talk. He remembered the superior, patronizing son of a bitch at the Michigan state prison where he'd done a nickel stretch for armed robbery in the early fifties, his only fall. Penal psychologist, they'd called him, penal meaning prick: probing with endless questions, rapping pure manure about detrimental adolescent environment and sociopathic attitudes and a hint of latent megalomania—leaving Kubion feeling irritated and unsettled each time, alienating him completely. The hell with that crap.

He'd decided finally that he would just have to take care of it on his own— control himself when the headaches came on, work it out the same way he worked out a difficult score. He hadn't been able to do it yet, but he would because he had to in order to keep on working and keep on balling. Things would smooth out all right. Hadn't they always smoothed out for him in the past?

Kubion did not think of any of this as they drove along the snowswept and deserted main street of the village. There was only the throbbing pain in his head, and the jangling of his nerves, and the bitter frustration of the ripoff that had gone sour in Sacramento, and the overpowering, irrational need to smash something or somebody. He lit another cigarette, staring out through the windshield at the Christmas lights which still burned above the street, the buildings all unlighted save for more Christmas bulbs decorating the facade of the Valley Inn and two squares of yellow which came through its misted front windows. The red and blue and green glow of the bulbs limned his dark face surrealistically—a lean face fashioned of hard, vertical lines that gave it a somehow unfinished appearance, as if it had never been properly planed off and you could, if you looked closely enough, see the marks of a sculptor's chisel. In normal light the darkness of his skin coloring, the sooty black of his hair and eyebrows, the heavy beard shadow combined to create about him a charred look, like a man recently emerged from a coal fire.

Beside him Brodie said the first words any of them had spoken in thirty minutes: "Not even eight thirty and they've rolled up the sidewalks already."

Kubion said nothing, sucking at the filter of his cigarette.

There were rustling sounds in the rear seat, and Loxner said, "Jesus, we finally here?" His voice was thick; Brodie had bought him a pint of gin when they stopped to put on the chains in Nevada City—antiseptic for his arm and anesthesia for the pain, not wanting to chance buying bandages or pharmaceuticals with the word out that one of them was wounded.

"Finally here," Brodie answered.

"All right if I sit up now?"

"Come ahead. There's nobody on the streets."

Loxner sat up, blinking. He was the same age as Kubion, running to fat in the middle from too much ale and food; he had thinning hair the color of tarnished copper and the beginnings of bulldog jowls. "My arm feels kind of numb now," he said. "But I got to get something on it as soon as we get to the cabin, iodine or something. You don't treat a gunshot wound and take care of it, you get infection. Gangrene, maybe."

"Shut up with your whining," Kubion said.

"Hey, I'm not whining. It's just that I—"

"Shut up! I've been smelling your blood for five hours now, and I don't need to listen to you shit at the mouth."

"Take it easy, Earl," Brodie said.

"Stop telling me to take it easy, you son of a bitch!"

Brodie took his foot off the gas and turned his head and looked at Kubion. He was tall, fair-haired, narrow-hipped, and looked like one of those smiling pretty-boy types Kubion had seen around the Miami resort hotels, looking for middle-aged and moneyed pussy; he had violet-blue eyes that were normally soft but which could harden until they resembled chunks of amethyst quartz—and they were like that now. "I'm no son of a bitch," he said slowly, "and I don't like being called one."

"Fuck you, Brodie. You hear that? Fuck you!"

Brodie stared at him a moment longer, his hands tight on the wheel. Then he seemed to shake himself slightly, and his fingers relaxed; he put his foot back on the accelerator and his eyes fully on the road again. They were beyond the village now, at the junction of Macklin Lake Road and Mule Deer Lake Road. Silently he swung the car right, the tire chains making thin crunching sounds on the packed snow which covered the road, and almost immediately they began to wind through thick stands of lodgepole pine. The car's headlights, made furry by the falling snow, tunneled through the darkness.

Kubion said, "Well, Brodie?"

Leaning over the back seat, establishing a small barrier between the two men in front, Loxner said, "You remember if there's bandages and iodine at the cabin, Vic?"

"Yeah, I think so," Brodie answered. "The place is stocked up with everything else."

"We haven't eaten anything since breakfast, you know that? Once I do something about this arm, it's maybe a good idea to put some food in my gut."

"We could all do with a little food. Steaks maybe."

"The hell with it," Kubion said. Ice crackled loudly as he wound down his window and threw the cigarette out; the chill mountain wind blew snow against the side of his face, put an edge on the heater warmth inside the car. "The hell with it, the hell with both of you."

They rode the rest of the way to the Mule Deer Lake cabin in heavy silence.

# Eight

Shortly past nine o'clock, in the familiar darkness of a Whitewater motel room, Peggy Tyler sighed and rested her cheek against Matt Hughes' hairless stomach. "Did you like that?" she asked. "Did I please you, Matt?"

"Oh my God!" he said.

Smiling, she moved up into the fold of his right arm. Tawny blond hair, tangled now, flowed over his chest and shoulders; her amber-colored eyes contained an expression, tinged with amusement, that was completely contrary to their normally demure one. Statuesque and heavy-breasted, her body shone like finely veined marble in the darkness.

She was twenty-one years old and had for four years known exactly what she wanted from life. And when the boy she had been dating at age seventeen offered to buy her a new ski sweater if she would take off her clothes and let him play with her, she had known exactly how to go about getting it.

Her goal was twofold: to get as far away from Hidden Valley, California, as it was possible to get; and to marry a man with position, wealth, and a passion for warm places, snowless places where you could lie at the foot of a clear blue ocean in the middle of January and let the sun bake away all the cold, cold memories. But she was not impatient as so many of her school friends had been. She saw no point in leaving immediately, prematurely, after high school graduation for San Francisco or Hollywood or Las Vegas or New York, as some of them had done. Once you were there, you had to play the game because everyone else played it—and all the while some of the excitement and some of the glitter were just around the corner, look but don't touch.

No, that wasn't the way to do it at all. There was a better way, a much better way. It required a large sum of money and a long period of self-sacrifice, but in the meantime you could mature, you could become well read and acquire a certain polish. You put every spare dollar into a special bank account until you had accumulated a minimum of twenty-five thousand dollars, and *then* you left. Then you went to Europe instead of to the mundane cities of America; you went to Paris and Rome and Monte Carlo, and you outfitted yourself in fashionably expensive clothes, and you stayed at the best hotels and frequented only those theaters and restaurants and clubs which catered to the whims of the select; you ingratiated yourself into the lives of the wealthy and the sophisticated, fitting in perfectly because you were perfectly prepared. That was where you would meet the kind of man you wanted, in his milieu, on exactly the right terms. It would not take long, with her looks and her sexual prowess. It would not take long at all.

So she remained in Hidden Valley, living with her mother in the family home on Shasta Street—her father, a county maintenance foreman, having died of a heart attack when she was eleven. She had taken the job with Grange

Electric in Soda Grove, and assiduously, she had sought out the right men with whom to sleep—the men with a little money who did not mind making small loans or cash gifts in exchange for the use of her body. Men like Hidden Valley Mayor Matt Hughes.

She had always believed Matt Hughes to be something of a puritan: righteous, religious, happily married, certainly not inclined to extramarital affairs. As a result, and despite the fact that he was the most well-to-do man in the area, she had never really considered him a possible stepping-stone. But then she had gone into the Mercantile one afternoon more than a month ago to buy some groceries for her mother, and he had been there alone; he kept looking at her, she could feel his eyes on her as she moved along the aisles, and when she had gone up to the counter to pay for her purchases, he made overtures that were at once carefully veiled and, to her, altogether obvious.

Concealing her surprise, accepting him immediately because of who and what he was, she had hinted that she found him attractive too, and that she would be willing to see him in more casual surroundings. Nothing more had been said that afternoon, but Peggy knew that she would not have to wait long until Hughes followed through; in point of fact, she was half expecting his call to her at work the ensuing Monday.

He said then that he was planning to be in Whitewater that evening, would she like to have dinner with him? She pretended to think it over and eventually allowed that she supposed it would be all right. He suggested she meet him, if she didn't mind the short drive, at a place called The Mill—a small restaurant on the outskirts of Whitewater; she said that was fine, and met him that night, and responded to his flattery and to his physical presence just enough to let him know she was definitely interested. After dinner, however, she demurely declined his suggestion that they go somewhere alone; she made it a practice never to seem too eager, which invariably made men like Matt Hughes want her that much more. When he asked if he could see her again, she feigned reluctance and then told him that even though it was probably wrong, dating him when he was a married man and all, she really couldn't bring herself to say no.

They had three other dinner engagements at The Mill before she finally allowed him to kiss her, to fondle her, to maneuver her to the small motel on the outskirts of Whitewater—one which did not ask questions or care to what exact purpose their units' beds were put, this being the middle of the winter off-season. He had been almost laughably excited when she accepted his proposal, as if he were an overeager teen-ager who'd never had a woman before, and she had thought he would probably be totally unsatisfactory as a lover. But he had surprised her in that respect, he was really very accomplished. Sex for Peggy had been a source of intense physical pleasure from the very first, and Matt Hughes was as proficient as any she had gone to bed with in the past four years. It made the arrangement with him all the more satisfying....

They lay without speaking for a time, and the only sound was the penetrating voice of the wind as it whipped through the pine and hemlock outside the motel. Finally, Hughes stirred and rolled onto his side and said, "You're fantastic, Peggy, do you know that?" in a voice still thick with desire.

She smiled again. "Am I, Matt?"

"Yes. Oh yes. Peggy—can I see you again tomorrow night?"

"We still have more of tonight, baby."

"I know, but I want to see you tomorrow too."

"Well, I'm not sure if I can...."

"Please? I'll have something for you then."

"Oh?"

"A Christmas present, a very nice Christmas present."

Peggy lifted herself onto one elbow, looking at him closely now in the darkness. "That's sweet of you," she said. "You're awfully sweet, Matt. What is it?"

"That would spoil the surprise."

"Couldn't you give me a hint?"

"Well...." He thought for a moment. "It's something small in size but not in stature."

"Jewelry?" she asked immediately.

"No, not jewelry."

"Something to wear, then?"

"No. No, you can't wear it."

"Matt, don't tease me like this. What is it?"

"I'll give you a broader hint. I'm not very good at buying presents; I mean, I'm always afraid I'll pick out something that won't be quite right. So I don't really buy *anything*, I leave that up to the individual person."

Money, Peggy thought—and said it aloud, "Money?"

Hughes misinterpreted the inflection in her voice. "You're not offended, are you?"

God! "No, I'm not offended, baby. I... just didn't expect anything like that. You've been so generous already."

Which was true enough. Peggy had waited until their fourth evening together at the motel before bringing up the subject of money; she had done it very casually and very deftly, as always, saying that her dentist had told her she needed some work on her wisdom teeth but that she really couldn't afford it and she supposed she could endure the minor toothache discomfort a while longer.... As she had anticipated, he had been sympathetic and had readily offered to pay for the dental work, a token of his affection for her, wouldn't even think of it as a loan; she had told him she couldn't possibly, and then allowed him to talk her into accepting. And when she said that her dentist would not accept credit from her, that she would need cash, he gave her a hundred dollars that same night and insisted that she tell him when she needed more. She had needed more two weeks later, another hundred dollars, and tonight she had been going to ask him for an additional fifty—proceeding cautiously—and here he was telling her that he was going to make her a cash gift for Christmas. Wonderfully beneficent, wonderfully pliable Matt Hughes!

He said, "I don't think I've been generous enough. And besides that, I want to do it, I want to give you something nice for Christmas."

"You give me something nice every time we're together," she said, but the words were automatic, disassociated from her thoughts; she wanted to ask him how large the present was going to be—the way he talked, it was a substantial sum—but she did not want to seem overly expectant. Three hundred? Five hundred? Just how generous was he going to be?

"And you to me," he said. "Tomorrow night, then?"

"Yes, Matt. Tomorrow night and any night you want."

He drew her full against him, kissing her eyes as if in gratitude. Excitement stirred in her loins again, as much a result of anticipation of his Christmas gift as in response to his warm and naked masculinity. He clung to her, whispering her name, as she began to stroke him, make him ready again. And while one part of her mind concentrated on their rekindled passion, another part dwelled on the twenty-one thousand dollars she had saved thus far and the concomitant knowledge that if his present was as large as he had led her to believe, if she could prolong the affair with him and he continued to supply her with money, the time when she would finally be able to leave Hidden Valley was very close at hand. Another six or eight months, maybe even less; certainly no later than mid-fall of next year, before her twenty-second birthday, before the cold winter snows came.

Oh yes, long before the snows came....

# Nine

Wrapped in mackinaw and muffler and waterproof boots, Lew Coopersmith had just finished shoveling thick powder drifts from his front walk when Frank McNeil came to see him shortly past nine Tuesday morning.

It had stopped snowing sometime during the night, and the air had a crystal quality, clean and sharp like the slender ice daggers which gleamed on the front eaves of the house. A high, thin cloud-cover shielded the winter sun; but visibility was good, and you could see portions of the white-laced peaks marking higher elevations to the east. You could also see the thickening black snow-clouds which obscured their crests, and you knew—sourly, in Coopersmith's case—that there would be another heavy snowfall later in the day.

He leaned on the long handle of his shovel as McNeil's ten-year-old Dodge plowed through the snow on Alpine Street and drew up just beyond his front gate—thinking irascibly: Fine, can't think of anyone else I'd rather have come calling this morning. With McNeil, he saw, was the café owner's son; the two of them got out of the car and came over to the gate.

"Morning, Frank, Larry." Coopersmith's voice was blank, without particular interest. "Something I can do for you?"

"I sure as Christ hope so," McNeil said. His eyes shone with dark outrage, and his blunt face was flushed. "Somebody broke into the café last night."

"What?"

"That's right. Broke the lock off the rear door and then propped the goddamn door wide open. Storeroom was filled with snow when Larry and me went in to open up a few minutes ago—snow all over everything."

Coopersmith abandoned his careless manner. "What was taken, Frank?"

"Nothing. Not a single thing."

"You positive about that?"

"Hell yes. First thing we did was check the register and my cash box. They hadn't been touched."

"No supplies missing, either?"

"No."

"Vandalism?"

"Just the rear door, that's all."

Coopersmith frowned. "Any idea who could have done it?"

"Damn it, no. It doesn't make a bit of sense."

"You report it yet?"

"I wanted to talk to you first."

In spite of his dislike for McNeil, Coopersmith felt mildly appreciative of the implied confidence. He said crisply, "All right, Frank. Let's go have a look."

He propped his shovel against the cross-slatted fence and went with father and son to the Dodge. McNeil started the car and drove the four blocks to the

Valley Café, pulled into the narrow, snowpacked alley that ran behind the building. He parked close to the Café's rear entrance, and Coopersmith got out immediately and went to look at the door.

The lock, old and flimsy, had been cleanly snapped by means of inserting a crowbar or some similar tool between the door edge and the jamb. There were splinter and gouge marks in the wood there which told him that much. The door was closed now. Coopersmith said, "You wedge it closed from the inside, Frank?"

"No. Latch still holds, even with the busted lock."

Coopersmith opened the door and stepped into the small, somewhat cluttered storeroom. The floor inside was wet, still mounded in places with the snow—melting now—which had blown in during the night. To one side was a half-filled crate of oranges; indicating that, McNeil said, "Crate there was holding the door open."

"That where you usually keep it—by the door?"

McNeil shook his head. "It's supposed to be over there with the other fruits and vegetables."

"Way it seems, then, whoever did it had nothing in mind except letting a lot of snow whip in here."

"Yeah. But what the hell *for?*"

"Could be a practical joke."

"Some joke, if that's it."

"Or it could be somebody wanted to harass you a little."

"Why'd anybody want to harass *me*, for Chrissake?"

"Well—you ruffle any feathers lately?"

"Not me. I get along with everyone, you know that."

Yeah, Coopersmith thought. He moved slowly around the storeroom, found nothing, and pushed open the swing door that led to the front of the café.

Following him, McNeil said, "Like I told you: nothing taken, nothing disturbed."

They went back into the storeroom, and Coopersmith said, "Best thing for you to do is report what happened to the substation in Soda Grove; but if you want, you can tell them not to bother sending a deputy over. Tell them I'll look into it—ask around, see if anybody saw anything last night, and then check in with them later on."

"What about fingerprints, stuff like that?"

"Frank, nothing was stolen, nothing was vandalized. Now I've got a fingerprint kit at the house, and I can get it and come back here and dust the door and the orange crate and everything else in the place, wet as it is. But what's the point? Like as not, whoever did it is a valley resident, and I can't go around taking prints of everybody who lives here. Besides, cold as it was during the night, he was probably wearing gloves anyway."

"I'm supposed to just forget about it, then, is that it? Who's going to pay for the damned lock?"

"I told you I'd look into it," Coopersmith said. "When I find out who did it, he'll pay for the lock or he'll find himself up in front of a county judge."

"He'll go straight to jail, I got anything to say."

Coopersmith pursed his lips. "You want to do it the way I said, or you want to call in a deputy from the substation?"

"Oh, you handle it. I guess you know what you're doing."

"Thanks," Coopersmith said dryly. "You going to open up now?"

"Might as well, I suppose."

"Well, I'll walk home then. Exercise'll do me good."

"You'll be asking around right away, won't you?"

"I will. And if I find out anything, I'll let you know."

Coopersmith started for the door, and McNeil said abruptly, "Listen, Lew, I just thought of something."

"What is it?"

"All of us who live in Hidden Valley, we know one another pretty well, and there's none of us who'd pull a shitty trick like this. But there's one person we don't know nothing about. You understand who I'm talking about, Lew?"

"That Cain fella, I reckon."

"That's right. Maybe you'd better talk to *him* right off; maybe he's the bastard who did this."

"Why should he do it? You have some trouble with him?"

"Not exactly. But it could be he found out I asked you to run that check on him, it could be he's got a hard-on for me over that."

"I ran the check three months ago," Coopersmith reminded him.

"Well, maybe he just found out about it. Anyhow, I don't like that bird; I don't trust him. Living up in the Hughes' cabin all alone, don't talk to nobody, walks around with his nose up like a dog just pissed on his leg. You can't tell what somebody like that will do."

Coopersmith thought about offering further words of reason, decided there was no point in reasoning with a man like McNeil, and said, "I'll see what I can find out." He nodded to the café owner and went out into the valley.

As he walked through the snow to Sierra Street, he realized that there was a certain purposeful spring in his step and that he felt better than he had in weeks. It was, he supposed, damned perverse of a man to feel good as a result of somebody else's troubles, but he could not help himself; if only for a little while, and only on a very small scale, he was involved again, he was useful to others and to himself.

# Ten

Kubion spent the morning prowling the large, slant-beam-ceilinged interior of the cabin at Mule Deer Lake: upstairs, downstairs, front and rear, smoking too much, drinking too much coffee. He no longer had the savage headache of the night before, but he felt restless and edgy—an impotent, caged kind of feeling. Two sticks of marijuana hadn't helped either, although the joints he had blown after their arrival last night had dulled his proclivity for violence and allowed him to sleep. That was the problem with pot: sometimes it did for him, and sometimes it didn't. As a result, he didn't use it often, but he liked to keep a supply on hand; liquor soured his belly, and everybody needed some type of high once in a while—ease the pressure, get rid of the down feeling.

Neither Brodie nor Loxner had said anything about the near blowoff in the car coming in, and he hadn't mentioned it either; all of them pretending it hadn't happened. So he'd lucked out of another of those bastard headaches, but unless he could learn to hold himself in check, he couldn't keep lucking out of them indefinitely. He'd wind up killing somebody, sure as hell, and when you killed people without good reason, you were as good as dead yourself. Well, he'd learn; he had to learn, and he would, and that was all there was to it. He just wasn't going to do to himself what all the fuzz in the country hadn't been able to do to him in seventeen years. No way. No frigging way.

Kubion came down the side hall from the rear porch into the living room. Loxner was sitting in one of the chairs grouped before a native-stone fireplace. He was his old bluff, stupid self today—pretending, too, that he hadn't let his yellow show through when he'd taken the bullet at Greenfront. His left arm was suspended in a handkerchief sling; he'd found merthiolate and bandages in the bathroom medicine cabinet and had wrapped it up as soon as they'd come in. The bullet had missed bone, exiting cleanly, and he'd be able to use the arm again in a few days, once soreness and stiffness decreased.

In Loxner's right hand was a bottle of Rainier Ale, and he was listening to the table model radio which had originally been in the kitchen—staticky country-and-western music, fading in and out at irregular intervals. The three of them had picked up a newscast on the radio over breakfast, and there were no fresh developments in Sacramento; the cops still hadn't found the dummy car. The news announcer had no further information on the suspected whereabouts of the holdup men, but the implication was that local law enforcement officials figured they were still confined to the immediate Sacramento area. Which was fine, except that it didn't change things much as far as they were concerned. Sure, the odds were good that they could leave today and make it to Vegas or L.A. without trouble and begin looking around for another score, a quick score; but when you're wanted for Murder One, and one of you has a shot-up flipper, and you know how the little unforeseeable things can screw you up—like that security guard coming in at just the wrong time to screw up the Greenfront job—you don't gamble, you don't put your ass on the line.

Kubion wandered around the room and then stopped short near one of the front windows. Damn it, this aimless pacing back and forth wasn't doing him any good. What he needed was to get out for a while: cold air, a sense of movement and activity. He went upstairs and got his coat off the floor in his room, where he'd thrown it last night. When he came down again, Brodie was standing with a paring knife in one hand and a potato in the other, talking to Loxner.

"You going out, Earl?" he asked as Kubion walked across to the door.

"That's what it looks like, right?"

"For a walk, or into the village, or what?"

"Why?"

"Well, if you're going into the village, I could use a couple of cans of tomato sauce. I want to make Veal Milanese for supper tonight."

Tomato sauce, Kubion thought, Jesus Christ. Brodie had this thing for cooking—*culinary art,* he called it—and he was always making crap like Veal Milanese and baked stuffed chicken and pineapple glazed ham. He said it was a hobby with him—he'd gotten interested from his mother, who'd won some kind of national prize once. Some hobby for a man; it was more the kind of hobby you'd expect a fag to have; and Kubion wasn't all that sure about Brodie. Vic had a reputation as a stud, Mr. Supercock, but with that pretty-boy face of his and this *culinary art* business, maybe underneath his hard professionalism he was Mr. Superqueer instead; you never knew these days who was taking it up the ass and who wasn't.

"All right?" Brodie said.

"Yeah, all right," Kubion said, and went out into the chill, rarefied air. When he got to the enclosed garage tacked onto the lakeward side of the cabin, he saw that snow had piled up in two-foot drifts against the doors. Shit. He stood staring at it for a moment and then lifted his eyes and looked down a long, gradual slope and across a white meadow at the frozen, snow-coated surface of Mule Deer Lake. Pines and taller firs crowded in close to the southern and western shores, but congregated along the eastern shore, where a row of white-fingered piers reached out into the water, were several other cabins and houses and summer lodges. Most of them were unoccupied now, abandoned-looking beneath canvases of snow.

Some bitching country, he thought. The exact center of nowhere. How anyone could live in a place like this the year round was beyond him. Nothing but snow and ice and bitter wind and maybe an influx of stupid fishermen and hunters in season—no action, nothing to do, a goddamn prison with trees and rocks and snow for bars.

He turned and went into the woodshed—looks like an out-house, he thought, *some* bitching place—which was situated at the rear of the property. The cabin, a double-tiered A-frame fashioned of bark-stripped redwood siding, sat on a projection of granite at the long slope's upper edge. Flanked by trees to the north and east, through which its private and currently snowpacked access lane wound upward from Mule Deer Lake Road, it was completely isolated; the nearest dwelling was a fifth of a mile away. The cabin belonged to a man named Brendikian, a long-retired bunco gambler who had amassed a small fortune during and after the Second World War with trimmed and shaded cards and suction-bevel missout dice; then he had gone into score financing and safe housing for the independents working outside the Circle. This was just one of several secluded safe houses he had bought and on which he paid taxes through dummy California and Nevada corporations—totally untraceable should one of them be knocked over. Loxner had once done a job of some sort for Brendikian and had had no difficulty arranging for the cabin's use at three bills a week.

Kubion found a curve-bladed snow shovel in the woodshed, came back, and cleared the area in front of the doors. Then he threw the shovel to one side and pulled the two halves open. Even though the car had been sheltered overnight, there was a thin film of ice on the windows; the garage felt like the interior of a frozen-food locker. He scraped away the ice, got the car started and out of the garage, and went down to Mule Deer Lake Road.

The village plow had been along there earlier in the morning, clearing it and pushing the snow into windrows at the shoulders; the pavement was slick with ice in parts, and Kubion drove slowly into the village. On Sierra Street, he parked in front of Tribucci Bros. Sport Shop, wedging his car against the long snow mound at the curbing. Music drifted down to him as he stepped out. The hicks always went in for Christmas in a big way—carols and trees and decorations and stockings on the mantel and sleigh rides, all the horse-shit. And this was a hick village if ever there was one. Populated by a bunch of half-witted Eskimos in wooden igloos. Christ!

He went into the shop, and a four-eyed balding guy was behind the counter, wearing a shirt with the name Vince stitched over the left-hand pocket. This Vince smiled at Kubion—friendly, vacuous, sure enough a damned Eskimo. Kubion smiled back at him, playing the game, and bought three packages of cigarettes. Vince wished him a Merry Christmas as he turned to leave, and Kubion said, "Sure, Merry Christmas," thinking it was anything but, after the bust in Sacramento.

Outside again, he walked toward the overloud singing. Tomato sauce and Veal Milanese, you'd think everything was beautiful and they were having a big celebration. Still—what the hell. You had to eat, and there was no point in creating a hassle with Brodie; let him make his Veal Milanese, let him make anything he wanted as long as he didn't try to make *him.*

Smiling faintly, Kubion entered the Mercantile. The store was fairly crowded, noisy, and smelled of wool and dampness and pitch pine burning in the potbellied stove. Kubion had seen most of the people there at one time or another during the previous week, though he did not know or care to know any of their names. But Pat Garvey was the dumpy blond woman being waited on by Maude Fredericks, and the three men grouped around the potbelly rapping about a forthcoming blizzard were Joe Garvey—big, work-roughened, with fierce black eyes and a sprinkling of pockmarks on his flushed cheeks; stooped and fox-faced Sid Markham, who operated a fix-it shop from his Mule Deer Lake home; and Walt Halliday. Matt Hughes stood inside the Post Office enclosure, sorting the mail which had just come in from Soda Grove.

Kubion went to stand near the front counter, close to the trio by the stove. They stopped talking about the weather and were silent for a moment; then Halliday said, "Either of you been over to see McNeil this morning?"

"Yeah, a little while ago," Garvey said. "The way he's yelling, everybody in the county knows the café was broken into last night."

"Funny damned thing: nothing stolen, nothing damaged."

"Don't make much sense, I'll grant."

"Lew Coopersmith find out anything yet, you know?"

"Talked to him just before I came in here," Markham said. "He hadn't learned a thing then."

"He been to see that Zachary Cain?" Garvey asked. "McNeil seems to think Cain might have done it."

"Didn't say if he had or not. But you ask me, Cain didn't have nothing to do with it. Sure, he keeps full to himself, but that don't make him a criminal. And keeping his own counsel is more than you can say for that fart McNeil, always running off at the mouth the way he does."

"I don't know," Halliday said. "It doesn't seem natural for a man to live all alone like that, never saying a word to anybody. You—"

He broke off as the door opened and a bearded, faintly bearish man came inside. He moved up to the counter, bloodshot eyes fixed directly in front of him, and stood next to Kubion; the three men at the stove watched him, silent again. This must be Cain, Kubion thought—they act like the poor bastard had leprosy. What a bunch of silly turds. If I were in his shoes, I wouldn't stop with breaking into their café; I'd burn the whole village to the ground, do them all a favor.

Pat Garvey finished with her purchases, detoured around Cain, and tugged at her husband's sleeve. "Sure, all right," Garvey said, nodded to Halliday and Markham, and followed his wife out of the store. Maude Fredericks came down to where Kubion was standing, asked him if she could be of service; he told her he wanted two cans of tomato sauce, and she smiled as if he'd ordered a side of beef and fifty pounds of canned goods and went over to the grocery section.

The door opened again, and Verne Mullins came in briskly. He raised a hand to the three men around the stove, went directly to the Post Office enclosure, and said loudly, "Morning, Matt." He was fat and had a huge red-veined nose and the bright, darting eyes of a bird; a bluff, somewhat testy exterior masked a soft Irish heart. Like Lew Coopersmith, he did not look his age: sixty-nine, come February.

Hughes turned, smiling. "Morning, Verne."

"Any mail for me?"

"Couple of things. Wait—here you go."

Mullins took the envelopes and shuffled through them; then he held one up—thin and brown, with the words "Southern Pacific Retirement Bureau" in the upper left hand corner—and said, "About time they decided to send my check along. Man works forty-five years for the same company, never late and never sick a day of it, and then when he retires, he's got to fight for the damned money he paid into the retirement fund all along."

Hughes winked at him. "That's big business for you."

"Now ain't that the truth?" Mullins said. "Bank open this morning, Matt? Figure I better cash this right off, so it doesn't bounce on me."

"Bank's always open for you, Verne."

Hughes came out of the enclosure and over to the counter. Mullins tore open the envelope, took the check out, endorsed it, and handed it across. "Put it mostly in twenties if you can," he said. "Got to send a few off to my grandkids for the holidays."

"Sure thing."

Hughes took the check into his office, closed the door. Maude Fredericks said to Kubion, "Will there be anything else, sir?"

"What?"

"I have your tomato sauce. Was there something else?"

"No," Kubion said. "No, that's it."

He gave her a dollar bill, and she rang up the purchase on the old-fashioned, crank-type register. She handed him his change, put the two cans into a paper sack. Hughes came out of his office with a sheaf of bills in his hand and counted them out to Verne Mullins—four hundred and fifty dollars. Mullins tucked them into a worn leather billfold, said, "Thanks, Matt, you're a good lad," and started for the door.

Hughes called after him. "Don't forget church on Sunday, Verne."

"Now would a good Irish Protestant like me be forgetting church on the Sunday before Christmas? I'll be there, don't you worry; somebody's got to put a dime in the collection plate."

Hughes laughed, and Mullins went out as Maude Fredericks said to Cain, "Yes, please?"

"Bottle of Old Grandad." Cain said.

Kubion picked up his paper sack and left the store. Bank, he was thinking. Safe in that office. Four hundred and fifty dollars without even looking at the check first. If this Hughes operates a kind of unofficial banking service, if he regularly cashes checks for people who live here, how much does he keep on hand?

Hell, Kubion told himself then, you're starting to think like a punk. A hick village like this, for Christ's sake, the amount in that safe *has* to be penny-ante. We need a score, sure, but something big, something damned big now. And you don't crap on safe ground to begin with, especially not with the kind of heat we're carrying. Forget it.

He went up the snow-tracked sidewalk to his car.

# Eleven

When the telephone rang at four o'clock, Rebecca knew immediately that it was Matt and that he was calling to tell her he wouldn't be home again that night. She put her book aside and stared across the living room to where the unit sat on a pigskin-topped table. Ring. Silence. Ring. Silence. Ring. I won't answer it, she thought—and then stood up slowly and walked over to the table and picked up the hand-set.

"Yes, Matt," she said.

"Hello, dear. How did you know it was me?"

"I'm psychic, how else?"

He laughed softly. "I just called to tell you I won't be home again until late tonight. Neal Walker wants me to go to the City Council meeting in Coldville, and I—"

"All right," she said.

"I'll try not to be too late."

"All right."

"Rebecca—is something the matter?"

"Now what could possibly be the matter?"

"Well, you sound tired. Are you feeling well?"

"Lovely," she said. "Have a nice time, won't you?"

"Yes. Don't wait up."

"I wouldn't think of it. Good-bye, Matt."

Rebecca put the receiver down without waiting to hear if he had anything further to say. She stood there stiffly, thinking: How many times have we played that same little scene? Fifty, a hundred? And such trite dialogue, like something written by a third-rate playwright. Rebecca Hughes: character in a pointless drama. Reciting her lines, going through the motions, while the unseen audience watches in boredom and suppresses snickers because the entire episode is so totally and ridiculously conventional.

She went to the main hall and along it into the kitchen. Earlier in the day she had gone down to the Mercantile to get coffee, and she had had the per-colator on ever since she returned; she poured another cup—did that make ten for the day, or was it fifteen?—and stood drinking it by the table. Through the window over the sink, she could see white-flecked darkness: snowing again, a whipping veil of snow. Beginnings of a heavy storm. She could remember a time when she relished one of these mountain winter blizzards—curled up with Matt on the rug in front of the fireplace, insulated against the turbulence without, drinking hot eggnog and perhaps making a little love in the crack-ling glow of the fir-log fire. Soft, shared warmth and soft, shared love.

And wasn't that, too, as trite as the rest of it?

I don't want to be alone tonight, she thought. I don't think I can stand being alone again tonight. But where could she go? The Valley Inn? No, there would be friendly, probing questions as to Matt's whereabouts, and she would have to repeat his lie and then listen to them talk about what a fine, upstanding man he was, and all in all it would be worse than being alone. Ann Tribucci? Ann was her closest friend in the valley, though Rebecca had at no time been able to talk to her about personal matters; she had wanted to often enough, to purge herself woman to woman, but she could never quite manage the courage. Tonight would be no different. If anything, seeing Ann tonight would make things worse: the previous weekend, she and Johnny had moved temporarily from their home near Mule Deer Lake to Vince and Judy Tribucci's house—Ann hadn't wanted to be alone out there with the baby coming—and Rebecca would have to face all four of them; she would have to witness the solicitous way Johnny looked at his wife and the happiness that was theirs with the baby due so soon now....

Abruptly, Rebecca wondered if things might have been different if she and Matt had had a child. Well no, probably not, and anyway, the question was academic. He had told her during their brief engagement that he was sterile—their childless marriage was in no way responsible for his infidelity, either—and she had said then that it didn't matter, they had each other and that was enough. There had been some talk at that time of adopting a baby later on, but neither of them had mentioned it again in the seven years they had been man and wife.

Her eyes strayed to the window again, and she could just make out the familiar, iridescent glow of light in the cabin above. And she found herself wondering about Zachary Cain again, wondering as she had on the previous night if he too was lonely. Would he welcome some company on this stormy night, the same as she? Would he be receptive to a visit from a young-old and cuckolded wife?

Oh, stop it, she told herself. The only thing you'd accomplish by going up there is to make a fool of yourself; remember Reno, remember that, and it doesn't matter that it's not the same thing. There's nothing up there for you, nothing at all.

Rebecca finished the last of her coffee, put the cup down, and went back into the living room. She was cold again—odd how she couldn't seem to keep warm lately. Picking up her book, she climbed the stairs and ran a hot bath and undressed and slipped into the tub. The steaming water helped a little; she could feel herself beginning to relax.

The book she was reading was one of those sex-and-big business best sellers—not really absorbing, just something to read—and she opened it again as she lay soaking. After two pages, she came to another in a long series of boudoir scenes; but this one, as coldly clinical in detail as all the others, had a curiously and intense erotic effect on her. Her nipples grew erect beneath the warm bathwater; her hips moved featheringly against the smooth porcelain; her thighs opened and closed in a gentle, involuntary rhythm. God, it had been such a long time now! Dry-throated, she closed the book sharply and put it aside, shutting her eyes, willing her body still. After a time the sexual need began to ebb—but she was cold again, even in the warm bath she was cold again....

Half an hour later, fully dressed, she sat with a tasteless sandwich—she could not recall the last time she had taken a genuine pleasure in the consumption of food—and a cup of coffee at the kitchen table. Seven o'clock now. Blizzard flinging snow at the window, wailing emptily. It was going to be such a long, long night—

—and I don't want to be alone, she thought.

The window seemed suddenly to develop a magnetic pull for her eyes. After a moment she stood from the table and went there and saw again the diffused yellow light in the cabin. She looked at it for a full minute, and then she thought: Well, I *could* go up there, I could go up and talk to him for a while; there's nothing wrong in that. Just two people, landlord and tenant, talking together on a stormy, lonely winter night. And she was curious about him, there was that too.

She kept on standing there, thinking about it—and then she walked into the hall, to where the coat closet was located near the Dutch-doored front entrance. You'd better not do it, she told herself—and knew that she was going to do it anyway. She opened the closet and put on fur-lined snow parka and fur-lined ski boots (presents from Matt in one of his contrite and attentive moments); then she tied a scarf tightly around her head, put the parka's hood over it, drew on a pair of wool mittens. And went out into the blizzard before she could change her mind.

The tails of her parka and the flared legs of her slacks slapped and ballooned in the chill white wind as she crossed the front yard to Lassen Drive. She started up the road, struggling through the dry shoulder drifts. The cold numbed her lips and her cheeks; the night and the snow pressed down on her, sealing her in a thrumming vacuum. Finally, she reached the cabin and stepped off the road, bracing herself against the heaving wind, moving toward the dull warm light in the facing window.

As she drew opposite, she could see beyond the ice-frosted glass, and Cain was there, sitting here in the window. He was smoking, looking down at the table: remote, grim-visaged in his thick grayish beard. Rebecca stopped abruptly, and she was less sure of herself now, less convinced that coming here was a good idea. What did she know about Zachary Cain, after all? He was a complete stranger, she hadn't spoken twenty words to him since he'd arrived in Hidden Valley; what could she say to him tonight, where would she begin? She thought of retracing her steps to the road, leaving as quickly as she had come. But she did not move. Home to the big, empty house had no appeal; being alone tonight disturbed her more than the unknown qualities of Zachary Cain.

The wind slackened and began to gust, and the cold penetrated her clothing to chill her skin. Through the hazy window, she saw Cain rub one hand over his face and through his unkempt hair a tired, despondent gesture that cemented her resolve. She moved forward again to the front door.

Rebecca knocked loudly several times. When there was no immediate response, she thought he hadn't heard above the sound of the storm and reached up to knock again. And the door opened with a jerky suddenness, and Cain stood holding it against the force of the wind, peering out at her with red-flecked eyes. There was a surprise in his gaze, but it dulled and faded almost instantly. She saw pain there, too, and what might have been irritation. He did not look drunk, but it was evident that he had been drinking.

She tried a tentative smile and felt the tightness of it on her mouth. He did not return it—except for his eyes, his face was totally impassive—and the doubts began to wash over Rebecca again. Her mind seemed to have gone blank; she could not think of anything to say. She had a foolish impulse to turn and run away into the snow-riddled night.

Cain said finally, "Yes, what is it, Mrs. Hughes?"

She found words then and pushed them out diffidently. "May I come inside? It's terribly cold out here."

He hesitated, and then shrugged and moved aside so that she could step in past him. The cabin was warm, fire in the hearth; but it smelled of liquor and stale cigarette smoke, and when he closed the door, cutting off the scream of the wind, it seemed too quiet. She was conscious of the snow that had blown into the room, that still fell fluttering from her parka; she wanted to say something apologetic about it, but the only words that came to her were acutely inane: *I'm getting snow all over your floor.*

Cain was standing with his back to the door, watching her, waiting silently for her to tell him why she was there. Instead, Rebecca said, "Quite a storm, isn't it?" and those words seemed just as inane as the other, unspoken ones. She began to feel awkward and incredibly silly.

He said, "Yes, I suppose it is."

"Well—I hope I'm not intruding. I mean, you're not... busy or anything, are you?"

"As a matter of fact, I was."

"Oh. Oh, I see. I'm sorry, I didn't know...."

"It doesn't matter. What did you want to see me about?"

"Nothing in particular. I just... I thought you might like to have some company tonight."

His barlike eyebrows lifted slightly. "Oh? Why?"

"I don't know, I just thought you might. I'm alone too this evening, you see, my husband is... away, and it seemed like a good idea to—" She broke off, realizing how wrong that sounded; she looked away from him and then said almost desperately, "I was feeling lonely, and I wanted someone to talk to."

"Why me, Mrs. Hughes?"

"I had the idea you might be lonesome too, that's all."

Something flickered in the depths oaf his eyes. "I'm not lonesome," he said harshly. "I live the way I do by choice."

"Does that mean you don't like people?"

"I prefer my own company."

"Would it be prying if I asked why?"

"Yes, it would."

"Well I'm sorry."

"Do you make a habit of calling on men you hardly know when your husband is away and you're feeling lonely?"

"Of course not."

"What would he say if he knew you'd come here tonight?"

Rebecca felt her cheeks begin to flush. "What are you getting at? Do you think I came for some... special reason?"

"Did you?"

"No. I told you, I only wanted some companionship."

"You won't find it here, in any variety."

"So you're inviting me to leave."

"To put it bluntly, yes."

Bitter, defensive anger welled inside her; words tumbled out unchecked, mirroring her thoughts. "Oh, we can *really* put it bluntly if you like. We can say, 'You're a bitch, Mrs. Hughes, I don't want anything to do with you, Mrs. Hughes, find someone else to go to bed with, Mrs. Hughes.' That's what you're thinking, isn't it?"

Cain seemed to wince slightly. His voice a little softer, he said, "There's no need to—"

"Of course, how thoughtless of me to bring it out into the open like that. Well, I'll just be going. Thank you so much for your time, Mr. Cain. It's been very pleasant; it isn't every day I get to feel like a cheap whore."

She moved gropingly to the door, fumbled at the latch, and got it open. The sudden gust of wind and snow was like a slap. She ran out and across the yard and down the road: staggering and reeling in a surrealistic coalescence of white and black, the sound of it now raging in her ears like mocking, hysterical laughter.

When she reached the house, an interminable time later, she was asthmatically breathless and trembling uncontrollably. Inside, she stripped off parka and scarf and mittens and boots and flung them into the closet; ran upstairs and into the bedroom. Slacks and sweater and undergarments were icy-damp against her skin, and she shed them urgently and located the warmest nightgown she owned—a heavy flannel—and put that on and got into bed. The shaking refused to abate; her teeth chattered, her body crawled with chills. She tried to smoke a cigarette, could not get it lighted, and finally threw it to the floor, burrowing deeper under the blankets. Cold, cold, trembling, cold....

And after a while, when it became unbearable, she turned her face into the pillow and slid one hand down beneath the covers and pulled the hem of her gown up over her hips; parted her thighs and began to massage herself harshly with her fingertips—a kind of rhythmic self-flagellation. In less than a minute, she climaxed; and her body, at last, was still.

Rebecca rolled onto her side, drew her knees up to her breasts, and willed herself into a sleep fraught with dismal dreams.

# Twelve

The blizzard continued to gather strength as the night progressed, dumping huge quantities of snow on Hidden Valley and on the high, steep cliffs through which County Road 235-A passed down into the valley. The last two cars to traverse the road—crawling ten minutes apart shortly before 1 A.M., like yellow-eyed animals in the storm—belonged to Matt Hughes and Peggy Tyler, returning from the Whitewater motel. Both sets of tire tracks were obliterated almost immediately.

More hours passed, and still the blizzard remained relentless. Drifts built higher and higher along the cornice at the near, lee side of the western cliff crown, while the screaming wind dislodged other snow from unsheltered places and hurled it downward into the pass in lacy white spumes. Long since rendered impassable, 235-A had a covering of more than eighteen inches by five o'clock.

At five thirty the blow reached its ultimate savagery. The scattered lodgepole pines clinging to the top of the western cliff were bowed double like genuflecting pilgrims, and the swollen cornice collected ever-greater amounts of heavy snow. It went on that way for a time—and then, just before dawn, the low-hanging clouds that sailed continually eastward on the high-altitude currents began to develop fragmentation lines, like amoebae about to reproduce. The snowfall decreased steadily until it was a thin, fluttering curtain. Gray light filtered into the sky, lengthening visibility, giving substance to the bloated shadows along the crown of the western wall.

The blizzard was over; but the destruction it had fomented was only just beginning.

First there was a rumbling—a low-pitched, throat-clearing sound. The overburdened cornice shuddered, shaking whiteness as if a buried giant had awakened and were trying to rise; slender vanguards spilled free in frothy cascades. The rumbling grew louder, and louder still.

And the entire cornice gave way.

Billowing snowclouds choked the air like white smoke, and a massive tidal wave of snow and ice and rock flooded downward with a thunderous, vibratory roar that was as loud as a bomb blast in the early-morning stillness. Granite outcroppings were ripped loose as though they were no more than chunks of soft shale; trees were buried, uprooted, or snapped like matchsticks and carried along. And in a matter of seconds, the plunging mass filled a section of the pass the way a child would fill an excavation in the sand....

Lew Coopersmith sat bolt upright in bed. The deafening noise rattled the bedroom windows, reverberated through the big, shadowed room. He struggled out from beneath the bedclothes and moved in sleep-drugged motions to the window; but from the vantage point he could see nothing to explain the sudden explosion of sound, now lessening into small, receding echoes.

The door connecting his bedroom with that of his wife's burst open, and Ellen rushed in. Her round, handsome face pale and frightened, silver hair braided into a long queue down her back, dressed in an ankle-length white nightdress, she was a ghostly figure in the semidarkness. "Dear heaven, Lew," she said, "what is it, what *is* it?"

Cleared now of all vestiges of sleep, Coopersmith's mind began to function normally, and he remembered what John Tribucci had told him in the Sport Shop Monday afternoon. He turned fully from the window. "I think," he said grimly, "that we've just had an avalanche."

John Tribucci knew instantly that they had just had an avalanche.

An early riser by nature, he was in the bathroom shaving when it happened. The magnitude of the noise startled him, caused him to cut his cheek. He put down his razor, tore off a strip of toilet paper, and blotted perfunctorily at the thin ribbon of blood. He could hear Ann's voice calling to him from the spare bedroom adjacent, the voices of his brother and his brother's wife in their room down the hall.

Ann was sitting up in bed when he came hurrying in. He sat beside her, took one of her hands. "You all right, honey?"

"Yes But you've cut yourself...."

"Just a nick. I'll live."

"It was a slide in the pass, wasn't it?"

"I'm afraid so."

"It sounded like a bad one."

He nodded: "I just didn't think it'd happen this soon, before Christmas, before the baby came."

"You'd better go have a look."

"Will you be okay?"

"I'll be fine. Our child is kicking the devil out of me, but I don't think he's ready to put in an appearance yet."

Tribucci kissed her, went out into the hall, and met Vince on the stairs. Neither of them said anything as they hurried down and out into the cold, gray morning.

In the first moment of wakening, Cain thought it was an earthquake.

He had been born in San Francisco, and natives of that city are sometimes consciously, always subconsciously aware of the network of faults on which they live and of what happens when the pressure in those faults become too great and the earth begins to shift as if in orgasmic release. The deep guttural rumbling, the rattling, skittering vibration of windows and boards and bed which pulled him up out of sleep were sensations not new to him. Immediately, fuzzily, he thought: Quake, big one, Christ it's finally happening—and flung the covers away from his body and rolled out of bed. He was without equilibrium and fell jarringly to his knees. Pain burst through his left kneecap, and the sharpness of it flooded his mind with abrupt reality.

He struggled to his feet and felt sweat icing on him in the cold room. The cabin was no longer trembling, and the sudden roar had given way to a strained quiet. He thought then, sluggishly: *What the hell?* and walked naked into the front room. Leaning against the windowsill, he peered beyond crystallike glass.

Lights on all over the village below. Sky clearing, lightening, and a gentle snowfall now; the storm was finished. To the north there was a sifting cumulus of what appeared to be snow, like a white dust cloud settling. It meant nothing to him.

He turned away from the window. His head had commenced to throb with hangover, and he felt vaguely nauseated; he was shivering from the cold. Maybe something blew up, he thought, but it was a dull speculation. He did not really care what it had been; it was over now, it was unimportant, it could have no bearing on his existence.

Cain went back to bed and lay waiting for the sleep he knew would not come again.

Matt Hughes said, "I'd better get down there. If that slide is as bad as it sounded, I'll be needed in more ways than one." He crossed to the bedroom closet, shedding his pajamas, and began to dress quickly.

Rebecca drew the blankets tightly against her throat and did not look at her husband. The sheets were sleep-warm, but she was still touched by the same cold as on the night before. The masculine odor of Matt's body and the faint lingering perfume he had brought home with him were vaguely repellent in her nostrils.

The sound of the avalanche and the spasming of the house had startled her badly at first; but once she had known what it was, once Matt had jumped up and run to the windows and begun shouting about a pass-cliff slide, the apprehension had left her, and she was calm. He hadn't seen that, though; with maddening condescension he had told her not to be frightened, that everything would be all right—as if *she* were the intrinsic child and not he.

He said now, as he buttoned one of his soft-wool shirts, "John and Vince Tribucci were right, after all. But there's nothing we could have done; you can't control nature or counteract the will of God."

I wish you'd stop talking about God, Rebecca thought. You're always talking about God, you make such a mockery of religion. But she did not say anything.

Hughes put on his mackinaw and stepped around the foot of the bed to kiss her absently on the forehead. "Depending on how bad it is, I'll come back home or call you from the Mercantile. Either way, I'll let you know soon."

It had not even occurred to him, she knew, to ask her along—or to question why she was not eager of her own volition to accompany him. She said, "All right."

When he was gone, Rebecca lay thinking about the slide to keep from dwelling on last night's experience with Zachary Cain—and on what she had done in this same bed after returning from the cabin. If the pass had been blocked, it meant they were now snowbound for, probably, several days. Was that bad or good? A little of both, she supposed. Nobody could come into Hidden Valley, which meant no mail and no fresh supplies: a minor inconvenience. And nobody could leave the valley, another inconvenience for most, particularly since this was the Christmas season. It also meant that Matt could not meet his current mistress and that he would therefore be forced to spend tonight and the next few nights with his wife. Forced, that was the key word; forced. Still, it was what she wanted—wasn't it?

I don't know, she thought then. I don't know *what* I want anymore.

And got up listlessly to face another day.

Peggy Tyler's mother—a faded prototype of her daughter—came running upstairs and opened the door to Peggy's room without knocking. She was fully dressed and had been in the kitchen making coffee. "It must have been a slide," she said breathlessly. "It must have been a terrible slide in the pass, I don't know what else it could have been."

"I guess that's what it was," Peggy said. She was normally a heavy sleeper, and while she had been awakened by the roaring and the quaking, her mind was still wrapped in languid dreams of a warm sun and a warm sea. Her body ached pleasantly; there was a gentle soreness in her loins, and her breasts and nipples tingled from the remembered manipulations of Matt Hughes' hands and lips. The fucking had been very good last night: some of the best she'd ever had. Of course, the reason for that was Matt's magnificent Christmas present, which he had presented to her with a kind of shy expectation, as if he had been afraid she would not be pleased, the moment they had entered the motel room.

One thousand dollars—cash.

Dollar sign-one-zero-zero-zero.

After a gift like that, the fucking just *had* to be very good.

Her mother said, "Thank the Lord it didn't happen earlier. You didn't get home until after one; suppose it had happened while you were driving through the pass? You might have been killed!"

"It didn't happen while I was driving through the pass."

"It might have. Where were you so late again?"

"I told you before, Mother," Peggy said. "I've joined a group in Soda Grove that's putting on a Christmas pageant, and there's a lot of work to be done."

Mrs. Tyler sighed. "We might be snowbound; there certainly is the chance of it. You won't be able to go to work today or maybe for the rest of the week."

How awful, Peggy thought. She said, "I have some sick leave coming. Look, Mother, let's not get into a panic, okay? If we're snowbound, then we're snowbound. It's no big thing."

"Well, we'd better go see, we'd better go find out right away. Get dressed now, don't dawdle." Mrs. Tyler went out of the room and closed the door behind her.

Peggy had no desire to leave the warmth of her bed; but if she didn't, her mother would come back up and there would be an argument, and she felt too good today to want to argue about anything. Oh hell, she might as well get up then, and anyway, the time was not far off when she could spend whole days in bed if she felt like it—not far off at all, now.

Leisurely, she swung the covers back and stood up and padded across to where her purse sat on the dresser. She took out the sheaf of fifty-dollar bills Matt Hughes had given her and stroked the money with one finger, smiling; then, reluctantly, she tucked it away again in the compartment where she kept her bankbook and began to dress. When she went downstairs to join her mother a few minutes later, she still wore the same smile.

In the cabin at Mule Deer Lake, Kubion and Brodie and Loxner slept unaware of what had happened at the entrance to Hidden Valley; the thunderburst of the avalanche, diminished by the distance, had not disturbed them.

Loxner and Brodie were quiet in their beds, sleeping soundly. Kubion dreamed of spiders—black, cold, feathery-soft; crawling over him with mouths gaping in wet red hunger—and trembled and trembled and trembled.

The Tribucci brothers and Walt Halliday were the first Hidden Valley residents to reach the slide. They met on Sierra Street where it narrowed into County 235-A, and from there they could see it clearly through a light sifting of snow. Solemnly, wordlessly, the three men tramped up the sharp incline of the roadway and stopped when they could go no further, staring at the solid blockage rising up into the gray morning sky.

Sheer slabs of granite and splintered trees with branches and strips of bark torn away, protruded from the irregular surfaces like shattered bones. The western cliff face seemed steeper than it had been, scarred with an inverted fanshell chute that shone blackly against the dove-colored surroundings. In the stillness you could hear the mounded snow and ice and rock settling with a soft rumbling sound, like a thin echo of the slide itself.

Halliday said, his voice subdued, "Bad. Jesus, about as bad as it could be."

Both Tribuccis nodded gravely; there did not seem to be anything else to say.

Several other Hidden Valley residents began to arrive, among them Lew Coopersmith and Frank McNeil and Mayor Matt Hughes. They, too, were quietly stunned by what they saw.

Hughes said finally, "My God, do you suppose anybody was in the pass when it happened?"

"Not likely," Vince Tribucci answered. "What with the amount of snow dropped by the blizzard last night, I doubt if the road was passable even before the slide. If it had to happen, this was probably the best time for it."

Hughes blew on chilled hands; in his haste he had forgotten his gloves. "I'd better get on the phone to the county seat and let them know about this and ask them to get men and equipment out as quickly as possible." He turned and hurried back to where he had left his car.

Frank McNeil turned to John Tribucci. "How long you figure it'll take to clear through?"

"From the way it looks, I'd guess at least a week. But if we keep getting heavy snows, it could take two or more."

McNeil pursed his lips sourly. "Merry Christmas," he said, "and a Happy god-damn New Year."

# Thirteen

By nine o'clock the clouds had thinned and scattered to the east, and the whitish eye of a pale winter sun dominated a widening swath of sky. There was no wind, and the thin air had lost most of its chill. On the inner valley slopes and in parts of the valley itself, some of the deep powder drifts created by the night's storm began to slowly melt, forming little cascades in intricate, interconnecting patterns. Ice unprotected by pockets of shadow crackled intermittently in the warming day; the snow on the village streets commenced liquefying into slush.

Kubion started in from the Mule Deer Lake cabin just before noon, handling the car cautiously, squinting through the streaked windshield. The glare of sun on snow hurt his eyes and intensified the dull ache in his temples. He felt lousy today, badly strung out. Not much sleep last night, that was one of the things responsible—and that dream he'd had, the spiders crawling over him with their red gaping mouths. Jesus! He loathed spiders; they were the one thing which terrified him. He'd never had a nightmare like that before, and it worried him; it was as disquieting as the recurring headaches and his irrational inclination to violence.

The headaches were another source of his uptight feeling. The dull pain in his temples and forehead hadn't developed into one so far, but he knew it could happen easily enough, he knew he could lose control again. He could feel the impulsive need to destroy lying just below the surface of his emotions, like something ineffectually chained in a dark cave, waiting for the opportunity to break free and come screaming into the light.

And there was the need to get out of this frigging wilderness, to get back to civilization, where they could set up another score; the attendant frustration of knowing they couldn't chance it the way things were. According to the morning radio reports, the Sacramento cops had finally found the rented garage and the dummy armored car; there would be no lessening of the heat for some time yet.

Kubion drove down onto Sierra Street and noticed that there was more activity in the village than usual—that two people were walking up the middle of the road toward the pass. Then he became aware of the huge mound of snow and rock and splintered trees which blocked the valley entrance in a long downward fan. What the hell? he thought.

He kept on past the Mercantile—he had come in for a few minor supplies, to get out of the cabin again for a while—and pulled the car into the Shell station and parked it on the apron. He went up the rest of the way on foot, stopping next to the man and woman he had seen trudging along the road: a couple of senior citizens in plaid mackinaws and woolen hats. "What happened here?" he asked them. "Avalanche, is that what it is?"

Lew Coopersmith looked at him, frowned slightly, and then seemed to place him. "That's what it is," he said at length.

"When did it happen?"

"Just at dawn. Woke up the whole village."

"Yeah, I can imagine."

"If you and your friend planned on leaving before Christmas, I'm afraid you won't be able to do it. According to estimates, we'll be snowbound at least a week and maybe more."

"You mean nobody can get in or out of the valley?"

"Not unless they use snowmobiles around and through ten or fifteen miles of heavy timber. The pass is blocked solid."

Some country, all right, Kubion thought: the frozen bunghole of creation. Well, what difference did it make? If anything, it was a favorable occurrence; for the next week or so they would be cut off completely from all the fuzz on the outside.

But he said, playing it cautious, "My friend's wife is going to scream like a wounded eagle. She was expecting us for the holidays, back in San Francisco. We were leaving Saturday."

Ellen Coopersmith said, "Oh, that's too bad."

"Yeah."

"Phone lines are open," Coopersmith told him, "so it isn't like we were completely isolated. Your friend will be able to call his wife and tell her the circumstances."

"He'll want to do that, okay. Thanks."

Coopersmith nodded. "Sorry about the inconvenience, but it's just one of those things that happens. Nothing you can do."

"I guess not," Kubion said. He turned away and walked back to his car and sat unmoving behind the wheel staring up at the slide. An idea began to nudge his mind. Snowbound, he thought. Nobody can get in or out of the valley. No contact with the outside except by telephone. Made-to-order kind of situation, by God. And he remembered the check Matt Hughes had cashed for the old man in the Mercantile the previous afternoon: unofficial bank and how much *was* there in that office safe? Ten thousand? Maybe not even that much, and then again maybe more—maybe a lot more. How many people in Hidden Valley? Seventy-five or so, wasn't it? Hicks; but hicks sometimes had plenty of money, you were always hearing about some old fart who kept his life's savings in a fruit jar because he didn't trust banks. Might even be as much as thirty or forty thousand in the valley....

Abruptly, Kubion shook himself. Christ! He was thinking like a punk again, there was no score for them here, how could there be? *They* were trapped along with the rest of the damned people, and there was the safe house to think of. The hicks knew him and Brodie by sight, if not Loxner, and realistically there just didn't figure to be nearly enough in it in the first place. Even if there was a hundred grand in cash and jewelry in Hidden Valley, it wouldn't be worth it. Still, it was a wild concept: rip off an entire valley. Wouldn't that be the cat's nuts! But three men couldn't execute a caper like that—or could they? Well there was probably a way to do it and get away with it, all right; the snowbound business took care of any outside interference, it would be like working in a big sealed room.... Oh shit, it was crazy and stupid to even consider it. They needed a job like Greenfront should have been: safe, clean, big take, no loose ends, no people who knew what they really looked like and could identify them afterward.

But a whole valley, a whole goddamn valley.

*Could* it be done, with just three men?

Kubion lit a cigarette and sat drumming his fingers on the hard plastic of the steering wheel. Come on, come on, he thought, it's a pipe dream. And then: Okay, so it's a pipe dream, so actually doing it is all the way out. The thing is, can it be done on paper? Is it workable at all?

He sucked at his cigarette. Well, why not find out? He was uptight, wasn't he? The waiting—at least another ten days of it for sure now—and the worrying about those bastard headaches and that dream about the spiders: all of it pressing in on him, flooding his mind. What he needed was to focus his thoughts on something else, something that would keep him from blowing off, and there was nothing better for that than the working out of a challenging score—even an imaginary one.

Kubion started the car and drove back along Sierra Street and parked across from the Mercantile; got out and slogged through the liquidy snow to enter the store. Except for the white-haired old lady who had waited on him the day before, the place appeared empty. Recorded Christmas music still blared away from the wall loudspeakers: some clown singing about a winter wonderland. Yeah.

Maude Fredericks said when he reached the counter, "Isn't it terrible about the slide? Such a thing to happen just before Christmas."

"Sure," Kubion said. "Terrible. Tell me, you have a detail map of this area?"

Her brow wrinkled quizzically. "Well, we have a specially printed tourist brochure that includes a comprehensive Hidden Valley map. We also have a county topographical map."

"Fine. I'll take both," Kubion said, thinking: And wouldn't you crap your drawers, lady, if you had any idea what I want them for....

# Fourteen

Cain spent most of that day snowshoe walking among the lodgepole pine on the upper east slope, where the stillness was almost breathless and the air was thick with the cold, fresh, sweet scent of the mountain forest in winter.

He knew these woods well, the series of hiking paths which crosshatched them, because he had spent a considerable amount of time exploring the area during the summer and fall months. When he was having a particularly bad day and the weather permitted, he had found that taking long walks served as an effective tranquilizer. Alone deep in the forest, you were mostly able to shut off your thoughts and to allow only your senses to govern; and, too, you made yourself physically tired, a weariness that acted like a supplemental narcotic to the liquor.

But on this day, as on the previous two, the forest did nothing to erase the continuing feeling of loneliness which had come over him on Monday night—which lingered like a sudden bright and maddening stain on the fabric of his mind; if anything, the absolute solitude of the surroundings increased it. He felt confused, restless, irritable. And to make it worse, now the damned people in this valley were starting to bother him.

Two unwanted and unexpected visitors yesterday. First that old man, the retired county sheriff named Coopersmith: pleasant, apologetic, asking politely if he knew anything about a door having been jimmied open at the Valley Café. It hadn't been the indirect implication that he was a malicious vandal which had caused him to snap angrily at Coopersmith; it had been the visit itself, the intrusion on his aloneness. The same was true of Rebecca Hughes' appearance last night. Perhaps she *had* come simply because she was lonely and wanted some innocent companionship, but that had not mattered at the time. He had only wanted to be rid of her; he didn't want conversation, and he particularly didn't want conversation centered on the subject of loneliness; so he had made the obvious insinuations, he had treated her, cruelly, like a tramp.

But this morning when he'd reexamined the incident not long after being awakened by the still-unidentified earthquakelike concussion, he had felt a sense of shame. He'd hurt her, her tears had been genuine when she'd run out, and the last thing he truly cared to do, after what he had done to his own family, was to inflict pain on anyone. Alone and fully sober, he'd thought that he could have got her to leave some other way and was sorry he hadn't. Briefly he'd considered going down to the Hughes' house and apologizing to her, but the embarrassed intimacy of a personal apology was something he simply couldn't face. And if yesterday were any indication, it would become necessary to leave Hidden Valley. There were plenty of similar places in the Sierra; it made no difference at all in which of them he lived just as long as he was left alone.

Cain returned to the cabin in late afternoon—and discovered ten minutes after his arrival, when he went into the kitchen for a fresh package of cigarettes, that the carton there was empty. His mouth twisted ironically; all the walking today, empty walking, and now, because tobacco had become a necessity rather than a habitual indulgence, he would have to walk yet another half mile or so round trip to the Sport Shop.

There was no need for snowshoes on Lassen Drive; he donned only his coat and a muffler before leaving the cabin again. The sun was well hidden now behind the mountain slopes to the west, but the sky in that direction held a faint lavender alpenglow. The temperature had dropped considerably, as it did every day around this time. There was still no wind.

When Cain reached the Hughes' house and drew parallel with the entrance drive—eyes cast down on the icing snow beneath his feet—an awareness touched him and he paused, raising his head, looking into the front yard. Rebecca Hughes had just come out of the house and was moving toward the road.

She saw him at almost the same instant, stopped, and visibly stiffened. One hand came partway up in front of her breasts in a gesture that might have meant anything or nothing. They stood fifty feet apart, motionless, for a long awkward moment. The sense of shame nudged Cain's mind again, and he thought once more of apologizing to her; happenstance had created the situation for it. But he could think of nothing to say; he still did not want a connection of any kind.

She was the first to move. Her hand dropped, and then she turned sharply and went back to the house with quick, jerky steps. At the Dutch-doored front entrance, she fumbled a key out of her purse, got it into the lock, and disappeared inside. The door made a dull slamming sound.

Cain was immediately thankful that there had been no dialogue between them; and yet at the same time he was contrite for not having spoken. More ambivalence—damned ambivalence! With an effort he forced Rebecca Hughes from his mind and continued down Lassen Drive.

He had gone five hundred yards farther, nearing the job in the road which would bring him into the village proper, when he heard the sound of a car approaching. He did not glance up. The sound grew louder, and the car came around the job and pulled abreast of him. It braked to a halt, and the driver's door opened, and Frank McNeil stood up, peering over the roof. His mouth was drawn so thin that it appeared lipless.

"You—Cain!" he shouted.

Cain kept on walking.

"Listen, goddamn it, I'm talking to you!"

He felt the muscles bunch on his neck and across his shoulders, and irritation came thickly into his throat. Finally he stopped and turned and looked at the car, recognizing McNeil vaguely, recalling the man's name. He said, "What do you want?"

"Where you been all day? I been up here three times now."

"What business is it of yours?"

"You think I don't know who's been doing it?" McNeil said in a voice that quivered with outrage. "Two nights in a row now, and you think I don't know it has to be you? Well I know, Cain, and I want you to know I know. I want you to sweat, because as soon as the pass is open, the county deputies will be here to arrest you. I've already called them, and the hell with Lew Coopersmith. You hear me, Cain? You hear me?"

Cain stared at him. "I don't know what you're talking about."

"You know, damn you, and you're going to pay."

The irritation boiled over into anger. Cain took several steps toward the car. McNeil slid back inside, and the door banged shut, and the rear wheels sprayed freezing slush in a long grayish fan as it skidded forward. Well up the road, it swung into the Hughes' driveway, backed and filled, and came down toward Cain at an increased speed. He moved deep onto the shoulder as it passed, but the wheels churned up more slush and flung it at him in an icy spume, spattering his jacket and trousers.

Cain stood trembling, watching the retreating car. Nothing McNeil had said made immediate sense to him; it seemed like gibberish. Then he remembered Coopersmith's visit the day before: somebody breaking into the Valley Café. Two times, McNeil had said. It must have happened again last night, and for some reason McNeil thought he was the one who'd done it. For Christ's sake, why would *he* do anything like that? Why single *him* out for the blame? He'd done nothing to give these people the idea he was that kind of man; he'd never bothered them at all.

And now there would be police, and there would be questions—further intrusion on his privacy—and while they would realize his innocence sooner or later, it might take days before they were convinced. The bastards, the bastards, why couldn't they let him be?

Why couldn't he be left *alone?*

# Fifteen

Late Thursday morning Lew Coopersmith sat in front of the quartz-and-granite fireplace in his living room, drinking hot, fresh coffee with John Tribucci.

An hour and a half earlier he had gone to the Mercantile on an errand for Ellen, and Tribucci and Matt Hughes had been discussing slide developments. The latest report from County Maintenance was that a second dozer had been brought in—there was also a rotary snowthrower on hand—and the crews were beginning to make some progress. But at a conservative estimate it would still be the day after Christmas before they had the pass road cleared, weather permitting. Coopersmith and Tribucci had eventually left the store together and then walked up to the slide. You could hear the sound of the machines from there, although the work itself was invisible from within the valley.

After a short time they came back down again, and Coopersmith invited the younger man to the house for coffee since Frank McNeil had decided to keep the Valley Café closed as long as they were snowbound and Walt Halliday did not open the bar in the inn until 4 P.M. Tribucci had readily consented, saying smilingly that as much as he adored his sister-in-law, her coffee was on the same qualitative level as that of an Army mess cook's.

Now Coopersmith began filling one of his blackened Meerschaum pipes from the canister of tobacco on the low table between them. "You think the weather will hold, Johnny?" he asked.

"Hard to say. Forecast is clear for the next couple of days, but we may be in for another storm either Saturday or Sunday. If you want a pessimistic opinion, Lew, it will be two or three days after Christmas before the pass is open again." He paused and frowned into his cup. "I just hope the baby doesn't decide to arrive until New Year's now."

"Even if it does, Ann will be fine. Doc Edwards has delivered dozens of babies in private homes."

"I know, but I'd feel better if she had hospital care when the time comes."

"We'll all feel better once things are back to normal. I don't like being cut off from the outside world for so long a time, even if it isn't total isolation. It makes me feel helpless and vulnerable."

"Vulnerable to what?"

Coopersmith fired his pipe with a kitchen match. When he had it drawing to his satisfaction, he said, "Well I don't know exactly. I guess it's just that I don't have complete control of my own life at the moment. It's like being up in an airplane—you've got to depend on somebody else. And when you're dependent, you're vulnerable. That make any sense to you?"

"I think it does," Tribucci said. "In fact, I suppose in a way that's why I keep worrying about Ann and the baby."

Leaning back in his armchair, Coopersmith sighed and chewed reflectively on the stem of his pipe. At length he asked, "What do you make of the café break-ins, Johnny?"

"I don't know what to make of them. It's a damned peculiar business, happening two nights in a row like that."

Coopersmith nodded. On the second occasion, as on the first, the rear door had been jimmied and propped open; but the damage had been considerably heavier, owing to the magnitude of Tuesday night's storm: bottles and jars blown off shelves and shattered on the floor, cans and perishables ruinously frozen. Frank McNeil had been livid, far more concerned about his private property than the avalanche which had left the valley snowbound. That was the primary reason he had decided to close the café until after Christmas.

"I talked to most everyone in the valley yesterday and Tuesday," Coopersmith said, "and drew a complete blank. Whoever did it pulled it off clean both times."

"Well, at least it didn't happen again last night."

"That's something, anyway."

Tribucci made a wry mouth. "McNeil says that's because yesterday he told Zachary Cain he knew he was the one responsible and was going to have him arrested as soon as the pass is cleared. Says that put the fear of God into Cain."

"Horse apples," Coopersmith said.

"Yeah. Cain is a funny sort, that's true enough, but he just doesn't strike me as the type to go in for malicious mischief."

"Me neither. He hasn't bothered a soul since he's been here. Besides, the idea that he would do it because McNeil asked me to investigate him when he first came is ridiculous. I told Frank there wasn't any way Cain could have found out about that in the first place, but trying to talk sense to McNeil is like trying to talk sense to a ground squirrel. He'll be lucky if Cain doesn't sue him for slander."

"That's for sure," Tribucci agreed. "Thing is, though, I can't picture anyone else in the valley doing the break-ins either. Not for any reason."

"Same here. But somebody did it, and for some reason." Coopersmith's pipe had gone out, and he relighted it. "Well, whatever the answer, I'll see if I can't ferret it out sooner or later."

The two men had a second cup of coffee and talked briefly of Christmas, of what gifts they had gotten for their wives—Ellen was in the kitchen, out of earshot—and determined they would get together at Vince's house on Christmas Eve for some traditional eggnog and cookies and caroling.

When Tribucci had gone to relieve his brother at the Sport Shop, Coopersmiith finished his pipe and brooded mildly over the slide and the café break-ins. He poured himself a third cup of coffee and, tasting it, decided it could use a little sweetening. He stood up and went quietly to the sideboard for the brandy decanter.

# Sixteen

Wearing warm old clothes and a pair of fur-lined boots, the Reverend Peter Keyes left his cottage at the rear of the All Faiths Church at one thirty to do his daily shopping.

He was not as deeply concerned about the pass slide as some of the other valley residents, although it *would* prevent him from spending Christmas afternoon and evening with his relatives in Soda Grove. Coming so close to Yuletide, it was of course an unfortunate thing; but no one had been killed or injured, for which thanks could be given, and the Reverend Mr. Keyes was not one to question an act of God in any circumstance. For all the inconvenience to his friends and neighbors and to himself, it was nonetheless the season of joy and charity and great faith: the celebration of the birthday of Jesus Christ.

The Reverend Mr. Keyes walked along the side of the church, beneath the three slender, obelisk-shaped windows and the sharply pitched alpine roof with its squared, four-windowed belfry and tall steeple at the rear: a simple frame church which, he felt, suited perfectly the simple life of those who made the Sierra their home. As he started toward the street, he noticed a medium-sized, unfamiliar man standing at the signboard adjacent to the front walk, reading the arrangement of glassed-in plastic letters which told of the coming Sunday services.

The minister altered his path and approached the stranger—no doubt one of the San Francisco businessmen he had heard were staying at Mule Deer Lake. Perhaps, since the man was reading the signboard, he was thinking of attending services; the prospect, if true, was a pleasing one.

When the newcomer heard the Reverend Mr. Keyes' steps in the snow, he turned. Very dark, he was, almost sooty-looking, with a hard cast to his face and a feral, overbright quality to his eyes. But the minister well knew how deceiving appearances could be, and as he reached the man, he smiled and extended his hand. "Good afternoon. I'm Reverend Peter Keyes, the pastor of All Faiths Church."

"Charley Adams is my name," Kubion said. He took the proffered hand. "Nice to meet you, Reverend."

"I noticed you reading the signboard, Mr. Adams. May I ask if you'll be joining our congregation on Sunday?"

"Well, I just might do that, all right."

"We'll be more than pleased to have you."

"There's only one service, I see."

"Yes—at noon. The village is really too small to make more than one feasible during the winter, although we have two throughout the summer season."

Kubion glanced at the church. "Are the doors open now?"

"Oh, of course. They're seldom locked."

"I'd like to step inside for a minute, if I could."

"Certainly, please do."

Kubion nodded a parting and moved away along the front walk. The Reverend Mr. Keyes watched him climb the five front steps and enter the church and then smiled gently to himself. Appearances were indeed misleading; Charley Adams was an agreeable sort of person—and no doubt a good and devout, if somewhat diffident, Christian.

He thought Kubion had gone into the church to pray.

John Tribucci was alone in the Sport Shop, stocking shelves in the tobacco section, when the dark stranger came in at two o'clock.

"Something I can do for you?" Tribucci asked pleasantly.

"Well, maybe there is," Kubion said. "I was wondering if you've got any snowmobiles in stock."

"Snowmobiles?" Tribucci managed to conceal his surprise. "Why, yes, as a matter of fact we do—just one. It was given to us on consignment by a chain sporting goods outlet in the county seat."

"Be okay if I looked at it?"

"Sure." He led Kubion around to the rear of the store, where the machine sat in the center of a small display of skis, snowshoes, and ice skates. It resembled a two-seat scooter mounted on skis and wide roller treads—black chassis, white cowl, red and white trim. "It's a Harley Davidson, fast and durable. Plenty of features: dual headlights, eighteen-inch molded track, shock-dampened steering, ski-mounted hydraulic shocks. Engine is twenty-three horsepower, good enough for cross-country slogging, and one of the quietest on the market."

"How much gas will it hold?"

"It has a six-gallon tank."

"Okay—what does it sell for?"

"A little better than fifteen hundred, plus tax. That's a good price for the quality, considering what some of the bigger mobiles cost these days."

Kubion frowned. "I didn't know they ran anywhere near that much," he said. "This the only one in the valley?"

Tribucci said dryly, "You mean, does anybody own an older model they might want to sell for a few hundred?"

"Yeah, I guess that's what I mean."

"I'm afraid not. The only other mobile in Hidden Valley is one my brother owns, and it's a Harley similar to this one—last year's model. He'd be willing to sell it, I think, but I doubt if he'd take less than a thousand."

"Still pretty stiff," Kubion said, and shook his head. Then, in a self-conscious way, he laughed. "You're probably wondering why all the sudden interest in a snowmobile."

"Well—yes," Tribucci admitted. "With the valley being snowbound, it's not exactly the time people think of winter sports."

"Winter sports didn't have anything to do with it; being snowbound is the reason. See, this friend of mine and me—we're staying out at Mule Deer Lake, you probably know that—we're expected back in San Francisco for Christmas. So we got to thinking last night that we could split the cost of a snowmobile and use it to get to one of the towns in the area, where we could rent a car. But we didn't figure the things to be so expensive; we just can't afford that kind of money for something we might not even use again."

Tribucci said, "You could get to Coldville all right in a mobile, swinging east by northeast; it's rough country, fifteen miles of it, but with a map and the mobile's compass and fair weather it could be done safely enough. Still, you'd have to have quite a bit of knowledge of mountain country like this."

"Couldn't we walk out, too, the same way?"

"You could, but I wouldn't advise trying it. That's a hell of a trek on snow-shoes—and if a storm hits, you'd freeze to death."

"No shorter way to do it, like going over or around those pass cliffs and then picking up the county road into Soda Grove?"

Tribucci shook his head. "The upper approaches to both cliffs, where the trees thin out, are made up of snow- and ice-covered talus and walls and pin-nacles of granite. To the west the terrain drops sharply and there are gullies and declivities filled with drifts of loose snow—you must have noticed com-ing in how deep and wide the canyon is on the other side of the pass. To the east, you've got a long series of smaller ridges and more deep snow pockets."

Kubion said, "And I guess it would be dangerous to try scrambling over the slide itself?"

"Suicidal is the word. That mass may seem like a solid pack, but it isn't. You couldn't scale this end, and even if you could, your weight on all that imbal-anced, down-slanted snow and rock would start a shifting and resettling that'd bury you in seconds. That's why the clearing process is such a slow and methodical one." Tribucci paused. "About the only practical way you could get out of Hidden Valley immediately is by helicopter, assuming the weather holds. But unless your leaving is a definite emergency, I wouldn't count on it. The county only has one chopper, and there are priorities."

"Then I guess we're stuck good and proper, and we'll just have to make the best of it. Sorry to take up your time."

"Not at all."

When Kubion had gone, Tribucci resumed stocking the tobacco shelves. It would have meant a not inconsiderable profit if he'd been able to sell the mobile, and with the baby due so soon, the money would have been more than welcome. But then, he hadn't really expected to make the sale from the first—not under the present circumstances and having correctly assumed the reason for the dark man's sudden interest.

City people, he thought, have the damnedest ideas....

Kubion spent another hour in the village—mainly at the foot of the east slope, beyond Alpine Street, where the telephone and power lines stretched downward into Hidden Valley—and then drove back to Mule Deer Lake. He parked the car in the cabin garage and went inside and directly up to his bedroom.

The dull ache in his temples and forehead was still with him, no better and no worse than it had been the previous day. Last night he had dreamed of spiders again, the same dream, the same ugly black spiders with their redly gaping mouths. But he hadn't thought of these things at all; his mind had been focused for the past twenty-four hours on the theoretical score—attacking it with a vengeance, just as if it were the real thing.

He sat on the rumpled bed and took one of the thin brown marijuana cigarettes from the tin on the nightstand. Leaning back against the headboard, he lit the stick and sucked slowly on it, holding the mawkish smoke deep in his lungs. When the joint was ash against his fingers, he could feel the lift, he could feel his thoughts coming clear and sharp. Then he began putting it all together, everything he had learned from the valley and topographical maps and everything he had found out in the village today.

And he knew it could be done.

The knowledge excited him, stimulated him. It could be done, all right, it actually could be done with just three men. Still a few details to be worked out, still a few angles to consider, but he had the basics completely assembled. It hadn't been much of a problem, not nearly as much a one as he'd first thought; the fact that the valley was snowbound was what made it all so simple.

Kubion lit a second stick of pot and smoked it, working out the details carefully. Time passed—and he had it all then, the entire operation from beginning to end. Nothing left unconsidered, no flaws in the progression. All of it neat, clear, workable.

Darkness settled outside and came into the room in slow, lengthening shadows; and with it came the letdown. The stimulation vanished; an empty flatness replaced it. He became aware of the dull throbbing in his head, and he could feel his nerves pulling taut again. He tried a third stick of grass, but this time it did nothing for him. The sudden downer was heavy and oppressive, and he knew the reason for it; sitting there on the bed, he knew exactly what was the matter.

He'd figured the score, and it could be done, and they couldn't do it.

From the beginning it had been nothing more than a mental exercise, something to occupy his mind for a while. But he couldn't forget it, now that he'd figured it; there would be nothing to do, nothing to focus on, and the pain in his head, and the spiders, the black red hungry spiders, and the blowoff that would surely come, the violence; he couldn't forget the score even though it was useless thinking about it further. Frustration now, and the pain centering behind his eyes, pulsing, pulsing....

Rapping on his door. He jerked slightly, irritably, at the interruption and called out, "What the hell is it?"

"Supper's ready, Earl," Brodie's voice said from outside.

"I don't want any goddamn supper, leave me alone."

Silence. Then, "All right, Earl."

"All right, all right, all *right.*"

Kubion stretched out full length on the bed. The room was completely dark now, and cold, and he put one of the blankets over him. It can be done, he thought, we can do it, go over it again and keep going over it, make it even more solid, cancel some of the risks but there are too many of them but the hicks keep money in fruit jars sometimes but they can identify us but a whole valley but this is safe ground but it can be done....

The spiders came.

They came out of the darkness, big ones, big black ones, crawling over the floor and up onto the bed. One of them crept upward along his leg, mouth opened redly, hungry mouth, saliva dripping, he could feel the saliva dripping like hot slime through the blanket and through his clothes and onto his naked flesh. No! But the room was filled with them now, coming for him, one on his arm, one on his chest, one on his neck, black and red and feather-legged with their hungry devouring mouths, get away from me, *get away from me!*

He screamed, and screamed again, and woke up, and came off the bed in a convulsive jump. He stood shivering in the darkness, and the spiders were gone; it had been the dream again and the spiders were gone. Or—were they? What was that, there in the dark corner? Something moving, something crawling. Spider! No, they were gone, mind playing tricks, no spiders here, no spiders, but something was crawling, he could see it crawling there....

He squeezed his eyes shut, nothing there, and slitted them open again, nothing there, nothing there. Think about the score, remember the score that can be done, that we can't do, that can be done. He could not keep his hands quiet; his body was soaked in sweat. The pain in his head was raging now, he could feel himself losing control, his thoughts were wrapped in a gray floating mist and he wanted to smash something, kill something, kill the spiders, the filthy spiders crawling there in the dark corner, and he ran to the corner and killed one spider, and killed a second, and twisted panting toward the bed and suddenly they were all around him, scurrying over the walls and floor and furnishings, they were real and they were after him and all the pain in his head the pain and the spiders coming the red black hungry spiders coming the spiders the—

He stopped shaking.

The pain went away.

The spiders went away.

Just like that, as if a bubble had burst inside him, it all went away, and he was calm again. He stood still for a moment, until his breathing returned to normal, and then bathed in sweat from his face and walked slowly to the bed. Sitting on the edge of it, he switched on the lamp and looked around the room.

Good-bye, spiders, he thought, good-bye forever because you're not coming back, I'm not going to let you come back.

And he began to laugh.

He laughed for a long time, tears streaming down his cheeks, drool overflowing the corners of his mouth, stitches in his belly and both sides. Then, just as suddenly, the laughter cut off, and his head came up, and he sat staring straight ahead, lips still stretched in a wetly fixed grin. His eyes were brightly feverish, glowing like round black stones daubed with phosphorescent paint.

He was thinking about the score again, the score, the big big big big score. Oh, there was no question about it now, oh no question; there had never *been* any question.

It could be done—and they were going to do it.

# Seventeen

As she stood ladling thick vegetable soup from a tureen into two serving bowls, Rebecca heard Matt come downstairs and then call along the hallway, "Dinner ready yet?"

"Yes," she answered.

"Fine, I'm starved."

He came into the kitchen, showered and shaved and cologned and wearing a clean shirt and slacks. But not for me, she thought; habit, personal hygiene—nothing more. He had been home for a little more than an hour, and the only other words he had spoken to her were, "Hello, dear."

He sat at the table, sighed gustily, and said as if to himself, "Soup smells good."

She did not say anything. She placed one of the serving bowls in front of him, and another at her place directly opposite, and laid out a basket of bread and a plate of Cheddar cheese and took a bottle of Mosel from the refrigerator because Matt liked chilled white wine with soup. Then she sat and watched him uncork the bottle and pour their glasses full; and glance at her briefly, almost blankly; and pick up his spoon and begin to eat.

Rebecca despised that look. It was the way he always looked at her during one of his affairs: as if she were not a woman, not even a person, as if she were merely an inanimate object which he owned and could ignore at will. Zachary Cain had seemed to look at her yesterday with that same blank negation, when chance had taken her out of the house—she had been going into the village to visit with Ann Tribucci—at precisely the moment he was passing on the Drive. It might not have been so bad, seeing him again that soon after Tuesday night's humiliation, if he had only paused and then kept on walking down the road, or if, in coming to a standstill, he had said something, anything, to her. But instead, he had looked at her that way, just stood there silently and *looked* at her.

She had wanted to scream at him, just as she sometimes wanted to scream at Matt, that she was a human being with feelings and rights and she deserved to be treated accordingly. I'm *not* a bitch, she had wanted to tell him; I went up to see you for nothing more than a little fellowship, a little kindness. It would have been pointless, however—exactly as it would have been and would be pointless to verbalize her emotions to Matt. And so she hadn't spoken either, had simply turned and fled his gaze like a frightened sparrow.

Tuesday night's misadventure and yesterday's mute confrontation, while essentially immaterial in themselves, had combined with Matt's affairs, his rejection, the emptiness, the emotional need—all of it—to compound and deepen her mental depression. She felt as though she were suffocating. Things could not continue as they had for so long; she could not allow them to continue this way.

Rebecca stared at her soup, at the tissuey pieces of green and yellow and white vegetables floating in it, at the thin sheen of fat-eyes which coated the surface. Her throat closed nauseatingly, and she pushed the plate aside and folded her hands around her wine goblet. Lifting it, holding it without drinking, she watched Matt eat his soup and two slices of bread and a wedge of cheese. He did not once raise his eyes to her.

She waited until he had begun helping himself to a second bowl of soup; then, slowly and deliberately, she said, "Matt, let's go up to bed after supper."

He looked at her then, frowning slightly, poising the ladle over the tureen. "Bed?" he said. "It's only six thirty."

"I want to make love," she said. "It has been more than a month since we made love."

Matt lowered his gaze immediately and went on ladling soup. "That's hardly dinner-table conversation. There's a time and a place, after all...."

"I want to make love tonight, Matt."

"Rebecca, please. I've had a long, hard day, and I'm exhausted."

"Which means you don't want to have sex with me, not after supper and not later this evening."

"I wish you'd stop talking like that," he said. "It isn't like you to be so forward."

"Will you make love to me tonight?"

"Now that's enough."

"Don't you understand what I'm saying? I want you, I need to feel a man inside me again. Damn you, I want to be *fucked!*"

Matt's spoon clattered to the table; his eyes went wide, and his mouth dropped open in a tragicomic caricature of surprise and shock. "Rebecca!"

She stood up and went out of the kitchen, walking slowly. Upstairs in their bedroom, she took off her clothes and stood naked by the bed, listening, looking at the door. Matt did not come. When she was sure that he wouldn't, she got into bed and pulled the covers up to her chin and lay there staring blindly at the ceiling, trying to think, trying to find the strength to make a positive decision because things could not, *they could not,* go on this way.

# Eighteen

Brodie was making Spanish omelets, and Loxner was watching him and drinking a bottle of ale, when Kubion came downstairs Friday morning and said he had something important to talk over with them.

They took chairs around the kitchen table. Brodie did not like the way Kubion's eyes looked; they seemed to have tiny burning lights far back in their depths, and it was like seeing a pair of bonfires through the wrong end of a telescope. A sudden uneasiness crept through him.

And Kubion put his hands flat on the table and said, "We've got a new score."

It startled Brodie; it was the last thing he would have expected. He looked at Loxner and then back at Kubion. "I don't follow. Where could you find a score? We haven't been out of this valley since Monday night. Hell, we're snowbound here; nobody can get out."

"Or in," Kubion said, "and that's it, that's the whole thing right there. The valley is snowbound, and the valley is the score. We take it over and we clean it out store by store, house by house. Everything and everybody."

Loxner seemed about to laugh; his mouth curved upward at the corners, but then stayed that way—a rictus. He made no sound. Brodie stared at Kubion for a long moment, said finally, "Earl, you can't be serious...."

"Sure I'm serious, what do you think? It can be done, I've worked it all out and it can be done—no sweat, no sweat at all."

"For *what?*"

"For forty or fifty grand and maybe more, that's for what. The guy that owns the Mercantile runs an unofficial bank: a safe in his office. He cashed a check for one of the other hicks, a couple of days ago, four hundred and fifty dollars without even looking at it first. He's the big man here, it figures they all go to him when they need ready cash; he'll have thousands in there. And these hicks keep money in fruit jars under their beds, they got the family jewels in lock-boxes on their dressers—you're always hearing about crap like that."

Brodie and Loxner just stared at him.

Kubion wet his lips; his eyes burned more brightly, now. "Listen," he said, "listen, I know what you're thinking. There's only three of us, right? Seventy-five people in this valley and only three of us. But that's no problem—no problem. We do it on Sunday. Now where do most hicks go on Sunday, where do they always go on the Sunday before Christmas?"

Automatically Loxner said, "Church."

Brodie said, "Oh *Christ....*"

"You see how simple it is? At least fifty or sixty of them are all together in the church: a bunch of sitting ducks. We wait until after the service starts at noon, and then we go in and take them over. We tell them to look around and see who's not there; we make a list of names and addresses. Then we lock the front doors and go round up the rest of them house to house: ring their, doorbells, put a gun in their faces; easy. Once we've got everybody penned up in the church—there's no back exit, it's a box—one of us watches the front doors with a rifle just to make sure none of them tries to get out, and the other two rip off the buildings. Ten to twelve hours, and we can strip this valley like a chicken bone."

Brodie started to speak, but Kubion made a silencing gesture with one hand and went on with it.

"Okay, now you're wondering about a getaway with the valley being snowbound. We can't just sit around and wait until the road's open again, right? So what we do, we leave here on snowmobiles—those little motorized scooters that run on skis and treads. The two brothers that operate the Sport Shop have one in stock, brand-new. One of them owns another. That's two, that's all we need."

"Snowmobiles," Loxner said. Without seeming to taste it, he drained the last of his ale.

Kubion was smiling now—an excited, unnatural smile. "One of the brothers told me it could be done; all you need is a compass and a topographical map. I've got maps already, and a route traced out, and the mobiles are equipped with compasses. It's maybe fifteen miles east by northeast to a town called Coldville: four or five hours at the outside. The hicks say the road will be open the day after Christmas; that gives us at least two full days' start if we leave at dawn Monday."

Brodie said, "Goddamn it—"

"How do I figure two full days' minimum?" Kubion said. "Well, we take a hostage or two not long before we go, and we tell the rest that the hostages are dead if anybody even puts his head out while we're still in the valley, and they won't have any way of knowing when we actually do leave. We tell them we're going to take the hostages with us, too; we won't do it, we'll tie them up somewhere or off them, what the hell, but the others will believe what we say. They'll keep right on sitting in the church until somebody comes and lets them out. Another thing we do is cut the telephone lines late tomorrow night; that isolates the valley completely and eliminates any threat of a phone call to the cops if anybody that isn't in the church gets suspicious before we've got them all rounded up. So even if they did get out before the pass is open, what could they do?

"Now: once we reach this Coldville, we buy a used car—they've got a dealership there, it's listed in the phone book, and shagging one is too risky—and then we head for Reno or maybe Tahoe. A little of the blister from Sacramento should be off by next Monday; we play it careful on the road, we're okay. In Reno or Tahoe, we split up and take separate planes south or east or north. We get off the West Coast entirely, relocate somewhere else."

Kubion moistened his smile again. "So there it is—all laid out. Simple, beautiful, a score like nobody ever pulled off before. Well? What do you think?"

"I think you been blowing too much weed," Loxner said, trying to make a joke of it. "Man, that ain't a score, it's like plain fucking suicide."

The smile vanished.

Loxner laughed nervously. "This is *safe* ground, you don't pull a job on safe ground no matter how good it is. Christ, Brendikian would never stand for having this place blown that way. And he's got Circle connections, Earl, you know that."

"The Circle isn't going to pick up on small-time crap like having an independent safe house blown, I don't care what kind of connections Brendikian's got. Screw Brendikian."

"You don't know him, man, he ain't anybody to fool with."

"Screw Brendikian," Kubion said again.

Brodie leaned forward. "Earl, the people here know your face and mine; disguises or masks wouldn't be worth a thing. The cops would have those Identikit drawings on every front page in the country once the ripoff was reported. Our cover identities would be blown, that's one thing. And we've all taken falls; they'd come up with our names sooner or later, they'd have mug shots out in addition to the composites."

"I thought of that, I told you I thought of everything. The hell with it. It's not that hard to build a new cover somewhere. And the FBI's been looking for Ben Hammel for eight years for the bank job he was in on in Texas. He's still walking around."

"I'm not Ben Hammel, and I don't want my ass in that kind of sling. There's a damned good chance the cops would connect us up with Greenfront, too—and the chance we'd run into trouble taking over here and people would get killed. Murder One heat, either way. We wouldn't last a week anywhere in the country."

"Oh, bullshit," Kubion said. "How much play can a thing like this get in Connecticut? In Florida? In goddamn Puerto Rico? A few days and it dies off. Sure, the fuzz keeps right on looking. But you both know how simple it is to change what you look like. You grow a beard for a while; half the men in the nation wear beards these days, and how can some cop identify you when you're wearing a face full of whiskers? You cut your hair or let it grow or dye it another color. You gain weight or you lose weight or you wear padding. You live quiet, don't spread any money around. You know all the tricks as well as I do. And we're split up, that's another thing; three guys in three different parts of the country who don't look anything like the ones who ripped off Hidden Valley, California."

Brodie said, "Damn it, none of it makes *sense*. Even if we could stay on the loose, where are we? Say we could take as much as thirty grand out of here: that's only ten thousand apiece. How long is ten bills going to last each of us? We'd have to look for a new score inside of three months, and with all the heat still on. How many pros are going to want one of us in on a job carrying that kind of blister?"

"So we play it solo for a while. We've all worked solo before. The heat will die, it always dies sooner or later."

"For God's sake, they'd have our *names;* they'd know exactly who did the job. That kind of heat doesn't die."

"Hell no, it don't," Loxner said.

"I'll tell you a way the cops won't get our names at all, a way to come out of it free and clear and to hell with this cabin," Kubion said.

"What way?"

"Set fire to the church or blow it up before we go on the snowmobiles. Don't leave *any* witnesses who can identify us, waste them all."

Loxner gaped at him the way you would at something under a decaying log. Brodie's shoulders jerked involuntarily. "Hey, hey, hey," he said. His voice was incredulous. "What kind of freaky talk is that? Jesus, what do you think we are?"

"Okay, okay, then forget that. But listen—"

"We listened enough already," Loxner said, "I don't want to listen to no more. We don't want no part of what you're laying down here, no part of it."

Brodie said, "Earl, what's got into you? You're all of a sudden after this valley like you got a hard-on for the place, you're acting like a crazy amateur—"

Kubion was on his feet in one swift motion, upsetting his chair. His cheeks had suffused with dark blood, and his eyes were like a pair of live embers. He slapped the table with the flat of one palm, hard enough to topple Loxner's empty ale bottle and send it clattering to the floor. "Call me a crazy amateur, you son of a bitch, call *me* a crazy amateur!"

Loxner and Brodie were standing now as well, backed off a couple of steps, muscles tensed.

"You stupid pricks, can't you see the kind of thing this is? A whole valley, a whole valley, nobody ever did anything like it. Well? Well?"

Watching him, Brodie and Loxner remained silent.

Kubion took a breath, released it sibilantly—and as suddenly as it had come, the rage drained out of his face. "All right," he said, quiet-voiced, "all right then, all right," and turned and walked out of the kitchen.

Very softly Loxner said, "Oh man!" He went to the refrigerator and took out another ale and popped the cap and swallowed half of it without lowering the bottle. Then: "Things are bad enough without shit like that. The last thing we need is shit like that, Vic."

Brodie did not say anything.

"He gave me the creeps with all that crazy talk," Loxner said, "that funny look in his eyes. It was like he's a different person all of a sudden, you know what I mean?"

Brodie's mouth was pinched in at the corners, his eyes grimly reflective. "Yeah," he said slowly. "Yeah, I know what you mean."

# Nineteen

Black-edged clouds began to drift over Hidden Valley Friday afternoon, obliterating the pale sun and giving the air a dry, ice-tinged quality; but it did not snow again until very early Saturday morning, and then nothing more than a light dusting which would not interfere with work on the slide. When Matt Hughes came down Lassen Drive a few minutes past 8 A.M., the village seemed bathed in a soft luminosity created by the snow's whiteness reflecting light filtered through the low cloud ceiling. Under normal circumstances, such a view would have pleased him—the serene beauty of a mountain valley, his valley, in literally its best light—but he barely noticed it now; he had too many divergent things preying on his mind.

There was the slide, of course: all the problems it had caused, the extra work it made for him as mayor. There was Peggy Tyler, whom he had seen several times since their lovemaking in Whitewater Tuesday night but whom he had not spoken to for their mutual protection; whose lush and eager body glowed in his memory, exciting him with fresh and consuming desire and filling him with a sense of frustration because he could do nothing about it. And, finally, there was Rebecca.

Her sudden outburst Thursday evening at dinner had upset him considerably. He loved her deeply, and yet it was a kind of reverent, detached love: the love of an art connoisseur for a masterpiece which he alone possesses. From the moment he had met her, Hughes had never been able to think of her in sexual terms; the act of physically entering her body had never given him pleasure or satisfaction—just as fondling the fragile surfaces of his masterpiece would give the art connoisseur no pleasure and no satisfaction. Sex for Matt Hughes was a savage, primitive urge totally disassociated from love. It was sweating flesh and moaning frenzy and animalistic release with women like Peggy Tyler, women who instilled no reverence in him, women who dazzled his senses and sated completely his carnal hunger.

He wanted only to have Rebecca near him, to know that she was there and that she was his; he wanted only to believe in her and worship her in some of the same way he believed in and worshiped God. He wished desperately that he could explain this to her, but of course he had never tried; she would not have understood. And he lived in constant fear that she would find out about his continual affairs—as she had found out about the Soda Grove waitress several years ago—and that she would, instead of once again forgiving him, decide to leave him. He couldn't bear that. But still he yielded each time the primitive forces inside him demanded it, as if he were two different men, as if he were a kind of sensually emotional schizophrenic.

Did she suspect the current affair with Peggy? Or had her outburst Thursday only been the result of neglect and some of those same base desires which were present in all beings? The latter, of course; he refused to think otherwise. After he had recovered from his initial shock, he had tried to make himself go upstairs and take Rebecca into his arms and make love to her, but he had not been able to do it. He had never been able to correlate the primitive with the reverent; it was one or the other, and he simply could not touch or devote himself to his wife during those times when he was pouring out his lust into the bodies of other females.

The situation had grown worse over the past two days. Rebecca had not spoken a word to him since Thursday, and the atmosphere at home was strained and uncomfortable. The careful juxtaposition of his two lives had been momentarily and maddeningly imbalanced; he needed both Rebecca and Peggy now, he needed the status quo, and he did not have any of them. There had to be an answer, a way to restabilize things, but he had not as yet been able to figure out what it was.

Maude Fredericks had already opened the Mercantile, as she did on most mornings, when Hughes arrived. He went into his office and put through a call to Soda Grove. The slide status, at least, was still quo: progress slow but steady, no fresh slides to complicate matters. He came out into the store again, built a fire in the potbellied stove, and went to work.

The day seemed to drag on interminably. Rebecca and Peggy, Peggy and Rebecca—first one and then the other, endlessly cycling in his thoughts. He found himself wishing Peggy would come in and was both relieved and disappointed when she did not. He thought of calling Rebecca but didn't; there would have been no point in it, there was nothing he could say to her yet. Depression formed inside him like a thick, damp mist.

At four o'clock Hughes stopped trying to find things to do to occupy himself, left Maude to close up, and drove home through the same light, steady snow which had fallen all day. When he entered the house, it seemed filled with a tangible emptiness, and he knew immediately that Rebecca was not there. Gone into the village, he thought; probably to visit with Ann Tribucci. He listened to the empty silence and felt his depression deepen. In the kitchen he made a light scotch and water and took it into his study and sat tipped back in his leather recliner, sipping the drink and brooding.

And after a time he began to think about Peggy again, about Tuesday night in the Whitewater motel room. His scrotum tightened painfully, and sitting there, he had a full and pulsing erection: the primitive in him screaming for her—now, today, tonight. But there was no way, not until the pass was cleared. Too dangerous for them to meet in Hidden Valley and no place to meet even if they dared to risk it. She couldn't come here to his house, and he couldn't go to hers, and the Mercantile was no good because of its central village location. No other place

Mule Deer Lake, he thought suddenly. The Taggart cabin.

Hughes leaned forward in the recliner, pulling it into its upright position. The Taggart cabin. Yes—and it wasn't all that dangerous if they were very, very careful. But did they dare? Would Peggy be willing? Some of the depression had evaporated now, and an almost boyish recklessness throbbed inside him. They could get away with it, and he needed her, he *needed* her. Call Peggy, call her right now, take the chance....

Impulsively he stood up and started across the study to the extension phone on his old rolltop desk. And stopped halfway there, touched by abrupt fear. No; it was utter foolishness. They could be seen, they could be recognized, and what then? The affair would become public knowledge, and Rebecca would leave him for certain then; she would have no alternative. Public disgrace, his position in the valley irreparably damaged—he could lose everything that mattered in his life. Besides, it would only be another few days until the pass was open again. They could resume their Whitewater meetings in a week or so, perhaps next Friday or Saturday night. He could wait that long, couldn't he?

He felt the burning, demanding ache in his genitals and was not sure that he could.

Rebecca, he thought with a kind of desperation, if only I could make love to Rebecca tonight. It would solve both his immediate problems; it would make things all right again. But the savagery of his need made it impossible; it was Peggy his body craved, Peggy, Peggy, and he would be completely and unquestionably impotent if he—

Impotent.

Impotence!

*That* was the answer to his marital dilemma; it had been the answer all along. Of course: impotence, it was so obvious he had never even thought of it before. All he had to do was to tell Rebecca that certainly he wanted to make love to her, but that it was, at the moment, physically impracticable—he had for some time been suffering from sexual incapacity. He had wanted to tell her long before now, he would say, but had been too ashamed to admit it; he was seeing a doctor in Soda Grove, taking hormone treatments to rectify the problem—although to date they had been frustratingly ineffective. She would believe him; there was no reason why she shouldn't believe him. She would be sympathetic and understanding, and there would be no more outbursts, no more periods of uncomfortable silence between them. Then, when the affair with Peggy came to its inevitable conclusion in another few weeks and he was once again able to bring himself to make love to his wife, he would tell Rebecca that the treatments had finally produced positive results. It would be just as simple as that.

Hughes felt immediate relief—one problem taken care of, he was sure of it—but the mitigation was tempered by his urgent desire for Peggy. He thought again of the Taggart cabin, of how easy it would be for them to use it as a meeting place. Nothing *could* go wrong, nothing would go wrong; the gamble was no greater than any of the others he had taken during the past seven years, and in that time no one in Hidden Valley had suspected a thing, they would have no reason to suspect anything now. A cautious hour or two, that was all, and just tonight, never again in the valley. After tonight he would be able to wait until next Friday with no difficulty at all. If he went through with it, there would be no more immediate quandaries with his personal life; he could have Rebecca and Peggy and the status quo, all his again and all tonight.

The recklessness, the excitement swept through him again. Rationalization and his hungry loins had decided the argument: he knew he was going to call Peggy and make the suggestion to her. Quickly, he went to the extension phone—and from there he could look through the study window at the darkened, restlessly clouded sky. It would keep on snowing for some time yet, the night would be very dark. Very dark. He caught up the receiver and then hesitated. What if her mother answered? Disguise his voice, that was it; put his handkerchief over the mouthpiece. He fumbled the folded square of cambric from his back pocket and draped it around the handset, at once realizing that he was being melodramatic and taking a kind of adventurous ebullience in the fact. Then he flipped open the county directory and found the Tylers' number and dialed it rapidly.

Peggy's voice said, "Hello?" on the sixth ring.

Hughes pulled the handkerchief away, releasing the breath he had been holding. "Peggy?"

Pause. "Matt, is that you?"

"Yes. You can talk all right?"

"My mother is over at the Chiltons. But you took a chance, calling like this."

"I know. I had to talk to you."

"That damned slide," she said. "It's going to be such a miserably long time until we can be together again."

"It doesn't have to be," Hughes said fervently. "Peggy, listen, I've just thought of something—a way and a place we can meet."

"You mean *here*, in the valley?"

"Yes. Tonight. I've thought it out, and it's safe as long as we're careful. Do you want to do it?"

"I don't know, Matt...."

"Peggy, I keep thinking about you, I can't get you out of my mind. I have to see you. Please, Peggy."

Pause. "Tell me your idea."

"The Taggart cabin at Mule Deer Lake," Hughes said. "The first one on the eastern shore, the one that sits by itself at the edge of the lake. Well, I've got the keys to it; the Taggarts always leave them with me when they go back to Red Bluff in the fall. We can spend a couple of hours there early tonight, say seven o'clock. And we won't turn on any lights, so that if somebody does pass the cabin, they won't know anybody is inside."

"We couldn't take both our cars."

"No, just mine. You can walk to the stand of trees where Sierra Street forks into the two lake roads, going along the west slope where nobody would see you. I'll pick you up there."

"What if somebody notices your car at the cabin or sees it drive up? The

Markhams and the Donnellys live on the eastern shore of the lake."

"Their homes are both well down the shore. It'll be dark at the lake—no moon; the snowing will keep visibility down—and we'll drive to and from the cabin with the headlights off. Somebody would have to be outside and peering along the road in order to see us, and that's hardly likely. The only other occupied place at the lake is the cabin where those two San Francisco businessmen are staying, and it's sheltered from the road by trees. As far as the car goes, I'll park it in the Taggarts' garage; the entrance is open and faces away from the road, and you can't see into it from there."

"Somebody could still notice you leaving the village or returning," Peggy said. "They'd wonder about it."

"If I'm ever asked, I'll say I decided to go for a short drive, just to get some air, and stopped for a while and walked around. That's why we'll meet so early—for that reason, and because of my wife and your mother too. Nobody would question an explanation like that; why should they? It'll look like I'm alone in the car anyway, since you'll be scooted down on the seat. Peggy, I'm desperate to see you, and I'll take the gamble if you will. We'll be very careful; nothing can happen if we're careful."

There was a prolonged silence this time, and Hughes said her name questioningly. Peggy said then, "I really don't think we ought to chance it, but I'm desperate to see you, too. And terribly horny. Are you terribly horny, Matt?"

Hughes had an erection again. "Yes!"

"Then—all right. You'll pick me up at the fork at seven?"

"At seven. I don't want to have to stop but a second, so hurry as fast as you can when you see the car."

"I will."

They said good-byes, and Hughes cradled the handset. He was sweating. He crossed to the lamp table beside his recliner, lifted his drink, drained it, and then looked at his watch: five forty-five. Leaving the study, he went upstairs and took a shower and doused himself liberally with body talc and changed into fresh clothes; came downstairs again and ate a light supper. The kitchen wall clock told him it was six forty when he had finished—time to leave. He would have to stop at the Mercantile to pick up the keys to the Taggart cabin.

Rebecca had still not come home, and he was relieved that she hadn't. He did not want to face her now, with his thoughts and his emotions focused on Peggy Tyler's lush sexuality. She would be home when he got back from the lake at nine or so, and he would tell her then of his contrived impotence. In just a few short hours, he thought as he hurried out of the house, everything would again be exactly as it had always been.

# Twenty

Compulsively, Cain put on his coat at six fifty and went out of the cabin and started down into the village.

He walked at a desultory pace, only superficially aware of the cold night and the snow-hazed lights below. His destination was the Valley Inn, and his purpose was to buy himself another bottle of bourbon—he kept telling himself that this was his purpose. There was an unopened quart in the cabin's kitchen that he had purchased in the Mercantile that morning—enough to last him through the long Sunday ahead—but the desolation in him had become so acute the ache was almost physical.

The past two days had been interminable. After returning from the village Wednesday afternoon, where he had learned with indifference of the avalanche and the fact that the valley was snowbound until after Christmas, he had been completely exhausted. Sleep came immediately that night; but it had been restless and shallow, and he had awakened from it gritty-eyed and stiff-muscled and despondent. He'd thought again of Frank McNeil's accusations, and the threat of arrest for something he had not done, and the imminent arrival of probing county police. All right then, he'd decided, let them come and let them ask their questions, and when the episode was concluded, he damned well *would* get out of this Hidden Valley where people persisted in pushing their way into his privacy; he would go somewhere else, he would find a place where the people would leave him utterly alone.

Then he'd thought: But *was* there such a place? Was there anywhere in the world where people would leave you utterly alone? Or would it always be as it had become here: intrusions, invasions, interference? And would the loneliness, the ambivalence continue to plague him wherever he went? It had seemed so simple in the beginning: just go to a small mountain village where no one knew you and no one cared to know you, and live apart, and die by degrees. For six months he had managed to do that, but now it had all started to collapse; it was no longer simple at all.

And tonight, he was going to the inn to buy a bottle he did not need, because he might need it and because it was Saturday night and he was desperately lonely for companionship that he wanted but did not want.

When he reached Sierra Street, he crossed directly toward the inn. Two and a half stories high, and a full block wide, it was the largest building in Hidden Valley. It had a double-balconied, redwood-shingled facade designed to give the impression of comfortable rusticity—alight now with its Christmas decorations—and two separate entrances: one to the small lobby and one to the restaurant-and-lounge that constituted most of its interior at street level. The upper floors were divided into eleven rooms, including the large apartment in which the Hallidays lived.

Cain hesitated in front of the restaurant-and-lounge entrance. Light glowed behind a large frosted window, and there was the sound of soft music and muted conversation from within. Apprehension fluttered in his stomach, but he went woodenly to the door and opened it and stepped inside.

The interior had a low, beamed ceiling and was bisected by square redwood supports. Waist-high partitions, topped with planter boxes of wood ferns, had been erected between the posts. The restaurant area to the right was empty and dark, chairs stacked on tables, closed for the winter season. Only the lounge on the left side was open, dimly lit by two electrically wired wagonwheel chandeliers suspended from the rafters. Eight booths with high, varnished wood backs were set along the partitions; dark leather stools flanked a leather-fronted bar against the far left wall. The rear wall and part of that behind the bar were adorned with deer antlers and glass-eyed deer heads; a glass-fronted case containing two matching and ornate shotguns, replete with boxes of shells; fishing reels and rods and corkboard displays of colored trout flies. Some fifteen people occupied the lounge, most of those in the booths. Only one man—Joe Garvey—sat at the bar, at the upper end, talking with Walt Halliday.

Cain brushed snow from his coat and stamped it soft-footed from his boots. Then he walked slowly and directly to the bar, not looking at the people in the booths, and sat on the end stool staring straight ahead. A full minute passed before Halliday came down to him.

"Can I get a bottle off-sale?" Cain asked him.

A frown creased Halliday's plump face; he hesitated. "We don't usually sell off-sale," he said finally.

"I'll pay extra for it."

"No need for that. Okay—what brand?"

"Old Grandad."

"Set you up a drink too?"

"No, I don't... yes. Grandad straight up."

"Chaser of some kind?"

"Nothing, just the shot."

Halliday hesitated again, as if he wanted to say something further. Then he shrugged and poured the drink and set the shot glass in front of Cain, took a full bottle from the backbar display, put that down, made change from the twenty Cain slid across the polished surface, and went back to the other end of the plank. When Cain lifted the glass, he was peripherally conscious of Halliday and Garvey looking at him and talking in low voices. He turned slightly on his stool, so that he could see nothing but the rimed front window, and tasted his bourbon. It burned in his mouth, his throat, the hollow of his belly. He put the glass down again and lit a cigarette.

Some of the conversation seemed to have abated behind him, and he sensed that others in the room were also looking at him. He felt conspicuous, like something curious on display. Get out of here, he thought urgently, they don't want you and you don't want them, you don't want any of this; go back to the cabin, be alone.

He swallowed his drink, dropped the cigarette into an ashtray, caught the bottle off the bar with his left hand, and moved hurriedly to the door. Turning out of it, he walked with rapid steps and head down to the corner—and ran into the woman just coming out of Lassen Drive from the west. The left side of his body bumped hard against her and threw her off-balance, so that she seemed about to fall into the packed snow at the curbing. Automatically Cain flung out his right hand and caught her arm, steadying her.

It was Rebecca Hughes.

She stared at him through the lightly falling flakes, and her mouth crooked into a bitter smile. "Well," she said, "we do seem to keep running into each other, don't we, Mr. Cain? Literally, this time." She shrugged off his hand and started away from him.

The shame he had experienced on Wednesday returned all at once, the loneliness made a plaintive cry, and he heard himself say impetuously, "Wait Mrs. Hughes, wait, listen I'm sorry, I'm sorry I ran into you just now and I'm sorry for the way I acted the other night, I had no right to do that."

It stopped her. Slowly, she turned to face him again. Her features smoothed somewhat, and the bitterness was tempered now with surprise and a wary puzzlement. She did not say anything, looking at him.

The act of speaking seemed to have had a strangely cathartic effect on Cain. He said again, heavy-voiced, "I'm sorry."

Rebecca continued to look at him in steady silence. At length the wariness faded, and she sighed softly and said, "All right. I'm hardly blameless myself for the other night; it was foolish of me to have gone in the first place."

"You only wanted what you said—some simple companionship; I suppose I knew that all along. But it's not the same for me, can you understand that? I don't need it."

"Everyone needs it, Mr. Cain."

"All I need is to be alone—that's all."

Rebecca asked quietly, "Why did you all of a sudden decide to apologize to me? You just... looked at me on Wednesday afternoon. You didn't say anything at all then."

"I couldn't."

"Why couldn't you?"

"I don't *want* to talk to anybody."

"You're talking to me now, on your initiative."

"Yes," Cain said. And then, abruptly and without prior thought: "Maybe... maybe you do have to have conversations with somebody once in a while, maybe you can't help yourself. It's all a matter of words."

"Words?"

"They pile up inside you," Cain said. He felt vaguely lightheaded, now. "Thousands of words piling up and piling up until there are so many of them you can't hold them in anymore; they just come spilling out."

"I've never thought of it that way before, but yes, I can understand what you mean." She paused. "And I guess the same is true of emotions and needs and frustrations, isn't it? You can't bottle them up forever either; they have to find an outlet of some kind."

"No. No, just words. Too many unspoken words."

Rebecca studied him for a time. "I was on my way home," she said. "Are you going back to the cabin now?"

"Yes."

"We could walk together as far as my house."

No, Cain thought. And said, "All right."

They went across Sierra Street and started up Lassen. In a sporadic way they talked of the slide, only that and nothing of a more personal nature. The spontaneity was gone; the flow of words from within him had ebbed into a trickle of words. Cain felt himself retreating again—wanted it that way, did not want it that way. When they reached the drive of the Hughes' house, he said immediately, awkwardly, "Good night, Mrs. Hughes," waited long enough to glimpse the small, brief smile she gave him and to hear her say, "Good night, Mr. Cain," and then turned away. He sensed, as he continued rapidly along the road, that she was watching him; but he did not look back.

All the way up to the cabin he was aware of the sound of the wind in the surrounding trees—the lonely, lonely sound of the wind....

# Twenty-One

Peggy Tyler reached the stand of red fir just above the lake roads fork at ten minutes before seven. Her mother had returned from the Chiltons' just after Matt's telephone call, and Peggy had told her she was going for a walk and then to the inn for a while. At six twenty she had left the house, at the western end of Shasta Street, and had turned right instead of left and slipped through the thick growth of trees well to the rear of All Faiths Church, circling toward the fork. She had seen no one, and she was certain no one had seen her.

She positioned herself at the bole of one of the firs nearest Mule Deer Lake Road, shivering slightly inside her fur-trimmed parka, and looked down into the village. Shining hazily through the thin gauze of snow, the lights seemed more remote than they actually were. The streets were typically deserted, and car headlamps were nonexistent.

Now that she was here, waiting in the heavy darkness and the kind of whispering quiet you found only on mountain nights, she was more nervous than she had been earlier. But it was an anticipatory feeling, born not of apprehension but of exhilaration. The past few days had been oh-so-deadly dull, with nothing to do except to watch barely discernible images flickering on the television screen and nowhere to go except out into the very environment she so passionately hated. The prospect of an adventurous balling session in what was literally her own backyard was intoxicating: a lovely and audacious private joke to be played on all the smug little people who lived in this damned valley, one of the few experiences of her life in the Sierra that she would be able to look back on with fondness and pleasure.

Of course, there *was* a certain hazard involved, though not nearly as great for her as for Matt. She didn't give a hair what Hidden Valley thought of her, her mother included, and she didn't give a hair for Matt's saintly reputation; if their affair were discovered, it surely wouldn't have any real effect on her long-range plans. The only consequence of discovery, as far as she was concerned, would be that the goose who laid the golden eggs would be dead: no more generous cash presents like the thousand-dollar Christmas surprise. Still, she wasn't worried. If Matt was willing to chance it—and it wasn't really much of a chance, the way he had outlined it—then she was too....

A pair of lights moving in the village intruded on her thoughts, and she saw that a car had swung onto Sierra Street just beyond the Mercantile. It passed the church, and even though she was unable to distinguish the make, she knew it would be Matt's. Behind the car, the village streets still appeared empty. She swiveled her head to look south along Mule Deer Lake Road; the wall of night there was unbroken.

When the car approached the stand of fir, it slowed almost to a crawl. Peggy waited until it had drawn abreast of her hiding place and then hurried out and opened the door and slipped inside. The dome light did not go on, Matt had done something to the bulb—clever Matt! She curled her body low on the seat, whispering a greeting, as the car picked up speed again.

He reached out a hand and stroked her hair. "Peggy," he said, "Peggy, Peggy."

She smiled and moved over, resting her head on his thigh, the fingers of her right hand stroking over his knee. His breathing came fast and heavy and she sensed the front of his trousers begin to bulge. He said thickly, "There's not a soul on the streets. I made sure of that before I pulled out."

"No one saw me either."

Peggy kept on stroking his leg, higher now, one fingernail moving across the bulge and making him jump convulsively. The area between her own legs had begun to moisten, to pulse demandingly; damn, but she was horny! "Hurry and get to the cabin, Matt. I'm on fire for you."

"I know," he whispered. "I know."

It seemed to take a long time for them to reach Mule Deer Lake, a long time before he said, "We're almost there, I'm going to switch off the headlights now."

"Can you see the lake?" she asked as the dashboard went dark.

"Yes. No lights anywhere, except in the cabin where those businessmen are staying. It's just up ahead."

Three additional minutes crept away, and then Peggy felt the car turn and the wheels bounced jarringly; they came to a stop. Hughes said, "We're here."

Peggy sat up, looking through the windshield: a blank wooden wall, the inner wall of the Taggart garage. Hughes had the driver's door open, and she followed him out on that side. They clasped hands and left the garage and went around to the front door of the cabin, on the lake side. The flat, frozen surface of Mule Deer Lake, ridged with snow, stretched out into deep black; the opposite shore was totally obscured by darkness. The only light was a distant glimmer to the north: the businessmen's place. It was so still that Peggy could hear the beating of her heart.

Hughes keyed open the door. "You see?" he said against her ear. "Nothing to worry about, not a thing. Nobody saw us, and nobody can possibly know we're here...."

Kubion knew somebody was there.

He saw the darkly indistinct shape of the car coming without headlights along the lake road, saw it just as he was about to get into his own car parked in front of a two-story, green-shuttered frame house some distance down the shore. Through the thin snowfall he watched it swing off the road at the Taggart cabin and then disappear. Nobody was supposed to be living in that cabin—he'd found out in the village earlier in the day which of the lake dwellings were occupied and which weren't—and he thought: Well now, just what've we got here? Eskimo kids looking for a place to hump?

Smiling fixedly, he slid into the car and started the engine, also leaving his headlamps off, and drove to within fifty yards of the cabin and parked on the side of the road. The building's windows showed no light; whoever it was was probably still in the car. Kubion thought: Fuck her, I did—an old teen-age taunt—and laughed deep in his throat. He sat there for a time: still no lights. Finally he reached for the ignition key, started to turn it; hesitated and released it again. Oh hell, he thought, the more the merrier.

He opened the glove compartment and removed a flashlight and got out of the car. His eyes, wide and unblinking, shone like a cat's in the darkness.

The interior of the cabin was winter-chilled and subterranean black. Hughes closed the door and said softly, "We'll stay here for a minute, until we can see well enough to walk without banging into things."

They stood pressed together, waiting, and eventually Peggy could make out the distorted shapes of furniture, the doors in two walls which would lead to other rooms. Watchfully, they crossed to one of the doors, and Matt widened it and said, "Kitchen," and led her to another. Beyond this one was a short hall-way, with a door in each wall; the one on the left opened on the larger of the cabin's two bedrooms.

The bed was queen-sized and unmade, but folded across the foot of the mat-tress was a thin patchwork quilt; they would need that because of the cold, Peggy thought—later, afterward. They stood by the bed and kissed hungrily, undressing each other in the darkness with fumbling urgency, and then they fell onto the bed, kicking the last of their clothing free, their mouths still meld-ed together. Peggy took hold of his erection in both her hands and heard him moan, and he broke the kiss to whisper feverishly, "Put it in, put it in, I can't wait!," clutching at her breasts as if bracing himself, and she guided him over her and into the waiting wetness of her and he made a jerking, heaving motion as she drew her legs back and said, "Peggy, ah ah ah Peggy!" and came shudderingly.

The rigidity left all his body at once, and he was dead weight on top of her, his face pressed to her neck. Peggy's lips pursed in mild annoyance, but when he raised his head finally to tell her he was sorry, he just couldn't hold himself back, she said, "It's all right, we have plenty of time, baby, we have plenty of time." She held him flaccid inside her, moving her hips, seeking to make him hard again, and when she began to succeed she said smilingly, "That's it, that's my Matt," and he commenced rocking over her and into her, expertly now, and it was the way it had been in Whitewater, it was perfectly synchronized and wildly good, and she could feel the beginnings of her orgasm fluttering and building in her and flung herself upward at him, reaching for it, reaching for it—

—and then a bright white beam sliced away the blackness like a sudden spotlight and pinned their glistening bodies on the bed.

For a single instant they were blindly motionless, still locked together, still one instead of two. Then Hughes made a startled, whimpering sound and rolled away from her, twisting, sitting up. Peggy threw an arm reflexively across her eyes; fright and confusion replaced the passion inside her, dulling her mind, stepping up the staccato pounding of her heart.

A voice—harsh, amused, unfamiliar—said from behind the light, "Well, I'll be damned. It's the banker himself, by Christ, tearing off a nice little piece on the side."

Hughes said in a stark, trapped tone, "Who are you, how did you get in here?"

"You left the front door unlocked. You must have been in some hurry, Banker, some big hurry."

"You have no right to be here, you have no right! What do you want, why did you come in here, put out that light!"

"Hang loose, just keep your head together."

At the periphery of her shielding arm, Peggy numbly saw Matt Hughes swing off the bed, shambling almost drunkenly, ludicrous in his nakedness. His face a matrix of fear, he started toward the white hole in the darkness.

"Stay where you are," Kubion said sharply, "stand right there."

"Put that light out, put it out I tell you!" And Hughes took another step toward the beam.

"Okay, you stupid hick bastard shit."

There was a brief flame, like the flare of a match, to one side of the beam; there was a sudden roaring sound, localized thunder echoing in the confines of the room, and Peggy jerked on the bed as if she had been struck. Then she saw Matt stop moving, and saw part of his face disappear, and saw something red spurting, and saw his hands flick upward, and saw him begin to sag before the hands reached the level of his chest, and saw him fall into a loose wet naked pile on the floor.

"How about you, sweetheart?" Kubion's voice said softly behind the light. "How about you?"

Peggy started to scream.

# Twenty-Two

Loxner said, "It's after seven, Vic, he's been gone more than five hours now. Where the hell could he be for five hours? He don't drink, and we got plenty of food right here, and there ain't nothing in the village for him to do and no place for him to be riding around."

"I know," Brodie said. "I know it."

"Man, I just don't like the way he's acting. Not a word to either of us since all that crap about ripping off the valley yesterday morning, gone most of yesterday afternoon, sitting up in his bedroom all of today until he finally went out. I seen him when he come downstairs, and his eyes were still funny; he was smiling funny, too, showing his teeth. I tell you I don't like it, it's got me all uptight."

They were sitting in the living room, across a coffee table set in front of the fireplace. Up until a few minutes ago they had been playing gin rummy, but neither of them had had their thoughts on the game and they'd given it up finally by tacit consent. Brodie stood now and picked up a blackened poker and stirred the pitch-pine logs burning on the hearth; sparks danced, and the charred wood crackled loudly, like firecrackers going off.

He set the poker down again, turned, and put voice to what had been on his mind for the past hour.

"You ever see anybody freak out, Duff? Like where they come all apart in the head, go crazy, do crazy things?"

Loxner blinked at him, scratching nervously at the bandage on his left arm. The arm was still stiff, and the skin under the bandage itched constantly, but he'd found he could use the limb for normal activity and had taken off the sling that morning. "No," he said, "no, I never seen nothing like that."

"I saw it happen twice, more or less saw it—both while I was doing time. The first guy was a lifer, been in for maybe fifteen years. Happened right out of the blue, one night in the dining hall. He just jumped up and started yelling and foaming at the mouth, got onto the table and ran down it with a fork in either hand and stabbed a con and a screw before they could put him down.

"The second guy was something else again. He'd been a bank teller or an accountant or something on the outside and got caught with his hand in the till; quiet type, mild-mannered, maybe thirty and good-looking. He'd been inside about six months when they switched cells on him, put him right down the block from the one I was in. The two cons in his new cell were hard cases, and on top of that they were fags, buggers. They got to him right away and raped his face and his ass and told him they'd kill him if he didn't cooperate from then on. So he cooperated, and for maybe a couple of months they passed him back and forth like a private whore. He still didn't say much, and he didn't look any different; we thought maybe he'd had some fag in him all along and had gotten to like it. Then the word got around that there was going to be a break, that this guy had masterminded it for himself and the other two. Nobody paid much attention to it; you know how the grapevine's always humming with word of a break. But they did it, they pulled some fancy moves and went over the wall from the roof of the library, where the accountant had been working. Only the next day the screws found the two hard cases lying in a ditch five miles from the prison—with their balls shot off. The guy stayed loose a week before they caught him, and in that week he offed six other fags in two cities, shot all their balls off. He'd freaked out too, is what I'm getting at, but it had all happened inside where you couldn't really see it; and what it did was turn him into a machine with one thought in his head: kill the hard cases and kill as many other fags as he could before they got him. He was like supercrazy—ten times as dangerous as the other one I told you about, because he could still think and plan and nothing mattered to him except one crazy idea."

Loxner said, "Jesus," and wiped his mouth with the back of one hand. "You think something like that's happened to Earl? You think he's really freaked out?"

"Maybe," Brodie said. "And maybe *his* crazy idea is ripping off this valley."

"Jesus," Loxner said again. Sweat had broken out on his forehead, and his hands twitched noticeably.

"It could be he's still okay and it's nothing but the pressure getting to him and he'll snap out of it pretty soon. But if he has freaked, there's no way we can know for sure until maybe it's too late. We can't afford to wait, Duff. There's only one thing we can do; it'll make problems for us in other ways, but it's got to be done."

"You mean—waste him?"

"I mean waste him."

Loxner got to his feet and paced rapidly forth and back in front of the fireplace. "Yeah," he said. "Yeah, yeah, you're right, we can't take no chances, we got to think about our own asses." He came to a standstill. "When do we do it?"

"Tonight. Just as soon as he gets back. I've still got the extra set of car keys he gave me, and when he's inside here, I'll go out and unlock the trunk and get one of the guns out of the suitcase."

"You going to pull the trigger, then?"

"I'll pull the trigger."

Loxner looked relieved. "What about the body?"

"There's no place to bury it with all the snow. We'll wrap it in a blanket and put it in the garage; it'll keep until we're ready to leave."

"Then what?"

"Put it in the trunk of the car. When we're a few miles away, we'll dump it into a canyon. There're plenty of them in these mountains."

Loxner sat down, got up again almost immediately, and said, "I need a goddamn drink." He went into the kitchen.

Brodie stared into the fire with eyes that were, now, like chunks of amethyst quartz.

Kubion returned to the cabin at eight fifteen.

They heard the sound of the car coming up the access lane, and Loxner wet his lips and looked at Brodie. Brodie said, "Deal the cards"—they were playing gin again—and obediently Loxner dropped his gaze to the deck. He shuffled it awkwardly, dealt ten cards to each of them with diffident flicks of his wrist.

When the front door opened, Brodie did not glance up. But there were no footsteps, no sound of the door closing again. A cold prescience formed inside him, and his head lifted then, and Kubion was standing there smiling a skull grin and holding the .38 backup automatic. His eyes seemed huge, streaked with lines of blood, and neither they nor the lids above them moved. No part of him moved, he did not even seem to be breathing.

Brodie's lips thinned, his body tensed. He thought: Oh fuck yes he's blown out, I should have known it yesterday, I should have killed him yesterday; we waited too long.

Loxner saw the change in Brodie's face and jerked his head around. Color drained out of his cheeks. He struggled to his feet, sweat once more breaking out on him, mouth opening as if he were going to speak, closing, opening again, closing again—all like a huge fish caught on an invisible line.

There was a long moment of silence, heavy and menacing. Snow fluttered across the threshold behind Kubion, like a sifting of white flour; chill, biting air rushing into the room robbed it of warmth, made the flames in the fireplace dance and gutter.

"We're going down to the lake," Kubion said finally. "Got a little something I want you to see."

Brodie forced his voice to remain even. "What's that, Earl?"

"You'll find out when we get there."

"All right—sure. But what's the gun for? There's no need for throwing down on us."

"Isn't there? Well, we'll see about that."

Loxner began thickly, "Look, look now—"

"Shut up, you gutless prick!" Kubion said with sudden viciousness. "I don't want any arguments, get over here and get your coats on, we're going now right now."

Brodie got up immediately and walked with careful strides to the closet; sweating heavily, not looking at Kubion, Loxner followed. They donned coats and gloves, and when they were ready, Kubion gestured outside and trailed them at a measured distance around to where the car waited, engine running and headlights burning, in front of the garage. He said there, "Vic, you take the wheel. Duff, you sit in front with him." He waited until they had complied and then opened the right rear door and slid into the back seat. "Go. I'll tell you where."

Brodie drove down to Mule Deer Lake Road and turned right and went along the eastern lakeshore. The taut silence was broken only by Loxner's asthmatic breathing. They passed the Taggart cabin and several other winter-abandoned structures; then Kubion said, "That house there on the left—pull up in front."

The house—a two-story frame with green shutters—was set back from the road, inside a diamond-pattern, split-log fence. It was shrouded in darkness. Brodie stopped the car where he had been told, and the three of them got out, Kubion hanging back slightly. They stood at the open front gate.

"Go up there and look inside, both of you," Kubion said. "The door's not locked, and the light switch is on the left."

They stepped through the gate opening and made their way slowly along the ice-slick front path; Kubion again followed at a distance. Brodie climbed the porch steps first, stopped at the door, and Loxner said, "I don't want to do it, I don't want no part of what's in there...."

Not listening to him, Brodie spun the knob and pushed the door inward. There was nothing immediate to see except darkness. He reached inside and felt along the wall and found the switch and snapped it upward; light spilled into the room, forcing the night back into crouching corner shadows.

Loxner said, "Oh *Christ!*"

There were seven people in the room—two men, three women, a boy of nine or ten, and a girl a few years older. All of them were tightly bound hand and foot with heavy-duty clothesline, gagged with torn strips of bedsheeting, lying on the carpeted floor near a tinseled Christmas tree with a nativity scene and several brightly wrapped presents at its cotton-draped base. They were all alive and apparently unharmed. Their eyes blinked against the sudden illumination, wide with terror. Two of the women whimpered; one of the men made a strangulated retching sound.

Cold fury knotted the muscles in Brodie's stomach, and he had difficulty pulling air into lungs. He slammed the door violently, spun around. Kubion had come up the path and was standing at the foot of the porch steps; he held the .38 automatic with deceptive looseness.

"It took me about four hours," he said through his fixed smile. "Duck soup, taking them over, but I had to bring the two from the house down the way to this place and that took a little extra time. Then I shook both houses down. I was just getting ready to start back when I made out this car without lights pulling into the first cabin on the lake, and I went to have a look. You know who it was? The banker, Matt Hughes; he's been getting a little on the side from that blond bitch in there. So I had to bring her over here, too."

He stopped speaking, watching them. Brodie said, "What about Hughes?"

"Well, he gave me a little trouble. You don't have to worry about him anymore, not a bit you don't."

"You killed him, is that it?"

"That's it. I killed him, all right."

Brodie began to rub the palms of his hands along his trouser legs: a gesture of suppressed rage. Loxner said in a kind of whine, "Why? Why all of this?"

"The two of you made it nice and clear yesterday how you felt about ripping off the valley, and I knew I couldn't talk you into it, right? But you didn't know how bad I want this one, I want it like I never wanted any other score, it's the cat's nuts. The only thing is, I don't figure I can make it alone, so I had to force you into it, you see? It's simple."

He paused, and his smile became sly. "Those people inside, I did a little talking to them. I told them all about the ripoff, and that's not all I told them. I told them we were the ones who did the Greenfront job, I told them everything except our names—what do you think of that?"

Loxner had the same look on his face—that of a kid about to cry—that he had had after the security guard shot him at Greenfront. "Crazy cocksucker," he muttered under his breath, "oh you crazy cocksucker!"

If Kubion heard him, he gave no indication. The smile still sly, he said, "I know what you're thinking now, both of you, you're thinking you want to put a bullet in me, maybe you've been thinking it ever since yesterday and that's why I took the guns out of the suitcase in the car if you don't already know about that and why I watched you like a goddamn hawk every minute I was at the cabin, I did you know. But suppose you could do it, suppose somehow you're able to jump me, take this gun away, put one in my head? Where would it leave you? These hicks here know who you are but say you had the guts to kill seven people, three women and two kids, say you had the guts, well the rest of the hicks and the cops would figure damned quick who had to've done it and you know what kind of heat you'd have then, right? So you let them live and then you cut and run, use one of the snowmobiles to get out of the valley, but that's the same situation as if we do the job only worse because these Eskimos would be found almost immediately and even if you took the time to bury Hughes' body and cut the telephone lines and put the second snowmobile out of commission, even if you could do all of that without being hassled, you still wouldn't have a clear jump. And you wouldn't have any bread either, that's the important thing, you'd have to knock over a place for ready cash, you'd have to shag a car, you'd be taking risks every time you turned around and all with Murder One heat ready to blow you on your asses at any time."

Kubion paused again and studied them cunningly. Brodie said in a flat, soft voice, "Keep talking, Earl."

"Okay, you're getting it now. You do things my way, you help me make the score, and we come out fine just like I told you yesterday. Bread in our pockets and two full days' jump, time to travel, time and money to get a long way from Hidden Valley before the lid comes off." Kubion used his left hand to take a roll of currency from his coat pocket. "Listen, you think there's no money in this place? Nine hicks out of seventy-five and only two of the occupied buildings so far and I've already picked up fifteen hundred, two bills from the Eskimos that live in this house and eighty from the ones down the way and a hundred and twenty from Banker Hughes' wallet, and that blond bitch, she had a thousand in her purse, just sitting there in her purse all nice and crisp in her *purse* for Christ's sake. Fifteen hundred already and we haven't even started."

He shoved the money back into his coat and made a sweeping gesture with the gun. "So what do you say? I say we go inside the house here and work over the details again, and this time you listen good. I say we do the job tomorrow, just as I told it to you. I say when it's done and we've made the split, we leave on separate snowmobiles and you go your way and I go mine, we're quits. Well? Do we get it on together or what? You tell me, you tell me."

There was a long, brittle silence. Loxner looked at Brodie to keep from looking at Kubion. And Brodie said finally in his flat, soft voice, "You haven't left us any choice, Earl. We do it your way."

# Book Two

**Sunday, December 23**

> Oh ye gods! what darkness
> of night there is in mortal minds!
> —OVID

# One

At eleven fifty-five Sunday morning, in the vestry behind the candlelit altar, the Reverend Peter Keyes released the bell rope and ended the resonant summons in the steeple belfry above. Then, opening the vestry door, he stepped out onto the pulpit and went to stand behind the lectern on the far right, to watch the last of the congregation file into All Faiths Church. Opposite him on the pulpit, Maude Fredericks sat waiting at the old woodpipe organ, a hymnal propped open in front of her.

Seven of the twelve pews on each side of the center aisle were completely full, but the last five on either side were only partially taken. The Reverend Mr. Keyes had entertained little hope for a capacity attendance, but he had expected a larger turnout than this. He scanned the congregation—the women and girls in their warm, brightly colored winter finery (you did not see somber hues in church these days, which was, he thought, as it should be); the men and boys in carefully pressed suits and bright ties, to which they were for the most part unaccustomed—and a small frown tugged at the corners of his mouth. He did not see Matthew Hughes, and Matthew never missed Sunday services, was in fact always one of the first to arrive; very odd indeed that he was not present on this particular Sunday, two days before Christmas. He also did not see the Markhams or the Donnelly family, who rarely failed to attend as well; nor the San Francisco businessman, Charley Adams, to whom he had spoken on Thursday afternoon.

Maude Fredericks turned slightly on the organ bench and glanced at him, and he indicated that she should begin playing; it was just noon. Deep-toned chords, reverent and felicitous, filled the wide interior. The Reverend Mr. Keyes waited, looking out through the open half of the double doors at the empty, snow-dappled walk beyond; the Hugheses and the Markhams and the Connellys did not arrive. Finally, sighing inaudibly, he nodded to this Sunday's usher, Dr. Webb Edwards. The middle-aged physician returned his nod, stepped out to look both ways along Sierra Street, and apparently saw no late arrivals in the vicinity; he came back inside, closed the open door, and took a place in one of the rear pews. The time was twelve five.

When the organ music had crescendoed into silence, the Reverend Mr. Keyes offered a brief invocation; a moment of silent and conjoined prayer followed. Then he led the congregation in the singing of "O Jesus, We Adore Thee" and "Savior, Blessed Saviour" and "Joy to the World." Time: twelve twenty. He arranged his notes on the lectern, cleared his throat, and prepared to deliver his traditional pre-Christmas sermon, the Bible text of which had been taken from the first chapter of the Gospel of St. Luke.

Time: twelve twenty-one.

And the double doors burst apart, the two halves thudding loudly against the interior wall, and three men came quickly inside. Two of them held deer rifles and fanned one to either side along the coat-draped wall. The third, pointing a handgun, stood with his feet braced apart just inside the entrance.

Heads swiveled around; faces blanched with incredulity and nascent fear. Kubion, who had the handgun, called out in a sharp, commanding voice, "All right, everybody just sit still. We don't want to hurt any of you but I'll shoot the first one who makes a move in this direction, let's get that understood right from the start."

The Reverend Mr. Keyes stared at the man he knew as Charley Adams, the man whom he had thought to be a good and devout Christian, stared at the two strangers with the rifles—and he could not believe what he saw or what he had just heard. It simply could not be happening; it was utterly impossible. He felt an unfamiliar but suddenly acute sense of outrage; his round cheeks flamed with it, his fingers gripped the edges of the lectern until the knuckle joints seemed about to pop through the stretched white skin. "How dare you!" he shouted. "How dare you come in here with guns! This is a house of *God!*"

"Calm down, Reverend," Kubion said. He seemed to be smiling. "All of you calm down, keep your heads, and then I'll tell you what it's all about."

The command turned the Reverend Mr. Keyes' outrage to blind fury. He pushed away from the lectern and came down off the pulpit. Lew Cooper-smith, sitting in the right front pew, said, "No, Reverend!" but Keyes did not even hear the words. He started into the center aisle, his eyes fixed on Kubion.

"Hold it right there, preacher man."

Reverend Keyes brushed past the arm Coopersmith put out to restrain him and walked slowly and grimly down the aisle. He was not afraid because he knew he would not be harmed, not *here;* his anger was righteous, his position was sacrosanct, and he said, "I won't have guns in my church, I won't have you bringing weapons of destruction in God's house," and Kubion unhesitatingly shot him through the right hand.

The hushed, strained silence dissolved first into the hollow roar of the gun-shot and then into terrified screams and cries from women and children, shocked articulations from the men. The Reverend Mr. Keyes had stopped

moving. He held his hand up in front of him and stared at the blood beginning to stream from the hole just below the thumb: numbly, not believing
what he saw any more than he quite believed, even now, that any of this was
actually happening.

"Dear God," he said then, and fainted.

Lew Coopersmith was on his feet and three steps into the center aisle before
he realized he had moved at all. Abruptly he stopped and allowed his hands to
unknot at his sides, standing rigidly. Others were on their feet now as well,
faces stricken—John and Vince Tribucci, Webb Edwards, Verne Mullins—but
none of them had moved from their places. The whimperings of the women
and children intensified the atmosphere of horror which now pervaded the
church.

Kubion said, "When I say something I mean it, you'd all better get that
straight right now, the next one that makes a funny move I'll shoot his face off.
Okay—one of you's the doctor, which one?"

"Here," Edwards said.

"Get out here and tend to the Reverend."

"I don't have my bag. I'll need—"

"You'll need nothing. Get out here."

Edwards went to where Reverend Keyes lay inert on the floor, knelt beside
him, and examined the bullet-torn hand; it was still bleeding heavily. He used
his belt as a tourniquet, his handkerchief to swab the wound.

Kubion said, "He got a key on him to the church doors?"

"I don't know," Edwards answered woodenly.

"Well look through his pockets and find out!"

Edwards probed quickly, gently, through the minister's dark-gray suit and
discovered a ring of keys. He held them up. Kubion made a tossing motion, and
Edwards flipped the key ring underhand, as carefully as he would have thrown
a ball to a three-year-old child. Making the catch with his left hand, Kubion
turned and pulled the entrance doors nearly closed. He probed at the latch on
one with three of the keys, found one that fitted, and then dropped the ring
into the pocket of his coat. He faced the congregation again.

"Couple of you pick the Reverend up and put him on one of the benches."

Coopersmith came forward, and Harry Chilton stepped out. With Edwards'
help, they lifted Keyes gently and laid him supine in the nearest pew.

"The rest of you men—shut those women and kids up," Kubion said. "I want
it quiet in here, I want every one of you to hear what I'm going to say, and I
don't want to have to say it more than once, you got that?"

While husbands and parents did what they had been ordered to do, Coopersmith retreated a few steps and glanced over his shoulder to where Ellen was
sitting; she was motionless, hands pressed against her white cheeks, her eyes
round and glistening wet with tears. He saw Ann Tribucci sitting near Ellen,
one arm wrapped in an unconsciously—or perhaps consciously—protective
way around the huge convexity that was her unborn child, her other hand

holding tightly to one of her husband's. John Tribucci's face, unlike most of the others, was as stiff and empty of expression as a store mannequin's.

Kubion said as the congregation quieted, "That's better. Here it is, then, plain and simple: we're here because we're taking over the valley and everybody in it and once we've got complete control we're going to loot it, building by building. Money and expensive jewelry, that's all we're interested in, and if you people cooperate that's all we'll take, nobody else will get hurt."

He paused to let the concept sink in fully. Then: "All right, now some details. When I'm done talking one of us will come around with a sack and you put your wallets and purses into it and anything else you've got in your pockets, don't hold anything out, turn your pockets. After that's done we'll want a list of names of everybody who lives in the valley that's not here right now, I mean everybody, because we're going to go round them up one by one after we leave here and if we find anybody whose name isn't on the list he's dead. You can forget about the Markhams and the Donnellys and Matt Hughes and Peggy Tyler; we've—"

Agnes Tyler's shrill, near hysterical voice cried, "Peggy? Peggy? Oh my God I should have known something was wrong. I should have known that telephone call last night was a lie!" She was standing, one hand clutching her breast, eyes like a pair of too-ripe grapes pressed into a lump of gray dough. "You've *hurt* her, you've hurt my daughter...."

Kubion looked at her and said, "Somebody shut that bitch the hell up."

Beside her, Verne Mullins took hold of her shoulders and eased her down again. Agnes buried her face in her hands and began moaning softly. Coopersmith said in a carefully expressionless voice, "What do you mean we can forget about those people? What have you done to them?"

Kubion's gaze shifted to him. "Nothing to any of them, old man—except Hughes. We'll bring them in later."

"Except Hughes?"

"He's dead," Kubion said, and the smile transformed on his mouth and made it look like an open wound. His voice was savage with impatience. "I killed him last night and he's dead, you'll all be dead you stupid hicks unless you shut up and listen to me and do what I say I don't want any more questions I don't want any more crap you understand me!"

The aura of horror had reached the point of tangibility now: it could be felt, it could be tasted, it lay like a pall of invisible mist inside the church. No one moved, no one made a sound; even the children and Agnes Tyler were silent. The Reverend Mr. Keyes shot in his own church, the valley about to be taken over and looted, Matt Hughes—their mayor, their friend, their benefactor—inexplicably murdered, all their lives suddenly in the hands of three armed men and one of whom was nothing less than a psychotic: they were literally petrified with fear.

Coopersmith swallowed against the rage and revulsion which burned in his throat, struggling to maintain calm and a clear head, and looked at each of the other two men, the ones with the rifles. Neither of them had made a single motion since their entrance; they were like wooden sentinels. But there was sanity in their faces, and the big heavy one was sweating copiously, and the fair-haired one, despite a guarded, stoic expression, appeared to be tensely uneasy as well. Why were they a part of this? he thought.

Merciful God, why *any* of this?

Kubion was smiling again, and when he spoke his voice was once more controlled, matter-of-fact. "Now like I said, once we have the list of names two of us will go round up the other people and bring them back here, and when everybody is in the church we go to work on the buildings—just two of us, the other one will be out front with a rifle, watching. We figure it'll take us most of today to get the job done, but when we're finished we might not be leaving right away, we might stay one day or two or even three before we go, and the way we'll go is on snowmobiles so don't get the idea we're trapped in the valley until the pass is open. But *you'll* wait until it's cleared, you'll stay in here until the day after Christmas. We'll bring in some food later and some water and you'll be nice and comfortable as long as you don't try any stupid tricks. The important thing for you to remember is that you won't know when we'll be leaving, you won't know when we're gone, and if you try to break down the front doors or knock out a window before the day after Christmas and we're still here, we'll kill everybody we see. Clear? All of that clear?"

Figures in stone.

Kubion said, "Good, we're going to get along fine now; you keep on sitting there like you are now and we're going to get along just fine." He looked at the heavy, dull-faced rifleman and made a gesture with his free hand. Loxner came over and put the weapon down against the wall, moving mechanically, using his left arm as if it were stiff and sore; then he took a folded flour sack from under his coat and walked up the center aisle. Coopersmith watched him as he passed down to the end of the right front pew; his damp face contained what might have been a kind of masked fear of his own.

When Coopersmith faced front again, he saw that the fair-haired rifleman had also set his weapon against the wall and had produced a pencil and a pad of paper. Kubion said, "Names now, everybody not here and where they live in the village." His eyes rested on Coopersmith. "You, old man, start it off. Who's not here?"

Coopersmith hesitated. Then, because there was nothing else he could do, he began in a leaden voice to recite. And all the while he was talking the same cold, voracious thought kept running through his mind: I wish I had my gun now because I would kill you, I think God forgive me I would kill you right where you stand, right here in church, and sleep tonight with a clear conscience....

# Two

When Brodie and Loxner had preceded him out of the church and gone halfway along the front walk—holding the rifle barrels down against their legs as he had instructed them to do—Kubion stepped out and shut the doors and locked them. His watch said that it was one fifteen. Very good: fifty-five minutes, five minutes less than he had anticipated. You couldn't do much better than that, bet your ass you couldn't.

He went down the steps and followed Loxner and Brodie to where his car was parked eastward of six others in the fronting lot; the automatic rested in his coat pocket now; his hand lightly gripping the butt. Sierra Street was still deserted, he saw with satisfaction, and there was no sign of activity anywhere else in the village. It had begun to snow thinly from a silky gray sky, but the drifting clouds to the west were black-bordered and pregnant; it would snow much more heavily before long.

Brodie and Loxner stopped beside the car, and Kubion halted ten feet away. "You see?" he said to them. "Easy, easy, no sweat at all."

"Why did you shoot the Reverend?" Brodie asked tautly. "You didn't have to do any shooting in there; it wasn't necessary."

"Don't tell me what was necessary and what wasn't, I know exactly what I'm doing. You got religion now, maybe?"

Brodie said nothing more. His fingers caressed the stock of the rifle, one of the three taken from the Markham and Donnelly houses; but it, like the one Loxner carried, was empty. Empty! Kubion laughed out loud. They had done the church scene with just his automatic, one loaded gun was going to take over the entire valley, and that was funny when you thought about it, that was a real gutbuster when you thought about it.

For a while yesterday he'd considered wasting Brodie and Loxner and ripping off the valley all by himself. The idea of that appealed to him all right, but he'd finally decided against it. Hicks would be more afraid of three men with guns than one man with a gun, the old psychological advantage—that was one thing; another was that he might need some help in rounding up the rest of the hicks, maybe in other, areas too; a third, and this had been the main deciding point, was that he liked the idea of keeping the two of them alive as long as he felt like it, playing with them a little, hamstringing them, using them to prolong the score because the longer it lasted, the sweeter it would be. And there wasn't a shred of doubt that he could handle the two of them—stupid gutless Loxner and culinary fairy Brodie; he could handle anybody and anything, he was like ten feet tall and nobody could touch him with all the power he possessed, the power that had been there all the time if only he'd recognized it for what it was and let it come free.

What it was, this new outlook of his, was like being on a perpetual grass high: you saw everything crystal clear, inside yourself and outside yourself, and you didn't worry about shit like headaches and spiders (they'd never come back again; he'd killed every last one of them), and you didn't worry about violence either. If you had to do something violent, why then you just did it and it was all right; in fact it gave you a kind of release, it made you feel loose again like you felt after you'd popped your cork into one of those big-assed black chicks. So when the impulse came over him, the way it had last night when he'd found Hughes and the blonde bitch together, he'd just let it tell him what to do and then followed orders. It had come on again in the church, just a little, but it told him not to kill the Reverend because that might have led to hysteria and the hicks had to be kept docile until the ripoff was completed, so he'd put one through that preacher man's hand. When it came on again, and sooner or later it would, it'd tell him just the right time to waste Brodie and Loxner and he'd do that; and maybe it would tell him to waste all the hicks too and he'd do that, a bunch of Eskimos like that were better off dead anyway. Right? Right on.

"Okay," he said, "let's get to work. Put the rifles in the back seat. Duff, the flour sack, too."

Brodie opened the rear door, and they tossed the weapons inside. Loxner laid the sackful of wallets and purses and other items on the floor matting, threw the door closed.

"Now we get those other hicks out of the pickup and into the church," Kubion told them.

They moved out silently, went around the south side of the building and along to the rear wall of the minister's cottage. The battered Ford half-ton belonging to Sid Markham was parked in close to the cottage wall, the glass in its rear window broken out at Kubion's instructions, its bed draped and tied securely with a heavy tarpaulin.

At the Donnelly house last night, with Loxner and Brodie under control, Kubion had first considered what to do about the families of Matt Hughes and Peggy Tyler. Go in and take them over too, bring them out to the lake? Too much extra hassle, he'd concluded; he had enough hicks under wraps as it was, and he didn't want to risk jeopardizing the operation planned for Sunday. Better to use the telephone and make excuses as to why Hughes and the blonde wouldn't be home that night, didn't really matter what kind of excuses because nobody was going to figure special trouble with the valley snowbound and they would accept anything that sounded halfway reasonable. He had had Brodie ungag Peggy Tyler; but she'd just sat there like a damned dummy, and slapping her hadn't done any good. He'd told Brodie to gag her again anyway and then to untie Martin Donnelly. Donnelly hadn't given any trouble; he had answered all of Kubion's questions about Hughes and Tyler and their people, and agreed to do and say exactly what he was told. So they took him to the Markham house—Kubion had disabled the Donnelly phone—and he called the blonde's mother and told her her daughter wouldn't be home until the next day because Donnelly's wife and both his kids were sick and he had seen Peggy in the village when he'd gone for the doctor and asked her to spend the night; the mother grumbled a little and finally said okay. Then they tele-phoned Rebecca Hughes, and Donnelly told her Hughes had come out for a visit and that a tree had fallen across the road in the interim, and Hughes was out with Sid Markham trying to do something about it but they didn't know if it could be gotten off the road tonight, don't worry if he doesn't make it home until tomorrow sometime. She didn't question the explanation. And that took care of that.

Later, past midnight, the three of them had driven into the village, and at Kubion's direction Brodie had climbed one of the utility poles beyond Alpine Street and cut the telephone lines. The remainder of the night was spent in the kitchen of the Donnelly house, going over details and then just sitting there and waiting: each of them wide awake and watchful, Kubion not even tired because he had slept most of Saturday morning in preparation for the all-night vigil. After a late, cold breakfast, which Kubion had eaten with relish and Brodie and Loxner had barely touched, they'd loaded the seven captives into the pickup; then, at exactly noon, they had come into the village again—Brodie driving the half-ton, Loxner driving Kubion's car and Kubion in the back. The streets had been completely empty when they reached All Faiths Church. Brodie had pulled the pickup around here to the blind side of the cot-tage, and Loxner had parked the car in the lot, and then they had met at the steps to begin the takeover.

Now Kubion stood to one side while Brodie and Loxner started untying the tarpaulin. When they had it off he could see the seven people lying just as they had been placed earlier, shivering with cold, their bloodless faces like those in the church: masks of crippling fear. He smiled across at them.

Loxner dropped the tailgate, and he and Brodie dragged the seven from the bed and put them on the snow-covered ground. Kubion took out his heavy, thick-bladed pocketknife and tossed it to Loxner, told him to cut the clothes-line bonds and remove the gags. He said when that had been done, "Close it up and toss it back, nice and careful," and Loxner obeyed instantly.

Sid Markham and Martin Donnelly rubbed circulation into their stiffened limbs and then moved to help the women and children; no one looked at Kubion. The little Donnelly girl began to cry, and her mother held her tightly, crooning into her hair. Peggy Tyler sat slump-bodied in the snow, lips moving in a soundless monologue, eyes wide and glistening like bright wet agates. Markham could not seem to get her on her feet, and Kubion finally had Brodie do it—stupid little bitch.

Once all of them were up and walking, he made a motion with his left hand. Brodie and Loxner prodded them down and around to the front entrance, where they stopped and huddled together in a knot. Kubion went up and unlocked the doors, calling out, "Stand back in there, you've got company." Then he looked at the seven hicks—and they mounted the stairs with the resigned, mechanical movements of condemned prisoners climbing a gallows.

Kubion relocked the doors after them, returned the ring of keys to his coat pocket; he could hear but did not pay any attention to voices rumbling within, the thin, sharp cry of a woman. He came down off the steps and told Brodie and Loxner to move over to the car.

When they reached it, he said, "Duff, you'll stay here and start emptying out that sack so we can see what we've got to start with. Vic and I will go after the rest of the hicks. And Duff—if you're gone any of the times we come back, I'll kill Vic first thing and then I'll go inside the church and shoot five of the women. You understand me?"

Loxner looked at a point several feet to the right of Kubion. "Yeah. Yeah, I understand."

"Give me the car keys."

As carefully as Edwards had tossed the keys inside the church, Loxner threw him the leather case containing the car keys; then he opened the door and slid into the front seat. He sat there with his hands splay-fingered on his thighs, staring through the snow-dappled windshield. Kubion said to Brodie, "Put that list of names and addresses on the roof, Vic, and then back off fifteen or twenty steps and keep still like a good boy."

Brodie did as he was told. Kubion lifted the pad, took out the tourist brochure that had the village map on it, and alternately looked at those items and at Brodie standing well out away from the car. Nineteen names, ten houses, maybe seven trips in all; start with the places nearest the church and move outward until he had them all. He picked out their first three stops, tucked the list into his coat, paused, and then called to Brodie, "Okay, Vic, move out, around to the pickup again."

Once Brodie had pivoted, Kubion told Loxner, "Get to work on that sack, Duff, take it out of the back and get to work—come *on.*"

A moment later he slammed the car door, thinking, Now then, now then, and hurried, glitter-eyed, after Brodie's retreating back.

# Three

Frank McNeil was on his hands and knees in front of his old Magnavox radio-and-record player console, fiddling with the radio dials in an effort to tune in the AFL pro football play-off game, when the doorbell began ringing insistently. He looked up in irritation. "Now who goddamn it is that?"

His son, sitting on the living-room sofa, said, "You want me to answer it, Pa?"

"Well what do *you* think, dummy?"

Larry stood up and went out into the hallway. McNeil heard voices at the front door and paid them no mind. Damn these mountains sometimes; you could seldom get a decent picture on television even in the best of weather, and today the damned *radio* was too badly static-ridden to be intelligible. If he could at least....

Footsteps in the hallway, and Larry's voice—high-pitched, frightened: "Pa? Pa?"

McNeil looked up again and saw the two men standing on either side of the youth; one of them was familiar, the other a complete stranger. And then he became aware of the gun in the hand of the dark familiar one, and his irritation dissolved into disbelief. He jerked awkwardly to his feet, flutter-eyed and gape-mouthed.

"No problems if you keep your cool," Kubion told him, "no problems at all."

McNeil continued to blink at him, almost spastically now. With impossible suddenness there was death in the room, *his* death—he could feel it, he could see it staring at him from the eyes of the dark one with the gun—and he began to shake his head, as if by doing that he could make the men and the gun and the stultifying presence of death vanish.

Kubion said, "Who else is here in the house?"

McNeil kept on shaking his head. His mouth and jaws worked soundlessly, as if in exaggerated pantomime of a man chewing gum; he was incapable of speech.

Larry said, "My mother... just my mother."

"Where?"

"In the kitchen."

"Call her in here."

"You... listen, you won't hurt her?"

"Now why would I hurt your old lady, get her in here."

"Ma," Larry called; then, louder: "Ma!"

"What is it?" a woman's voice answered.

"Come into the living room."

"Who was that at the door?"

"Ma, come in here, will you!"

Sandy McNeil—a dark-haired, soft-featured, harassed-looking woman wearing an apron over a faded housedress—appeared in the doorway. "What—" she began, and then stopped speaking and stopped walking as she saw the men, the gun Kubion held. Her eyes grew very round, and the intake of her breath was loudly sibilant, like the hiss of valve-bled steam. The dish towel she had been holding slipped loose and fell unnoticed to the floor.

Larry went to her and put a protective arm around her shoulders, partially shielding her body with his own. "What are you going to do?" he asked. "What do you want with us?"

Kubion said, "We're going to take you to a party."

"Party?" Sandy McNeil said blankly.

"At the church. A little party at the church."

"I don't understand," she said. "I don't *understand.*"

"You don't have to understand. You just do what I tell you. Let's go."

Larry guided his mother toward the hallway. But McNeil stood frozen in front of the console, eyes glazed with terror; he couldn't move, he could not make himself move.

Kubion looked at him, and then stepped quickly forward and cupped a hand around the back of McNeil's neck and sent him reeling across the room. McNeil made a strangled, bleating sound, caught his balance, and groped sightlessly into the hall—pushing his wife and son out of the way as if they were bundles of sticks. His face was the wet dirty color of slush.

A small stain began to spread on the front of his trousers, and Kubion laughed when he saw it. "Well, if you aren't a pisser," he said. "If you aren't a real pisser." He kept on laughing all the way out to the pickup waiting in the side drive.

Somebody began pounding on the downstairs lobby door just as Walt Halliday and his wife finished making love.

"Oh for goodness sake," Lil Halliday said drowsily. She was a thick-bodied woman with butter-yellow hair and a pleasantly homely face. Lying naked on the rumpled double bed, her husband's balding head pillowed comfortably on her heavy breasts, she looked younger than her forty-two years.

Halliday raised his head and listened to the pounding—louder now, demanding—and finally sat up in annoyance. His nose began to run, and he reached one of the Kleenex off the nightstand and blew into it. He had awakened that morning with a sore throat and the runny nose and a slight fever and knew he was coming down with the flu; instead of getting up and dressing for church, as he might have done, he had decided to stay in bed. Lil, who was not much of a churchgoer and went only when he did—fifteen or twenty Sundays in any year, most of those during the quiet off-season months—had brought him a tray breakfast and had then come back to bed with him. They had dozed for a while, talked for a while, been leisurely in their lovemaking: a good Sunday, a fine Sunday. Until that damned persistent pounding on the door.

Standing, Halliday put on his glasses and pajamas and robe and slid his feet into ankle slippers. "Whoever that is," he said, "is going to get a piece of my mind. There's no need to beat on the door like that."

"I'm just glad they didn't start that racket about five minutes ago," Lil said.

"That's something, anyway," Halliday agreed.

He went to the door and glanced back at his wife, and she was still lying there uncovered; she knew he liked to look at her that way. He gave her a broad wink and left their apartment, which was on the first floor of the inn, at the head of the stairs, and started down to the lobby. He shouted, "I'm coming, stop that hammering!" but the sound continued. It was heavy enough now to rattle the glass in the adjacent window.

More than a little irritated, Halliday unlocked the door and jerked it open and said, "What's the idea of—" The rest of the sentence died when he saw the two men and the automatic one of them was pointing at him.

Kubion said, "Back inside, hurry it up, you kept us waiting too long already."

Halliday did what he was told, rapidly, putting his hands up over his head. His mind, all at once, was wrapped in dreamlike confusion. "What do... what do you want?"

"You'll find that out soon enough. Nothing will happen to you as long as you do what you're told. You've got a wife—where is she?"

"Upstairs. She... but she...."

"Take us to her."

"She's in bed, my wife's in bed."

"So what? Come on, get your ass in gear."

Halliday stared at the gun, at the face behind it, and turned instantly to the stairs. As he began to ascend, he could not seem to think of anything except the way Lil had been lying when he'd left her moments ago; and he found himself hoping almost desperately that she had covered herself. Whatever was about to happen, he did not want these two men to see his wife naked....

Joe Garvey opened his front door, and one of the two men standing on the porch outside showed him a gun and said, "Back off, we're coming in; do what you're told and you won't get hurt."

Garvey said incredulously, "What the *hell!*" and stayed where he was. The fingers of his right hand still clutched the edge of the door.

"Inside," Kubion said. "Move it."

"Listen, what is this, you can't come around my house waving a gun—"

Kubion kicked the door out of his hand, jarring loose the candle-festooned holly wreath which hung from the outer panel, and crowded forward. But instead of giving ground as he was expected to do, Garvey braced himself in anger and indignation and made a reflexive lunge at the extended automatic. Half turning, pulling the gun in against his body, Kubion blocked the sweeping arm with his shoulder and made a horizontal bar of his left arm and hit the other man across the chest with it. Garvey banged into one of the inside corridor walls, came off it again like a ball bouncing, and Kubion clubbed him full in the face with the barrel of the weapon.

Bawling with pain, broken nose spraying blood, Garvey staggered into the wall a second time and then went down hard to his knees. Kubion took four more steps into the corridor without breaking momentum and swung around in a crouch and said, "Don't do it, Vic."

Brodie was through the doorway, one arm upraised like a bludgeon, moving in a rush. He brought himself up three feet from the muzzle of Kubion's gun and dropped his arm and backed away immediately, around the kneeling figure of Joe Garvey. His face, momentarily savage, became blank again; only his eyes maintained their polished amethyst shine.

Pat Garvey's voice began calling in querulous alarm from somewhere in the house. "Joe? Joe?"

"Stupid, Vic," Kubion said. "Stupid, stupid."

Brodie said, "All right, I lost my head."

"You'll lose it permanently if you do something else that's stupid. I need you to work the rest of the takeover, you're still in for a third of the take, but I'll make you a dead lump of shit if you push me. You'd better have that straight now."

"Okay," Brodie said. "Okay."

Garvey took his hands away from his face and stared at the blood on them, at the blood dripping from his pulped nose to stain the white front of his shirt. Throbbing pain ringing in his ears, nausea in the back of his throat. What's happening here? he thought dazedly. I don't know what's happening here.

His wife came running into the corridor, saw the two men, saw the gun, saw Garvey kneeling on the floor with the bright red fluid all over him. One hand came up to her mouth, and she screamed softly. "Joe, oh my God, Joe!" She started toward him.

Kubion stepped in front of her and caught her arm; she shrank back away from him, struggling vainly to release the grip, her eyes darting from his face to her husband. "He'll be all right," Kubion told her, "and so will you if you both keep your mouths shut, I mean *shut,* you hear?"

Leave her alone, you filthy son of a bitch! Garvey thought. He tried to put voice to the words, but there was blood in his throat; he began to cough instead.

The blood and the coughing saved his life.

Greg Novak wondered where the hell everybody was.

Sierra Street was deserted all the way up to the slide, and there was no sign of life anywhere else. He hadn't seen a soul since he'd left his parents' home on Modoc Street five minutes before.

For that matter, where were his father and mother? They'd gone to church at a quarter to twelve, and it was three o'clock when he came out of the house for a little fresh air, and they still hadn't returned. He supposed they'd gone to visit somebody, though they didn't usually do that on Sundays. Usually they came straight home and his mother fixed a light lunch and then they played canasta. Church and canasta were both a drag, as far as he was concerned.

Sometimes he got pressured into both, because it was easier to give in than to start a hassle; but he'd stayed in bed this morning, and for a change his mother hadn't tried to talk him out. All things considered, his folks were pretty good people, even if they were hung up on religion and canasta.

So where was everybody, anyway?

Novak felt as if he were walking in a village that had been abandoned, and the feeling made him oddly uncomfortable. He stopped and turned and looked back down Sierra—and a Ford pickup had swung out of the lane to the north of the church and was coming up toward him. Sid Markham's pickup. The uneasiness left him, and he stood watching the half-ton approach, waiting for it.

When it had come close enough so that the two men in the cab were visible through the windshield, he realized that neither of them was Sid Markham. He began to frown. The pickup slewed over to him, and the passenger door opened; the guy on that side jumped out with a gun in his hand, vaulted the packed snow at the curbing, and said, "Stand right where you are, kid, don't move a muscle."

Novak did not even breathe.

Emily Bradford was seventy-five years of age, a thin and frail old woman confined by chronic arthritis either to her bed or to a wheelchair for the past eight years. She lived with her daughter and son-in-law, Sharon and Dave Nedlick: six months in the Macklin Lake hunting lodge which the Nedlicks owned and operated, and six months in the two-story frame house on the corner of Alpine and Modoc streets, where she now lay in her upstairs bedroom.

Sharon and Dave had left for church just before noon, and Emily had spent the next hour faithfully reading her buckram-bound Bible. She had long ago learned to live with her invalidism, but she was still bothered by the fact that she could no longer attend church. Reading the Bible for the length of a Sunday service compensated somewhat, although it was simply not the same thing and never would be. At one o'clock she had resumed her current crocheting project, waiting for her family to return home.

It was presently three thirty, and they had still not come back.

When Sharon and Dave planned to be away for any period of time, they always asked one of the neighbors—mostly an obliging Ellen Coopersmith—to stay with her; but Sharon had said this morning that they would return immediately after church, because they were having turkey for Sunday dinner and she wanted to get it into the oven by one thirty, and Emily never minded being alone for an hour or so. Almost four hours was something else entirely, particularly when the prolonged absence had no apparent explanation, and as a result, Emily had fretted herself into a state of acute anxiety. Something was wrong, she felt it in her bones. She could not imagine what it could be, what with the valley being snowbound as it was, but that only made her all the more apprehensive.

She reached out to the telephone on the bedside table, the third time she had done so in the past hour, and lifted the receiver to her ear. There was no dial tone, it was *still* not working, and why did there always have to be problems with the telephone when you needed it most? She dropped the handset back into its cradle, keenly aware of the stillness of the house and the quick beating of her heart. Why didn't Sharon and Dave come home? Why didn't they come home?

Something made a crashing, shattering noise downstairs.

Emily started violently. One of her veined hands flew up to clutch at the high neck of her nightdress, and her eyes widened behind the lenses of her glasses until they were like luminous brown-and-white pellets. She sat tensely, listening.

More sounds came from below, heavy footsteps. Sharon always walked softly, as did her husband, and Emily thought: Somebody else, there's somebody else in the house! Her breath made a rasping sound in her throat, and her heart began to pound now like a fist within her thin breast.

The heavy footfalls were on the stairs now, ascending.

"Who is it?" she cried, but her tremulous voice was a whisper instead of a shout. "Who's out there?"

The bedroom doorknob rattled—and then the door popped open, and she was looking at two men she had never seen before; men with hard, dark faces and the tangible aura of malevolence about them, one of them brandishing a gun—a *gun!* That one came into the bedroom, sweeping it with deranged eyes, looking at Emily as if she were just another of the room's furnishings.

The other one said, "For Christ's sake, they told you in the church she was an invalid. What's the point of coming up here like this?"

"To make sure," Kubion said. And to Emily, "Take it easy, old woman, nothing's going to happen to you."

"We're not taking her out of here, Earl—not her."

"No, she won't be any trouble."

Kubion stepped back into the hall, motioning, and Brodie swung the door shut. Their footsteps retreated along the corridor, on the stairs.

Emily did not hear them for the thunder in her ears, the loud loud thunder of her heart. And then the thunder began to fade—fading, fading, becoming only a stuttering whisper—and her free hand lifted and fumbled at the air as if imploring. A moment later, like an autumn leaf drifting from tree branch to earth, it fluttered slowly back to the bedclothes and lay still.

The house was once more silent, once more empty; but now the silence was sepulchrally hushed, and the emptiness complete.

# Four

Restlessly pacing the living room, smoking her fifteenth cigarette of the day, Rebecca was intensely aware of the metronomic ticking of the antique pendulum clock on one wall. Ordinarily she did not even hear the familiar tempo, but today, this afternoon, now, it seemed to have grown in volume with its marking of each passing second, so that it filled the room and hammered at her consciousness and at her nerves in the manner of a steadily dripping faucet.

Twenty till four, the clock hands said.

The cigarette tasted raw and noxious, and she turned to the coffee table and jabbed it out in the cloissoné tray. I can't go on with this passive waiting any longer, she thought. I've got to find out where Matt is and why he hasn't come home.

When Martin Donnelly had telephoned her the previous evening—she'd been in bed at the time, thinking about the curiously intimate encounter with Zachary Cain; that he was a man tortured by a personal crisis greater than her own and that she had selfishly misjudged him—Rebecca had unhesitatingly accepted Donnelly's account of a fallen tree likely stranding Matt overnight at the lake. There was no reason to doubt Martin's word—he was a scrupulously honest man—and no reason to suspect anything wrong.

But when Matt did not return this morning or call as he always did when legitimately or illegitimately detained somewhere, she had experienced a vague presentiment of things being not quite right. There was little to support such a foreboding, other than the fact that a team of men should certainly have been able to clear the road of a down tree by midmorning, but it had nagged at her until, finally, she had gone to the telephone with the intention of calling the Donnelly home. The phone had not been working—lines down some place probably, it happened occasionally during the winter months—and that, she told herself, was obviously the reason Matt hadn't called. Everything was quite normal, otherwise. After all, what could happen in a snowbound little place like Hidden Valley?

And yet....

At eleven forty, with Matt still not home, Rebecca had briefly considered going to church. But then she thought that Matt would never think of setting foot inside All Faiths Church on Sunday unless he had dressed for the occasion in his best suit and tie and shirt and shoes. Since he hadn't come home to change, it was axiomatic he wouldn't be in church—and was then, supposedly, still out at the lake. Too, formal religious observance had been destroyed for her some time ago by Matt's hypocrisy: seeing him in fervent, righteous prayer on those Sundays when she knew he had lain with another woman the previous night; she continued occasionally to accompany him when he insisted and for the hollow sake of appearance, but while she still believed in God, actively worshiping Him had been and was impossible. And so she remained in the house, busying herself with prosaic chores, waiting.

One thirty had come. No Matt. She'd tried the phone again, and it was still out of order. Two o'clock. Three. Three thirty. The premonition of wrongness had steadily amplified until, now, it made further waiting unconscionable. Perhaps it was only a case of too much imagination—the making-mountains-out-of-molehills syndrome—and there was some simple and innocuous reason why Matt hadn't returned; but she had to find out, she had to know.

Rebecca went into the hall and opened the door of the coat closet. Boots, hat, parka, mittens. She would, she thought, go to the Tribuccis first. They would know about the fallen tree business, and if there *was* more to it than that, if they weren't aware of his whereabouts, John or Vince would drive her out to Mule Deer Lake so she could talk to Martin Donnelly. Quickly she buttoned her parka and then opened the front door and hurried outside.

She was halfway across the front yard when Sid Markham's old pickup pulled into the drive and the dark, smiling stranger stepped out to confront her....

Beneath the lean-to which ran the full rear width of his cabin, Cain stood at a round, flat, tablelike stump and used a hatchet to split halved pine logs into kindling. The logs were stacked evenly along the rear wall, several cords of them flecked with icy snow; the area covered by the long, shake roof was otherwise bare. He worked mechanically, breath puffing white and hazy, and the thudding, splintering sounds he made reverberated hollowly in the brittle late-afternoon stillness.

Inside him, with an intensity that had mounted throughout the day, guilt fought with memories and despair grappled with rebirthing personal need.

He had had a recurring dream last night, so sharply vivid that it had half awakened him three or four times and had left him, when dawn finally came and ended all sleep, feeling weak and shaken. In the dream he was walking alone on a huge, sere plain, under a copper colored sky. Far ahead of him he saw that the withered grass gave way to a stretch of bright green, and he went toward it and recognized as he approached that someone was standing just beyond the separation line between green and brown. The someone was one-half of himself—and he realized that there had only been half of *him* the entire time he'd been on the burned section of prairie, that he had been hopping on one leg instead of walking on two. Frightened, he stared with his single eye as though transfixed by his second eye.

And the other half of him said, with half a mouth, *Why do you keep fighting me? Sooner or later we're going to merge, you know that. We're going to become whole again.*

We can never be whole again, he said.

*We can and we will. And when we are, we have to go back—back to architecture, back to San Francisco, back so we can pick up some of the pieces. It has to be that way; you can't run away from me any longer.*

You're dead, do you hear me? You're dead!

*I'm alive, we're alive. Listen, now, listen.*

No.

*Question: Would Angie have wanted you to do what you've done to us? Would Lindy and Steve, as young as they were, have wanted it?*

That doesn't matter. They're gone, it doesn't matter.

*Yes it does, oh yes it does. Question: Why weren't you able to suicide us? Wasn't it because I stopped you? Wasn't it because I, you, we want to go on living, after all?*

Enough, I don't want to hear any more.

*Question: If you truly wanted to turn us into an alcoholic, moribund vegetable, why did you come to Hidden Valley—why did you choose to live among people—in the first place? Aren't there hundreds of totally sequestered areas in this country where you could have become a literal hermit? Didn't I stop you there, too, even though you were stronger then?*

Shut up, shut up.

*You're not stronger anymore, I'm stronger. The incident with Rebecca Hughes was more than a spilling over of words, it was me taking over at last, it was the beginning of the end of these past six months. You know that, why won't you accept it?*

I can't. I won't.

*You can and you will. It's inevitable. Come to me now, come to me and we'll be whole again.*

No!

He turned and tried to run, but with his single leg he could only hop; and the plain shimmered and suddenly became a quagmire that made accelerated motion impossible. Darkness took away the copper light of the sky, folding around him, and he could feel warm breath against the back of his neck—the other half of him pursuing, unimpeded by the boggy ground, coming closer, touching him then, touching him....

At this exact point he would come out of it—only to sink back into slumber and have it start all over again.

When Cain had gotten up at dawn, and the shaken feeling had passed, he tried not to think about the dream; but it was fixed in his mind, each detail as ineradicable as the stain of loneliness. He dressed and went into the kitchen and fried two eggs, and couldn't eat them; poured bourbon into his coffee, and the smell of it gagged him. It was cold in the cabin, and he made a fire with the last of his kindling. The cold seemed to remain. He sat at the table by the window, chain-smoking, but the sitting began to gnaw at his nerves. Pacing did not help, and he thought of going for a walk and didn't want to do that either.

Sunday, today was Sunday. And on Sundays he and Don Collins would go out to Sharp Park or Harding and play eighteen holes of golf. On Sundays he would watch that intricate war game known as professional football on television. On Sundays he would take Angie and the kids to Golden Gate Park, where they would eat a picnic lunch at Stow Lake and then visit the De Young Museum or the Steinhart Aquarium or the Japanese Tea Garden or the Morrison Planetarium. On Sundays—

Shivering, Cain got a broom from the closet and swept out all the rooms; emptied an overflow of garbage into the can outside; made the bed and straightened the bedroom; washed the bathroom sink and shower stall and walls and floor. In the front room again he put more wood on the fire—and was acutely aware of how incredibly still it could get in there, how sterile and empty the surroundings actually were. He found himself wishing that he had a radio, that he could listen to some music or the news; realized he had not heard a newscast or read a paper in all the months he had been in Hidden Valley; realized he did not know, except for snatches of disinterestedly overheard conversation between valley residents, what was happening anywhere in the world.

I need to talk to someone, he thought, like I talked to Rebecca Hughes last night. I need—*I need*....

He made a sandwich and forced himself to eat it. He could not think of anything else to do after that, and spent five minutes smoking six cigarettes and coughing up as much smoke as he exhaled normally before he remembered that there wasn't any more kindling. He got the hatchet then and came around here to the lean-to and began splitting logs.

There was, now, enough kindling lying in the snow at his feet to last him for weeks.

Cain buried the hatchet blade in the stump, wiped perspiration from his forehead with one gloved hand. Take all this inside, come back and carry in more halved logs to stack by the fireplace; keep busy, keep finding things to do. Stooping, he gathered up an armful of the kindling; straightened again, turned, took two steps—and came to a standstill.

Rebecca Hughes and two men he did not recognize were standing in the falling snow just outside the lean-to.

Cain opened his mouth to speak, closed it when he saw that the darker of the men, positioned well apart, was grinning oddly and holding a gun. The other one had his arms down at his sides, fingers curled in against the palms. As still and pale as a piece of marble statuary, Rebecca looked at Cain with eyes that were wide circles of fear. A feeling of unreality fled through him, as though the three of them had been conjured up from his subconscious—a kind of snow mirage.

"Drop that wood and get over here," Kubion said.

Cain found words, pushed them out. "Who are you? What's going on here?"

"You'll find out soon enough. Now shut up and do what you're told."

"What do you want with me, with Mrs. Hughes?"

"Get the fuck over here, I said!"

Cain sensed, incredulously, that the man would not hesitate to shoot him if he failed to comply; the feeling of unreality modulated into one of surreality. He let the kindling fall out of his arms in automatic reaction, walked forward stiffly and came out from under the roof and stopped again. Kubion's eyes followed him, and when Cain stared into them he saw unmistakable dementia shining there. His stomach contracted, and a brassy taste came into his mouth; he could not seem to think clearly.

"That's better, that's fine," Kubion said. "Now we go for a ride."

He gestured with the gun, and the second man—tight-mouthed, sane-looking—prodded Rebecca's shoulder. She moved forward, paused in front of Cain, and there was bewilderment commingled with fright in her expression; she seemed to have no more idea than he of the two men's motive or intent. Her dread was palpable; he could feel it as he could feel the knife-edge of the wind blowing along the cabin's side wall, and a rush of anger took away some of his own confusion—caring anger, an emotion (like the brassiness in his mouth) he had not experienced in a great long time.

He did not want her to be hurt; he did not want to be hurt himself.

I don't want to die, he thought almost detachedly. It's true, I really *don't* want to die....

"Step out!" Kubion yelled at them. "Move!"

Rebecca edged close to Cain as they trudged forward through the snow. He said in a low voice, "Are you all right? They haven't hurt you?"

"No. No. But God, I—"

"Shut the hell up," from behind them. "I don't want to have to tell anybody again, you understand?"

Cain clamped his teeth together; Rebecca stared straight ahead, walking like a life-size windup toy. They went around to the front and across the yard to where an old Ford pickup was parked nose downhill on Lassen Drive. Brodie half circled it and got into the cab on the driver's side, and Kubion came forward then and said, "Both of you now, woman in the middle."

When Cain had pulled the door open Rebecca climbed awkwardly onto the front seat, drawing up a full twelve inches away from Brodie. The door slapped against Cain's hip as he wedged in after her, then latched under the pressure of Kubion's hand. Kubion swung onto the running board, over into the bed, and his face appeared in the broken-out rear window. He said to Brodie, "Nice and slow, Vic, you know how to do it."

"Yeah," Brodie said, and reached out to switch on the ignition.

Like a child huddling impersonally for warmth and support, Rebecca leaned against Cain with hip and thigh and shoulder and one breast—soft, yielding flesh through the parka she wore and despite the trembling tension in her. It was the first time he had been in physical contact with, conscious of, a woman's body since Angie, and defensively he felt his muscles stiffen.

But he did not withdraw from her as the truck glided forward and down through the empty afternoon.

# Five

Coopersmith was one of the first to move when the three gunmen left the church and the key turned in the outside lock. He hurried to where Webb Edwards was bending over the still-unconscious form of the Reverend Mr. Keyes and holding his limp left wrist between thumb and forefinger.

"How is he, Webb?"

"Pulse is holding steady," Edwards answered shortly. "Get me a couple of coats, Lew. Only thing we can do is keep him warm."

At the front wall, Coopersmith dragged two heavy winter coats off the canted wooden pegs. Others were milling about now, as if in a kind of posthypnotic confusion. You could smell the sour odor of fear, Coopersmith thought; and you could feel the ripplings of panic like a dark undercurrent beneath the surface of sound and movement. Voices shrill and questioning assailed his ears as he took the coats to Edwards.

Judy Tribucci: "How can a thing like this happen, how can it happen to us...."

Minnie Beckman: "A spawn of the devil, did you see his eyes, those terrible eyes...."

Harry Chilton: "Why are they doing it? Why, for God's sake, why, why...."

Verne Mullins: "Who are they, they're not businessmen, where did the third one come from...."

Maude Fredericks: "Matt can't be dead, he can't be...."

June Novak: "Oh my Lord please don't let Greg be harmed, please...."

Sharon Nedlick: "Dave, Mother's heart won't stand any kind of shock, if they break into the house and try to bring her here even after what we told them...."

Agnes Tyler: "Peggy *has* to be all right, they haven't hurt her, they haven't hurt her...."

Edwards' nurse, Sally Chilton, had joined him at the minister's side. She took one of the coats from Coopersmith, folded it, and carefully pillowed Keyes' head; Edwards covered him with the second and then began unwrapping the blood-soaked handkerchief from his torn right hand, telling Sally to find a clean scarf or something to use as another makeshift bandage.

Coopersmith pivoted away—and Ellen was there, coming into his arms, pressing her wet face against his shoulder. He held her clumsily, felt the tremors fluttering through her body, and had no words to comfort her. Acrimony, helplessness formed an acidulated knot in his chest.

After a moment he lifted her chin with gentle fingers, brushed his lips across her forehead, took her slowly back to where they had been located in the right front pew. Opposite, on the left forward bench, Ann Tribucci was still sitting in the graceless, spread-legged, flat-footed posture of the pregnant woman in her final month; her abdomen, moving with the quickened tempo of her breathing, seemed enormous. Tie pulled loose, shirt unbuttoned at the throat,

John Tribucci squatted in front of her.

He was saying, "You're *sure* you're okay, honey?"

"A little queasy, that's all."

"It's not the baby...."

"No. No."

"Do you want to lie down?"

"Not just yet. Johnny—"

"What, honey?"

"If... Matt has been killed, do you think Becky—"

Inadequately he said, "Shh, now, try not to worry about Becky or anything else."

"How can I help it? I'm so frightened—for all of us, for the baby...."

Tribucci took her hands in his and held them tightly. "I know," he said, "I know, I know. But nothing will happen to any more of us; we're all going to come out of this just fine."

There's no conviction in his voice, Coopersmith thought—and I don't think I believe it either, not after the things that homicidal lunatic said and has done already. He looked at Ellen and then swiftly averted his gaze again; he did not want her to see on his face what was in his mind. Spontaneously, he went up onto the pulpit and stared at the wooden crucifix on the wall above the prayer cloth-draped altar. The constriction in his chest had tightened, and he realized that he was short of breath. A new apprehension tugged at him. He had had a physical checkup three months before, and Webb Edwards had pronounced his heart as strong as ever; but he was sixty-six years old—*old,* not young—and an old man's heart could give out at any time under stress, wasn't that a medical fact?

Knock it off, he told himself sharply. You're not going to have a stroke. Whatever else will happen today, you're not going to have a stroke.

He kept on standing there, staring at the crucifix. A minute or two passed, and John Tribucci came up beside him. Some of the younger man's control had clearly begun to slip; his normally amiable face was dark-flecked with an admixture of anxiety and savage fury. "Lew," he said in a voice liquid with feeling. "*God,* Lew."

"Easy, son."

Tribucci closed his eyes, released a heavy shuddering breath and opened them again. "I've never hated anybody or anything in my life, but those three men, that maniac...."

Coopersmith knew what he was thinking: exactly the same thing he himself had thought when the dark gunman ordered him to reveal which valley residents were not present inside the church. He did not speak.

"It's so *senseless,*" Tribucci said. "Reverend Keyes wounded and Matt Hughes murdered and maybe others dying, maybe all our lives in jeopardy—for what? For what, Lew? There isn't any money or valuables in Hidden Valley worth stealing."

"Johnny, don't try to find reason in the actions of a madman."

"All three of them can't be crazy."

"No, but it was obvious who's running the whole show. I can't figure why the other two are in it. Maybe for some other cause than what little the valley can be looted for."

"Well alone or not, that psycho has been planning it for days. He came into the Sport Shop on Thursday and asked me a lot of questions about snowmobiles and ways to get out of the valley. I believed the excuse he gave, told him everything he wanted to know. He looked all right then, I didn't suspect anything to be wrong...."

"How could you? How could any of us? We—"

*"Stand back in there, you've got company!"*

The shouted command from outside sliced off conversation, jerked heads around, turned Tribucci and Coopersmith and brought them down off the pulpit. There was the sound of the key in the lock, and then one of the door halves swung open and the Donnelly and Markham families, and Peggy Tyler, filed inside. The door banged shut, and the key scraped again.

Agnes Tyler cried, "Peggy!" and rushed down the center aisle. The blonde-haired girl had stopped just inside the entrance and was standing as immobile and expressionless as a mannequin. When her mother reached her and flung arms around her, moaning her name, she blinked several times but did not otherwise move; she seemed only vaguely aware of where she was. Coopersmith saw, as he and Tribucci approached, that the others seemed in better condition and apparently unharmed, although the adults were all haggard and eviscerated and shaking with cold or fear or both. The two Donnelly children clung to each other like waifs lost in the night.

Webb Edwards pushed his way forward and swept each of them with a clinical glance that concluded only Peggy Tyler was in immediate need of medical attention. He stepped to her, disengaged Mrs. Tyler's enfolding arms, and probed the damp ivory face, the vacuous eyes. His mouth thinned; he took one of her lax hands.

"What is it, what's the matter with her?" Agnes Tyler said frantically. "God in heaven, what did they do to you, baby, what did they *do* to you!"

Taking Peggy's other arm, Sally Chilton helped Edwards steer her to one of the rear pews; her mother hovered nearby, hands clenched together at her breast, teeth biting deeply into a tremulous lower lip. The Markhams and Donnellys found benches near the south-side wall heater, and Coopersmith and Tribucci and Harry Chilton brought extra coats for the women and children.

Minutes later, in subdued and exhausted tones, Sid Markham and Martin Donnelly related some of the grim details of their ordeal. When they were finished, Coopersmith said, "So it was just the lunatic at first."

Markham nodded. "I don't think the other two knew anything about it. He didn't bring them around until he had us all tied up in Martin's living room, and they were shook when they saw us—plenty angry."

"Why did they join in with him, then?"

"They didn't have much choice. For one thing, the crazy had his gun out and they didn't seem to be armed, and he looked like he'd use it on them if they gave him any trouble. For another, he'd told us everything about the three of them except their names—and I guess told them that he had. He sat there grinning after he had us tied and said how he planned to take over the valley and that they're professional thieves and that they tried to rob some place called Greenfront in Sacramento last Monday and killed a security guard and didn't get any money. He said that lake cabin where they've been staying is what he called a safe house." Markham's foxlike face remained desolate, but his words took on a sardonic edge. "We've had criminals hiding out in Hidden Valley off and on for years, seems like. Right under our noses the whole time."

Coopersmith was not surprised that the three men were professionals; despite the madman's actions, they had taken over the church in a phlegmatic, businesslike manner with which he was all too familiar after forty years of law enforcement. But the fact that the Mule Deer Lake cabin had been an established hideout for the criminal element was an unexpected and galling revelation. Right under our noses, he thought. Right under the nose of a retired old fool of a county sheriff named Lew Coopersmith, who kept bemoaning a severed involvement in his profession while God knew how many wanted felons camped with impunity in his backyard and maybe drank Saturday afternoon beer with him in the Valley Inn bar. The knot in his chest tightened again, and he felt now every one of his sixty-six years; he felt incredibly tired and used-up and incompetent.

Tribucci asked, "Do you know about Matt Hughes?"

"He's... dead," Donnelly answered, purse-lipped.

"We were hit with that much, but not where or how or why."

Markham and Donnelly exchanged silent glances. "Have you got any idea how it happened?"

"I guess we do," Donnelly said.

"How, then?"

"Better if we don't talk about it," Markham said.

"We've got to know, Sid."

"There's enough on everybody's mind as it is."

Doris Markham—a thin, shrewish woman whose hands jumped and fluttered as if wired to invisible electrodes—swung around to look at her husband. She said stridulously, "Oh for Lord's *sake*, Sid, what's the use of trying to hide the truth? They'll find it out anyway, sooner or later. Tell them and have done with it."

"Doris—"

"All right then, I will. Matt was killed at the Taggart cabin. He was with Peggy and the crazy found them together and shot Matt and then brought her to Martin's and tied her up with the rest of us. She saw Matt killed; that's why she's the way she is now. There—it's all out in the open."

Audible intakes of breath, murmurs. A gaseous sourness bubbled in Coopersmith's stomach.

Maude Fredericks said, "You can't mean they were—I don't believe it! Matt... Matt wouldn't have...."

"Well I couldn't believe it either at first, but it's true. The crazy told us how he found them"—her mouth twisted—"and told us exactly what they'd been doing. He laughed about it. He stood there and laughed—"

"He was lying!" Agnes Tyler, on her feet now, stared at the other woman saucer-eyed. "Not Peggy... Peggy's a good girl, Matt was a good man... no!"

Doris looked away. Markham started to say something to her, changed his mind, and spread his hands toward Agnes in a gesture of mute deprecation.

"No, no, no, no," she said and began to sob, one hand fisted against her mouth. The sound of her weeping and the susurration of voices grated corrosively at Coopersmith's nerves; he turned on legs that, always strong, now felt enervated and frail-boned, and returned to the forward pew and sank onto it and stared at his liver-spotted hands.

Matt Hughes: paragon of virtue, energetic and benevolent community leader, the man everyone looked up to and wanted their sons to emulate. Matt Hughes: unfaithful husband, hypocrite—and dead because of it. The Reverend Mr. Keyes was still unconscious, but he would learn the harsh truth about the murdered head of his flock eventually. And so would poor Rebecca. Everything seemed to be crumbling around them on this cataclysmic day—secrets revealed, illusions shattered, beliefs shaken, and no one spared in the least. All for the Greater Good? Could they still believe in that now and in their collective salvation?

Coopersmith looked up again at the crucifix above the altar. And a passage from Proverbs in the Old Testament flickered into his mind: *Be not afraid of sudden fear, neither of the desolation of the wicked, when it cometh. For the LORD shall be thy confidence, and shall keep thy foot from being taken.*

"All right," he murmured aloud. "All right.'

Peggy Tyler lay quiescent on the hard wooden pew bench, tangled blond hair swept away from her face. A small part of her was aware that she was inside the church, that her mother and Dr. Edwards were beside her, but a much larger part was still in the Taggart cabin at Mule Deer Lake. It was as if she were coexisting in two separate realities, two separate time streams. Jumbled voices from both seemed to whisper distantly, hollowly in her ears, images from both were strangely superimposed on one another.

Shivering, she said, "I'm cold, I'm cold."

Mrs. Tyler tucked the heavy fur coat tighter beneath Peggy's chin; then, tears still trickling along her cheeks, she leaned down and said imploringly, "It's not true, is it, baby? You weren't sinning with Matt Hughes, tell me you weren't.... "

"Stop it, Agnes," Edwards said. "I told you, she doesn't seem to be able to comprehend anything we say to her. You're not doing either of you any good."

Matt? Peggy thought. Matt—Matt? You killed him! You shot him in the face, his face is gone, oh the blood the blood... no, don't touch me! Don't touch. me, don't you touch me!

"Mother?" she said.

"I'm here, baby, I'm here." Mrs. Tyler lifted her entreating gaze to Edwards.

"Can't you do something for her?"

"If they bring me my bag, I'll give her a sedative. There's nothing else I can do, Agnes, I'm only a village doctor. She needs hospitalization. And, the way it looks, psychiatric care."

"*Psychiatric* care?"

Edwards said gently, "What she saw last night seems to have had an unbalancing effect on her mind. It may only be temporary, but—"

"I won't listen to that kind of talk. There's nothing wrong with her mind, she didn't see Matt Hughes killed, she wasn't with him at the Taggart cabin or anywhere else."

"Agnes...."

"No. She was captured by those murderers and had a terrible experience and she's in shock, that's all, just simple shock. She'll be fine in a little while—won't you, baby? Won't you?"

He took my money, Peggy thought, he took my thousand dollars. Give it back, it's mine. I earned it, I need it, I almost have enough to leave now. Leave these mountains forever, go to Europe, lie under a hot sun by a bright blue ocean. Warm places, snowless places. Soon. Matt? Soon.

"I'm so cold," she said.

The next two and a half hours passed in grim cycle.

"Stand back in there!" the voice outside would shout, and talk would instantly fade, and eyes would fasten on the entrance; the lock would click, the door would open—

Frank McNeil, sweating, shaking, face and eyes like those of a woman on the brink of hysteria; in sharp contrast, Sandy and Larry McNeil following as if narcotized.

—and the door would close, the lock would click; vocalization and constrained activity would commence again, questions would be asked, questions would be answered; the waiting tension would mount; and then it would all begin anew:

"Stand back in there!"

Walt Halliday, rubber-legged, sniffling and coughing into a mucus-spotted handkerchief; Lil Halliday, lower jaw paroxysmic, hands clasped in front of her as if in prayer.

"Stand back!"

Joe Garvey, face bloody, clothing bloody, staggering slightly but waving away the proffered assistance and attention of Webb Edwards; Pat Garvey, lachrymose and looking as if she were near collapse.

"All right, stand back in there!"

The Stallings family.

"Stand back!"

Bert Younger, Enid Styles, Jerry Cornelius. "You people stand back in there!"

Greg Novak, more dazed than frightened, immediately enfolded in the tearful embrace of his father and mother....

Through it all John Tribucci was in constant prowling motion, like a panther in a zoo cage. He paced from back to front, from side to side, pausing only to make sure Ann was still all right or to exchange brief dialogue with his brother or Lew Coopersmith or one of the new arrivals. Veins pulsed along his forehead, on one temple; impotent frustration was toxic within him. Trapped, trapped, no way out, nothing any of them could do, no way out—

Abruptly, near the lectern on the left side of the pulpit, he came to a standstill. His head snapped up, and he stared at and mentally beyond the high, wood-raftered ceiling.

The belfry, he thought; the belfry.

And the voice outside shouted, "Stand back in there!"

# Six

Waiting beside the Ford half-ton, Brodie watched Kubion lock the last two valley residents—Hughes' wife and the big bearded man—inside the church. His mind was still sharply alert, but physically he had begun to feel the effects of the long sleepless night, the constant tension; his eyes were sandy and his neck ached and fatigue leadened his arms and legs. The chill mountain weather made it worse. The wind was up now, and it kept getting colder, and snow fell in turbulent swirls of fat, dry flakes. Night shadows, thickened by the density of the bloated gray clouds overhead, crept rapidly through the village and across the valley.

Brodie turned his head to look toward the car parked sixty yards distant, and through the snow and the rimed windows Loxner was a blackish outline behind the wheel. He'd been visible there each of the times they'd brought prisoners back here to the church, probably hadn't even got out of the car in all that time; no guts and no brains, Brodie couldn't have asked for any worse an ally. Well, he hadn't expected Loxner to try to take Kubion, had thought that if Duff did anything at all, it would be to run his ass into the woods somewhere and hide. The only way Brodie was going to get out of Hidden Valley alive was to handle Kubion himself.

He'd been in tight situations before, been under the gun before, but making a move against an armed man and making a move against an armed super-crazy and super-deadly psycho were two different things entirely. You just didn't want to gamble, because when you got desperate around a maniac, you got dead—period. So you hung on grimly to your cool, and you waited for a mistake or some other clear-cut opportunity. Only Kubion hadn't made any mistakes—his whip hand had been unbreakable so far—and there just hadn't been any openings. What had seemed like one when Kubion pistol-whipped the pockmarked guy had turned out to be a blind corner instead, and he'd been within a half step, a half second of taking a bullet for his effort. Since then he'd been able to do nothing except to wait and keep on waiting.

And now maybe he had waited too long.

They'd rounded up all the valley people, and Kubion didn't need him or Loxner to loot the village. It could be he intended to let them both keep on living a while longer; but he was totally unpredictable, and there was no way you could second-guess him. If this *was* it, Brodie's only option was that desperate gamble; he wasn't going to die a frozen target, any way but a frozen target. The only other thing he could do was to try to buy himself time, and the way to do that was to remind Kubion of the Mercantile's safe.

When they'd first taken Hughes' wife, Kubion had asked her for the combination; she'd said she didn't have any idea what it was, no one knew it except her husband and he had committed it to memory. Too scared to be lying, even

Kubion had seen that. So the safe had to be cracked—and Kubion was no jug-
ger, he didn't know the first thing about busting a box. Brodie did, though. Jug-
ging was a nowhere business these days, owing to modern improvements in
safe-and-vault manufacturing: drill-and acetylene-resistant steel alloys and
self-contained alarm systems and automatic relocking devices to help guard
against lock blowing with nitro or plastic gelatine; but there were still a few
old hands around, and Brodie had worked a couple of scores with one of them,
Woody Huggins. Kubion was aware of that and had to be aware, too—made
aware, convinced—that Brodie could open that box a hell of a lot quicker and
surer than he could do it himself....

Kubion returned to the pickup, which straddled the front walk thirty feet
from the church entrance, and stopped by the tailgate. He said, "All of them
now, all of them, didn't I tell you the way it would be? You should have listened, you and Duff should've listened from the start."

"That's right, Earl," Brodie said, "we should've listened from the start."

"Now the gravy, eh Vic? Now the gravy."

"The safe in the Mercantile first?"

Kubion gave him a sly look. "Could be."

"I hope it's one I can jug without any sweat."

"Maybe I could jug it myself, you know?"

"Maybe you couldn't, Earl," Brodie said slowly. He watched the automatic the
way you would watch a coiled rattlesnake.

"Yeah, maybe not," Kubion agreed, and laughed.

"Do we move out now?"

"How come you're so anxious, Vic, how come?"

"I just want to see how much is in that safe."

The slyness vanished. "Well so do I. Let's get to cracking." He paused, realizing what he'd said, and found it to be funny; his laughter this time was loud
and shrill, echoing on the wind. "Pretty good, hey? Let's get to cracking."

Brodie relaxed a little, not much. "Pretty good, Earl," he said.

He watched Kubion go around to the passenger door, open it; they got into
the cab simultaneously. So Kubion wasn't worried about Loxner any more than
Brodie was counting on him; he was giving them *both* some extra time. Well,
screw Loxner, Loxner just didn't figure to matter at all. What mattered was an
opening, a mistake. And it would come, he had to keep telling himself that; it
would come, it would come.

Brodie started the engine, drove across the front church-yard and onto Sierra Street and up to the Mercantile. They got out of the pickup, climbed over
the windrows onto the icy sidewalk. The wind hurled snow in gyrating flurries, moaned in building eaves, rattled boarding and glass, singingly vibrated
the string of Christmas lights spanning the street. In its emptiness the village
had an almost eerily desolate feel, like an Arctic ghost town.

"Kick the doors open," Kubion said.

Brodie looked at the holly wreath and mistletoe decorating the two glass
halves, over at the cardboard Santa Claus and cardboard reindeer in one of the

windows. Then he tongued cold-chapped lips and stepped up to the entrance. Raising one foot, he drove it against the lock in the wooden frames where the two leaves joined; the doors held. He kicked again, and a third time, without being able to snap the lock.

Impatiently, Kubion told him to break the pane out of one of the halves.

He did that, and the holly wreath flew inside with splinters of glass and scattered berries and leaves across the floor. He used his foot to punch away the remaining shards, ducked through the open frame and into the semi-darkened interior. When he was eight steps across the wooden floor, Kubion came in and said, "Light switches are on the wall over there, behind the counter."

Moving slowly, Brodie passed the potbellied stove and went around and found the metal control case and flipped the row of switches within. Warm yellow illumination flooded the store. Kubion waved him a short way along the aisle between the counter and wall shelves of liquor and other bottled goods; then, without taking eyes off him, he rang up No Sale on the cash register and rifled the drawer. Seventy or eighty dollars, if that much. He wadded the bills into his trouser pocket, made another waving motion, and they went down to where the office was located.

The door was locked, but this one gave and bounced inward the first time Brodie slammed the bottom of his shoe against the wood above the latch. While Kubion stood watching from just outside the doorway, Brodie crossed to the heavy oak desk and put on the lamp there. The glass top held no potential weapon, not even a letter opener, but would Hughes have kept a gun in one of the drawers? Not likely—and Kubion wouldn't let him into the desk anyway. He gave his attention to the safe. A cheesebox, it could be opened in a maximum of thirty minutes; all you had to do with one of these old one-pieces was to knock off the combination dial.

Kubion said, "How long?"

"I'm not sure. I might have to peel it."

"A crate like this?"

"It's more solid than it might look."

"I don't want any bullshit, Vic."

"No bullshit."

"All right, what you need?"

"Hammer, chisels, pry bar, maybe a high-speed drill."

"Nice and convenient hardware section out front, right?"

Out of the office, around the counter, through the grocery section. "Hold it," Kubion said.

Brodie stopped immediately. "What?"

On top of one of the shelves was a cardboard carton of paper towel rolls; Kubion motioned to it. "Dump out that carton and bring it along."

"What for?'

"So you don't get any ideas, baby."

"I don't know what you mean."

"No? I'll lay it out for you then: I don't want you carrying hammers and chisels and pry bars loose in your hands, I don't want you even touching any of that stuff until we get back into the office, now do what I told you."

A tic fluttered one corner of Brodie's mouth. He turned and took the carton down and emptied the paper towel rolls onto the floor. In the hardware department, Kubion instructed him to put the box down and then turn around and lace his hands behind him. After Brodie complied, he heard tools begin to clatter into the carton, Kubion's voice calling off the name of each. Then: "Okay, that everything you need?"

Brodie considered asking for an awl, because of the tool's thin sharp-pointed blade; telling Kubion he might need it for work on the lock mechanism. But if Kubion saw through the lie, there was just no telling what he'd do; the last thing Brodie could afford now was to antagonize him. And Christ, even if Kubion let him have one, he'd never get close enough to stab him with it; and the round, beveled handles on the things made them too awkward for throwing, overbalanced them.

He said, "That's everything, Earl."

"Turn around and pick up the carton."

Wordlessly, Brodie carried the heavy container back into the office. He set it down in front of the safe, took off his coat and gloves, and knelt beside it. He could feel Kubion's eyes on his back as he began to sort through the jumble of tools, lifting them out of the carton one by one, trying to stall without seeming to do so.

"Vic," Kubion said finally, "Vic baby."

Brodie stopped stalling then and went to work on the safe.

# Seven

The moment Rebecca stepped inside the church she knew that Matt was dead.

She felt it like a chill in the strained, hushed atmosphere, and saw it reflected in the staring faces of the people huddled throughout. Everyone who lived in the valley seemed to be there, everyone except Matt, and he was not there because he was dead; he had been killed somehow by the men who had kidnapped her and Zachary Cain and all these others, too. The presentiment of things being wrong, Matt's unsatisfactorily explained absence, had planted the seed in her mind, and it had germinated swiftly with the appearance and actions of the wild-eyed gunman and his demands for information about the Mercantile's safe. A kind of creeping mental numbness—a defensive barrier erected against the sharp stabbing edges of fear—had kept her from dwelling continually on the possibility, but now there could no longer be any resistance because there was no longer any doubt.

Matt was dead.

She stood very still and tried to feel grief, some sense of personal loss. There was only the terror and a hollow despair. Dreamlike, she watched people converging on her and felt Webb Edwards' hand on her arm and heard him asking if she were all right, if she wanted to sit down; heard other voices murmuring but none of them saying anything about Matt, uneasily avoiding the inevitable, and so she said it for them, she said, "Matt's dead, isn't he?"

Ann Tribucci was at her side now. "Becky, you'd better come and sit down...."

"*He's dead,* isn't he?"

"He... yes. Oh Becky—"

Woodenly, "How did it happen?"

"You don't want to know, not now."

"I have to know. I don't know anything about what's going on. Why are we here? Who are those men? How did Matt die?"

In hesitant, succinct words they told her who the men were and what had occurred last night and today. Rebecca was beyond the point of shock; she comprehended the facts, accepted them, abhorred them automatically with a small part of her mind, but they had no immediate or cohesive impact on her and she registered no external reaction. She waited for someone to tell her about Matt, and when no one did she repeated her question:

"How did Matt die?"

"Come and sit down," Ann said again.

"I don't want to sit down, will you stop asking me to sit down and please please tell me what happened to my husband?"

Awkward silence. Rebecca sensed dimly that their hesitancy was not solely the result of a desire to spare her the specifics of Matt's death, that there was something else they were reluctant to reveal and which they wanted to spare her. What? she thought—and then she guessed what it must be, but this also had little distinct impact on her. Like an anesthetic, the numbness had begun spreading through her mind again.

She said in a barren tone, "Where was he killed?"

Lew Coopersmith, slowly and resignedly: "At the lake."

"Last night?"

"Yes."

"They shot him, is that it? Was he shot?"

"Yes."

"Was he alone?"

The awkward silence.

"Was he alone?" Rebecca repeated.

"No one else was shot last night."

"That isn't what I asked. Was Matt alone?"

Pleadingly Ann said, "Becky, Becky...."

"He wasn't alone, was he? He was with another woman, together with another woman. Isn't that right?"

Silence.

"Yes of course," she said, "of course he was. Who was it? No, it doesn't matter, I don't want to know, it doesn't matter."

Shuffling movement around her, toward her, away from her. Faces averted, faces staring. Pity touching her like fat, soft, unwelcome hands. She did want to sit down then and found a place without assistance. Head bowed, she thought dully: Well, that makes it all very simple, doesn't it? No need for a decision now, no need for anything now. Matt was dead, and the truth was out; they all knew the truth at last: Matt Hughes a philanderer, Matt Hughes consorting with a local woman and doing it right here in Hidden Valley (even she would never quite have expected him to be that brash, that foolhardy; even she did not really know all of what had been concealed beneath his generous, boyish, pious exterior). How surprised they must have been—and how fitting that they should have learned it in this of all places. And what would they say if she were to tell them of the long, long line of other women, all the past deceits?

Oh yes, there had been quite a bit of goodness in him, and his death was violent and premature, and she had lived with him and slept with him for seven years; but she could not now or ever grieve for him. The well of Matt-directed emotions had run dry. She had given him everything she knew how to give, and he had left her with nothing whatsoever of value. How could she possibly mourn an unfaithful husband who had even died in the company of another woman?

Ann sat down beside her and covered one of her mittened hands, not speaking. Rebecca was grateful for that; she did not want dialogue of any kind. She sat without moving or thinking for several moments. Then, gradually, some of the numbness began to recede, and she became aware of the heavy tumescence

that was Ann's unborn child, of her surroundings, of why she and all the others were here in the church, of the things the three men outside had already
done: the full horror of the situation penetrating for the first time. Fear surged
consumingly in her stomach again: her fingers closed tightly around Ann's
and clung to them. Matt was dead, murdered—and what of Ann and her baby
and everyone else in the valley? What of Rebecca Hughes?

What was to become of *them?*

# Eight

Cain sat on the far edge of the pulpit, spine curved to the outer organ casing, forearms resting on his pulled-up knees. It was warm enough inside the church, but his skin crawled with cold—the kind of cold that has nothing to do with temperature.

The dark gunman's clearly homicidal dementia had prepared him for most any contingency on the ride down from the cabin, yet the magnitude of what was actually taking place in Hidden Valley—recounted to Rebecca Hughes while he had stood listening and ignored on the periphery—had stunned and repulsed him. The concept was monstrous; you could not immediately reconcile your mind to it. Things like this can't happen, you thought; they can't happen to *you*. And then you remembered men like Hitler and Richard Speck and Charles Manson, and that all their victims must have at first experienced the same staggering disbelief, and you understood that such things could and did happen at any time, at any place, to anyone.

*Anything* can happen, Cain thought now; madness doesn't have to have a thing to do with it. A man can get drunk to celebrate some great good fortune and run over a child while driving home. A man can send his wife out for a package of cigarettes, and she can be raped and murdered on the way to the corner grocery. Yes, and a man can repair a home appliance and make an unconscious error that causes the death of his entire family....

He raised his head and looked toward the rear, to where Rebecca Hughes sat. Compassion moved through him, as it had minutes earlier. It was bad enough for himself and each of the others, but she had taken a vicious triple blow: the nightmare itself, the death of her husband, the fact that he had been killed during a blatant affair with another woman. Or maybe she had already known about his infidelity, and that was the underlying source of her confessed loneliness; she had almost instantly guessed what they were holding back from her.

Cain's eyes roamed over the other women, the men, the children. They were strangers to him; none of them seemed even to be aware of his presence at this moment, except for Frank McNeil, who stood but gave the impression of crouching against the near wall, mutely hating him with eyes like water-shiny pebbles. And yet Cain's involvement with all of them—even McNeil, he could no longer seem to feel animosity toward the man—was the same as if they had been relatives or friends of long standing. He *cared* whether they lived or died, as he had realized at last that he cared intrinsically whether *he* lived or died.

At the upper edge of his vision he saw one of the stained-glass windows, and centered his gaze on it, and thought then of God. A full year since he had been inside a church, last Christmas with his family; six months since he had denied to himself the existence of a benign Deity. If there was a God, would He allow a gentle wife and mother and two small innocent children to die so cruelly and unnecessarily? Would He allow wars and poverty and racial hatred and the kind of wanton terrorism which had exploded here in Hidden Valley? Rhetorical questions. You believed or you didn't believe: simple as that. Once Cain had believed; and now, here, he was not sure he had ever really stopped believing.

On impulse he got to his feet and crossed slowly to the altar; looked at the open Bible on the prayer cloth, at the melting votive candles in their silver holders. And standing there, he grew conscious of low but discernible voices coming from inside the vestry, the door to which stood ajar a few feet distant. He recognized them as belonging to John Tribucci and Lew Coopersmith, recalled that he had seen Tribucci say something to the old man a minute or two earlier and then both of them step up onto the pulpit.

"...got to do something, Lew," Tribucci was saying. "We *can't* accept the word of a lunatic that nothing will happen to us; he's psycho enough to have carried out this whole fantastic scheme and committed one brutal murder already, and that makes him psycho enough to slaughter us all. He could do it in a rage when he finds out just how little of value there is in the valley or because he knows we can identify him or even because he gets some kind of warped thrill out of killing. And I can't believe those two partners of his would be able to stop him; for all we know he may be planning to kill them, too, he may have done it already." Beat. "Mass murder isn't the only threat, either; there's a good possibility he intends to take hostages anyway when he leaves, to make sure we don't sound the alarm right away. Kids, women—Ellen, or Judy, or Rebecca... or for God's sake, even Ann. He wouldn't hesitate to shoot them when he had no more use for them, you know he wouldn't."

Coopersmith said, "Don't you think all of that's been preying on my mind, same as yours? But what can we do, Johnny, trapped like we are?"

"There's one thing we can do," Tribucci said, "one thing he overlooked: a way out of here."

"What? What way?"

"Through the belfry up there. Go up the ladder and break out one of the windows; then cut the bell rope—I managed to hold out my penknife when they were collecting our belongings—and tie the rope around a bell support and climb out and down the rear wall."

"And you're thinking of going after help, is that it? Johnny, even if you could get away from the church without being seen, how would you get out of the valley? Snowmobile, the way they're planning to? What are the odds of you reaching one undetected? Of getting it out of the village undetected? Of making it clear to Coldville in the middle of a stormy night with the temperature at zero or below? And suppose you *did* manage all that—the county couldn't get men back here before morning, except by helicopter, and if the storm holds, a chopper wouldn't be able to get off the ground at all."

"Lew, listen to me—"

"Suppose you didn't make it out of the village in the first place? Or suppose you did and the psycho discovered one of the mobiles missing? What do you think he'd do then?"

With deceptive calm Tribucci said, "I'm not talking about trying to go for help, Lew."

Nothing from Coopersmith.

"That was the first thing I thought of when I remembered the belfry," Tribucci said, "and I rejected the idea for the same reasons you just gave. The idea I didn't reject involves me and one or two others, and we don't leave the valley once we get out of here."

Cain, listening, knew all at once what Tribucci was getting at; he realized he was breathing heavily, if silently, through parted lips.

Coopersmith knew it too, now. He said, "Go after weapons and try to take them head to head."

"That's it, Lew."

"You realize what that would mean?"

"It's kill or be killed, and you can't argue with that morally or otherwise—not with all the lives at stake. I'm not a killer, any more than an eighteen-year-old soldier forced to fight in an alien jungle is a killer, but I can do what that kid has to do for some of the same reasons and for some that are a lot better."

"Maybe you can," Coopersmith said. "And I can too, because I've spent my life in the kind of job that requires a man to be ready to kill other men if he has to; but I'm sixty-six years old, I'm an old man—it's taken me a long time to admit that to myself but I'm admitting it now; I'm an old man with slow reflexes and brittle bones and if I tried climbing out of the belfry I'd probably break a leg, if not my neck. Who else is there, Johnny? Vince, maybe, only I don't have to tell you how poor his eyesight is. Joe Garvey? He's been hurt already, and while he's got the courage, he hasn't got the caution or the patience; he'd be a bull in a china shop. Martin Donnelly? He can't kill a fly without flinching. Dave Nedlick? Greg Novak? Walt Halliday? Doc Edwards? There's nobody but you and me, and that means there's nobody but you."

"Then I'll go alone."

"Against three professional hard cases, against a madman? What chance do you think you'd really have?"

"A better chance than we've got sitting in here waiting to be slaughtered." Thick, desperate rage surrounded Tribucci's words. "I've got to try it, Lew, don't you see that? *Somebody* has to do something, and that somebody is me."

"What about all the others? Some of them—McNeil, for instance—would vote to do nothing, wait it out, take the psycho's word. Have you got the right to make a decision for seventy-five people? Because if you do go, you're going to have to do it without telling anybody else; you're going to have to make that decision."

"You know the answer to that as well as I do, Lew: if my going can mean saving the lives of everyone in the valley—my family's lives—then yes, *yes*, I've got the right...."

Cain had heard enough. He moved away from the altar and stopped by the organ. Tribucci's right, he thought, one look at that dark one's eyes is enough to tell anybody he's right; it has to be done, one way or another. Anger stirred inside him again, began to burn with increasing candescence. His eyes wandered the oppressively silent room, located Rebecca Hughes again, rested on her bloodless face—and she reminded him of Angie; she did not resemble Angie in any way, but she might have been Angie. The children, too, the huddling children were little boys who might have been Steve and little girls who might have been Lindy. And what if it *was* them sitting out there? What if they were alive and they were here now, the way Tribucci's family was here now?

Sweat formed a thin beaded mosaic on Cain's forehead, trickled down along his cheeks. No, he thought then. No, no.

*Yes,* the other half of him said.

No I'd freeze up, I'd panic, I'd—

*We'd do what has to be done.*

Before he quite realized what he was doing, he had turned and taken two steps in the direction of the vestry door. And when his foot lifted for the third step, the back of his neck prickled and a tingling sensation washed down through his groin. His mind opened, like a blossom, in epiphany.

Forward, he thought, walking forward. I've been walking backward for six months, and I've just taken my first forward steps in all that time.

*Yes!* the other half of him said again, and the two halves remerged spiritually at last and made a bonded whole. Without hesitation, he kept on walking forward.

# Nine

Tribucci and Coopersmith, still debating in low, taut voices, lapsed into immediate silence when Zachary Cain came into the vestry. He stood in front of them, arms slack at his sides, bearded face and gray eyes animate with not quite definable emotions.

He said, "Can I talk to both of you for a minute?"

Tribucci frowned, the cords in his neck bulging like elongated ribs. Coopersmith had to be on his side, to handle things here in the church once he set out on the recon, to help him plan out a course of action, and he was close to convincing the old man now; Cain's surprising intrusion—the man had never spoken directly to anyone, except to make a purchase, in all the time he'd been in the valley—could not have been more ill-timed.

And Cain said to him, "I overheard you talking a couple of minutes ago—about the belfry, about what you want to try to do. No one else heard it; I was alone by the altar."

Tribucci exchanged a quick look with Coopersmith. He said then, "Well?"

Cain held a breath, released it slowly. "I want to go with you."

They stared at him—and a kind of low-key electrical tension developed among the three men. None of them moved for a long moment.

"I mean it," Cain said finally. "I want to go with you."

Unlike some of his neighbors, Tribucci had never resented or disliked or mistrusted Cain; although he was an odd sort in a lot of ways, there had always seemed to be a gentleness and a basic decency beneath his eccentric taciturnity. But now he was immediately suspicious. How could Cain possibly care enough about the people of Hidden Valley to want to risk his life for them? Did he have some idea of pretending to join forces just so he could get out of the church and save himself? And yet—that didn't make sense either. If he wanted to escape in order to run away, coming to them as he had just done was pointless; all he would have had to do, now that he knew about the belfry, was to wait until he, Tribucci, was gone and then sneak in here and leave in the same fashion....

Coopersmith, studying Cain probingly, said, "Why? Why do you want to go?"

"Because I think Tribucci's right, I think that madman wouldn't hesitate to commit mass butchery, I think the only alternative is to go after him and the other two. Tribucci might be able to pull it off alone, but his chances are twice as good if there are two of us."

"That doesn't exactly explain why you're volunteering."

"You said it yourself: there isn't anybody else."

"Not what I meant. Look Cain, we don't know a thing about you. Since you came to the valley, you've taken pains to keep to yourself. I respect a man's right to live his life the way he sees fit, as long as he doesn't hurt anybody else, but in a crisis like this, where the lives of so many people are in jeopardy, we've got to *know* you before we can put any trust in you."

"That's right," Tribucci agreed grimly. "Who are you, Cain? Why do you want to put your life on the line for people you hardly know, people you've shunned?"

A long, still hesitation. Then, staring at the wall to one side of them, Cain said very softly, "The reason I came to Hidden Valley, the reason I've lived here as I have, is that I was responsible for the deaths of my wife and two children this past June."

Tribucci winced faintly; Coopersmith's hand lifted, as if to rumple his dusty hair, and then fell across and down his shirt front. But there was nothing for either of them to say just yet.

Still talking to the wall, Cain went on, "I was one of these do-it-yourself people, don't waste money on plumbers and electricians and repairmen when I could take care of what needed to be done with my own hands and enjoyed the work besides. We had a fairly old house with a fairly new gas stove in the kitchen, and it developed a minor gas leak and I fixed it one night—thought I'd fixed it okay, there didn't seem to be any more problems. The following Saturday I went bowling in a tournament, and when I got home there were... there...."

His voice had grown heavy and liquid, and he broke off and swallowed audibly. When he was able to go on with it: "I came back and there were fire trucks and police cars and an ambulance and a hundred or more people on the street, and the house... it was burning, there had been an explosion, one wall was blown out. My wife and son and daughter were... they were inside when it happened and there was nothing anyone could do, they never even knew what hit them, and their bodies... I saw their bodies...."

A shudder went through him; he shook his head a single time as though to erase the mental picture of that scene. "When I'd fixed the stove leak," he said, "I unknowingly twisted or bent the gas line fitting at the baseboard somehow and caused another leak, one of those slow ones that you can't smell because it all builds in the walls; that was the official verdict, and that's the way it had to have been. It was my fault, my carelessness, that caused the deaths of the only three people in the world I loved. I didn't want to go on living either, not then. Committing suicide was... impossible, and yet I thought staying in San Francisco was impossible, too. So I quit my job, I'm an architect, and made arrangements with our bank to send me a small allotment every month—we'd saved more than twenty thousand dollars toward a new home—and I came here because it was a place I knew, I'd done some fishing and hunting in this area.

"For six months I've been in a kind of coma, drinking too much to numb the pain and guilt, never really numbing it at all. I didn't care about anything, I didn't want contact with you people, I thought I could exist in that coma forever because I thought it was what I wanted. But it wasn't and it isn't, I've come to realize that now; I'm lonely, I'm terribly lonely, I need to start living again. If I got out there to face those men, I might die, but if I do nothing in here I might die too; and if I'm killed out there, it will be in a cause worth dying for. I want you people to live too, caring for myself has made me start caring for others again and I don't want to see women and children die as helplessly as my family died. There was nothing I could do to save them, but maybe I *can* help to save your wives and your children. That's why I want to go, that's why I need to go...."

Cain fell silent but continued to stare unseeingly at the wall. Tribucci moved his head slightly and once more looked at Coopersmith.

Do you believe him? Coopersmith's eyes asked.

I believe him, Tribucci's eyes answered, and Coopersmith dipped his head almost imperceptibly. They had just witnessed the laying bare of a man's heart and soul, and the sincerity of his confession was to both of them unquestionable.

Turning, Cain met their gazes again. "I've been in the Army," he said, "so I know the principles of seek-and-destroy and I know how to use a handgun. I'm not in the best of shape, but I think I can climb down a rope all right. I'm also afraid, I can't lie to you about that, but I'm as sure now as any man can be without having been tested that when the time comes, I'll be able to stand my ground and pull the trigger on any of those three men."

Tribucci believed him about that, too. All doubt had vanished now; his instincts told him what type of man Cain was, and he had always implicitly trusted his instincts. The two of them, he thought insightfully, were of the same basic nature: they felt things deeply, they loved and hated deeply, and when a crisis arose they could not be passive or indecisive, they were compelled to act. And these character traits, for better or worse, were of course the reason why (he understood this for the first time) he had taken on the two cyclists thirteen years ago. If Cain had been with Charlene that night on the beach, he might have done the same thing; and if Tribucci had lost his family as Cain had lost his, he might have reacted in much the same fashion as Cain—when it happened and right now.

"Do I go with you?" Cain asked him.

Tribucci had made his decision. "Yes," he said simply. And then pivoted to Coopersmith.

Eyes steady and penetrating, features set in hard, perceptive lines, the old man was not old at all; except for the flesh-and-bone shell in which the essence of him was trapped, he was young and strong and sagacious. But it was that shell which meant so much now, that shell which prevented him from leading the kind of assault he had been trained for, that shell which had forced him into an admission a few minutes ago that his pride and his spirit had never previously allowed. But he was not old; he had never been old, and he would never be old.

"All right," he said, as Tribucci had known he would, "I'm in it anyway, so I might as well be in it all the way. With both of you."

Cain said, "When do we go?"

"As soon as possible. But there's some talking out to be done first. You don't rush into a situation like this without planning strategy; too many things can go wrong as it is. First consideration is the two of you getting out of the belfry and away without being spotted."

"Well if there's still a guard," Tribucci said, "it figures he'll be in front in one of the cars. With the storm that's up and howling out there, he's not going to be walking around. And the storm itself is all in our favor; it'll cover any noise we make breaking out the belfry window, fill in our tracks before too long, keep visibility down to a minimum."

"It's not going to cover the sound of breaking glass here in the church."

"There's the organ," Cain said. "If you could get somebody to play a few hymns, the music should be loud enough to drown splintering glass."

"Okay—good. I'll talk to Maude, and if she won't do it, Ellen will. I'll try to get as many people singing as I can, too; that'll keep them all together out front, so no one wanders in here at the wrong time."

Tribucci said, "Second consideration is weapons. We can't take the chance of going to the Sport Shop, but we can circle through the trees on the west slope, to the houses along Shasta. Joe Garvey's got a Walther automatic that he brought back from Europe a few years ago and uses for hunting small game. And Vince keeps a pair of target revolvers."

"That leaves the big question," Cain said. "How do we deploy once we're armed?"

"Only one way to handle it," Coopersmith told them. "Come back here, so you're in a position to protect the church; don't try to do any stalking, that'd be like playing Russian roulette. If there's a guard, take him first—as quietly as possible, maybe with a knife if you can get close enough to do it that way." He studied the impassive faces of the two younger men. "Shooting a man is one thing, stabbing him with a knife is another—you know that, don't you?"

"We know it," Tribucci said thinly.

"All right. Next thing you do is set up in ambush and wait, and keep on waiting no matter how long it takes. But not both of you in the same place, and I don't have to tell you the reason for that. You'll have to figure your exact positions once you get to that point."

Cain nodded, and Tribucci said, "Agreed on all of it. Anything else?"

"One thought," Cain said. "If we're going to be waiting in that snowstorm, we'd better put on hats and mufflers and as much extra clothing as we can handle while we're at Garvey's place."

"Right." Tribucci's mouth quirked. "Lew—Ann and Vince are going to miss me pretty fast, even if nobody else does. I'd tell them beforehand, but I'm afraid there'd be a scene...."

"There's liable to be a scene anyway, sooner or later, but that's my problem; I'll tell them once you're gone. You just leave this end of things to me; you're going to have enough to worry about outside."

Tribucci exhaled heavily through his nostrils, looked down at his watch.

"Five oh five. It's dark now, but it'll be darker still in another half hour. Go at five thirty-five?"

"Five thirty-five," Cain said.

Coopersmith said, "That covers just about everything, then. We'd all better wait out front until it's time; leave now one by one. The two of you come back in here, separately, between half past and twenty-five to. I'll have Maude or Ellen playing the organ as soon afterward as I can manage it."

The three men stood for several silent pulsebeats. Tribucci wanted to say something to Cain, to tell him he was sorry about the tragic loss of his family, to thank him for the choice he had made; but he had no words, it was not the time for words like that. Later, he thought, when it's over. Later....

He moved first to the closed vestry door.

# Ten

There was $3,247 in the Mercantile's safe.

Brodie had taken too much time getting the box open, and Kubion's patience had ebbed away finally and he'd told him to quit diddling around, quit diddling *around* you queer bastard, and Brodie said he was doing it as fast as he could, and Kubion just looked at him over the raised muzzle of the automatic. Six minutes later Brodie had the combination dial punched out with hammer and chisel and the safe door open wide. Inside were sheafs of papers and some ledger books and a key-type strongbox. With Kubion watching him closely, Brodie snapped the lock on the strongbox and counted out the money it contained onto the desk's glass top.

$3,247.

Kubion stared at the thin piles of currency. Three thousand lousy goddamn lousy dollars! He had figured ten grand at least, maybe fifteen or twenty, some banker Hughes had been some hick banker son of a bitch. If he wasn't dead already he'd be dead right now, just like all the hicks were going to be dead pretty soon, pretty soon.

He centered his gaze on Brodie standing by the desk in a litter of tools and bits and pieces of safe metal. Brodie's face was stoic, but those purple eyes of his were like windows and you could see what he was thinking, you could hear we-told-you-so-didn't-we running around inside his head as plainly as if he were saying it aloud. Kubion shouted, "Shut up, shut the fucking hell up!"

"I didn't say anything, Earl."

"This is only the beginning, you hear, there'll be more in the other stores and in the houses, plenty more."

"Sure there will."

"Plenty more," Kubion said again. The impulse, the need, had begun whispering to him; the ball of his index finger moved tightly back and forth across the automatic's curved trigger.

Brodie said quickly, "I'd better gather up the tools before we leave here. We might need them again."

Kubion's temples throbbed. His finger continued to slide across the trigger, increasing pressure.

"Did you hear what I said, Earl?"

"I heard you."

"There's probably other safes in the valley: the inn, the Sport Shop, the café, the Hughes' house or one of the other houses. I can't open them without tools."

"There won't be any other safes."

"We can't know that for sure, not yet."

"If there are I'll get combinations or keys from whoever they belong to, I don't need you for that."

"Suppose whoever it is gives you trouble and you have to kill him before you find out a combination? Suppose there's a safe at the Hughes' house and the wife doesn't know that combination either? Could be Hughes kept a spare bundle at home, some of these guys don't like to keep it all in one place, right?"

Kubion's finger became still. The impulse was still whispering to him, but it was saying now: Don't kill him yet... he's right, you might need him... don't kill him yet, soon but not yet....

He said, "Put the tools back in the box, hurry it up, shag your ass."

Brodie let breath spray inaudibly between his teeth. Immediately, carefully, he knelt and put on his coat and gloves and then began feeding the scattered tools back into the cardboard carton. When he was finished, Kubion ordered him to lace his hands behind him again; stepped forward and scooped the bills off the desk top left-handed and wadded them into his trousers. He went back to the doorway, told Brodie to pick up the carton and come out. A moment later, following him down the aisle between the counter and the wall shelves of liquor and bottled goods, Kubion felt the chill breath of the wind that came stabbing through the glassless door half. Snow whipped in the darkness outside, eddied into the store; the cry of the storm was like that of something alive and in pain.

Kubion's mouth twisted into a vicious grimace. Snow, wind, cold, goddamn Eskimo village with wooden igloos, and three thousand in the safe and have to keep Brodie alive and Brodie's back like a target in front of him, urge saying don't kill him but then saying smash something else, smash something! He stopped moving, smash something do it *now*, and transferred the automatic to his left hand and swept his right through the bottles of liquor on the nearest of the shelves, driving a dozen or more to the floor. Glass shattered, dark liquid splashed and flowed. Brodie whirled and stared at him, carton held up at chest level, and Kubion yelled, "Don't say a word, don't move I'll kill you if you move," and picked a bottle off the shelf and threw it into the grocery section, toppling a pyramid of canned goods in another banging, clattering counterpoint to the shriek of the wind. He caught up a second bottle and pitched it at the gated Post Office window, missing low, this one not breaking, and a third bottle was in his hand and he flung that across the store at the left front window. The heavy bottom struck the cardboard replica of Santa Claus at the base of the spine and drove it and exploding fragments of glass outward to the sidewalk. One of the torn reindeer clung to a jagged piece of window, flapping in a sudden gust that hurled more flurries of snow through the opening.

The impulse grew silent then, momentarily satisfied, and he leaned panting against the counter. After several moments the smile reappeared on his mouth, and he straightened up again and returned the automatic to his right hand.

"We'll hit the Sport Shop now," he said. "Then the inn and the café and the rest of the buildings along here. Then the Hughes' house."

"However you want to do it," Brodie said carefully.

"That's right, Vic, however I want to do it."

They went out into the sharp white wind.

# Eleven

The interior of the church had grown progressively duskier with the coming of night. The votive candles on the altar had melted down, and the filtered daylight shining through, the stained-glass windows had faded and then disappeared altogether. Spaced at intervals along the side walls, brass-armed electric candles burned palely, cheerlessly, and did little to dispel the pockets of grayish shadow forming on the pulpit and along the front wall.

In one of those pockets, by the peg-hung garments at the south front corner, Rebecca stood alone and wished that she could cry. Crying was a purge, in the same way vomiting was a purge, and it would get rid of some of the nauseating dread that persisted malignantly inside her. But there was no emetic for tears. You could cry or you couldn't, and even as a child she had rarely wept. Once she had considered this a sign of inner efficacy; in truth, however, it was nothing more than a simple incapacity, like not being able to sing on key or stand on your head or perform backflips.

A voice beside her said softly, "Mrs. Hughes?"

She had not heard anyone approach, and she blinked and half turned. Zachary Cain was standing there. She searched his bearded face briefly and found no pity; empathy, yes, but mercifully, no pity. She thought then that he seemed *different* somehow. She hadn't noticed it at the cabin earlier or on the ride down, she had been too frightened to notice anything; but there was a definite strength in him only hinted at previously, and the haunted irresolution which had ravaged his features last night had been effaced. It was as if he had undergone some sort of tangible metamorphosis; and today's ordeal had had no apparent effect, or possibly some esoteric fortifying rather than weakening effect, on that change.

She said, "Don't say you're sorry. Please don't."

"All right. I... know how you must feel."

"Do you?"

"I think I do."

"Nobody can know how I feel right now, Mr. Cain."

"I can, because I've been through it—some of it."

"What do you mean?"

He said slowly, "I lost my wife and two children six months ago, in San Francisco. My carelessness caused the deaths of all three of them."

Rebecca stared at him.

"That's why I came to Hidden Valley," Cain said, and told her briefly what had occurred and the way it had been for him since.

The only words which came to her when he stopped talking were the same emptily condolent ones she had just asked him not to say to her. She moved her head slightly from side to side, right thumb and index finger worrying one of the buttons on her open parka.

At length she found other words and her voice. "Why did you tell me all that? Why now?"

"I'm not sure. Maybe... well maybe because of what you're going through and will keep on going through for a while, the similarities of the things that have hurt both of us."

"Keep my chin up, roll with the punches, don't let happen to me what happened to you—is that it?"

"I didn't mean it exactly that way."

Rebecca looked away from him. "No, of course you didn't," she said, and then, in an undertone: "It's just that everything seems so hopeless now. What's the use of thinking about the future when there might not *be* any tomorrow for any of us? We might all be killed today, just as my husband was killed."

"We're not going to die," Cain said.

"I wish I could really believe that."

"You can. You have to."

He extended a hand, as if to touch her and transmit by osmosis some of his own conviction; but he did not make contact, and his arm lowered and dropped again to his side. He held her eyes for a long moment, and Rebecca once more felt the new strength in him, felt some of the same intimacy they had shared the night before.

He said finally, "You're going to be okay, all of us are going to be okay," and one corner of his mouth spasmed upward in what might have been half of an ethereal smile. He moved past her and away along the front wall.

Rebecca watched him stop in front of the entrance doors and stand there staring straight ahead; watched him for a full thirty seconds. Then she thought that she wanted to sit down again and took a place in the nearest pew. She looked at the round whiteness of her joined knees, saw them mistily—and realized that the eyes which never cried were suddenly brimming with tears.

Cain waited gravely, leaning against the locked doors, for it to be time to go into the vestry.

His nerves jangled now and then, as if in reaction to a silent alarm bell, and a clot of fear existed parasitically just under his breastbone. But his earlier self-composure and the sharp anger remained forcefully dominant. He had only to look deep within himself again to know that he would be able to do whatever had to be done.

He thought of the unburdening of himself to Tribucci and Coopersmith. He had known, of course, that he would have to tell them, and he'd been both reluctant and willing. Like the words which had piled up inside him and finally spilled over to Rebecca last night, the entire tragedy had reached the limit of containment—she had been perfectly right in her comments about bottled-up emotions needing an outlet, too, sooner or later—and with self-perception there had come the need to relieve some of that pent-up pressure. The telling had been much easier than he might have thought, and even easier still when he'd related some of the facts to Rebecca minutes ago, and would be progressively easier each subsequent time he did it—if there were to be any subsequent times. The onus became so much more bearable when you confided to somebody, he knew that now: not because you wanted their pity or reassurances, but because it was like lancing a festering boil and letting some of the hurt drain away with the pus.

He had come to Rebecca with at least a half-formed intention of doing exactly as he had done—and he was not quite sure why. There were surface reasons, but there was also an underlying motivation that was elusive and amorphous. Perhaps it had something to do with Rebecca herself rather than Rebecca as just another person, something to do with empathy and mental concord and the way she had huddled against him in the pickup....

Abruptly he told himself: You're doing too much thinking, there's just no point in it now. Remember what the military taught you about survival in combat: concentration on fundamentals, on the external and not the internal; instinct, training, death as an abstract, doing the job at hand. The military was wrong about a great many things, but not about that.

Cain glanced down at his watch, and it was five thirty-two. He located Tribucci with his eyes, alternately pacing and standing along the northern wall. Coopersmith had been sitting by his wife, but now Cain saw him stand up and come toward the front, stop by the woman who worked in the Mercantile—the church organist.

Time, he thought. And walked with careful, though apparently aimless, strides to the opposite aisle and past Tribucci and up onto the pulpit.

Coopersmith bent at the waist, resting his left hand on the pew back, and said *sotto voce* to Maude Fredericks, "Maude, I think it would be a good idea if you played some hymns for us."

Pouched in red, tear-puffed hollows, her eyes moved dully over his face. Ordinarily she was a strong-willed woman, but the day's life-and-death crisis, coupled with the twin shocks of Matt Hughes' death and unfaithfulness—Coopersmith knew she'd maternally worshiped her employer—had clearly corroded that inherent strength.

"You mean now?" she said.

"Yes."

"Why?"

"It would give us all a little comfort," he told her, and it was at least part of the truth. "A hymn is a prayer, you know that, Maude."

"Is He listening? If our prayers reach Him, why has He allowed us to suffer like this?"

"I don't know, Maude. But I haven't lost hope or faith, and I don't believe you have either."

Faint color came into the crêpy whiteness of her cheeks. "No," she said, "no, I suppose I haven't."

"Will you play some hymns then?"

She nodded and rose, and they went together to the pulpit. Sitting at the organ, Maude reached out to touch the open hymnal with the tips of her fingers, then she began to flip the pages slowly toward the rear of the book. Coopersmith did not see Cain, and Tribucci had just entered the vestry. He turned and announced quietly what he had requested of Maude. A few nods or murmurs of acceptance followed his words, though most of the drawn faces registered a kind of benumbed apathy. There was a single vocal objection.

"What for?" Frank McNeil demanded in shrill tones. "What's the sense of it? We don't need any damned hymns."

The Reverend Mr. Keyes, conscious for some time now, struggled onto his feet. Pain-narrowed eyes sought out McNeil and pinned him with a look of uncharacteristic vehemence. "We are prisoners here, yes, but this is nonetheless a house of *God*. I won't have further blasphemy, I won't have it!" His voice was surprisingly strong and galvanic.

"The Reverend's right," Verne Mullins said. "Watch that mouth of yours, McNeil."

More softly, Keyes said to Coppersmith, "Thank you, Lew. The playing of hymns, the singing of hymns—conjoining ourselves in prayer—is exactly what is needed now. Only Almighty God can put a swift and righteous end to this siege of wickedness."

God and two men named John Tribucci and Zachary Cain, Coopersmith thought. He saw McNeil's pinched mouth form words without voice, could read them plainly: "Hymns, prayers, religious mumbojumbo—ah *Christ!*" Pursing his own lips, he went to sit once more beside Ellen; took one of her large, rough-soft hands in both his own, and gazed over at the vestry door.

"They'll do it," he thought, and then realized that he had spoken it aloud.

Ellen said, "What, Lew?"

He did not have to fabricate an answer; in that moment, Maude Fredericks began to play.

As he came into the vestry, Tribucci saw that Cain was standing like a sentry beside the ladder which led up into the belfry. He went over next to him, taking the penknife from his trouser pocket and thumbing it against his palm while he buttoned his coat. They did not speak.

Long minutes dragged away, with the only sound that of the wind hammering beyond the outer wall. Tribucci was a simple, if intelligent, man who did not think in terms of metaphysical or Biblical symbolism, but standing there, waiting, he was struck with a wholly chilling perception: In its snowbound isolation, invaded by godless forces, this tiny valley had been transformed into a battleground; All Faiths Church was the focal point, its ultimate sanctity to be preserved or irrevocably destroyed along with the lives of seventy-five individuals; the conflict being waged and about to be waged here seemed in an apocalyptic sense to transcend the human element and become a battle between random representatives of Good and Evil.

Hidden Valley, California—on a Sunday two days before Christmas—was a kind of miniature Armageddon....

Raised voices came suddenly from inside the church proper. Tribucci tensed, listening. Another minute passed, and then the organ burst into swelling sound out on the pulpit; the Reverend Mr. Keyes commenced to sing in a shaky contralto, and Lew Coopersmith's voice and a few others joined in. The chill deepened within Tribucci as he turned ahead of Cain to start up the ladder.

The hymn was "Onward, Christian Soldiers."

# Twelve

When Cain emerged into the belfry behind Tribucci, he saw that there were four obelisk-shaped windows: two set side by side in the western and eastern walls. They were a foot and a half wide, of plain glass puttied into wooden frames. The church bell itself was not visible, exposed high above, but its four heavy redwood supports slanting outward to the walls beneath the windows filled most of the enclosure. The bell rope hung down between the supports.

He stepped from the ladder onto the narrow catwalk which hugged all four walls, and peered through one of the frosted panes, westward. There was nothing to see except snow-embroidered darkness, the vague shapes of the cottage at the rear and the rising line of red fir well beyond.

Opposite him, Tribucci was looking through an eastern window. Cain asked, "Can you see the church front?"

"No. Too much roof. Lights in half a dozen buildings on Sierra and in a few of the houses, but the house lights have probably been burning since the roundup. It figures at least the psycho is still somewhere along Sierra."

Cain gloved his hands. "We'd better break the window first."

"Right."

"I'll punch a hole low center, so most of the glass stays in the frame. Then we can work it loose and set the shards in here on the catwalk."

"Good," Tribucci said. He had come around the catwalk and was drawing on his own gloves. "We don't want to be dropping down onto jagged glass in the snow."

Standing in close to the window, Cain started to draw his arm back. Tribucci caught it and said, "No, wait, the hymn," and Cain realized the organ was crescendoing through the last few bars of "Onward, Christian Soldiers." He nodded and sleeved sweat from his forehead, thinking: Close—go slow, no mistakes, no mistakes.

There was silence for a full fifteen seconds, and then the organ began playing "Cross of Jesus," and the singing voices lifted once more. Cain waited another ten seconds, held a breath, and jabbed his fist against the pane. The single, measured blow was enough; he had had just the right amount of force behind it. In the narrow confines of the belfry, the sound of the glass breaking seemed overly loud—but there was no cessation of the organ or the singing. The hole in the pane was jagged but clean, webbing the remaining glass into fragments that held the frame.

Carefully, Cain slipped fingers into the hole and wiggled one of the shards until the old, stiff putty yielded and the splinter came loose; he set it to one side. Tribucci followed suit with another fragment, and together they managed to clear the opening in something less than two minutes. The last section of glass that Cain jerked free was razor sharp, and in the darkness he gripped it wrong; the spine sliced through his glove, cut deeply into his right palm. He felt blood gush warmly and set his teeth against the lancing pain.

Wind-driven snow pelted through the aperture—icy pinpoints against their faces—and fluttered down into the vestry below. But there was nothing to be done about that. Tribucci leaned out of the window, checking both ways along the rear of the church; then he put his head back inside, dipped his chin to Cain, and began pulling up the bell rope, coiling it around his left arm. When he had all of it, he used his knife to saw through it as high up as he could reach.

The organ now, after another brief pause, was playing "Faith of Our Fathers."

Tribucci looped the cut end of the rope over one of the thick supports at its juncture with the wall, tied it securely, and tested the strength of the knot. He dipped his chin again, to indicate that he was satisfied it would hold their weight, and played the coiled length out and down the outer wall.

"Doesn't reach all the way to the ground," he said. "There'll be a drop of six or seven feet, but the snow'll help cushion our landing."

"You'd better go first," Cain said. "I cut my right palm on a piece of glass, sliced a tear in the glove, and blood leaking through will make the rope slippery."

"Can you hold onto it? Is the cut deep?"

"I'll manage somehow. Go ahead."

Tribucci climbed onto the windowsill, facing into the belfry, and gathered up slack in the rope and made a loop around his right wrist, then he leaned back and swung out against the steeple wall. Shoes sliding on the snow-slick boards, body stretched back into an almost horizontal plane, he went down with quick agility. When he reached the last foot of rope, he hung for an instant and then let go. His feet disappeared ankle-deep into the surface snow, and he went to one knee; but he was up again immediately, thrusting his right thumb upward, moving in close to the wall and toward the north corner.

Cain ran his right gloved palm gingerly along one trouser leg, to clear away some of the blood. The organ stopped again as he stood up into the frame, and he waited tense-bodied until it resumed with "God of Mercy." He wiped his right glove a second time, took up the rope and looped it around his left wrist. And went out the way Tribucci had.

The pressure of the rope against his palm made the glass cut burn hellishly; long-unused muscles strained, wrenched, in his armpits and across his shoulders. He felt his grip begin slipping before he had gone halfway, held on desperately until he was ten or twelve feet above the ground. The instant he felt the rope slide irreclaimably through his knotted fingers, he willed his body to relax. There was a moment of giddying free fall, then solid impact that stabbed pain upward through both legs to his groin and hips. He toppled forward, sprawling. Snow clogged his nose and mouth, and he spat it out soundlessly as he pulled himself up onto hands and knees. The pain in his legs had begun to decrease; he had not broken or sprained anything.

Tribucci caught his arm and helped him upright. He asked urgently, "Okay?"

"Okay," Cain said.

A short exhalation of breath plumed like smoke from between Tribucci's lips. He said, "North and south walls are clear. So far, so good."

"I'll follow your lead."

As he trailed Tribucci along the side of the cottage, its attached garage, Cain flexed his arms and shoulders to loosen the taut-stretched musculature; his right glove seemed filled with flowing, sticky-cold blood. The line of trees began a hundred yards beyond, and they crossed the sloping open space at a shuffle-stepped run. The storm lashed at them, surrounded them with dancing skeins of whiteness as nearly impenetrable as the curtain of night itself. Cain's face started to numb, and his feet were wet and chilled inside his boots; his ears ached, his eyes burned.

They reached the wood finally, and its density cut off some of the storm's tumult. There was no movement along their backtrail—or at least none visible through the flurries. Tribucci set a lateral course a few short yards inside the timber, so that the church and the village buildings remained dimly perceptible on their right. Minutes later they reached a point from which they could look down the two-block length of Shasta Street. Most of the houses were dark, but two showed lights; the illumination there and on Sierra was blurred by the fluxing snow. They went farther north, until they were on a line with the side wall of the nearest, completely dark house, and then followed the line down and across a bare yard to a rose trellis at the house's front corner.

The neighboring dwelling was one of those that showed light in some of its windows. Tribucci said against Cain's ear, "That's Joe Garvey's place."

"Doesn't seem to be any tracks out front."

"The Garveys were among those picked up in the canvass. It should be empty."

"We've got to make sure before we try going in."

"Yeah. Best if we come up to it from the rear."

They went along the side of the dark house, into its back yard. A waist-high wooden fence separated the two adjoining properties, and they crossed to it in a humpbacked run, passed over it one leg at a time in a low profile. A check of the two lighted windows in the western wall revealed an empty kitchen and an empty bedroom; they looped. around past the back stairs and along the eastern wall and looked into an empty living room through the only illumined window on that side.

When they saw no activity on Shasta to the immediate east, they edged around to the front and past another living-room window and came up to the roofed porch. The entrance door was standing wide open, rattling in the wind; thickly undisturbed snow overlaid the inside hallway floor. Cain said, "Empty," and Tribucci repeated the word in accord. They climbed the steps quickly and entered the hallways, the living-room.

"Garvey keeps his gun in a cabinet in the washroom," Tribucci said. "I know that because I've gone fishing with him a couple of times, and he stores all his sporting equipment there."

The washroom was located off the kitchen, and the cabinet—four by six feet, made of metal, door unlocked took up half of an end wall. The Walther automatic, a .380 PPK, lay wrapped in chamois cloth on an interior shelf, clean and well cared for. Its butt magazine was empty, but on the same shelf Tribucci found two full clips in a cigar box containing gun oil and other cleaning accessories.

He said, "You want to take this one?"

Cain nodded, accepted the weapon and the two clips, fitted one into the butt, and put the other into his left coat pocket. The gun was light for an automatic of that caliber, compact; its plastic grips felt cold and rough. He dropped it into his right coat pocket, and they moved back into the lighted kitchen.

A utensil drawer under the drainboard yielded a pair of narrow-bladed, eight-inch carving knives. Another drawer held a ball of string, and Tribucci cut off three pieces and tied the blade of one of the knives to his right thigh beneath his coat, leaving the handle free: a makeshift sheath. Cain did the same with the second knife.

In the front hallway again, Cain said, "Next step is to find extra clothing. I need another pair of gloves, too; my right one is full of blood from that glass cut."

"You won't have any trouble using the gun?"

"No. Cut seems to've stopped bleeding now, and it's in the fleshy part of the palm."

There was a closet in the hall, and inside was an old gray overcoat with a pair of cracked-leather gloves stuffed into one of the pockets. But that was all: no mufflers or hats of any kind. Tribucci said, "I'll see what I can find in their bedroom," and hurried away.

The gray overcoat was knee-length, heavier than the shorter one Cain wore; he made the exchange and found that it fit him well enough. Once he had it on, he peeled off Coopersmith's gloves, wiped his dark-stained right hand—the blood, coagulating, felt as viscous as liquid adhesive—and tried the new pair. They were a size too small, but not so tight that they would hamper free finger movement.

At the open front door, he looked out and down Shasta again. All that moved was the wind-hurled snow. Cain turned as Tribucci reentered the hall wearing a thick muffler and a woman's fox-pelt cap pulled down over his ears; his own light-colored overcoat was heavy enough so that he hadn't needed to replace it with another, but he'd put on a wool sweater beneath it. In one hand he carried a second muffler, a second sweater, and a man's lamb-wool Cossack-style hat.

He gave those items to Cain, watched as he put them on. "Best way to do it now, I think, would be for the two of us to split up: you back to the church and me after the other guns at my brother's. One of us has got to get into a protective position as quickly as possible."

Cain weighed the proposal for several seconds. "Agreed," he said then. "If there is a guard out front, I'll see if I can locate his whereabouts. But I won't make a move until you come—unless there's a definite threat and I don't have any choice."

"I'll make it back as fast as I can." Tribucci held his wristwatch up to his eyes. "Six twenty. Figure less than half an hour. You'll be along the church's south wall?"

"Right," Cain said. "We'd better have a signal, though. We won't be able to recognize each other from a distance, and things are going to be tense enough as it is."

"Suppose I stop in front of the cottage door and give a left-handed wave over my head."

"Good. I'll make the same gesture in return."

"Split up in the wood; it'll be safe if I go that way."

They moved out of the hallway and down off the porch, climbed the wooden boundary fence, and retraced their original route into the trees. Once there, Tribucci put a hand on Cain's arm, squeezed it, and then slipped away quickly and was swallowed by the heavy fir shadows. Cain turned in the opposite direction—and he was immediately conscious of being alone. When two or more men were working together, interacting, in a crucial situation, the unit they formed became an entity unto itself—stronger than each individual because it fused their strengths into the whole. You thought as part of the unit, and as a result, you were able to maintain rigid control over your own personality. But when the unit was temporarily disbanded, and you became a man alone, a little of that control began to slip; you tried to continue blocking out emotions, to keep your mind functioning as calculatingly as it had been, but a few inevitably, if dimly, seeped through: fear, anger and hatred, enormity of purpose.

And for Cain, too, a repulsion of—a reassurance from—the weapon that seemed to have become a sudden immense weight in his right coat pocket....

# Thirteen

Brodie came out through the broken mouth of the Valley Café, braced his body against the force of the storm, and then stepped beyond the perimeter of the fluorescent light spill and started across Sierra Street. Behind him, Kubion trailed like a sentient and menacing shadow.

They had ripped off the Sport Shop and the Valley Inn and now the café, and the total take had been slightly more than four bills. Counting the fifteen hundred Kubion had taken from the people at Mule Deer Lake, he now had a little more than five thousand on him. At the outside there would be another grand in the flour sack of purses and wallets Loxner had collected in the church, and no more than a couple of thousand in all the village homes combined.

All of this, the whole puking business, for maybe eight thousand—*eight thousand dollars!*

Kubion had worked himself up into another destructive rage, the way he had in the Mercantile, and had made a broken shambles of the café: smashing glasses and crockery and two wall mirrors. Watching him, Brodie had had to struggle to maintain a grip on his ragged control. Kubion was far over the edge now; all you had to do was look at him to see how much he wanted to start killing people. There just wasn't any way Brodie was going to buy himself any more time than he'd already been allotted. The café hadn't had a safe, and neither had the Sport Shop or the Valley Inn; he'd said there was still the Hughes' house and the filling station and the other buildings in the village, and Kubion said, "There's only the Hughes' place and that's it, that's our next stop. We're going up there now and there'd better be a safe, Vic, there'd better be a safe for you to open with those tools in the pickup, you hear me Vic, there'd better be a safe."

It didn't make any difference whether there was a safe or not; the Hughes' house was intended to be Brodie's execution chamber.

But Kubion still hadn't given him even the smallest of possible openings, and in the two hours since they had started looting the village there hadn't been any sign of big stupid gutless Loxner, eliminating the last faint hope of help from that quarter. Kubion's freaked-out head had forgotten all about Loxner— they hadn't gone anywhere near the church in those two hours—and that was the closest he'd come to any sort of mistake. Brodie kept telling himself that Kubion getting crazier and crazier would work both ways, that it would make him careless as well as more dangerous; he kept telling himself the opening would come, don't take a last desperate gamble because the opening would come.

He reached the window on the eastern side of Sierra, started along it toward the pickup in the next block. The surface snow there was freezing and slick;

he walked it with slow, cautious steps, risked a glance over his shoulder. Kubion's dark face stared back at him: no smile now, lips moving as if in silent monologue. Brodie told himself again that an opening would come.

And one came.

Just like that, with startlingly coeval suddenness, Kubion made the kind of mistake Brodie had been waiting for.

Thoughts and eyes focused elsewhere, he had not been paying any attention to his footing; his right shoe came down on one of the patches of glassy snow, found no traction and slipped, and the leg kicked up rigidly like a football placekicker following through. His left arm flailed at the air and his body jerked into a horizontal plane and he fell bellowing, landing heavily on his buttocks, left leg twisted slightly as he skidded sideways into the snowpack at the curbing.

Brodie's reaction was almost instantaneous. Instinct obliterated surprise and fatigue, and when he saw that Kubion had managed to hold onto the gun, it rejected any effort of trying to jump him across the ten icy steps which separated them. He spun and ran, diagonally back the way they had come because Kubion's body was bent toward the south and because Lassen Drive to the west was the nearest release street, the nearest shielded path of escape. He fled in a headlong, weaving crouch through the less treacherous snow which blanketed the middle of the street, coming on the far windrow near the corner of the inn. Another bellow sounded behind him, and then the flat wind-muffled explosion of a shot. Nothing touched him but the flakes of obscuring snow.

He leaped over the windrow, muscles hunched and rippling along his back, head tucked down against his chest. Sliding on the ice-quilted sidewalk, he lunged against the building wall, caught the corner, and heaved himself around it as a second shot echoed dimly and a bullet slapped into the boarding a foot or two to his left. He vaulted the ragged snowpack on Lassen Drive, to evade more sidewalk ice—lost his balance this time and sprawled out prone on the street and planed forward half a dozen yards like a man on an invisible sled before he was able to drag his feet under him again.

There were no more shots, but he did not look back; he stretched his body forward into the wind, summoning reserves of stamina, and kept on running.

# Fourteen

Coopersmith was standing at the foot of the vestry ladder, looking up into the belfry, when the door swung open and Frank McNeil came inside.

Pivoting abruptly, he saw the café owner bump the door closed with one hip and press back against it. McNeil gaped with frightened, furtive eyes at the wetness on the floor directly under the belfry, at the flakes of snow which sprinkled down and liquefied on Coopersmith's head and shoulders. Sweat beaded his upper lip like a thinly glistening silver mustache.

Face void of expression, Coopersmith crossed to him and said evenly, "What are you doing in here, Frank?"

"I knew it," McNeil said, "I knew something was going on. You and John Tribucci and that Cain alone in here before, had to have your heads together about something, and then you with the organ music and hymn singing and neither one of them is out front now, I looked when I saw you slip in here a minute ago and they're not there and not in here either. They got out, didn't they? They broke out through one of the belfry windows, didn't they?"

A tic made Coopersmith's left eyelid flutter in arhythmic tempo, so that he seemed incongruously to be winking. "Keep your voice down," he snapped.

"For Christ's sake, why did they do it, why did you help them do it, what's the matter with you, they'll be killed out there, they'll be killed and we'll be killed too, we're all going to be *killed*—"

Coopersmith slapped him across the face. "Shut up, McNeil, shut up!"

McNeil's eyes bulged exophthalmically, and his fingertips trembled over the reddened surface of his cheek. He made a soft, choking sound that might have been a sob and turned to fumble the door open. Coopersmith reached for him, caught his shirt sleeve, but the rough material slipped from his grasp; McNeil went through the door, onto the pulpit beyond.

He backed away to the left and leaned up against the curved outer edge of the organ, still touching his cheek. Coopersmith came out grimly and shut the door. The silence in the dim room was funereal now. Maude Fredericks had played eight hymns and said then that she could not do any more; the Reverend Mr. Keyes had stood up immediately, shakily, and offered a long prayer to which Coopersmith only half listened because he was not sure Cain and Tribucci had had enough time to get out. When the minister finally subsided, he had gone instantly into the vestry to make sure. He knew now that he should have gone first to Ann and Vince; knew as well that the open-handed slap he had just given McNeil was a second misjudgment, that he should have hit him with a closed fist instead, knocked him unconscious. McNeil was half out of his head with fear—a coward, something less than a man at this moment—and his eyes and the quivering white slash of his moth made it plain he was going to tell everyone Tribucci and Cain were gone.

Coopersmith said, "Frank," sharply, aware that some of the others were looking at the two of them now and sensing the tension between them. He took
three quick steps toward the café owner, said his name a second time.

And McNeil told them: loudly, running his words together, putting it all in
the worst possible perspective.

The immediate reaction was just as Coopersmith had known it would be.
There were spontaneous articulations of alarm, a half-panicked stirring as men
and women got to their feet—some turning to their neighbors, some pushing
forward onto the pulpit. Ellen came up beside him, took his arm, but Coopersmith's eyes were on Ann Tribucci. She was standing between Vince and
Rebecca Hughes in a rear pew, face milk-white, and her lips moved with the
words "Johnny, Johnny, oh Johnny!" Vince caught her by the shoulders, steadied her; his features were set in hard lines of concern, but they betrayed little
surprise.

Questions, remarks pounded at Coopersmith from several directions. He
waved his arms for quiet, shouting, "Listen to me, all of you listen to me!"

The voices ebbed. He faced his friends and neighbors steadily, let them see
nothing but assurance and authority and self-control. Then, keeping his voice
calm, low-keyed, talking over interruptions, he explained the situation to
them: why the decision had been made, why the secrecy, how it was being
handled by Tribucci and Cain, exactly what they were now attempting to do.

More apprehensive vocalization; a soft cry from Ann that cut knifelike into
Coopersmith and made him wince. The Reverend Mr. Keyes stepped forward,
supporting his bloodied scarf-bandaged right hand in the palm of his left.
"'Give them according to their deeds, and according to the wickedness of their
endeavors: give them after the work of their hands; render to them their
desert.'" Then: "'The righteous shall rejoice when he seeth vengeance; he shall
wash his feet in the blood of the wicked.'" No longer benign, no longer
clement, he spoke harshly the passages from Psalms in the Old Testament; his
spirit, now, seemed to seek communion not with the God of Love and Charity, but with the God of swift and merciless Wrath.

McNeil pointed a spasmodic, accusatory finger at Coopersmith. His face was
lacquered with sweat. "You had no right, you had no *right* to make a decision
that might cost me my life!"

"The decision was the Lord's," the Reverend Mr. Keyes said. "The Lord granted them the wisdom and the courage to do what must be done, and the Lord
will grant them the strength to carry it through."

"The Lord, the Lord, I've heard enough about your Lord—"

The Reverend Mr. Keyes started toward McNeil angrily. Webb Edwards
restrained him. Eyes touched the minister, touched McNeil, returned to Coopersmith; the preponderance of expressions revealed a vacillation between hope
and deepening terror.

Joe Garvey, his nose puffed into a discolored blob from the pistol whipping
he had taken earlier, said thickly, "Lew, I can understand why Johnny would
risk his life for us, and I can trust him and believe in him. But what about this

Cain? He's an outsider, a man who's made it plain all along he wanted nothing to do with any of us. How could you and Johnny be sure of what *he'll* do out there?"

"That's right," McNeil cried, "that's right, that's right! A bird like that, a lousy vandal, he'll run away and try to save himself the first chance he gets. Oh you crazy old man, you crazy old fool!"

Blood surged hotly in Coopersmith's temples. "What right have you got to judge and condemn a man you don't know anything about—a man with guts enough to fight for your miserable life and everybody else's life here? Cain won't run away, any more than Johnny will. And he isn't the one who broke into the café; whoever it was, it wasn't Zachary Cain."

"The hell it wasn't, he's the one all right—"

"That's enough!" a voice shouted suddenly. "I won't listen to any more against Mr. Cain, I'm the one who broke into the café, *I'm* the one."

The voice belonged to McNeil's son, Larry.

Coopersmith stared down at the youth; of all the Hidden Valley residents who might have been responsible for the breaking and entering, Larry was one of the last he—or any of the others—would have suspected. Sandy McNeil said something to her son in a hushed voice, but he shook his head and pushed out into the center aisle. She came after him, one arm extended as if beseeching, as he stepped up onto the pulpit and approached his father.

McNeil was looking at him incredulously. "You, boy—*you?*"

"Me, Pa." To Coopersmith, Larry's thin face seemed for the first time to contain maturity, a kind of determined manliness. "I slipped out of the house around 3 A.M. both mornings, when everyone in the village was asleep, and used an old tire iron you had in the garage to jimmy the door. Then I propped it wide with the orange crates so the snow could blow in and ruin as much stock as possible. I'd have owned up to it sooner or later anyway, with you threatening to have Mr. Cain arrested; but now that I know he's gone out there to try to save us, I just can't hold it inside me anymore."

McNeil's lips worked soundlessly for a moment. Then, in a low voice that cracked as brittly as thin ice: "My own son, Jesus, my own son."

"Always talking about Ma," Larry said, "always talking about her in front of other people, putting her down, saying dirty things. And the way you treated her, both of us, like we were nothing to you and we're not, all you care about is yourself. That's why I did it. I thought it would be a way to hurt you. I'm sorry for it now, I wish I hadn't done it—not only because it was wrong but because I was thinking and acting the way *you* do, I was being just like you. And I don't ever want to be like you, Pa, not ever...."

His voice trailed off, and the silence which followed was thick and uneasy. Sandy McNeil looked at her husband, at her son, and then she moved closer to Larry and took his hand; the gesture, the stolidity of her expression told Coopersmith she had made a decision for the future, if there was to be one for the two of them, which she would not compromise.

McNeil's cheeks were gray and damp and hollow. He watched his wife and son walk away from him; searched the eyes of the others and found no sympathy, found nothing at all for him. He seemed to fold in on himself, to shrivel and age perceptibly until he became like a gnome whose eyes glistened wetly with the cancer of cowardice and self-pity. He groped his way to the organ bench and sat on it and put his head in his hands.

The collective gazes turned from him and settled again on Coopersmith. Quietly, he told them about Cain—who the man was, why he had come to the valley, why he had volunteered to join Tribucci. And when he was finished, he saw a grudging acceptance of the situation on the majority of faces. The palpable, fear-heavy tenseness was more acute than ever, but there would be no panic, no chaotic infighting. Things in here, at least, appeared to again be under control....

*"Webb!"*

The cry came from Vince Tribucci, jerked heads around once more, brought Dr. Edwards running down the center aisle in immediate response. Vince was leaning anxiously over his sister-in-law, helping her into a supine position on the pew bench; Rebecca held her head, pillowed it gently on one thigh. Ann's swollen abdomen heaved, convulsed, and her face was contorted with pain.

She had her lower lip clenched deeply between her teeth, as though to keep herself from screaming.

Ellen clutched at Coopersmith's jacket. "She's gone into labor; the shock put her into labor. Dear heaven, Lew, she's going to have her baby...."

# Fifteen

At the approximate point where he and Tribucci had first entered the wind-combed trees, Cain stopped against the bole of one fir and studied the area. The tracks they had made coming across the sloping snowfield had been partially obliterated by the storm; through the flurries he could make out nothing except the dark outlines of cottage and church, the vague illumination of the church's stained-glass side windows.

With his gloved fingers opening and closing steadily, agitatedly, around the butt of the Walther PPK, he started down and across the open area. The wind shoved harshly at his back, bending him forward from the waist, and the tails of his coat flapped against his legs like the wings of a fettered bird. Firn crackled and crunched beneath his boot soles. He kept his head up, watching the cottage looming ahead, breathing shallowly.

Long moments later he reached the rear of the attached garage, took the gun out of his pocket, and went along the building's southern, front wall. Icicles hung from its eaves like pointed giant's teeth; shutters closed across one of the facing windows rattled loudly above the storm's querulous skirling. Cain stopped at the forward corner, and from there he could see the gray-black opening of the glassless belfry window and the ice-coated rope hanging down out of it; but neither was discernible from any distance.

Crossing to the church, he edged slowly and carefully toward the front. When he had come midway, he could see all of the near third of the parking lot. Three cars, each of them shrouded in white, were parked nose up against log brakes set on a line with the church's southern wall. Snow had built little ledges on the sills of their windshields and near passenger windows, and was frozen to the glass itself in streaks and spatters.

Cain went another dozen steps, and two more cars came within range of his vision—both parked with their front bumpers extending to the edge of the church walk, one in the center of the lot and the other down near Sierra Street. Their windows, too, were like blind white eyes. Within a foot of the corner, he squatted and leaned his left shoulder on the icy boarding and stretched out just enough so that he was able to see the area immediately fronting the church. One last car, as frozen and abandoned-looking as the other five.

A muscle in his left leg began to cramp with cold, and Cain straightened up again. A guard in one of those cars would logically keep at least one window facing the church clear of snow and ice, so he could watch the entrance doors; too, it was likely he'd have the engine running and the heater and defroster on, with a wing open or window rolled partway down to circumvent the threat of carbon monoxide poisoning. There were no puffs of exhaust smoke, no sounds above the wind, no car windows open or clear. No other sheltered place in the vicinity. No tracks anywhere.

No guard.

Okay, Cain thought. Okay.

He craned his head forward a second time and swept his gaze over the parking lot, Sierra Street and the wind shaped drifts in the meadow beyond. The lights shining farther into the village were all there was for him to see; the snow flurries continued to place visibility in a constant flux. Pulling back, he tugged the fur hat down tighter over his ears and rubbed at his cold-deadened face. The wiry beard hairs were like brittle threads of ice, and he imagined that in the rubbing he had depilated part of the growth. He swallowed a nervously humorless laugh, shook himself mentally to keep his thoughts in tight check.

How do we deploy when Tribucci gets back? he asked himself. One of us here, one of us by that car nearest the entrance? That seemed the best way to do it, all right. They would be separated, but not so far apart that one would be unable to offer protection for the other or to minimize the potential advantage of a crossfire. And they would be positioned at the closest possible points to the doors, so as to guard the entrance fully and effectively. They'd have to figure a way to cover the tracks from here to the car, though; they couldn't afford to wait for the storm to do it. Maybe there was something they could use in the cottage—a whisk broom, a trowel, something.

The wind began to gust, whistling mournfully, sweeping snow in misty sheets down close to the ground. Cain bunched the collar of his coat tighter against his throat with his left hand, repocketed the gun with his right. Minutes passed. Again he checked the area fronting the church; again he saw nothing. His feet were so achingly chilled now that he had almost no feeling in his toes; he lifted first one leg and then the other, like a man doing calisthenics in slow motion, to keep the blood circulating. The movement of time seemed to have slowed down to an inert crawl, as if the bitterly cold night had managed to wrap it, too, in a cloak of ice.

Time, Cain thought.

Abruptly he pushed back the left sleeve of his coat and squinted at the luminous numerals of his watch. It was seven five. Tribucci had said it would take him less than half an hour to get the guns from his brother's house and return here, but it was nearly forty-five minutes since they had parted in the wood. If nothing had happened, he should have been here by now. If nothing had happened....

The clot of anxiety under Cain's breastbone expanded. He made one last quick and fruitless reconnaissance of Sierra Street and then hurried back to the rear corner and across to the cottage and along its facade again to the garage corner. He stared beyond the snowfield at the trees: black-and-white emptiness everywhere.

Where was he?

Where was Tribucci?

# Sixteen

Moving through the familiar darkness inside his brother's home, John Tribucci went from the rear porch into the downstairs study. At an antique sideboard along one wall, he bent and opened the facing doors and rummaged through the interior until his fingers located the cowhide case he knew Vince kept there. He took the case out, set it on top of the sideboard, and worked the catches to lift the lid.

Inside was a matched set of .22 caliber, nine-shot Harrington & Richardson revolvers—a gift from Vince's father-in-law some three years earlier. One of Vince's favorite all-weather pastimes was target shooting, and he preferred Western-style pistols such as these to automatic target weapons like the Colt Woodsman. Tribucci had done some shooting with his brother, with these guns, and knew the feel and action of the model. Both were loaded, safeties on; he put one into the left pocket of his coat, clutched the second firmly, and went out of the study and started back through the house.

As he came into the kitchen, he grew aware for the first time of the subtle, homely fragrances which lingered in the warm black: his wife's Lanvin perfume, Vince's after breakfast cigar, the batch of Christmas *pfeffernüsse* cookies Judy had baked just before the four of them left for church. A vivid image of Ann entered his mind then, and his throat closed and his stomach twisted with a rush of emotion that was almost vertiginous. He leaned against the refrigerator for a moment, holding onto the image, trying to think of her laughing and happy instead of the way he had left her in church, the way she would be now that Coopersmith had surely told her what he and Cain were doing. Then, deliberately, he forced his mind blank of everything but his immediate purpose and stepped out onto the wide back porch.

He pushed through the door there—it had been customarily unlocked, and he'd come in that way initially—and hurried around to the front yard, into the deep shadows beneath one of the twin fir trees flanking the walk. The house was located on Eldorado Street, slightly more than half a block off Sierra; he peered eastward, then down the length of Shasta Street. The falling snow was like a huge, wind-billowed lace curtain that combined with the darkness to obscure anything more than fifty yards distant. A thin haze of light from the buildings on Sierra tinged the sky in that direction.

Tribucci moved out from beneath the fir and ran in long, light strides across Eldorado, coming up against the broad entrance doors of the building which fronted Placer on the east; owned by Joe Garvey, it served as a garage for extensive automobile and truck repairs and also as a storage shed for the village snowplow. On the opposite side of the street was a wide, bare hummock of ground, deep-drifted, that extended south to Lassen Drive and north to the beginnings of the pass cliffs—a shorter path into the wood higher up, but a slow and precarious one because of the snow depth. He would follow the longer but quicker route by which he had come: first down to the corner, to make sure Lassen was clear, and then traverse Placer and traverse Lassen and go up slantingly into the trees.

He was three steps from the corner when the dark figure came running at fly speed out of Lassen Drive.

Startled, Tribucci stood immobile for an instant; then, instinctively, he took a step back hard against the building, embracing the heavy darkness there. The running man crossed Placer—not looking back, not looking anywhere except straight ahead of him. When he reached the low picket fence enclosing the front yard of Webb Edward's house, he jumped it without slowing and disappeared around the screened-in porch.

It all happened so quickly that Tribucci had been able to distinguish nothing of the fleeing man's physical characteristics; but he had been hatless, and that meant it couldn't have been Cain, wasn't Cain. One of the looters... running from the psycho? You ran that way when somebody was after you, and maybe the maniac had tried to kill him—already killed the third one?—and he had broken away somehow. Was the psycho in close pursuit then? Was he just around the corner on Lassen? Tribucci worked saliva through his dry mouth, momentarily indecisive. Retreat or stay where he was? He might be seen either way, and this wasn't the place for a fight; he had to get back to Cain and the church—

A new movement caught his eye through the storm, kept him hugging the garage wall: an indistinct shape running through the yard of the Beckman property adjacent to Edwards'; cutting back across Placer at an angle, obscured white face turned to the north but with the screening snow and the ebon shadows, not seeing him, Tribucci, from that distance; vanishing once again into the Modoc Street corner lot belonging to the Chiltons.

Urgency tugged commandingly at Tribucci's mind, vanquishing the indecision. Get away from here, he thought. Get away from here now.

And the second figure appeared in the middle of Lassen fifteen feet away, oblong pointing finger of an automatic darkly defined in one hand, stalking—limping—in the runner's snowtracks.

Tribucci stiffened again; his ears seemed suddenly filled with the thrumming of his pulse. The second one stopped, looked across at Edwards' house—and then, as if with sixth sense, turned and stared north along Placer, stared right at him, could not miss seeing him across that short a span of ground. Tribucci recognized the charred, savage face immediately, confirmation of what he already knew, and a mixture of fear and hatred and fury constricted his anus and opened his jaws in a wolflike rictus. He had waited too long, it was too late to run, and he had no place to run to; he had to fight *now.*

Kubion took two steps toward him, gun arm leveled. Tribucci fired from in close to his chest, missed in his haste, saw the other jerk to a halt as if in surprise and then lunge to one side, onto his right knee with his favored left leg dragging. Moving sideways, Tribucci snapped his arm out and locked the elbow and braced his body; fired again—missed again, snow kicking up like a puff of white dust near the trailing leg. Damn you to hell damn you damn you! and started to squeeze off a third time, but the automatic in Kubion's hand flashed then and

stab! in his chest,

and flashed again and

stab! in his chest,

the stock of the bullets' impact driving away his breath—no no I blew it— and his legs buckled, the nerves in his gloved right hand were like filaments of ice. The revolver fell free, he felt his body slumping and heard the wind and the vague echoes of the shots as he toppled loosely into the half-frozen snow. I blew it good but oh *please* God don't let me have blown it completely—and a congealing red-black haze formed and thickened inside his head, spinning him, spinning him, obliterating all sound and all feeling and the sudden bright image of Ann that clung to his last shred of consciousness....

# Seventeen

Kubion stared down at the snow-spattered form of the man he had shot, recognized him as the one brother from the Sport Shop. Savagely he said, "You fucking hick Eskimo son of a bitch!" and drove the point of his shoe into yielding flesh just below the ribs, did it a second time. Then he backed up against the wall of the garage and probed the night around him with slitted, restless eyes.

Despite the direction of the snow tracks, he'd thought at first it was Brodie there in the building shadows and then the bastard had plugged away at him with that horse gun and Brodie hadn't had time to locate a weapon but Christ on a crutch he'd almost walked into it, the first bullet had missed him by a foot but the second had almost gotten him but he was ten feet tall and nobody could kill him least of all a lousy hick, but still it had been close. *Goddamn* it he'd been positive none of them would try to get out of the church and here this one was stupid stupid, not through the locked front doors not that stupid but maybe some other exit he'd overlooked when he'd examined the interior on Thursday or by breaking out the glass in one of the windows, and how many others were there? Oh, there'd be at least one more that was certain because one alone was too much of a risk even for stupid Eskimo hicks but now Tribucci was a dead hero and he'd make the other one or two dead heroes too. And Brodie, he'd kill Brodie slow and painful when he found him the fag shit, all that crap about safes but the urge telling him no and he'd thought he had everything nailed down and then that lousy ice and not watching his footing and falling and twisting his ankle, sprained and hurting and swelling up and hobbling him, and Brodie getting away and things all of a sudden screwing up just like the Greenfront job, things you couldn't figure ahead of time. But there was no way things were going to screw him out of this score no way because there'd be a fruit jar somewhere with the big money he *knew* it, and it was only a matter of time before he was back on top and killed Brodie and killed them all.

The urge moaned and trembled inside him, softly, softly. He opened his mouth and pulled freezing air and flakes of snow into his lungs. Things screwing up sure but Tribucci was dead, and it was a good thing he'd had the shootout because now he knew some of them were free; coming after Brodie with the idea he could spot him on the run had been smart then but not now, no point in trying to trail him like a goddamn Indian and maybe walking into an ambush. Maybe Brodie'd try for the Sport Shop, he'd be after a weapon first thing all right, but it was too obvious and maybe he'd go somewhere else; still, the thing to do was check it out quick and careful and even if he couldn't flush him he knew what Brodie would do after he was armed no question about that. He knew what the other hick heroes would be doing too, they'd want to protect those in the church and too many men running around in the village would increase chances of discovery and they'd be smart enough to understand that so they'd be waiting by or near the church for Tribucci to come with the guns that he wouldn't be bringing. The church was the lay okay, all the way all the way.

Not looking at the motionless figure in the snow, Kubion sidestepped to the corner and went around it and ran limpingly back along Lassen Drive to Sierra Street.

# Eighteen

As soon as he was sure the immediate area was clear, Brodie climbed over a
five-foot boundary fence into the north-south alley bisecting the block
between Modoc and Lassen and kicked open the back door of the Valley Inn.
The wind muffled the sounds of splintering wood and snapping metal, sent
swirls of snow into the heavily shadowed storeroom ahead of him. Directly opposite and to one side, he could make out a narrow corridor leading into the
front of the building. He ran down there, came out in the restaurant kitchen,
and crossed to a swing door in the far wall. When he had pushed through, he
was in the inn's darkened dining room.

Lights burned a pale amber in the lounge area beyond the center partitions.
On the wall behind the far end of the bar, Brodie could see the glass-fronted
guncase he had noticed earlier—and the twin, ornately scrolled shotguns
shining dully within. Spread across the bottom of the interior shelf, just as he
remembered, were boxes of shells.

He ran around into the lounge and swung his body up onto the bar, over
behind it. With a heavy decanter from the backbar display, he broke the glass
out of the guncase door and cleared clinging shards from the opening. The
shotguns were .12 gauge pumps with 26-inch barrels, three-shot Savages.
Brodie pulled one of them loose from its clip fastenings, pawed open a box of
cartridges, fed three into the magazine, and worked the slide to jack the first
into firing position.

Despite the deadliness of the piece, it was cumbersome—and the storm
would retard accurate shooting at any range over twenty yards. There were
plenty of handguns in the Sport Shop, but once Brodie was certain he'd made
good his escape and could think calculatingly again, he had decided against
that objective. Kubion had to know that his first consideration would be to get
himself a weapon and that the Sport Shop was the one place to pick up on
guns and ammunition. Maybe Kubion would be following snow tracks, the
way you'd expect, but then again, since Brodie hadn't seen any sign of him
when he'd looped around and doubled back across Placer Street, it could be he
had gone to the Sport Shop instead. Christ, he could be anywhere, doing anything.

Brodie dropped a handful of extra shells into his coat pocket, went over the
bar again, and ran through the dining room and kitchen. He slowed there and
entered cautiously into the dark corridor, bringing the shotgun up so that the
stock butted hard against his shoulder, moving to where he could see the open
rear door. Snow still churned inside, blanketing a section of floor in an unbroken swath. He edged into the storeroom, circled silently around to the wall
beside the door. Then, swiftly, he stepped over in front of the opening, still
three paces inside, and fanned the pump across the fence. Nothing showed,

nothing moved. He saw that the only tracks in the alley snow were his own, hesitated for a moment, and then ran out through the doorway to the left; pulled back to the building wall, sweeping the shotgun's muzzle from the fence northward along the alley and back again. The narrow expanse was empty in both directions.

With the pump sighted once more on the fence, Brodie waded sideways through the snow to the south. Just prior to Modoc Street, the fence ended against a low line of shrubbery, and he could see a portion of the adjoining house's front yard: smooth-swept whiteness. He went over there, fanned the area behind the fence, and then swung the weapon outward in an arc to Modoc. Clear. Carefully, he backed farther into the yard at an angle that allowed him to see down Modoc to Sierra in one direction, and back deeper along the fence in the other. He was completely alone.

His moves so far had been the right ones; he'd been inside the inn less than five minutes—not long enough to have trapped himself if Kubion was follow-ing his tracks, just long enough to have balanced the odds a little. There was no question what his next move had to be: the church. Loxner figured to be long gone, hiding out somewhere, but there was still an off-chance he'd remained in the car and even a mush-belly was better than no help at all. And doing the cat-and-mouse bit in the village was pure stupidity; you didn't play games with a maniac. If he could get to the church before Kubion, and Loxner *was* gone, he could burrow in somewhere and try to pick Kubion off when he showed—and he would show all right, he could already be on his way there because he'd remember Loxner now. But that didn't change matters. Any way you looked at it, the church was where Brodie had to go.

He hurried through the facing yards of two houses, watching his flank as well as what lay ahead. Then he cut across Modoc and went into another yard and along the side of a dark frame house. There was no fence separating that property from the one which fronted on Shasta; he passed beneath a row of bare-branched fruit trees, paralleled a second dark house, and came to a stop beside a wooden pony cart the owners had put in for landscaping decoration.

He squatted there to catch his breath, to momentarily relieve the sharp ache of fatigued muscles. The shotgun seemed to have grown heavier, more unwieldy. Opening the bottom two buttons of his coat, he used the lining on one of the flaps to wipe his wind- and snow-stung eyes.

As far as he could see, then, Shasta Street was clear both east and west. He levered up again and ran at an angle across the roadway, plowed through thick drifts to a fir tree at the edge of the church acreage. Kubion's car was dis-cernible from there; like all the others on the lot, it was draped in white, wind-shield and windows ice-veiled. It looked as if Loxner were gone, all right, but he was still going to have to make sure.

Brodie slogged forward through the surface pack with his body humped over and the pump gun up against his shoulder, covering both front and rear cor-ners. When he had reached the near wall, he went to the corner and stared out into the lot. The snow everywhere was unmarred. If Kubion had managed to get there before him, he hadn't come across the lot and he wasn't in the lot.

Stepping out, Brodie moved to the front stairs and sat on his haunches next to them, fanning the shotgun from south to east to north. Then he looked down at Kubion's car again, came up, and scurried crablike across the walk to the nearest vehicle; went around behind it, half turned back toward the church. Once he got to the car, he raised his left hand and rapped hard against the cold metal of the door. No response from within. He knew that the dome light in the car didn't work, and he reached up and caught the handle and jerked outward. Ice seals crackled, breaking away from the metal; the door opened wide.

Brodie said "Jesus!" between suddenly clenched teeth, because Loxner hadn't gone anywhere, because Loxner was still sitting there behind the wheel—with his mouth hanging open and both hands wrapped around the blood-coated haft of Kubion's pocketknife embedded just under his breastbone.

# Nineteen

Cain was not startled when he put his head out to look around the church's southern front corner and the looter was less than twenty yards away, armed with a shotgun, moving across the front walk and into the parking lot.

He had been expecting one or more of them for several minutes, ever since he'd stood at the cottage's far end and waited for Tribucci to appear out of the trees. There was only one possible explanation for Tribucci's continued absence: something had gone wrong, he had been seen and killed or wounded and pinned down somewhere. And that meant the psycho was now aware at least one man had gotten out of the church, that he would want to find out as quickly as possible if there were others, that the element of surprise had at best been neutralized and at worst been transferred in part to the opposition.

He had forced down the stirring of a strong mixture of emotions, forced himself to remain calm and to think strategically. Deliberation had been brief. The only thing he could do was to situate himself at the south church wall, alternating between front and rear corners; that way he could cover all immediate approaches without leaving any more telltale tracks than he already had. He'd spent the past ten minutes moving back and forth along the wall, watching and waiting for something to happen, and now the waiting was over—part of it, or all of it.

The man in the parking lot was not the psycho; Cain was able, through the flurries, to determine that by size, coloring, and clothing before pulling back rigidly against the boarding. His fingers tightened convulsively around the butt of the Walther, and he brought it up against his chest, thinking: Why the parking lot, why not around on this side? He can't think I'm out there, there isn't any spoor.... All right, it doesn't matter; what matters is what he does next, where he goes—what I do and where I go. One mistake and it's all over: remember that, don't forget that for a second.

Cain inched his head out again. The looter had reached the vehicle parked by itself at the forward end of the lot, was pulling open the driver's door. He reacted to some thing inside the car; but the dome light did not go on, and because of distance and angle and the storm, Cain couldn't tell what it was. With taut movements, the man straightened and backed off two steps; swept the shotgun south to north across the front of the church, not seeing Cain— not yet.

But he's going to come back here now, Cain thought, and when he does it'll be in this direction; he came from the north, and he can't know what there is on this side. Retreat to the back? No—retreating won't accomplish anything positive, there isn't going to be any more retreating. Too late to go after him, and that would be a fool's move anyway with that shotgun he's got and across open ground. Stay here, then, right here. Don't take eyes off him, don't make any unnecessary moves because movement is the thing that'll give me away; he's not going to be able to penetrate stationary shadows until he gets closer—believe that. Wait, wait until the last possible second, play for one shot at dead aim and don't even think about missing....

The looter was moving now, shuffle-stepping toward the church and diagonally to the south. He held the shotgun centered on the building, ready to swing either way, but his head turned in a slow, intent ambit, coming out of profile. He seemed to be facing Cain squarely then, to hesitate—

don't move, don't breathe.

—and finally he swiveled his gaze slowly to the north again.

Sweat trickled down from Cain's armpits, froze along his sides; the brassiness was back in his mouth, sharp and raw. When the looter's attention was focused fully away from him, he lifted his left arm cautiously to eye level and anchored it against the corner edge of the church; brought the Walther up in the same motion and rested the barrel on his forearm. He released the held breath into his left coat sleeve, drew another. Squinting, he peered along the iron muzzle sight.

The looter took another step, and another.

Aim for the head or body? What did the Army tell you about something like this? Can't remember, can't think—make a decision! Body then, larger target, center on the chest, the heart.

Another step.

All right, steady now, steady. Slow, even pressure on the trigger. Squeeze it, don't pull it, when the time comes. The looter came to a standstill.

Not yet! He doesn't see me, he's not looking here. Wait. Last possible moment, one shot. Come on, you, come on, come on.

Moving again—one step, two.

Steady.

Twenty yards now, any second now.

Steady steady steady.

And the looter stopped again, jerkily this time. His body started to dip into a crouch, the pump gun swinging hard across in front of him.

He's seen me, Cain thought—and let his finger compress the trigger.

The recoil jumped the automatic's barrel off his forearm, the roar seemed to hammer deafeningly in his ears. He snapped the muzzle down again, trying to rebrace it—but the man was falling, Cain realized this with a kind of fascination and watched him fall as though in cinematic slow motion, one foot coming up, leg bending, body turning and then arching backward, falling with the shotgun still held in his hands, striking the yielding snow on his back, the pump jarring loose finally and rolling up over his head and away; the body settling, becoming still, lying there in twisted repose.

Cain leaned heavily against his left arm, weakness in his legs, weakness in the pit of his stomach. The illusion of slow motion vanished, and he thought: *My God, my God,* dully. He did not move from his position, staring at the sprawled figure in the snow beyond. Breath shuddered and rattled in his throat. The chill of it, the numbing wind against his face, sharpened his thoughts again: you did it, okay you did it, and now you've got to do it again. His eyes probed the parking lot, the church's facade, the area behind him to the west. Empty darkness.

He rubbed harshly at his face, stepped out bent-bodied, and went quickly, gun extended, toward the motionless body. The looter lay on his back, and when Cain came up to him he could see the sightlessly open eyes, the grimaced mouth, blood on the mouth, blood on the coat front. Dead—yes. Heart-shot. He backed around the body, swallowing a faint ascendance of nausea, and approached the car at which the looter had crouched.

The door still stood partially open. Nausea surged again when Cain squatted and looked inside and saw what the looter had reacted to: the body of the third man behind the wheel, the blood, the haft of the pocketknife—dead in there all this time. The psycho had done it, no doubt of that, and that was all the explanation he needed; details were meaningless. All that had meaning now was not one but two of the terrorists were dead, and in all probability Tribucci as well, and it was only the psycho and himself who were left. Just the two of them, one against one.

Sure—one against one.

Well suppose he sought help, suppose with the way things were now he went up to the church doors and tried to break them open or shouted for some of the men inside to break them open, told them what the situation was.... No, that was foolish thinking. He didn't know where the psycho was, and he would make a fine target up there on the steps. And the threat of a stampede was a real one, you couldn't predict the actions of each and every one of seventy-five trapped people once the doors to freedom were open to them.

He'd have to do it alone, then; nothing had changed, nothing could change. Remain here at the church, guard the entrance, and begin the waiting all over again. Back around the south corner? Or right here in the lot? The lot—behind the car nearest the front doors. The surface snow was full of tracks now, and without that problem to worry about, the lot was the more tactical location. From here he could see both front corners, and Sierra Street, and most of the village to the north, and all of the lot, and the open incline leading up into the trees beyond the lake road's fork.

Rising up, Cain ran in a low stiff crouch to that nearest car, an old finned Mercury. The flurries were less heavy now, and the force of the wind seemed to have abated somewhat; the darkness harbored nothing that he could see. He knelt in the snow at the right rear fin—and almost immediately he could feel the chill penetrating his trousers and the heavy skirt of his overcoat. He could feel, too, the aching cold-tightness of muscles and joints throughout his body and the beginnings of enervation in his limbs. It was as if the freezing night were sucking strength out of him like sweat through the pores of his skin.

Make it soon, damn you, he thought. Make it *soon*.

# Twenty

Crouched beside an evergreen shrub on Shasta Street, a half block off Sierra, Kubion watched skull-grinning as Brodie died in the church parking lot.

He had come across Sierra and made a rapid, though guarded, check of the Sport Shop, front and rear; then he'd recrossed the street at Modoc and gone up to Shasta, into it laterally through thickly concealing darkness. When he reached the shrub, he paused to reconnoiter the church and the short length of Shasta to the west. It was while he had been doing that that Brodie came out of one of the yards in the next block and ran across to the fir tree at the edge of the church property.

Going to the church all right, Kubion had thought. Got him a shotgun or a rifle, some piece in a snowstorm but he's running scared, and the first thing he'll do when he gets over there is go to the car looking for Loxner. Fifty yards closer and you wouldn't go anywhere you fairy son of a bitch, but maybe it was better this way maybe he'd flush any other stupid hero hicks hiding in the area. Big black blowfly, that's what Brodie was, big black blowfly circling around and when he landed he was going to get squashed flat, spill his guts all over the goddamn snow.

Brodie had stepped out from under the tree, and through the gusting snow-fall Kubion's slitted eyes had followed his progress to the church and to the car. Surprise! Surprise, Vic! Oh, Jesus his face must have been something to see right then, trying to figure out when and how it happened well I did it just after we took over the church, I put the knife in him while you were walking away with your back turned, the whispering told me it was time; one stroke clean when Duff was leaning over the seat to get the flour sack and he never made a sound and you thought all along he was alive, you could see him sit-ting behind the wheel all the while and you thought he was alive and he was just another dead lump of shit....

The grin had stretched Kubion's cold-cracked lips as Brodie turned and start-ed back toward the church. Now what, blowfly? Now what? And that was when he saw the brief muzzle flash from the church corner; Brodie falling, staying down without moving. Kubion stood up against the shrub, head craned forward; nothing changed in his face, the skull grin remained fixed. Seconds later the shadows at the corner separated, and he watched the figure of the man materialize.

Mothering bastard! Hick got him hick killed him; where did he get the gun? Well fuck that, he had it and he'd picked Brodie off with it, one shot lucky shot and Brodie was dead, he'd wanted Brodie for himself but it was okay this way too—okay, okay. Kubion kept staring over at the lot, saw the hick check the car and then come back and take a position behind another car and now show himself again. So—digging in out there this time, where he could cover all approaches and the church doors. No way to slip up on him but that was okay too because he knew exactly where the hick was and that the hick was armed and that there probably weren't any others or they would've come into the lot, or else he'd have gone to them to report if they were too far away to know what had happened with Brodie. Right on, he was right on top again ten feet tall; no more screwing up from here on in, no more screwing up.

The impulse was talking to him again, telling him exactly what he had to do because it was time now to finish everything.

Fire-bomb the church, it murmured. Fire-bomb the church!

Get material for Molotov cocktails from one of the houses and cross to the church from where the sharp-shooting hick couldn't see him and toss a couple through one of the stained-glass windows on the far side and the front. When the hick heard and saw what was happening, his instant reaction would be to try to help the ones inside, forgetting everything else because that was the way these silly Eskimos always reacted and always would react, and he'd run up to the doors and Kubion would stand out and pick him off and then dump another cocktail on the entrance to make sure nobody broke down the doors and nobody got out alive.

He could imagine vividly the way it would be, he could see the bright burning flames and he could hear the screams; and when he backed away through the shadows to Sierra, he felt a sharp hurting in his groin and realized that the urge's excitement had given him a stone-hard erection.

# Twenty-One

Within the church, balanced precariously on the edge of panic, the people of Hidden Valley waited for some indication of what was taking place in the storm and darkness outside—and for the bitter incongruity of the birth of a child.

At Webb Edwards' direction, the pews forward and rear of the one where Ann Tribucci lay had been cleared immediately after he'd satisfied himself that her labor was not false. With the exception of Lew Coopersmith, who had taken up a listening post at the front doors, all the men and all the children had grouped on or near the pulpit; most of the women were spaced in the pews between or along the walls. Edwards had taken the prayer cloth from the altar and draped it across the pew backs above Ann, to form a kind of awning that would offer a measure of privacy. Some of the heavier winter coats helped anchor the cloth. Sally Chilton had taken Rebecca's place, holding Ann's head in her lap, mopping perspiration from her paper-white cheeks, talking to her softly, soothingly. Once Edwards had removed some of Ann's garments, he had placed his own soft fur-lined coat beneath her hips; then he'd gotten two heavy shawls from Judy Tribucci and Ellen Coopersmith, had unfastened the string tie he was wearing and divested it of its thin, metal, caduceus-shaped slip ring—swaddling clothes and umbilical binding and surgical cutting tool, all poor unsterile substitutes that would have to do because there was nothing else, there was not even any water for cleansing. Kneeling at the edge of the prayer cloth, he massaged her heaving abdomen gently and timed the frequency of her pains.

Rebecca stood against the south wall, hugging herself, not wanting to watch this grim enactment of what must ordinarily be the moving spectacle of childbirth, watching anyway because Ann was her friend and because it was as momentarily inescapable as their prison itself. Would there be complications? It was a wretched possibility. And if there were, would Webb Edwards' simple medical knowledge be enough?

Would it matter to Ann and the baby even if there were no complications at all?

Minutes ticked away—empty, barren, Rebecca listened to the softly vocal praying of the Reverend Mr. Keyes, Ann's muffled cries, the monotonous droning of Sally Chilton's voice and that of Agnes Tyler crooning to her unresponsive daughter—and her nerves grew tighter, until they seemed on the verge of snapping like rubber bands stretched to the limit of their elasticity. She wanted to scream, to fling herself at someone, to run in circles until she collapsed: something, anything, to relieve the inexorably mounting pressure. She could not stand it much longer, she thought; none of them could stand it much longer. When she looked around at the others, she could see some of what she felt in their groping movements, in the way their eyes shifted from Ann to the front doors to one another, in the hollowness of their faces. It was like watching, being a part of, the beginnings of a collective nervous breakdown.

She swallowed thickly, thinking: I've got to get a grip on myself, I can't let go now, there's still hope—there is still hope. Cling to that, to faith in Johnny and in Zachary Cain, to *faith*. We're not going to die. We're not going to die....

And she remembered that Cain had spoken those same words to her earlier, remembered again the conviction in his voice and the new strength of him. Curiously, she had not been surprised when she'd learned he had gone out there with Johnny and what the two of them intended to do; her only surprise had been that they'd found a way to get out in the first place. Like Johnny, Cain—and this was something she now understood she'd seen in him from the first, dormant but perceptible—was a basically forceful, selflessly compassionate man: the kind of man who acted and reacted strongly to any given situation. The hell he had put himself through because of the death of his family was testimony to that, just as what he was doing now, for them, was testimony to it.

I wonder what Matt would have done if he'd been spared, she thought. For all his benevolence and professed love for the people of the valley, would he have volunteered to go out there and try to kill three men to save all our lives? She did not think so; no, she did not think so.

The entire nature of her relationship with Matt seemed to have become quite clear now. There hadn't been anything left of their marriage or of her love for him; the last binding threads had unraveled a long time ago, and she had been living a foolish lie, hiding the debilitating ugliness of that lie behind the guise of weakness and self-pity—not fully understanding what it was doing to her as a woman, as a human being. And yet she *had*, slowly, been coming to an understanding of the truth, would have reached that understanding sooner or later. And when she had, the strength so long repressed in her would have manifested itself and she'd have left him and gotten a divorce. It was a simple matter of self-preservation: if she had stayed with Matt, she would have died spiritually, died inside, and for all her weakness and timidity and indecisiveness she would never have allowed it to happen. Knowing that, she knew herself: she had at last rediscovered her own identity.

Only now, bitterly, it might have come too late.

There you go again, she told herself; stop it now, stop it. It's not too late, think about something else, think about anything else. Think about Zachary Cain; yes, think about him, and what he said, and the way he looked, and the way he was and is and will be when you see him again....

Fifty minutes after she had gone into labor, and mercifully without complications, Ann Tribucci gave birth.

From his position at the doors, Coopersmith saw Edwards lift the newborn infant by the ankles—long, finger-thick umbilical cord trailing down beneath the prayer cloth like a wet white rope, seeming to pulse faintly—and use a clean handkerchief to sponge away accumulated blood and mucus from mouth and nose; slap tiny buttocks sharply to begin normal respiration. The child's cries echoed piercingly through the grim silence.

Ann said weakly, tearfully, "Webb... oh Webb...."

"It's a girl, honey," Edwards said. His voice was thick. "Normal in every way and you can hear how healthy she is."

He laid the baby down on one of the shawls, took up his string tie and bound off the umbilical cord, used the tie's metal caduceus clip to saw through it. Then he wiped her dry and wrapped her in the other shawl and handed her across to Sally. His hands and clothing were spattered with reddish fluid as he knelt again to minister to Ann.

Coopersmith, as some of the others had already done, looked away; he had fathered two sons but had seen neither of them born, and he'd never realized that childbirth could be quite so messy—a messiness that only added fuel to the sick terror in the room. Facing the side wall, he heard Ann say, "I want to hold her, please let me hold her," and he thought: Life and death, in the midst of one you have the other, and you can't separate them; one Tribucci born and one ready to die, the Lord giveth and the Lord taketh away....

The tightness had returned to his chest, the sourness like trapped gas to his stomach. He passed a hand over his face. And standing there that way, with his ear close to the joining of the two doors, he heard something else, something outside—a faint cracking sound thinned by the storm. He knew immediately that it was a shot, strained to pick up further sounds; there were none. He turned his head to see if anyone else had heard the report. Each of their attentions, he saw, was centered on Ann and Edwards and the cries of the baby, or turned within.

Let it be Cain or Johnny who fired that shot, he thought fervently. Let them stay alive and do what they have to do—so all these people can live, so Johnny's baby can live. You've given, but don't take away; let Cain and Tribucci live....

# Twenty-Two

John Tribucci was still alive.

He was alive because the bullets which had entered his chest had both missed vital organs—one chipping the left collarbone and one lodging against a right upper rib—and because of the two vicious kicks in the side Kubion had delivered just after the shooting. Shock had been responsible for the red-black haze, the initial unconsciousness; but if it had not been for the kicks, the freezing wind and snow would have prevented him from coming to and eventually have done the job the bullets failed to do.

The sudden pain in his side brought him out of it gradually, into a vague awareness of where he was and what had happened, and he did not move perceptibly or make any sound. He lay there at first feeling only the cold and the pain in his side where he had been kicked and a bitter hollow helplessness, half expecting a final bullet, the *coup de grâce,* that he would never really feel or hear. Instead, there was the audible crunching of steps going away from him—not far, it seemed, just up to the garage wall a few yards distant, but far enough for Tribucci to begin to taste faint hope. His thoughts cleared somewhat then, and he clung with silent desperation to the threads of consciousness, giving thanks that he had fallen with his face turned downward against one arm, so that each thin expulsion of breath went into the snow and did not dilate upward in a telltale white vapor.

In his wounded and cold-stiffened condition, he knew it would be suicidal to go after the second .22 revolver in his left coat pocket or the knife strapped to his leg, or to make any sort of movement at all, while the psycho remained in the vicinity. He waited, playing dead—and kept on waiting. Pain began to seep through the numbness in his chest, muted at first but gathering a pulsing intensity; he was aware of the faint cold stickiness of blood on his upper torso.

And then, above the cry of the wind, he thought he heard steps crackling again, retreating to the south. But he was not completely sure, and still he kept his body immobile. One or five or ten more minutes ebbed away. He began to feel a kind of torpid warmth, lying there in the snow, and that was a certain sign you were on your way to freezing to death; he could not wait any longer, if he didn't move very soon now he would never move at all.

Tribucci forced his eyes open into slits, blinking the lids free of ice flakes, and then turned his head slowly up and around. He could see all right; the haziness was gone. It was snowing less heavily now, giving him greater visibility than he had had earlier, and there was no one at the garage wall and appeared to be no one to the south along Placer. When he had worked his head around to look to the north, he saw nothing in that direction either.

He got his hands under him and lifted himself slowly, weakly, into a kneeling position, setting his teeth against the rising agony in his chest. The depression in the snow where he had lain was spotted darkly with blood, but most of the fluid had been contained inside his clothing, caking his undershirt to his body. Trembling with cold and enervation, he lifted one leg and planted his shoe firmly and heaved upward onto his feet; staggered, fell to one knee again; pushed upward a second time and groped his way to the garage wall. He leaned against it heavily, panting.

How much time had passed? Tribucci dragged his left arm up and looked at his watch, and it was seven thirty-seven. More than an hour since he had left Cain, three-quarters of an hour since he had come out of Vince's house across Eldorado. He swallowed into a constricted throat and tried to collect his thoughts into coherent order.

The psycho knew now that at least one person had got out of the church, and he had to be thinking that maybe there were more as well. He would head there, then, he wouldn't keep on reconning the partner who'd been running away from him—and maybe that one would make for the church as well. Cain would have realized by now that something had happened, too much time had elapsed for him to think otherwise, and he would be extra-cautious; but so would the runner and so would the psycho, particularly the psycho.

Tribucci sleeved snow and chilled sweat from his face, breathing rackingly. I've got to get to the church, he thought, and I've got to get there fast: warn Cain, join him in a stand. There might still be a little time, but not enough for him to attempt the trek on foot; too dangerous with the psycho's whereabouts unknown, the runner's whereabouts unknown, and the frigid wind and snow would sap too much of his remaining strength. He had to do something overt, then; there just wasn't any other choice.

Take a car; a car was fast and direct, and it would give him some protection as well. Vince's Buick? It was in the garage across Eldorado—but God he didn't have a key for it, and he wasn't enough of a mechanic to be able to jump the ignition wires. His own car was at the church he and Ann and Vince and Judy had gone in that this morning. Was there another vehicle in the village somewhere that might have the keys in it? He could not think of one, there might not *be* any, and he would waste precious time, too much time, if he—

Snowmobile, he thought.

Vince's snowmobile.

It, too, was in his brother's garage, and the key for it was kept in a storage compartment under the cowl; friends were always borrowing the machine with Vince's carte blanche permission and he felt it was simpler to keep the key there than on his person. It was as good as a car in that it could travel just as quickly, better than a car because it was smaller and more maneuverable in the snow and would not be noticed as soon from a distance. He would be fully exposed driving it, a moving target, but there was nothing to be done about that; he had to get to the church, he had to get to Cain.

Tribucci pushed away from the wall, located the dropped .22, and bent for it. The motion made his head spin dizzily and sickness funnel into his throat, but when he straightened again the nausea receded. He shoved the gun into his free pocket, went back toward Eldorado Street with his left arm pressed hard across his chest, running drunkenly on legs which felt as if they had been rubberized. He fell once, dragged himself up; he could not seem to get enough of the biting cold air into his lungs. The pain in his chest was a fiery, pulsing counterpoint to the hammerlike tempo of his heart.

He went down twice more crossing to Vince's front yard, willed his body up again both times. Fresh blood welled from the two bullet wounds, and it was like a coating of viscid oil on his skin. He wondered dimly if he were bleeding to death. No. He wouldn't bleed to death and he wouldn't freeze to death, remember Ann, remember the baby, remember Vince and Judy and seventy of his friends and neighbors locked inside the church—and Cain, remember Cain.

He flung himself across the last few feet to the garage doors, banging hard against them with one shoulder. Gasping, he fumbled at the latch and got the doors open and shoved them wide against the powdery snow. He lurched inside. The odors of grease and winter dampness permeated the thick ebon interior, and Vince's old Roadmaster gleamed dully in front of him. To the rear, Tribucci could make out the familiar shapes of tool-littered workbench and power saw and drill press, the chain-supported wooden storage platform which protruded from the upper back wall. He leaned against the car, used it to uphold the weight of his body as he shuffled around it toward the area beneath the suspended platform.

The snowmobile, beneath a dun-colored canvas tarp, sat parallel to the wall. With numb fingers he pulled the tarp off, thinking: Let there be gas in the tank. He caught hold of the plexiglass windshield with both hands, turned and dragged the machine out from under the platform. It moved easily across the smooth cement floor on its waxed skis and heavy roller treads. Tribucci laid his shoulder against the windshield, his hip against the edge of the cowl, and pushed the mobile past the Buick and out into the snow in front of the garage.

His vision now was obscured with sweat and shimmering black pain shadows. He pawed urgently at his eyes. When he could see again, he swung one leg over the Etha-foam seat, sat down, and braced his feet, knees up, on the narrow metal running boards on each side of the frame. Then he pressed his forehead against the top of the windshield and fumbled under the cowl, located the storage compartment, found the key in its magnetized metal case.

It seemed to take him minutes to get the key threaded into the ignition slot. He turned it finally, hit the electric starter button, and the engine coughed and didn't catch and he thought, Oh, Christ, please! and pressed the button again—and this time the motor came to life in a low, throbbing whine.

Breath whistled through his nostrils. He took one of the Harrington & Richardson .22s from his coat, the one which had not lain in the snow, and wedged it between his crotch and the padded seat, butt outward, where he could get at it instantly; but he left the safety on to guard against accidental discharge. Then he caught the handlebars, shifted into Forward, worked the hand throttle, and sent the snowmobile skimming at an angle across the yard and out onto Eldorado Street.

The jouncing, accelerated motion made razorlike lancinations slice through his chest, and his thoughts were sluggish, his reactions were sluggish. The wind hurled snow back against his face, distorting his vision again. He fought desperately to keep the machine on a steady course, to hold away the congealing red-black mist which had begun again to form inside his head.

Hang on, give me the strength to hang on....

And Tribucci swings the snowmobile around the corner onto Sierra Street, weaving erratically, straightening out again. His arms have taken on the weight of stone. Down the center of the street, beneath the darkened Christmas decorations mocked and made ludicrous by the bleak savagery of a nightmare, between wedges of light that reach out dully through broken doors and shattered and ice-frosted windows. Warm reddish black within, cold whitish black without; ominous shadows, the valley of shadows, *Yea, though I go through the valley of the shadow of death, I will fear no evil....*

He comes past the Sport Shop then, and the church looms ahead of him through the now thinly sifting snowfall. He ducks his head against his left arm, to clear his vision again, as the snowmobile planes across Shasta Street. Cars in the parking lot all dark and icebound, nothing moving—take a chance. He bounces up over the sidewalk curbing—sharp cut of pain, pain and Cain, find Cain, get to Cain—and veers toward the southern front corner.

He sees something, something dark against the snow between Shasta Street and the north wall: man-figure, stopped, poised, not Cain, carrying something that looks like a sack.

The psycho, Tribucci knows instantly it is the psycho.

He makes an unconscious screaming-sobbing sound in his throat, wrenches the snowmobile back to the right. The psycho is running now, limpingly, toward the rear of the church, sack like an obscene caricature of Santa Claus's toybag bouncing against one leg. His right arm crosses his body; the gun which is in his hand flashes: wild shot, missing both Tribucci and the snowmobile.

Leaden fingers fumble at the dashboard, locate the headlight knob, pull it out and twist it to high beam. Bright yellow cones jab glitteringly through the snowy darkness. Tribucci swerves left too abruptly and then overcorrects; the snowmobile begins to yaw. Get him, get him, run him down! and he tries to center the psycho in the headlights but seems to have no more control over the machine, no more control over his own bodily movements. Breath heaves out in out in through his open mouth, pain boils in his chest, weakness spreads tangibly and the red-black mist grows and twists through his mind like a helix, no hold on, and his left hand slips off the handlebar throttle, his right undergoes a paroxysm and jerks forward and sends the smowmobile sliding sideways toward the church, the helix widens blackly and he can't hold on any longer, he can't hold on any

# Twenty-Three

When Cain first saw the blob of motive darkness coming unevenly along the center of Sierra Street, he did not know what to think. He stared at it through the thinning flurries: not quite distinguishable, the fuzzy patches of light from the buildings on either side failed to reach it. Stiffened joints protested painfully as he pulled his feet under him and flattened his upper torso across the layer of freezing snow which covered the Mercury's deck.

Drawing nearer, the blob began to take on shape and substance—and when it passed the Sport Shop, Cain recognized it as a snowmobile. But the driver, crouched low behind the snow-speckled windshield, was just another heavy shadow. The psycho? It didn't make sense that he would be coming so openly, coming on a *snowmobile*.... Weaving, the machine angled toward the parking lot on a direct line to where Cain was hidden; the whining sound of its engine reached his ears. He still could not make out the driver, but he was thinking then: Tribucci? Whoever was piloting the snowmobile either knew nothing at all about handling one or else was hurt, badly hurt—Tribucci?

Cain saw the mobile lurch again, due west; instead of coming into the lot, it was going parallel to the north wall. When it was fifty feet away, abreast of the Mercury, he was finally able to make out the driver in dark profile: wearing a cap, wearing what appeared to be a woman's cap, wearing a light-colored overcoat. Tribucci! Relief, and a sense of sharp exigency welled inside him— and moving spontaneously, he pushed out from behind the car, ran along its side with his left hand upraised in frenetic signal.

The snowmobile's dual headlights snapped on.

What's he doing, what's he doing? Cain thought, and ran another five steps; but Tribucci did not see him. The machine wobbled left, wobbled right, made a sudden right-angle turn toward the church, swirling a quadrant of light, and tilted up on its near side. Trubicci spilled off the seat, the howl of the motor cut off as it stalled. The snowmobile shuddered to a halt, full on its side, in a thin cumulus of dislodged snow.

Cain saw all this running, cutting toward the corner, coming out into the open—saw then the dark figure forty yards away, twenty yards from the rear corner, and knew why Tribucci had put on the headlights and realized with the abrupt taste of ashes in his mouth just how foolish his own actions had been. But it was too late now to reverse direction, the psycho could see him just as plainly, and without hesitation he threw himself forward and down in a flat running dive. He landed on his belly and left forearm, keeping the Walther up—heard a buzzing slap in the snow to one side of him, the muted sound of a shot. Frantically he propelled himself toward the snowmobile on elbows and knees, putting the machine between himself and the other man. A hole appeared in the plexiglass windshield, spurting ice crystals, making a loud cracking noise; a third bullet spanged somewhere into the undercarriage. He came up against the cowl, arched his body around the curved line of the windshield, and braced his right forearm in his left palm.

Kubion was running again—hobbled steps—toward the rear corner.

Cain fired after him, missed badly both times and saw him disappear into the shadows at the end wall. He pulled back, trembling slightly, dragging his left arm across his eyes, and crawled toward the motionless figure of Tribucci lying face down five feet away. Kneeling low beside him, Cain rolled him gently onto his back. Frozen blood and two charred holes in the upper front of his coat; shot twice, unconscious but still clinging to life: mouth open, breathing liquidly. Blood in his throat. Turn his head to one side so he doesn't strangle on it. Nothing else he could do for Tribucci, not now if at all. He had to concentrate on the psycho—but he couldn't stay where he was, he couldn't wait, he had to make some kind of offensive move....

And he knew then just exactly what it would have to be.

Half dragging his left leg, Kubion ran the length of the church's rear wall and came up hard against it at the south corner. Immediately, black eyes staring back to the north, he set down the gunny sack—four quart mason jars of gasoline siphoned from a car in one of the house garages on Shasta Street; a half dozen oily rags he'd found, along with the jars, in that same garage—and ripped the empty clip out of the automatic. He heaved it away furiously, located the extra clip buried beneath a wad of currency in his trouser pocket, bills spilling out unnoticed, and jammed that one into the butt.

The impulse, now, had reached a vertex of shrieking inside his head, making it pound thunderously, jumbling and interfusing his thoughts: No pursuit but let him come let him try cat-and-mousing blow his head off Christ! screwing up screwing up things keep screwing up snowmobile coming catching me in the open like that just two more minutes fucking snowmobile so sure only one other hick out and killed Tribucci so who was driving had to be Tribucci killed him but he wasn't dead and got to snowmobile oh these Eskimo bastards one in the lot alerted running out fat target but lousy snow cold darkness throwing off aim and clip empty had to run because him with the gun he'd shot Brodie with well all right nothing really changed and nothing more going to screw up ten feet tall can't stop me can't stop me come on hick give it to you burn all of you up watch you burn....

Kubion bent and caught up the sack again; turned his body with his weight on his good right leg and backed away from the building at an angle. When he could see all of the south church wall and that it too was clear, he ran along it and stopped beneath the nearest of the stainedglass windows. He lowered the sack a second time, looked up at the pale light in the window—looked back at the sack and reached into it and brought out one of the mason jars, one of the oily rags.

Wedging the jar between his right arm and body, so he would not have to release the gun, he unscrewed the cap and fed one end of the rag inside;

worked the cap back on to hold the cloth in place. His body shielded both from the falling snow, kept the rag dry. He glanced both ways along the wall—nothing stupid hick wasn't going to come but he would come later bet your ass he'd come later when he heard them yelling in there when the fire bomb exploded in there when they started dying in there—and then glanced up again at the stained-glass window. The need shouted, shouted, and his breathing grew heavier; the skull grin reformed on his mouth.

All right all *right.*

Kubion brought his left hand up and fumbled for the box of wooden matches in his shirt pocket.

Cain, leaving Tribucci, crawled back against the padded seat of the snowmobile. He peered closely at the dashboard, ran gloved fingers over both handlebars and located clutch, throttle, gearshift, brake. He had driven a snowmobile only once in his life, two winters before when he and Angie and the Collinses had spent a weekend at Mammoth Mountain; but they were simpler to operate than a car, and it had taken him, that time, no more than a minute to get the knack of it.

He leaned his shoulder hard against the seat, gripped the windshield in his left hand, and shoved upward. The machine rose, tilted, dropped with a flat heavy thud on its skis and roller treads. Cain waited for half a dozen heartbeats, but the shadows at the rear corner remained substantially solid. He opened the top three buttons of his coat, tucked the Walther into his belt, and then wrapped his left hand around the near handlebar and engaged the clutch lever; his right moved along the dash to the starter button, pressed it. The headlights dimmed slightly as the engine coughed stuttering to life, brightened again as the stuttering smoothed into a stabilized rumble.

Still nothing at the corner.

Cain lifted a leg over the seat, maintaining his grip on the clutch lever, and pulled himself into a hunched sitting position. He caught hold of the right handlebar, shifted into forward, opened quarter throttle, and let the clutch out slowly. The machine began to move forward. He spun a sharp turn to the northwest, spraying snow, and made sure he had full control before opening the throttle wider. Nearly abreast of the rear corner, he made another looping turn to the south; straightened out. The headlights were like probing yellow blades slicing into the night's dark fabric, and he could see all the area between church and cottage. No sign of the psycho. He'd gone around on the south side then, maybe all the way around to the front; whatever he'd been carrying in that sack was bound to be lethal, and God, if he had time to open the locked front door....

Grimly, Cain give the snowmobile full-bore throttle and sent it skimming to the south equidistant between the two buildings, leaning his head out to the left because frozen snow and the webbed bullet hole made the windshield impenetrable. When he came on the south corner, he circled out and made another hard skidding left.

And the sweeping beams found Kubion in close to the wall, halfway toward the front.

Having heard the engine, having seen the headlamp glow before the gleaming shafts cut around to him, he was backing away rapidly: sooty face nakedly hideous, right arm locked, gun leveled, left arm cradling a quart jar with a rag hanging down out of it like a brown-spotted tongue. Fire bomb, Cain thought, oh Jesus—and Kubion dipped his face along his upper right arm, to shield his eyes from the blinding light, and squeezed off a wild shot. Cain snapped his head back partway, hunching his body lower, gripping the handlebars with such pressure that his wrists ached and he could feel, vaguely, pain surge again through the glass cut in his right palm.

Kubion fired again, there was a screeching fingernails-on-a-blackboard sound as the bullet scraped a furrow across the right front edge of the cowl, and then Cain saw him glance feverishly over his shoulder and come to the realization that he was not going to be able to beat the onrushing machine to the front corner. He jerked to a stop, limned against the wall like a spotlighted deer, and triggered a third shot that sang high over Cain's head. The snowmobile was almost on top of him now.

Dropping the jar, twisting his body, he flung himself out of the way.

Cain tried to turn into him, missed by a foot and went by. He braked immediately, frenziedly, and swung the snowmobile in a tight turn, saw that Kubion had landed on both knees and was struggling up. The moment the head lights repinned him, Cain opened the throttle wide again. Kubion staggered sideways in the deep snow, lifted the automatic and fired a fourth time; glass shattered and the left beam winked out. But Cain sustained control, the snowmobile bore down relentlessly.

Kubion slowed and tensed for another leap. This time Cain was ready.

Almost upsetting the machine, he veered in the same direction—toward the church—at the instant Kubion made his jump. Kubion's right foot came down, left leg trailing aslant; the upthrust, rounded metal guard on the right ski hit flesh, snapped bone, just below the knee and sent him spinning and rolling violently through the snow.

Pain lanced white-hot in Kubion's leg and groin and lower belly, and ice granules filled his open mouth and pricked like slivers in his lungs. He came up finally on his buttocks, coughing, sucking breath, clawing at his eyes. The snowmobile, ten yards away, was swinging around once more and he heard the shrill howl of its engine as the single high-beam light struck him, again half blinded him.

Inside his head the impulse screamed and screamed and screamed—snowmobile hick son of a bitch with snowmobile Jesus Christ why won't things stop screwing up ten feet tall you *can't* do this to me kill you kill your snowmobile kill you all kill—and he twisted over onto his right knee, left leg useless, bones broken and grating, pain pulsing, and brought his right arm up

and he didn't have the automatic,

he had lost the frigging *gun,*

and the screaming was a rage of sound, the snowmobile's engine was a rage of sound, glaring yellow eye hurtling down on him and he pitched his body flat and rolled and rolled but then the screaming in his head and the screaming of the machine blended into one and a new, supreme agony exploded in the small of his back, surging metal hurled him broken-doll-like toward the church wall. His head struck the icy wood jarringly, more agony bursting like shrapnel through his brain. He lifted onto his right hand and tried to stand up, tried to just kneel, but his body was all searing pain, paralyzed by pain.

Six feet away the snowmobile had come to a stop, its one headlight shining over his head, and dimly he saw Cain rise up out of it, saw the gun in his gloved fingers as he came slowly forward. Spittle drooled from the corners of Kubion's mouth, freezing there, and he thought *You won't shoot Eskimo snowmobile shit not face to face;* began screaming aloud then, screaming, "Won't shoot hick bastard won't do it oh you fucking—"

Cain shot him three times in the head at point-blank range.

# Twenty-Four

They heard inside the church the initial exchange of shots, and they heard the accelerated whine of the snowmobile's engine, and they heard those final three, close-spaced reports beyond the south wall. A kind of breathless paralysis succeeded the first and carried them through the second, but when the last came and was followed by silence from without, the thin edge of panic finally crumbled away.

Bodies massed confusedly toward the front; there was a rising torrent of sounds and cries. Ann's newborn daughter began to wail. Gibbering, Frank McNeil stumbled onto the pulpit and tried to force his way into the vestry past Joe Garvey; Garvey threw him against the wall, hit him in the stomach in a release of pent-up emotion, and McNeil went down gasping and moaning and lay with his hands over his head. Coopersmith stood back hard against the entrance doors, arms spread, and shouted, "Stay calm, for God's sake stay calm, we don't know what's happening, we've got enough people hurt as it is!"

They didn't listen to him; they did not even hear him. They had lived in fear of the worst for all the long, long hours, and they expected the worst now. Have to get out! their faces said. Going to be killed anyway, have to get out....

Heavy footfalls on the stairs outside—and the a voice, a voice wearily raised no more than a few decibels above normal but still loud enough so that almost everyone could hear it and recognize it. That voice did what no other but one could have: it froze them all in place again, it stilled them, it transformed terror into incipient relief.

"This is Cain," the voice said. "This is Cain, I've got the key and I'm going to open the doors, give me room."

Key scraping the lock as Coopersmith swept them back, clearing space; doors opening.

Cain stood there with his feet braced apart and the limp form of John Tribucci cradled close to his chest. "They're dead, all three of them," he said. "You're free now, they're dead."

And the people of Hidden Valley surged around him like waves around a pinnacle of rock.

# Twenty-Five

For the first few seconds after consciousness returned fuzzy and disjointed, Tribucci did not know where he was. Someone was holding his hand, chafing it briskly, and there were faint garbled voices, and there was softness beneath him and warmth over and around him. He had no pain, only a tingling semi-numbness everywhere except in his face and in the hand that was being rubbed. Cain! he thought immediately, and made a noise far down in his throat, and wanted to sit up. Gentle hands held him still.

He fluttered his eyes open. Bright shimmering grayness, but then dissolving and images beginning to take shape—pale blue walls, fluorescent ceiling lights, face hovering over him as if disembodied and saying words that now he could comprehend: "Johnny, it's all right. You're in my emergency room, son, it's all right."

He squeezed his eyes shut, opened them again, and this time he could see more clearly. His throat worked. "Webb?"

"Yes, it's Webb."

"You... you're out of the church...."

"All of us, Johnny—we're all safe. Cain too."

"Thank God. But how? How did Cain...?"

"There's no time for explanations now. Sally and I are going to put you under anesthesia; you've got two bullets in you, and we've got to get them out. But we wanted you awake first, there's something you have to know."

*Ann,* he thought suddenly. "Oh, God, Ann, what about Ann, she—"

"She's fine, she's upstairs in my room; I gave her something to make her sleep. Johnny, listen carefully: Ann is fine. When she found out in the church what you and Cain had gone to do, she went into labor. And she gave birth; she gave birth there in the church to a healthy little girl. Do you understand, Johnny? Ann's fine and the baby's fine, you've got a daughter."

The fuzziness would not release his thoughts, but he understood, yes, and he tried to smile, lips cracking and stretching faintly. "A daughter," he said. "Ann's fine and we have a daughter."

"That's right, that's good. You've got everything to live for now. You're badly hurt, but you're going to live, you're going to keep on fighting; you're not going to stop fighting for a second, Johnny, do you hear me?"

"Not for a second," he said.

Edwards sighed softly and his face retreated, and Sally Chilton's wavered into Tribucci's vision. He felt the sting of a needle in the crook of his left arm.

"She looks like Ann, doesn't she?" he asked.

"Just like Ann," Sally said. "Wait until you see her."

Tribucci felt himself beginning to drift. "Marika," he said, "we're going to name her Marika." Drifting, drifting—and his last thought before the anesthesia took him under was that if it had been a boy, they would surely have called him Zachary....

The Reverend Peter Keyes waited in the adjacent anteroom, his now professionally, if hurriedly, bandaged right hand resting in his lap, left hand clutching his Bible. The shot of morphine Sally had given him minutes ago, to ease the pain, had also made him drowsy; but he would not sleep yet—not yet.

After a time, eyes tightly closed, he raised the Bible and held it against his breast. "Oh Lord my rock," he said aloud, softly, "thank you for not forsaking us all...."

In the parlor at the front of the house, Coopersmith sat in silent vigil with Ellen and with Vince and Judy.

As soon as Edwards came in to tell them Johnny was going to live—and he *would* tell them that, a man who had been through what Tribucci had would not be allowed to die now—Coopersmith thought he would find Cain and try to put into words some of what he felt in his heart. He had never had a feeling of love for a man before, other than his two sons; but now, tonight, he loved both Cain and John Tribucci. All the hate and all the pressure and all the terror were gone; tomorrow there would be pain and sorrow when he woke and remembered and saw the ravaged face of a Hidden Valley that would never be quite the same again—yet for what was left of this day, he would have nothing except love inside him.

Sitting there with Ellen's head against his shoulder, he was very tired—a physical weariness, nothing more. When the hate and terror drained away, they had carried with them the inner tiredness and the last remnants of those earlier feelings of uselessness and incompetence and emptiness. And he would not let them come back, any of them. He was sixty-six years of age, that was true, but he had lived a long and rich and fruitful life, and he was *still* living it, and he had his health and all his faculties, and he had the capacity to love, and he had the reciprocal love of an unselfish woman who had shared his bed and his dreams and his rewards for more than forty years. He hadn't realized it before, but that was so much more than some men had. So much more.

He smiled wanly across at Vince and Judy, gave them an encouraging nod, and they returned both in kind. Like him, they seemed to know that death and tragedy would not touch any of them again for some time to come.

And within the semi-darkened church, sitting slumped and thinking about many things and about nothing at all, Cain did not hear the doors open or the soft steps come forward to the pew. But after a time he sensed that he was not alone and turned his head, and Rebecca was standing there watching him.

"Hello, Zachary," she said. She was drawn and grave, but there was a kind of self-assurance, a kind of pride, in her eyes and in her carriage. "I thought you might still be here."

"Yeah," he said. "I was going to leave pretty soon, I want to find out how Tribucci is."

"I just came from Dr. Edwards' house. He's operating now to remove the bullets. He wants Johnny in a hospital as soon as possible because of the threat of pneumonia; Greg Novak is taking one of the snowmobiles to Coldville at dawn, so there'll be helicopters in some time tomorrow."

"He'll live," Cain said positively. "He'll live."

"I know he will; we all do."

"He's a fine man. They don't come any finer."

Rebecca sat down beside him, turning her body so that she was facing him directly. "You look exhausted, Zachary."

"I killed two men tonight," he said. There was nothing, no expression, in his voice.

"And saved seventy-five other lives. That's the only really important thing, isn't it?"

"Yes—it has to be."

"I don't suppose any of us will ever really forget what happened today," she said. "But I've got to believe that things do stop hurting after a while."

"They do," Cain told her. "After a while."

"Will you... keep on living here in the valley?"

"No," he said. "No."

"Where will you go?"

"Back to San Francisco."

"And then what?"

"See if I can get my old job back, or one like it. Start rebuilding my life."

"I'm not so sure I can keep on living here either. Too much has happened, too many things have changed." She paused. "What's San Francisco like?"

"It can be a beautiful city—the most beautiful city in the world."

"Would I like it if I came there?"

He looked at her for a long moment. "I think so," he said finally. "I think you might."

"I'll be staying at the Tribucci house for a few days," she said, "with Judy and Ann and the baby. Vince will go with Johnny. Now especially it's a time none of us should be alone."

He waited, not speaking.

"Will you come for dinner tomorrow?"

"Yes," he said, "I'd like that."

"Will you walk me there now?"

Cain nodded, and they stood together and strode slowly out of the church. It was still snowing lightly, but there was very little wind; the clouds overhead had begun dividing, and you could see patches of deep velvet sky through the fissures. The storm was nearly over.

In a few short hours it would be the day before Christmas.

## THE END

# games

By Bill Pronzini

*For the memory of my father,*
*Joseph Pronzini*
*(1908 – 1973)*

204BILL PRONZINI

# PROLOGUE

Friday, May 8:
WASHINGTON

*One must test oneself to see if one is meant for independence and for command. And one must do it at the right time. Never avoid your tests, though they may be the most dangerous game you can play, and in the end are merely tests at which you are the only witness and the sole judge.*

—NIETZSCHE, *Beyond Good and Evil*

□ □ □

In the private office of his suite on Capitol Hill, Senator David Jackman sat brooding out the window adjacent to his desk, elbows resting on the padded arms of his chair, fingers laced under his chin. A light rain pattered softly against the glass, slid down it in intricate configurations. The rain had been falling steadily for five days now, and it was beginning to depress him; Washington under wet skies was the grayest place in the world.

He swiveled abruptly to the desk, and his gaze moved in a restless turn around the office. Heavy, dark wood paneling and furnishings. Old-burgundy carpet. Bookshelves floor to ceiling on two walls. Subdued lighting, an absence of bright color. The overall effect was one of pure functionalism: no frills of any kind. On days such as this, however, it also developed an aura of mustiness, of almost Victorian austerity, like something out of Dickens.

His eyes lowered to the desktop and then held on the two framed photographs arranged side by side on the polished surface: one of Meg, taken ten years ago when there had been no artifice in her smile, no cupidity behind the guileless brown eyes; one of himself and the Old Man, taken in 1966 on the island.

It was amazing how much he looked like the Old Man, Jackman thought. Same long, broad, ascetic face. Same carefully brushed, carefully trimmed black hair. Same intelligent, alert expression and strong jaw and gleaming white teeth. Two generations of clean-cut, all-American men; good men, perhaps even great men, bearing the weight of public office on their squared shoulders, standing tall and indomitable and forever prepared to fight with unselfish zeal for the vital needs and causes of the country, of the world.

Bullshit, he thought.

And even though he did not turn his head, he was aware in that moment of the two dozen black-and-white film stills on the wall behind him. *I, Camera,*

*Eye:* an artistic, impressionistic slice of life seen from the interchanging points of view of a man and a camera, the man as a camera, the camera as a sentient eye. He had written it, directed it, and coproduced it with three friends in college in the late fifties, and it had won honorable mention at Cannes and been favorably received at the New York and San Francisco film festivals. The critics had said it showed great promise; the critics had said they were eager to see his next film. Only there had not been a next film. The Old Man had seen to that.

And here I am, he thought. For better and for worse, a mediocre and slightly tarnished, if conscientious, champion of the people. *I, Senator, Aye.*

He massaged his temples: his head ached dully. Christ, it had been a long day. Morning meeting of the D.C. Committee, at which two representatives of the NAACP had demanded that something be done about the severe underrepresentation of blacks on the Washington police force. Lunch with two Maine congressmen to discuss reforestation policies. A quorum call this afternoon for the military aid to Lebanon bill, and then a conference with two of his aides who were trying to convince him to attend a campaign-deficit dinner in California next month. Smile and agree, smile and disagree; silence when necessary, eloquence when necessary. Honest manipulation, forthright maneuvering. Move and countermove.

*It's all a game, David, never forget that. Life, love, politics—just games. Once you learn how to play them, once you become an accomplished gamesman, you'll never have to look up at any man or back on any decision.*

If he concentrated Jackman could hear, echoing in the dim corners of memory, the Old Man's voice saying those words a quarter of a century ago. Those words, and others like them. The Philosophy of Thomas R. Jackman, United States Senator and Unsuccessful Aspirant for the Presidency, Now Deceased. Maybe I ought to have that philosophy engraved on a plaque that I can hang in here next to my law degree, he thought, not for the first time and not frivolously.

Because the thing was, the Old Man had spoken the truth. Which was ironic when you considered that he had spent his career in the Senate bending and reshaping truth and honor to his own ends, making up his own rules for the games he played. Jackman recalled the Wendell Phillips quote again: "You can always get the truth from an American statesman after he has turned seventy, or given up all hope for the Presidency." Except that Thomas R. Jackman had died of a heart attack at the age of sixty-four, while engaged in yet another futile drive for a presidential nomination.

Still, the philosophy itself was basically valid. Everything *was* a game; you could translate any situation, any goal, any facet of life, into those terms. Play the games well and you were a winner; play them poorly and you were a loser. Simple as that. And Jackman had learned to play them well, all right—learned the intricacies and the strategies and the nuances. The only difference between him and his father was that he played by constitutional and lawful and mostly ethical rules rather than by rules he and he alone devised. Even his

opponents in and out of politics, men like James Turner and Alan Pennix who
bitterly refuted his liberal policies and spoke out against the "Jackman family
dynasty," had not been able to label him a total simulacrum of his father....

The intercom burred: his secretary, Miss Bigelow. Loyal and competent,
Bigelow, if not much in the way of window dressing; she was fifty-four, going
to fat in the middle and hips, and had a pronounced mustache because she had
stopped using depilatories when she reached the five-decade mark. He had
inherited her from the Old Man, for whom she had worked during the fifteen
years prior to his death: she was a team player all the way.

"Yes?"

"Your wife called, Senator."

"Called? She didn't ask to speak with me?"

"No sir, she said it wasn't necessary. She left a message."

"All right."

"She's decided to attend the Women's Caucus benefit tonight," Miss Bigelow
said. "She expects to be home rather late."

"I see. Was that all?"

"No. She asked that I tell you she made airline reservations for Boston this
afternoon. United Flight Fifteen, leaving May twenty-first at seven-thirty P.M.
You're to call her father if you feel you can get away."

Memorial Day weekend near Boston, with Meg's stuffy family on their stuffy
estate. Or was that really where she was going? She knew he had no intention of joining her there; he had made that clear to her when they discussed
the subject earlier in the week. Meg was very good at game-playing too, which
was one of the reasons why he had been attracted to her in the beginning.

"Fine," he said. "Thank you, Elaine."

He sat for a moment and then swiveled his chair again and looked at the
window, watched the rain stream down the pane, the grayness beyond. Memorial Day weekend. Three long days, free days, because he had no pressing
engagements. And he thought about sun, and about the smell of pines and the
smell of the sea, and about the summers of his youth.

He thought about the island.

□ □ □

It was 7:10 P.M. when Jackman left the Senate Office Building and picked up
his car and drove across the city. The headlights on the two-year-old Dodge
illuminated the misty rain, turned the droplets into glistening particles of silver, reflected blurrily off the wet street.

After twenty-five minutes he slowed at an intersection, swung into another
street, and drifted in to the curb in front of the third building on the right side
of the block. This was one of Washington's better neighborhoods, quiet and
expensive, not far from the Potomac; the building was ivied, and there was an
arched front door and round-topped windows and hanging carriage lamps—
not unlike the house in which he and Meg lived in Georgetown. Add a

sycamore here, a Dutch elm there, a decorative fountain in the center of a curving front drive, and he might have been coming home.

Might have been. Coming home.

He shut off the engine, the headlights, and got out into the drizzle and locked the doors and then ran up onto the colonnaded porch. There were two flats in the building; he rang the bell for the top one. A moment later the door buzzed softly, and he went inside and climbed the stairs two at a time.

Tracy was there and waiting for him, as Meg so seldom had been these past few years.

□ □ □

Like everything else, sex was a game. When two people played it well together, it was very good; and the aftermath was warm and filled with sweet fragrances and a kind of luxuriant repose. It had been that way with Meg at first, but not anymore; she played the sex game, at least with him, out of necessity rather than pleasure, duty rather than love or affection. Not so Tracy. Tracy took as much joy in giving as in receiving, and her enthusiasm and her inventiveness were boundless. You could immerse yourself in her. In Meg, you could only float emptily on the surface of feeling.

They lay quiescent in Tracy's bed, her head cradled against his chest, and he stroked her hair gently with the tips of his fingers. The room was feminine, but without coyness, and tastefully decorated in lavenders and whites. The only light came from a small, low-wattage bedside lamp.

After a while he said, "I've been thinking."

"That's good."

"Specifically, I mean, about Memorial Day weekend. I'd like to get away for it—a short vacation. I haven't had even that for months now. Senators should have vacations every now and then, don't you think?"

"Absolutely," Tracy said. "They absolutely should."

"How would you like to join me?"

"I'd like that very much. Can we arrange it?"

"We can."

"Did you have some place particular in mind?"

"Particular, and private. A private island."

"I didn't know there were such things anymore."

"There are lots of them off the north coast of Maine," Jackman said. "I seem to have co-inherited one, as a matter of fact."

She leaned up on one elbow so that she could look down into his face. "Are you serious, David?"

"Politicians are always serious."

"I didn't know you had an island."

"I don't advertise the fact."

"What sort of island is it?"

"Oh, not much as islands go. About three square miles, covered mostly by pine and spruce forest. My father bought it in the thirties and built a summer home on it; I spent most of my boyhood summers there. I haven't gone much since he died. Meg doesn't like islands."

"I love islands," Tracy said.

"So do I. We'll love it together Memorial Day weekend."

"It occurs to me that you must have someone living there the year round. You'd hardly leave a summer home unattended on a private island."

"There's a caretaker—the same one my father hired in 1937."

A puckish smile. "And he approves of you bringing your mistresses up for weekends?"

"You make it sound as if I've had a string a mile long."

"Haven't you?"

"No," he said seriously, and thought but did not say: There has only been you and a girl named Alicia, only two. "What I usually do is to wire a message to him in Weymouth Village a few days ahead and let him know I'm coming—"

"*Wire* a message?"

"There aren't any telephones on the island."

"How come?"

"Too far out from the mainland, for one thing. For another, my father didn't care to have his summers cluttered up with a lot of unimportant political and private business. Messages, important or otherwise, have always been taken out by boat from the village."

"Wow—the nineteenth century still lives."

"You won't think so after you've seen the house," he said. "Anyhow, if I tell the caretaker, Jonas, that I don't want to be disturbed, he'll take the family boat in to Weymouth and leave it in a boathouse we rent there. When I leave we reverse the procedure. Generally I look him up to say hello, but he won't think anything of it if I don't."

"So we'll be completely alone together."

"Just us, and the seabirds and the little beasties that live in the piny woods."

"It sounds idyllic."

"It is. Settled, then?"

"What about your wife?"

Liberated woman, Tracy: direct, frank, no mincing of words. Not at all like Meg, who played all of her games by circumlocution and euphemism. Jackman liked directness, had always liked it. Tracy was the kind of woman, in fact, that had appealed to him strongly since puberty; strange, then, now that he considered it, that he should have married someone like Meg. And why *had* he married Meg? They had had game-playing in common, but little else; and the love he had thought was binding had turned out to be weak and tenuous. They had grown in opposite directions, grown out of love and into an arrangement: no divorce by mutual consent, because it might harm both their images; elaborate pretenses at public and family functions and at media interviews; lovers acceptable by tacit agreement, just so long as the affairs were carried on with the utmost discretion. It was probably a good thing, he thought, that she had been born with a tipped uterus. Children would not have cemented their marriage, and children do not flourish in an arrangement....

"David?"

"Sorry," he said. "I was woolgathering. Don't worry about Meg; she's going to spend Memorial Day with her family in Boston. Or so she says."

"Then it's settled. When do we leave?"

"Friday the twenty-second, early morning?"

"Beautiful."

"We'll take separate seats on a flight to Bangor," he said. "Then we'll rent a car, or you will, and we'll drive up the coast—"

He stopped, because in that moment, with sudden objectivity, he saw and heard himself: United States Senator David Jackman, friend of the people, hater of political chicanery, deeply involved in just causes, lying naked in the bed and arms of a woman who was not his wife and planning a furtive weekend. God! It might have been funny in an ironic sense, like JFK's amorous adventures, but he could not seem to rationalize it that way. Not funny—pathetic, a little disgusting.

And then he thought: For Christ's sake, it's just a game—and the moment passed. Just a game: not one he wanted to play, one he was *forced* to play. Nothing to do with politics, that was a different game entirely. You had to play thousands of games during the course of a lifetime, and if one of them was less than moral or honorable, it could be forgiven, it did not have to affect the individual as a whole.

Tracy seemed to think he had finished naturally. She said, "And we'll spend the entire weekend balling, maybe even out among those beasties in the piny woods."

She sounded pleased and excited, and he told himself he felt the same way; in her arms he had lost the depression caused by the rain, and now he had the weekend, and Tracy, and the island to look forward to. "Yes," he said. "Anywhere you want, Ty. Anytime."

But when she laughed and said "How about again right now?" and drew his head to her breasts, the only real anticipation in him was for the island itself, and he had, inexplicably, the same vague kind of lost and lonely feeling he had experienced sometimes as a child.

# PART ONE

Friday, May 22:
THE ISLAND

*There is the isle of tombs, the silent isle; there too are the tombs of my youth. There I wish to carry an evergreen wreath of life.*
—NIETZSCHE, "The Tomb Song," *Thus Spoke Zarathustra*

Over the hammering pulse of the boat engine, Jackman said, "There it is, dead ahead."

From this distance the island appeared long and flattened down, fitted to the juncture of bright blue water and pale blue sky; the gradual hump to the right of center was ascendant forestland and the jagged line of cliffs which rose a hundred feet above sea level and formed part of the southern, seaward shore. Oblong in shape, as were most of these Maine coastal islands, it ran two miles northeast-southwest and slightly more than a mile northwest-southeast. The pine and spruce woods covering roughly three-quarters of its surface were a brownish-green smear through the late-afternoon haze.

Beside him at the wheel, Tracy leaned forward with her hands on top of the open windscreen. "How far away is it, David?"

"More than a mile." *Watch it grow, boy,* the Old Man had told him at the beginning of one of those long-ago childhood summers. *It grows right before your eyes.* "Watch it grow," Jackman said to her.

Except for the plumelike fan of the cruiser's wake, the surface of the sea was flat and unruffled; the day was unseasonably warm, temperature in the high seventies, windless. The smell of salt was so sharp that you felt as though you could taste it. Gulls wheeled in lazy circles overhead, but nothing else moved, no other boat.

The cruiser—a nineteen-foot Chris-Craft, mahogany finish and brightwork gleaming in the sun—planed smoothly past two bare-rock islets and drew abeam of another, wooded one to starboard. This area of the coast, north of Bar Harbor, was a bay of islands—more like a lake district, with its calm waters and archipelagic acres of woods and meadowland, than a part of the Atlantic Ocean. Jackman Island, nine and a half miles from the mainland, was farther out and somewhat more isolated than most.

The coastline itself was a complex labyrinth of bays and headlands, and the drive from Bangor, once they had left State Route 1, had taken them alongside and across saltwater inlets and marshes, bridges and causeways, peninsulas and inshore islands. Jackman remembered the drive with pleasure: sun and shadow, sea and sky, the cool salt breeze and the cries of gulls and great blue herons. All such a long, long way from Washington.

They had gotten to Weymouth Village shortly past three o'clock. Jackman had not been there in nearly two years, but it hadn't changed any in that time; it hadn't really changed any that he could recall since his first summer visit at the age of nine—aloof from progress, unspoiled by tourism. The nineteenth-century church and schoolhouse, the birdlimed Civil War monument in the village green, the line of old white houses ringing the narrow harbor, the clustered masts of the lobster boats bows-on to the tide, and the grizzled men who owned them grouped along the wharf to take in the sun: peaceful, what had once been called quaint before that word became overused. The Jackman family boathouse was on the northeastern side of the harbor, and the Chris-Craft had been locked inside when he and Tracy got there. Jonas, the caretaker, had not been around, nor had anyone else. Wearing sunglasses and the brand-new sports outfit, complete with canvas shoes and a jaunty sailor's cap, which Tracy had presented to him as a "weekend gift" the night before, Jackman had felt both a little foolish and a little furtive—the first attack of conscience he had suffered since the one in Tracy's flat two weeks ago.

As the boat drew closer, now, the island took on familiar contours: the cobble beaches and mudflats of the sheltered north shore, visible because the tide was at ebb; the dense pine and spruce forest, studded here and there with oak and white birch; the rocky cliffs and headlands, wet with spray from the open sea; off the southwest shore, the four tiny satellite islands, only one of which was large enough to support vegetation. The summerhouse and the wide bay, which it overlooked on the northwest shore, were still hidden by trees and by the long arm of land the Old Man had christened Eider Neck in honor of the ducks that nested there.

Approaching the island again after two years, Jackman found himself pervaded with nostalgia and a sense of wellbeing, and he wondered why he had denied this to himself for so long. It was the one place he felt truly at home, the one place he knew better than any other, and loved, and could become one with. Meg hated it because of its isolation, its primitive nature—the precise reasons why it attracted him. Opposites in every meaningful way, it seemed, he and Meg. Opponents. He would have found time to come to the island often if she had shared his feelings; as it was, he should have found time to come alone.

"Where do we land?" Tracy asked. "That shore looks pretty rocky."

"There's a bay around that arm of land there on our left, Eider Neck. It's one of only two places you can put a boat in to the island; the other one is around on the east shore. There are ledges jumbled everywhere else. You can see some of them when we get closer: it's low tide."

"Is that where the house is, at the bay?"

"Yes."

Jackman cut the wheel to port, to make the loop around the rock- and mead-

ow-carpeted hump of Eider Neck. There was still no other craft in the vicinity, and the aura of vast sun-swept emptiness, of being utterly alone, was enormous; and yet, there was no loneliness in it. Out here, Jackman had never felt
alone in any way.

The long ragged sweep of the headland on the far side of the bay came into
view as they neared the tip of the Neck, running at right angles to it several
hundred yards offshore to avoid the ledges and the uncovered mudflats. The
rich resin scent of the evergreens carried to him on the warm air—a sweet fra-
grance like that of Tracy, or Meg in the early years, after they had finished making love. Jackman's throat felt curiously dry.

Then he could see the bay, and the boathouse at the end of the wooden dock,
and the three white buildings set on high ground two hundred yards inland
from the half-moon, shale-and-cobblestone beach. A clipped, sloping lawn
stretched between the house and the beach, dotted with ornate black-iron
poles on which carriage-style lanterns had been hung in the old days; they
resembled, at least to Jackman's mind, uniform pieces scattered on a bright
green gameboard. Pine and spruce made a dark green backdrop to the northeast, east and south. Cleared paths, two of several on the island, wound
upward and away through the trees on both inner sides of the cove.

The Old Man had modeled the summerhouse after post-Revolution Maine
cottages, only double the normal size because that was the way he had always
done things. It had sixteen rooms, four fireplaces, a sharp-pitched roof, narrow
oblong windows—but he had spoiled the replica by adding a wide, pillared
veranda onto the whole of the front. The much smaller swelling a hundred
yards to the north and fifty yards below the main house was of a simple frame
type, built on a fieldstone foundation; this was where Jonas lived with his
wife. The other building, behind and to the southeast of the house, was a combination woodshed and storage barn.

Jackman took the boat carefully into the bay, cutting power, and angled it
across toward the boathouse. The wide entrance doors were latched open.
When he maneuvered the Chris-Craft inside, Tracy, good sailor, jumped onto
the narrow platform along the left-hand wall and made the bowline fast. He
shut down the engine, swung their bags onto the walk, tied the stern line, and
moved back to pull the doors closed with a long hooked pole kept there for
that purpose. Then they went out onto and along the dock, Jackman porter-
ing.

"That's quite a summerhouse," Tracy said. "It looks big enough to subdivide."

"My father liked a lot of room and a lot of people around, even in the summer," Jackman said. "We always had house guests, and two or three parties a
week. Catered, for God's sake."

"The good old carefree days."

"For me, maybe, growing up. Not for the world at large; we were at war part
of that time." The Old Man fiddling while the whole world damned near
burned, he thought. Liquor flowing while blood flowed on alien soil; mourning in radio speeches the American loss of life on Guam and Leyte and the

beaches at Anzio, with a Maine suntan and a voice made husky by too many gin rickeys and too much island laughter. And I wonder what would have happened to this country if Thomas R. Jackman had succeeded in his ambition to become President?

They came down off the dock and onto the path that skirted the rim of the beach. Seaweed and driftwood layover and among the rocks, deposited by high tides; the remains of two dead flounder added a faint stench of decay to the salt-and-evergreen scent. When they were opposite the house, Jackman led the way off the path and across the lawn and up onto the veranda.

The front door opened into a large foyer: an antique table and a gilt-framed mirror, a pegged coat rack in lieu of a closet, the staircase to the upper floor. To the right was a wide archway, and they went through there and into the parlor. This room was large enough to sit and stand thirty people comfortably; it had paneled walls and pine flooring, leather furniture, brass accessories, heavy wool-twist rugs, an antique grandfather's clock, a standing leather-fronted bar in the far corner. A native-stone fireplace covered most of the inner wall lengthwise.

He put their bags down beside the couch and then stood still for a moment. In his mind he could hear the ghostly echo of voices and clinking glasses and the muted strains of "Over the Rainbow" and "Twilight Time" as they had been played by the three-piece band the Old Man had hired out of Milbridge. Empty and immaculate, the room felt incomplete. An atmosphere of waiting seemed to linger within it, as if it needed people, gaiety, life, to give it a life of its own.

But the old days were dead and gone, buried along with the Old Man and with his submissive and perpetually smiling wife, who had preceded him to the grave by six years. Jackman's older brother, Dale, a New York cliff dweller who had forsaken politics for the parallel game of Big Business, brought his wife and family here for the month of July every year; and Jackman himself had come exactly five times since the Old Man's fatal heart attack eight years before. Aside from these visits, and aside from periodic dustings by Jonas' wife, the house stood deserted and alone: watching the seasons come and the seasons go....

He asked Tracy, "What do you think so far?"

"Impressive. When do the caterers arrive for us?"

He laughed. "Drink first, or the grand tour?"

"How about both? I'm thirsty *and* curious."

"Fair enough. Old-fashioned?"

"No, liberated." Standard joke between them.

Jackman went behind the bar—well-stocked as always, plenty of fresh ice in the portable icemaker—and made an old-fashioned for Tracy and a rum tonic for himself. Then, carrying their drinks, they went up the staircase to the second floor.

Two guest bedrooms, each with a private bath. Servants' quarters. Storage room. Master bedroom: canopied four-poster his mother had bought in a shop in Bar Harbor and which the Old Man had said was "too damned flimsy for a marital couch"; white rugs on the floor, white lace curtains. She had made this room her own, if none other in the house and little else in her married life.

Standing in the doorway, Tracy said, "God, it looks bloody virginal. We're not going to sleep here, are we?"

Jackman gave her an uncomfortable glance. Showing her these upstairs rooms, he had developed a vague feeling of guilt, as though he were committing a sacrilege by bringing a woman who was not his wife into the house—as though the house itself realized this, and disapproved, and transmitted that disapproval to him by osmosis. What would the Old Man have said about Tracy? Well, the Old Man had not exactly been a paragon of fidelity, if you could believe the rumors about him—and you almost certainly could. So he would probably have smiled in his sly way, given a knowing wink, and: *Just another game, David, a harmless diversion. Play and enjoy. But be careful of your moves....*

"No," Jackman said. "Not here. We'll use one of the guest rooms, the biggest one down at the end of the hall."

He took her into Dale's room. Walls covered with Harvard pennants, the model ship he had built one summer still sitting in the middle of the writing desk. Then, finally, they entered Jackman's boyhood room. Familiar view of the bay and Eider Neck and the island-dotted waters beyond, books placed neatly on the shelves against one wall: biographies of historical figures, volumes dealing with cinematography and film technique, adventure and classic novels, the collected works of Lewis Carroll bound in worn leather. Everything just as it had always been, because neither he nor Dale had wanted it changed. The memories of this place were too good and too perfect to want for alteration of any kind.

Tracy picked out one of the leather tomes. "I didn't know you were into Lewis Carroll."

"Pretty heavily a long time ago," he said, and smiled, and felt himself relaxing again. "'Twas brillig, and the slithy toves/Did gyre and gimbel in the wabe;/All mimsy were the borogoves'—"

"—'And the mome raths outgrabe,'" she said. "I was weaned on 'Jabberwocky.'"

"Can you still recite the whole poem?"

"I think so. Can you?"

"Well let's see...."

He began to quote as they went out into the hall again, and Tracy joined in, and the only line they stumbled over was "Long time the manxome foe he sought—" By the time they were finished, he had taken her through the library downstairs—hundreds of books, all of them law texts or political treatises; no fiction because the Old Man had been too unimaginative and too much of a plotter himself to take pleasure from the mind games of others—and then into the study.

This had been Thomas Jackman's retreat, and it was a completely masculine but somehow cold and impersonal room, as if it had been contrived to fit an image rather than suited naturally to a man's personality. Deep leather chairs, hunting prints, primitive art, the traditional stag's head mounted on the wall over the massive oak desk, the—

Jackman stopped five paces into the room, frowning. "Now that's odd," he said.

"What is?"

He pointed across to the free-standing, glass-door cabinet opposite the desk. The doors were open wide, and the cabinet was empty. "My father kept his collection of guns in there," he said. "Half a dozen rifles—he had deer brought to the island when he bought it—and twenty or so handguns."

"Well maybe the caretaker took them out to clean them, or whatever else it is you do with guns."

"I suppose so."

But he was thinking that Jonas was a fussy sort and so was his wife. He couldn't imagine either of them leaving the doors standing open like that. And there were gun oil and rags and such in the drawer at the bottom of the cabinet; Jonas wouldn't have had any reason that Jackman could see to take the weapons to his own house, or away with him to the mainland.

Someone else—an intruder?

No, of course not. Jonas never allowed visitors without direct permission, and he invariably made the rounds before he left the island. He wouldn't have left at all if there had been trespassers or indications of trespassers. Still, someone *could* have landed a boat illegally at the cove on the east shore, after Jonas and his wife had gone....

Well Christ, Jackman thought, there hadn't been any sign of forcible entry and nothing else was missing or out of place in the house. Prowlers would have taken other things besides the guns; there were at least a dozen items more valuable on the premises. For whatever reason, Jonas had removed the guns from the cabinet, no one else.

Tracy was looking at him. "You don't think anything's wrong, do you?"

"No, of course not." He pushed the missing guns from his mind and put his arm around her shoulders. "Come on," he said, "you haven't seen the room where you'll be spending most of your time."

"What room is that?"

"The kitchen, where else?"

She gave him a sweet smile. "Fuck you, Senator," she said.

□ □ □

They had second drinks on the veranda, sitting in wicker armchairs and looking out over the bay. It was almost five-thirty now, and the sun had drifted low in the west; the sky had a glazed, coppery look. There was a stirring of wind, edged with coolness, and later, during the night and early morning, Jackman knew there would be one of the summer mists he had watched fascinated from his bedroom window as a boy. *And a grey mist on the sea's face and a grey dawn breaking.* Masefield? Yes: *I must down to the seas again, to the lonely sea and the sky....*

Tracy said, "Is it always this still here? If it wasn't for a gull once in a while, there wouldn't be any sound at all."

"Usually, in weather like this."

"It's kind of eerie. I feel as though I'm somewhere at the end of the world."

"You'll get used to it soon enough," he said. "It's the most tranquil place on earth."

"I hope so. Right now I feel more edgy than tranquil."

He looked at her beside him, in profile, and thought again—exactly as he had the first time he'd seen her—that she possessed an almost classic beauty. Every feature flawless: full-lipped mouth, slightly rounded chin, Grecian nose, high cheekbones, silky complexion, thick-lashed hazel eyes that would turn a bright glittery green with passion or intense emotion. Midnight-black hair, worn long and flowing; immaculately proportioned body; unaffected grace in each movement. A fascinating woman, Tracy Haddon. And an enigmatic one.

In the ten months Jackman had known her, he had never been able to fathom the depths of her personality. She was a complex individual, fashioned of anomalies; a private person who offered no explanations and no excuses for what she was and what she did. She had a BA in history from the University of Virginia, and yet she had made a successful career for herself as a writer of film documentaries. She was a self-admitted feminist, and yet she had taken and seemed to relish an almost totally submissive role in their affair. She had said on one occasion that the lust for wealth was the greatest of all sins, and on another occasion that if money couldn't buy happiness, it could buy something very close to it. She hated deception of all types, but she took a kind of perverse pleasure in the machinations necessary to keep their relationship a secret. She thought politics was "ridden with corrupt fools, bullshit artists, and hamstrung martyrs," that it was ultimately a futile and frustrating exercise for the average citizen to become involved, and yet she had chosen to work with and among politicos in the Washington milieu: the bulk of the documentaries she wrote were concerned with political life or figures.

It was just such a documentary, for PBS, which had brought about their meeting. He was in the early stages of his first campaign for reelection, and the subject of the film was just such a campaign: a study of freshmen senators and congressmen and their feelings about reelection, why they had chosen to run again, what they felt they had accomplished in their first term, and what they hoped to accomplish if there was a second—that kind of thing. She had been one of the group who had approached him, had been present at each of a series of taped interviews; had spent a good deal of time with him, off and on, in Washington and in Bangor, until just a few days before the election itself (which he had won in a landslide; the Jackmans always won in Maine and always in landslides).

He had been mildly infatuated from the first, by her beauty and by her involvement in filmmaking: she was doing the kind of thing he had always wanted to do himself, would have done himself if it had not been for the Old Man. She had been impressed when he told her about *I, Camera, Eye,* and they had discussed film and film theory whenever the opportunity presented itself. But it had been too soon after the difficult affair with Alicia, and he had been too committed to his campaign and to his work in the Senate to make or even seriously consider advances. And her own attitude toward him had been one of interest in the senator but apparent indifference toward the man. Or so he had thought. She told him later that she had felt a growing attraction from the beginning, but that she had kept it hidden because she was not the kind of woman who got off on going to bed with a public figure, and because he had never given any indication of being open to a relationship.

Perhaps their affair would never have begun if it had not been for a chain of circumstances. His election victory, and Tracy being out of Washington when he returned there from Bangor. The bitter fight he had had with Meg two days later, over the quite minor question of redecorating their house in George-town. The fact that he had decided to work late at his office that same night, after Miss Bigelow and the rest of his staff had left, rather than go home to a continuation of the battle with Meg. The fact that Tracy had come in on a night flight from New York and had called from the airport with the intention of leaving a message on his answering machine that her company wanted to arrange a final interview for the documentary. The conversation they'd had, innocent enough but leading to an impulsive invitation to her to stop up on her way home to discuss that final interview. The look of her when she arrived, and the two drinks they had shared, and the easy rapport between them, and the quiet emptiness of the office, and the developing aura of intima-cy, and the long and sudden moment of silence in which they seemed to real-ize mutual willingness and mutual need. And then the first kiss, and the sharp urgency, and Jackman hearing himself say "I want you, I can't help it," and Tracy saying "Yes, right here, right *now,*" with her eyes shining green and shameless, and the tearing away of clothing as they sank to the soft carpet, and the feel of her naked body, and the column of her arched neck, and the soft wetness of her, and the orgasms, and the holding, and the admixture of guilt and excitement he had felt at the commencement of a brand-new game.

That night had always seemed vaguely surreal in retrospect, a kind of sen-sual fantasy trip. On the floor of his office, for God's sake; in the Senate Office Building. Sex and the democratic process, semen spilled in the sanctified halls of government. Just another fucking politician.

Now, ten months later, their affair was nearly as intense as it had been that first night. But both of them knew it would not last indefinitely. They were not in love, and each was aware of that fact; there was no feeling of commit-ment, no spiritual communion or understanding; they never spoke of the future. Passion was all, but passion dies and rekindles elsewhere. A few more months, maybe as many as six, and then there would be someone else for her and maybe someone else for him. End game. No recriminations. And that was the way it should be.

Tracy finished her drink and sat forward in the wicker chair. "I just can't seem to sit still," she said. "David...?"

"Mmm?"

"Have you ever been bothered by trespassers out here?"

He frowned slightly. "Summer explorers and deer poachers once in a great while. Why?"

"I don't know. Maybe this stillness is getting to me, but I keep thinking about those missing guns."

"Come on, Ty. You explained that yourself: Jonas took them."

"You didn't seem very convinced of that."

"I'm convinced. No sign of prowlers in the house, was there?"

"No."

"Case closed. Another drink?"

"I don't think so. Why don't you show me some of the island? Those cliffs we saw coming in looked interesting. Maybe if I get to know the environment a little better, I'll feel more secure."

The suggestion appealed to Jackman; it had been such a long while since he had communed with the island himself. "Guaranteed," he said. "We've still got more than two hours of daylight left. That's plenty of time to go all the way to the cliffs, if you won't mind a two-mile hike round trip."

"My mother always told me I came from pioneer stock."

"Then we're on our way."

They got light jackets from their luggage, in deference to the evening cool, and then took the path up across the inland edge of Eider Neck and into the woods. The trees—mostly pine here, with a few spruce and balsam—grew thick and tall, and the light within the forest was dusky. The earth lay concealed beneath fallen needles decomposing into black humus. Green and gray moss-covered trunks and down logs and big gray outcroppings of rock, and clumps of lichen hung from spindly lower boughs. There was more sound here than there had been at the house: the light southeast wind murmuring among the foliage, the occasional chatter of birds, squirrels scurrying, the soft crunch of their footsteps. The air was heavy with pine resin and the odor of decaying wood. Tracy relaxed almost immediately; she was hardly the skittish type, and the shadowy woods seemed not to bother her. Before long, neither would the stillness or the city-bred fear of prowlers.

Nostalgia crowded his mind as they walked. He and Dale playing day-long games of hide-and-seek among these trees; the Old Man's nature and botany lessons; the excursions to the long flat top of the cliffs, to pick basketsful of the blueberries and strawberries that grew wild there; the low-tide explorations of the caves carved out of the cliff base by eons of crashing surf. God, how good it had been then, how simple, how innocent. What you believed in as a child was so much better than what you knew to be the truth as an adult—and wasn't what mattered then, at the base level, so much more important than what mattered now? Wasn't faith and love and beauty and simplicity what made up the soul of Man?

After they had gone a mile or so, the terrain began to slope steadily upward. The trees thinned and gave way to patches of open ground. Where the path skirted one of several fernbrakes on the island—a mini-jungle of brownish ferns, young pines, dead trees and branches like splintered gray bones—they paused to rest.

Tracy said, "This is a regular wilderness. I didn't expect anything like this."

"Do I take that as a favorable comment?"

"Absolutely."

"Wait until you see the cliffs," he said.

The path rose higher, through a long cathedral of trees, and then crested onto the flat. Acres of high green grass, dwarf pine, red-leaved blueberry bushes, multicolored wildflowers—and beyond, the cliffs and the offshore islets nested by gulls and sandpipers, and the wind-crinkled sea stretching away to the horizon. To the west, the rim of the sun had dipped below one of the other large islands, but its rays were still strong enough to lay a firelike glow on the water and to bathe the flat in soft gold light.

"See what I mean?" Jackman said.

"It's beautiful, David."

"The most beautiful spot on the island, particularly at this time of day. I used to come here sometimes just to watch the sunsets."

He took her hand and led her across to the edge of the cliff, to where they could look down a hundred feet to rock walls and boulders made black by rockweed and algae and barnacles, white-edged waves hissing spray as they broke. They stood in silence, watching the movement of the ocean, and Jackman felt—not for the first time—a kind of mystical connection with it. It had always been for him a symbol of vast power and vast knowledge, considering what it was capable of and what it harbored in its depths; he imagined that it was a link between man and infinity, and that you could, if you watched it and listened to it long enough, comprehend some of the secrets of life and the universe, and thereby touch infinity itself. And maybe that was what every human being was trying to do, in one way or another: live his life, play his games, and touch infinity once before he died.

He said this to Tracy, on impulse, and she did not laugh (Meg would have laughed). Instead she said, "Maybe it is. Maybe that's why men have been going to sea for millennia, and why they'll keep on doing it for as long as the world lasts."

"Yes, exactly," he said. "You know, I'm glad I brought you here. Not everyone would understand the island, or how I feel about it and about the sea."

She nodded but said nothing, staring down along the face of the cliff.

"There are caves below," he told her. "How do you feel about spelunking?"

"I love it—but not in caves."

Smiling, he said, "There's a way down that's not too dangerous. We could try it tomorrow or the next day."

"*You* can try it. I'll just watch, thanks."

"Coward."

"When it comes to scaling cliffs, right on."

They stood for a time in silence. The sun sank lower in the west, until more than half of it was hidden and the firelight paled on the water. "It'll be dark in an hour or so," Jackman said finally. "We'd better get on back."

They turned and started back across the flat. And something Jackman had not noticed before, because of the angle at which they had come out of the trees and because his attention had been focused on the sea, caught his eye. It was a pile of stones, curiously shaped—from this distance, not dissimilar to a barbecue—and it stood on a hump of ground in close to the pines. Jackman had never seen it before.

Tracy noticed it at almost the same time. She said, "Did you used to have cookouts up here?"

"No," he said, and went over in that direction.

When he neared the stone pile he saw a small shape lying in the hollowed-out center of it. And then recognized the shape and stopped abruptly. A red squirrel, laid out on its back, eyes like bits of black glass reflecting the dying sun. Freshly disemboweled.

Tracy said, "My God," and Jackman felt her fingers dig into his arm.

A chill melted down between his shoulder blades. He took a step closer, and a second. Deeper into the hollow, at right angles to the dead and bloody squirrel, were a series of smooth yellowish-white spots. There was nothing else anywhere on or within the stones.

"David, what—"

"An eagle, maybe. There are eagle aeries on a couple of the islands in this area."

"An eagle wouldn't do something like that, would it? Eat the... guts of its prey and nothing else?"

"It might," he said. "And it might have been carrying the carcass back to its nest and dropped it here or left it here for some reason."

"Were these stones here the last time you came?"

"No, but Jonas could have built the pile since then."

"Why would he?"

"I don't know."

Tracy shivered slightly in the cooling wind. "I don't like this, David. It makes me twice as uneasy."

"You're not thinking of prowlers again—"

"Aren't you?"

Jackman said nothing. He continued to stare at the rocks, at the squirrel. The red-furred belly of the animal appeared to have been cut open, he thought then, not torn open by the sharp beak of an eagle. There was no other wound of any kind. Slaughtered alive, then.

After having been caught in some kind of snare?

And those yellowish-white spots—candle wax?

The chill on his back deepened. Up close like this, the arrangement of stones looked not like a barbecue at all.

It looked like a kind of altar.

□ □ □

Dusk was settling when they hurried out of the woods and across the meadow toward the house, the warmly beckoning lights in the parlor windows. The western sky had an apricot tinge, and the wan face of the moon seemed balanced on the inland treetops; thick night shadows crowded the forestland, gave the evergreen boughs a charred look. To the northwest, at least two miles distant, another light on another island showed blurrily through the twilight.

When they reached the porch steps, Tracy hesitated—as if she were not certain the house was as empty as they had left it. Jackman went up ahead of her and opened the door and walked through into the parlor. Their bags still sat next to the couch, exactly as they had left them; the room itself still had the aspect of incompleteness, of perpetual waiting.

Behind him Tracy said, "No visitors while we were gone."

"Did you really think there might have been?"

"Oh don't sound so goddamned masculine-condescending," she said. Her voice was nervously sharp. She came forward, to within a pace of him, and stood searching his eyes. "We both know there could be someone else on this island. Not come and gone, but here right now."

"All right," he said, "it is possible. Jonas is careful about watching for trespassers, but someone could have slipped a boat in on the east shore and hidden it and themselves so that he didn't notice anything out of the ordinary when he made his final rounds. Or someone could have come ashore after he and his wife had already gone."

"And built that stone whatever-it-is and killed that squirrel and maybe got in here and took your father's gun collection."

"But damn it, I still think there's some innocuous explanation for all of that."

"Well, Jonas could have taken the guns, that's credible. But you don't honestly believe he's responsible for the squirrel and the pile of stones, do you?"

"It's also a possibility."

"Then why wouldn't he have left you a note explaining them?"

"It might have slipped his mind. He's an old man."

"If you had a telephone here—"

"But we don't have. Look, Ty, why would trespassers trap and then kill a squirrel? Why would they break into the house—and do it in such a way that there's no sign of forcible entry—and steal nothing but a collection of guns? It doesn't make any sense."

"Some people don't need reasons for doing things," Tracy said. "At least not rational reasons. Remember the Manson family?"

A corner of Jackman's mouth twitched. "Let's not let our imaginations run away with the facts."

"Things like that *can* happen, that's all I'm saying."

"Not on Jackman Island."

"David, we can't just ignore what we've found."

"We can if it's harmless."

"How do we find out either way?"

"Ty, let's look at this calmly. We've been here better than three hours now, and nobody's bothered us. We haven't seen anybody or signs of anybody except maybe for what we found on the cliffs. If there *were* trespassers, they're long gone."

"They could still be here, on the other side," Tracy said stubbornly. "Maybe they don't know *we're* here yet."

"If there were people on the island, they'd have to know about the house; know there are full-time residents. And if they meant harm they'd be somewhere close by, waiting for the residents to come back—and they'd have put in an appearance by now."

"I don't want to stay here if there are trespassers, whether they mean harm or not."

"I still say we're completely alone and there's nothing to worry about," Jackman said. "There's just no evidence to the contrary."

"You're so damned confident," she said.

"I've been coming here most of my life, that's all, and there's never been anything to fear in all that time. This is my island; I'm not going to run away from it just because there may or may not have been trespassers in the past day or so." He paused. "If it'll make you feel any better, I'll take a look around outside. Check the storage barn and Jonas' cottage. If I don't find anything amiss, maybe it'll put your mind at ease."

"Suppose there is something amiss?"

"Will it make you feel better if I promise we'll take the boat and head straight back to Weymouth Village? Report strange goings-on out here to the authorities and let them handle it?"

"Yes."

"Then I promise. But it's not going to come to that."

"I'm going with you," Tracy said. "I'm not very good at sitting and waiting and wondering what's happening somewhere else."

He would have preferred to go out alone, but telling her that would only have indicated concern on his own part. And probably have raised hackles on the feminist in her as well. He said, "Tandem, then," and led the way out of the parlor and down the center hallway and onto the enclosed rear porch.

He opened a wall cabinet stocked with fuses and light bulbs and other household necessities. Took out two of four large-cell flashlights and handed one to Tracy. Then they went outside, into full darkness faintly silvered by the low-hanging moon.

There was nothing directly behind the house except a bare slope leading up to a line of trees a hundred yards away, and at the foot of the slope, a stone wall grown over with moss and ferns. Four feet high and extending parallel to the rear width of the house, twenty yards out on each side, the wall had been built as protection against heavy buildups of snow that sometimes led to slides in the winter. Jackman put his flash on and played the light along the length of the wall; then he went over and did the same along the opposite side. He swept the beam across the incline and up into the thickly shadowed woods.

Nothing anywhere except vegetation and emptiness.

They walked down to Jonas' cottage and circled it, Jackman checking doors and windows and finding each of them secure. He held the flash against the panes of three of the windows, one in back and two on the near side, bedroom and kitchen and parlor: clean, orderly, stocked with familiar anachronisms—Colonial cedar chest, horsehair sofa, Edward Howard Regulator clock, Chase trestle desk, each in its proper place.

"Everything's okay here," he said.

Tracy said, "Do you have a key?"

"No. There's never been a reason I should."

"I'm thinking about those missing guns."

"It's a pretty good assumption they're inside."

"But we won't *know* without looking, will we?"

"We're not going to break into Jonas' house, not without a better reason than that," Jackman said. "Even if the guns aren't inside, it doesn't prove anything. He might have taken them to the mainland. To a gunsmith for professional cleaning, something like that."

"I suppose so," she said, but her voice was dubious.

"The houses are undisturbed, that's the important thing," he said. "Now the storage barn."

They went back across the rear of the main house, flash beams cutting yellow patterns in the night. The wind hummed in the evergreen boughs, blew cold and already moist with sea mist over the open ground and against their faces. In one of the two apple trees that fronted the barn, a catbird imitated a robin's song and then followed with its own mewing call as if proudly identifying itself as a mimic. Summer insects made a faint pulsing wave of sound, like a distortional echo of what Maine natives called "the rote"—the sometimes muted, sometimes thunderous cadence of the sea breaking on rock.

There was no lock on the barn doors, and Jackman found one of the two halves slightly ajar when he and Tracy came up. Nothing unusual or sinister in that; if you didn't make certain the latch was firmly shut, the wind would tug it open. But he felt an involuntary tightening in his stomach as he widened the one half—and he swept his light over the shadowed interior without entering.

Cords of pine firewood against the back wall. Remains of the ancient carriage the Old Man had bought sometime in the mid-thirties with the impulsive and later abandoned idea of using it and an imported horse as island transportation. A stack of lobster pots and marker buoys and other gear which Jonas had stored here when he sold his fishing boat, the *Carrie B,* three years ago. Gardening and woodcutting and carpentering tools hanging within painted outline drawings above and beside the workbench along the left-hand wall. A bench saw and drill press. Five-gallon cans of extra gasoline. A pile of lumber in various sizes and lengths, including sheets of plywood. Roofing material. A farrago of discarded furniture and household odds and ends such as an old-fashioned top-coil icebox and a genuine wooden butter churn. And housed along the far-right wall, whirring softly, sending out faint vibrations, the heavy-duty generator which provided the island with its electricity.

Everything exactly as it should be; nothing missing, nothing added.

He said "Okay" to Tracy, and stepped back and shut the door, tested it to be sure it was completely latched. Then he looked up at the sky, at the soft moon and the bright cold stars; listened again to the commonplace night sounds; smelled the evergreens and the sea, the essence of the island itself.

Despite his assurances to Tracy, he had been edgy since their discovery of the disemboweled squirrel—and the edginess had increased as they searched the grounds. Hyperactive imagination, the power of suggestion. But now his stomach lost its tightness and the edginess began to disappear. He thought: Well of course it's okay. You expected it would be, didn't you? Nothing out here in the dark but the bête noire—old Mr. Bugbear....

*Ain't no bogeyman walkin round here in the dark, boy. Ain't no bogeyman, period. Nothin to fear at all cept old Mr. Bugbear, lives inside each of our heads. Mine, yours, he inside every person on this good earth.*

Charlie Pepper. A night long ago, sometime in 1943 when Jackman was seven years old, yet vividly recalled even now. He had wandered away from the family home near Bangor, in search of frogs or salamanders or something else equally boyish, and had lost track of where he was along the river, and when nightfall had crept up on him he realized suddenly that he wasn't sure of how to get home again. There was an old mill on the river a mile or so from the estate, and some of the kids said it was haunted, and that the haunts would bite the heads off little kids who ran around alone in the dark. He sat down under a tree and imagined he saw haunts and bogeymen and other terrible creatures hiding in the shadows, and he cried and trembled with fear. And that was when Charlie Pepper had found him, wiped his eyes dry, and told him about old Mr. Bugbear.

*Can't hurt nobody, old Mr. Bugbear, just talks and carries on. But if we listen long enough, he make us tremble and shake, make us see things ain't there, make us afraid and keep us afraid long as we let him do it, till maybe we end up hurtin ourselves. But when old Mr. Bugbear starts to talk, and we should stand up strong and say, Look here now, I know it's you and I ain't gonna listen—why, he got to shut up and leave us alone. So there ain't never any reason to listen to him, boy, you just remember that. Ain't never any reason to be afraid of what you don't know or what you don't understand or what you only think might be.*

Quite a man, Charlie Pepper, in his own quiet way. A huge black who had, until his death in 1960, worked for the Old Man for thirty-odd years as a chauffeur and general handyman. Who had spoken seldom and then mostly in a conventional Negro dialect, but who read W. E. B. DuBois and Langston Hughes and Richard Wright, among a number of other black and nonblack writers. Who looked a little like Stepin Fetchit and sometimes appeared to act a little like an Uncle Tom, but who fought all his life for equal rights through the offices of the NAACP, and maintained a great personal dignity which anyone who cared enough to acknowledge his humanity could recognize; the stereotypes existed only in the eyes and minds of bigots and fools. Who had had—Jackman hadn't quite grasped this until his midteens—an intense love-hate relationship with the Old Man, because each understood and grudgingly respected the other: master gamesman-by-design, master gamesman-by-necessity-for-survival. White king, black pawn—but on the gameboard they had been equals, and their thirty-year match had ended in a draw.

Jackman felt himself relaxing again. And as he relaxed, it occurred to him that in a perverse way he had been enjoying the melodramatics of the situation; had been stimulated by it, just as he had been stimulated by the island games he and Dale had played as children. He smiled wryly and said to Tracy, "Mr. and Mrs. North."

"What?"

"Fictional detective team. That's us—Pam and Jerry, out with our flashlights, searching for clues in the dark."

"David, don't for Christ's sake joke."

"Oh come on, Ty," he said. "We've been over the grounds and there hasn't been anything to find."

"And I'm supposed to be satisfied, right?"

"Meaning you're not."

"I don't know what I am except nervous."

Jackman took her arm and they moved back toward the rear of the house. When they got to the porch he said reluctantly, "Look, if it bothers you that much, we'll take the boat and put back into the mainland."

She did not say anything until they were inside the well-lit parlor. Then, turning to him: "I suppose you think I'm being a damned shrinking violet."

"You're anything but a shrinking violet."

"Normally. I'm a city person and I can cope with most of what a city throws at me; but I guess I'm out of my element here. That pioneer stock I told you about is so much crap."

"I won't think worse of you if you want to leave."

"But you'd be more than a little disappointed," she said.

"It's pretty evident how you feel about this island."

"I won't deny that."

She studied him. "You wouldn't stay a minute if you thought there was really any danger, would you?"

"No, of course not."

Tracy turned abruptly and went over to the bar and began mixing herself an old-fashioned. "I hate weakness and I hate indecision," she said. Then, "Oh shit, David, don't pay any attention to me. We're not going back to the mainland until Monday afternoon. We're not going to spoil this weekend—*I'm* not going to spoil it."

"You're sure that's how you feel?"

"Reasonably sure. Okay?"

"Okay."

He joined her at the bar. He felt relieved at her decision, and relieved too at the sudden dissipation of tension that came with it. "Make me a drink, barman," he said. "Then I'll build us a fire on the hearth for the evening's pleasure."

"Bar*person*," she said.

"Oh? Was I being sexist again?"

"You were."

"Tell me, do you suppose I'd get more of the feminist vote if I changed my name to David Jackperson?"

"Nuts," Tracy said, and made a face at him. "Who's going to make dinner?"

"I will, tonight. How does roast squab, asparagus vinaigrette and Caesar salad sound?"

"Great."

"We'll have it when we get back to Washington. Tonight it's ravioli and stewed tomatoes and whatever else we happen to have in cans."

"Typical politician." She handed him a rum tonic. "Promises the moon, delivers a hunk of stale green cheese."

For a moment, that remark bothered Jackman; there was a hint of mockery in her tone—a trait he disliked, and which she exhibited often enough to irritate him. But then he shrugged it away and lifted his glass. He gave her a passable imitation of a Bogart leer, lowered his eyes to her breasts. "Here's looking at *yours,* kid," he said.

□ □ □

They sat Indian fashion on the floor in front of the fireplace, backs against the leather couch, Tracy with her head on his shoulder. Pine logs blazing on the hearth made muted crackling, popping sounds, like sporadic bursts of distant gunfire; the only other sound in the parlor was the iterative ticking of the grandfather clock. All the lights were off, and the fireglow turned their faces and the room around them into a combination lightshow and shadowplay.

After Jackman had made sure that all the doors and windows on both floors were secure, at Tracy's behest, they had stuffed themselves with ravioli and Spam and tinned German pumpernickel, and had drunk a full bottle of Château de Viens '69 Bordeaux. He had hoped to recapture the light mood they had shared earlier in the day, because that was the way he wanted it between them here on the island. Uncluttered days and nights, untroubled thoughts. The proverbial weekend idyll. But while she seemed outwardly to have relaxed, he sensed that she was still a little uncomfortable; he had caught her twice listening to sudden night sounds, cat-tense. Well, maybe she would snap out of it in the light of a new day—unless she was more like Meg than he might have thought, unless she was incapable after all of accepting the island for what it was. The prospect depressed him.

During the meal they had discussed filmmaking, the credibility of the auteur theory; he had lost none of his fascination for this career game over the years, and he seized every opportunity to pursue the subject. Now they were silent— Tracy seemed to want it that way; watching the fire and basking in its warmth.

He found himself thinking of other fires and again of other summers—and heard once more the ghostly echo of voices. The Old Man's voice in particular: resonant, stentorian, raised in anger, softened by humor, rich with wisdom, bloated with fool's rhetoric. Everything the Old Man had believed in and had been, politically and spiritually, had come from his own mouth in this room during one summer or another, spoken to his family or to guests of various persuasions. A partial, encapsulated oral biography of Thomas R. Jackman, retained by the walls of the house he had built, whispered in the night like the mutterings of an apparition in one of those legendary New England haunted houses. No chains here, no scrapings or rustlings or wailings or midnight walks; only glossy orations played and replayed to the tunes of "Over the Rainbow" and "Twilight Time":

—FDR said a while back, "The country needs, and unless I mistake its temper, the country demands bold, persistent experimentation. It is common sense to take a method and try it. If it fails, admit it frankly and try another. But above all, try something." Well, he's right, you know. No country and no individual ever gets anywhere without showing guts and backbone, without utilizing new tactics and fresh offensives. It's the by-God difference between winners and losers and always will be.

—That was a fine speech Marshall gave at the Harvard commencement, and this plan he and Truman have cooked up is a damned good one despite the expense. But I tell you, Marshall made a mistake with that line about our policy not being directed against any country or doctrine. The major threat to Europe is Communism, and Marshall knows it and Acheson and Truman know it and everybody else in the country knows it. You can't keep skirting the issue; it's political suicide. Unless Truman and the rest of them lose their color blindness and start seeing Red where Red exists, Harry will be fortunate if he carries half a dozen states in the '48 election.

—Remember Youngman, owns that string of lumber mills in the northern part of the state, contributed heavily to my last campaign? He approached me just before I left the capital with a request for state funding on a ten-thousand-acre logging project. I see no reason why we shouldn't go along with him. If there's one resource we won't ever have to worry about exhausting, it's Maine timberland.

—You know that old story of Truman's: "Early on in my life I had the choice of becoming either a piano player in a whorehouse or a politician. And to tell the truth, there's not much difference between the two." Well, if I'd been faced with the same choice, I'd probably have made the same selection—unless of course it was a *first-class* whorehouse.

—I never took a dime under the table in all my years in public service, not a dime. But I don't mind telling you that I've taken a number of favors, and given a number more. There's nothing illegal or unethical in that. Hell, the entire political system would come to a grinding halt if everybody stopped scratching backs.

—Trouble with Kennedy is, he wants everybody to like him; he goes out of his way to get people to say "Well now, that JFK is a damned fine fellow." If he doesn't show a little brass and iron, and soon, people are going to realize he's too image-conscious to be a strong President. And that will be the end of him.

—Certainly I'm in favor of the U.S. intervention in Southeast Asia. The only game the Communists understand is force, I've said that for years. If we don't step in, Vietnam will fall and so will Laos and Cambodia and Thailand and Malaysia and eventually every other country in Asia. It's a tragic shame our boys have to lay their lives on the line because of this menace, but the cause of democratic freedom for all people is a just one. We should be proud and eager to do anything and everything we can toward that end.

—I'm delighted with my son's decision to enter politics; in fact, I don't mind taking some of the credit for it. All he needed was a little guidance from me, a little confidence in himself. He's the image of me when I was his age, you know: he sees things the same way, does things the same way. In the long run he'll turn out to be exactly the kind of congressman, exactly the kind of senator, that I was and have been to this day....

"What are you thinking, David?"

Jackman smiled humorlessly, still watching the flames jump and dance around the dry pine logs. "About my father," he said. "Some of the things he said in this room, long ago "

"Things worth sharing?"

"No, not really." He shifted position; his right leg, prickling, had gone to sleep. "Political comments, mostly, and this is supposed to be an apolitical weekend."

"Mind and spirit free of Machiavellianism?"

"That's a pretty big word there."

"I know. And don't you just hate educated women? They're as bad as uppity niggers, right?"

"Oh shut up," Jackman said, and lifted her head and kissed her roughly.

He intended it to be a brief kiss, to tease her, but Tracy would not let him play that game. Her contained nervousness, seeking an outlet, made her aggressive; she laced both hands behind his head and held his mouth on hers, moving her tongue over his lips and then between them and hard against his tongue. Desire stirred in him and he held her more tightly, and she leaned into him and pushed him away from the couch and down flat on the rug, half on top of him, and took one of her hands away from his head and slid it down slowly between his legs. Began stroking him gently with the palm. Her touch did not give him an erection—he no longer seemed to have instant erections, even with Tracy—but the desire deepened and his breathing quickened and his hands kneaded the curves of her buttocks.

He said against her mouth, "Why don't we go upstairs and continue this in bed?"

"What's wrong with right here?"

"It's not very comfortable."

"You didn't worry about that our first night in your office."

"Special circumstances."

"Mmm." She raised herself off him, kneeling, and started to unbutton her blouse. "Have you ever made love in front of a fire?"

Once, he thought, with Meg at her father's lodge in Massachusetts. But she was self-conscious about it, tightened up everywhere, and neither of us enjoyed it much.

"No," he said.

"Well I have. It's very nice."

"Is it?"

"You'll see," she said. She took the blouse off, and her bra off. Her breasts were medium-sized, the under curves deeply rounded, and the nipples and aureoles shone blackly in the firelight, like polished onyx. "Oh you'll see," she said. She reached down and unbuckled his belt and opened his trousers and stripped him from the waist down. Then she straddled him at the ankles. Her fingers touched his abdomen, cool and soft; moved downward in slow, diminishing circles until they centered on his groin, until he saw and felt himself begin to harden. Her eyes held his the entire time, her face a wicked mask of light and shadow.

And she said, "Shall I blow you, David?"

"Yes," he said.

"Now?"

"Yes."

"And you'll do me?"

"Yes."

"Slowly. Both of us—slowly."

"Yes. Yes. Yes."

They lay closer to the fire, spent, bodies heavy with the languor that comes with intense sexual completion. Jackman said, "Would you like to hear something not very funny?"

"What?"

"In all the years I've been married to Meg, we've never had oral sex of any kind. She considers it ugly and perverted, not to mention unsanitary."

"There's no accounting for taste," Tracy said, "you should pardon the vulgar pun. What turns one person's stomach, another gets off on. Perversion and pleasure are interchangeable, really."

"Meaning you condone sadism and the like?"

"Between consenting adults, as they say, why not? Isn't getting off, or the anticipation of getting off—not only physically but mentally—what really, basically keeps us all from reverting into savages, keeps us sane and in control of our lives? Life, liberty, and the pursuit of orgasm—that's the human way. When you stop to consider it, everything else is pretty empty and hopeless. We work and create for what? For posterity? For a better world tomorrow? Bullshit. What do we care about tomorrow's world? We'll be dead in another twenty or thirty or forty years, and it's those twenty or thirty or forty years that count because that's the only time we've got."

Jackman leaned up on one elbow. "Jesus," he said, "what turned on *that* metaphysical faucet?"

A crooked smile. "Sorry. I get carried away sometimes."

"Do you honestly believe what you just said?"

"More or less. Sometimes the human condition seems awfully damned pointless—or hasn't that particular little perception ever struck you?"

He lay back down. "It has," he said. Too many times, he thought. "But there's still more to life, to human endeavor, than different kinds of orgasm."

"Such as?"

"Touching infinity, maybe."

"A form of getting off."

"Not if you believe in an afterlife."

"Which I don't. Do you?"

"I don't know. I used to."

"But now you're older and wiser—true?"

He shook his head. "I'm just not an existentialist, Ty. Living until you die isn't all there is. I wouldn't be what I am and where I am if I thought that."

"Well I hope you're right, David. Man ought to be *some*thing other that what he appears to be, have something more than self-gratification; but until somebody proves it to me, I'll just have to go on being a skeptic and a cynic. And believing that orgasm is the big enchilada, as a Hollywood friend says." She reached out to stroke his lower belly. "Speaking of which—do you suppose you can get that fat gentleman there to stand up again?"

Jackman had no further sexual desire; her egocentric philosophizing had robbed him of it. He was aware in that moment of just how little they had in common emotionally, of how shallow their relationship might really be at the core. Like his former relationship with Alicia, a totally self-centered woman—

But he did not want to think about Alicia. He said, "No. Not tonight."

"Well how about if I hum 'The Star-Spangled Banner'? He'd have to stand for that, now wouldn't he?"

Jackman was not amused; the remark annoyed him instead. Wordlessly he got to his feet and padded naked to the bar and poured himself a brandy. He stood staring into it for a moment, then sipped at it without lowering the glass—what the Old Man had called "nibbling."

Tracy said, "Hey, did I say something?"

He turned. "No, it's all right. Want a nightcap?"

"Actually, I'd rather have a fuck."

That made him wince. The Look!-I'm-liberated language was just another of her less than endearing traits. He wasn't used to it from women, not so casually tossed out and not after having been married to Meg, with her proper Bostonian upbringing, for as long as he had. And maybe down at the core he was something of a prude himself, perhaps even the kind of male chauvinist Tracy teasingly accused him of being. The Old Man had been both of these things, of course, despite his extramarital affairs—

—and Jesus *Christ*, he thought, why do you have to keep bringing him into every memory or reflection lately? He's been dead for eight goddamn *years*.

"...up to bed," Tracy was saying.

He shook himself. "I'm sorry, Ty, what did you say?"

"I said, since it appears I'm not going to be able to seduce you again tonight, we might as well go up to bed. It's gotten chilly in here all of a sudden, even with the fire."

"That's the fog," Jackman said automatically. "This is the time of night it starts drifting in from the sea. It seeps inside the house, no matter how tightly you seal it; you can't see it but you can feel it, the cold and dampness of it."

"Oh you're wonderful," Tracy said, and stood and began to hurriedly gather up their clothing. "You must tell lovely ghost stories. Now I'm not only cold and covered with goosebumps, I'm being manhandled by invisible tendrils of fog."

He found a smile for that. "I'll protect you," he said.

They went upstairs and got into bed in the guest room. Tracy lay quietly beside him for a time, and he had the feeling she was looking at him in the darkness. Then he heard her sigh softly, and she began to rub against him for warmth. After a while, and after all the rubbing and the softness of her body gave him an erection, and she said "Well, well" dryly and knowingly and rolled on top of him, and he entered her, and not long after completion he went to sleep holding her that way, still imprisoned inside her.

And as he slept he dreamed, adrift within himself in the peculiar, almost cinematic way of all his dreams: both participant and narrator....

*I have just graduated from college and I am visiting the Old Man in Washington and I tell him I do not want to go into politics as has always been tacitly supposed between us, that the success of I, Camera, Eye at Cannes and on the art-theater circuit in New York and San Francisco has convinced me to enter a career in filmmaking. He is silent for a long while and then he says "No," just that one word, "No," and I realize with sudden agony just how much influence he has, how many people owe him favors, and I know there is no way I can win this game, I have no real choice except capitulation; and while he begins eloquently and persuasively to point out why I must continue his work, I weep inside for what I am unable to be and for what I will become*

*and it is my first term in Congress, my first full year in Congress, and I am sitting at my appointed place on the House floor listening to a roll-call vote on a bill to ban handguns from all but public and private police agencies. Up and down voting, so I cannot abstain. When the clerk calls "Jackman of Maine" I stand—but before I can speak the members around me begin to laugh, and the clerk and the Speaker join them, and within seconds everyone in the chamber, members and guests alike, are on their feet and* pointing at me and the combined sound of their laughter is thunderous, reverberating from wall to wall. I cannot understand why they should be laughing, and I look around and then down at myself, and I am naked. I am standing there naked and my penis is so shriveled that it appears to be crouching, hidden within my scrotum, and it is at my genitals that everyone is pointing, the source of their wild mirth. Then, before I can flee in shame, someone rushes onto the floor, I do not see who it is, and shouts something, and the laughter stops instantly, and he shouts it again, and this time I hear: he is shouting that the President has been shot, the President has just been shot in Dallas

and I am on the first of my two visits to Vietnam, a Senate fact-finding mission during which I have gone to My Lat and Chu Lai and several other places, and now I am back in Saigon. There are half a dozen of us—Senator Lawton from Iowa and three aides and a lieutenant from the Armed Forces Radio and Television Network—grouped outside a building in which we have just finished taping a television program: Lawton and I discussing the sentiments of the people at home, a brigadier general denying the widespread use of drugs among enlisted personnel and the rumors that innocent Vietnamese civilians are being slaughtered during search-and-destroy maneuvers. We stand sweating in the thick tropical heat, watching the ebb and flow of life around us, and then there is a sudden concussive sound and the sidewalk shudders under my feet and someone screams and there is a pall of smoke and someone else screams, and when I regain my senses I know that either a plastique bomb or a grenade has exploded. I see that none of us is hurt, none of us is hurt, but farther up the block a car is on fire and there are people lying on the street, women and children, and I run up there, shouting all around me, wailing, and I see a woman with no left arm, her left arm is propped against a fence ten feet away like something discarded, and near her is a child with blood all over him, so much blood I can't see his face, and I stagger and turn in midstride and run back again, away from all that, and I lean against the building wall and Lawton says Jesus that was close Jesus it almost got us, but all I can do is lean over at the waist and vomit, thinking It's all a game, it's all a game

and I am at a party in the home of Alan Pennix and I wish I was not there because I don't like Pennix, I don't like the politicians he controls or his reactionary policies; but it is the kind of Washington party which honors a visiting dignitary and which pretends to be apolitical, and Meg has insisted that we attend. I am in a corner, alone, one of those brief moments when you are between polite encounters with people who are trying too hard to play this game, or people like myself who wish they were engaged in another game altogether. I sip my second brandy, and Pennix comes up and with him is Alicia. This is Alicia, he says, and we talk and then Pennix drifts away and I am alone with her and I look at her closely, hair the color of the sun, good body, haunted eyes, oh haunted enthralling eyes, and I say I want to go to bed with you, Alicia, even though I know I am dreaming and in reality it did not happen quite like that, and she says Yes, David, and we go outside together and run through the night, we are naked and my genitals are shriveled but she does not laugh, she takes my penis in her hand and rubs it and says You have a magic cock, David, when I rub it wondrous things happen, and then she says Now watch it grow, David, watch it grow, son, and it grows and grows and now it is my turn to laugh and I enter her, we laugh together, we come together, and all at once she says I want to be with you always, I want to marry you, *and I say No, we don't love each other, Alicia, and she throws a tantrum and screams that she is going to kill herself and I realize how unstable she really is, and then she is gone, she disappears, her landlady says on the telephone that she has moved out without leaving a forwarding address. I try to find her, I spend weeks trying to find her, but she has vanished and in the end I go home to Meg with my genitals shriveled again and Meg giggles when she sees them*

*and I am addressing the May Day demonstrators in 1971, but they will not listen, We don't want words, they say, we want an end to that unholy war in Southeast Asia! I want it too, I tell them, but my hands are tied, my cock is shriveled. Then the country is dead! they shout. No, I tell them, the country is alive; as long as we're free, we're alive. Then we're dead for sure, one of the demonstrators says, because this is a goddamn police state, a fascist dictatorship, and I say You're wrong, you're wrong—and the police and the FBI agents and the CIA spooks come, a sea of blue uniforms and tan trenchcoats and tattered cloaks and gleaming daggers, and arrest all the demonstrators, they arrest 7,400 demonstrators, and every one of the 7,400 shouts at me Stop them, don't you see what they're doing, they're trying to arrest the world! But I only stand there, I cannot move, I can only say It will be all right, you'll see, everything will be all right*

*and I am back in Saigon, kneeling beside the boy with the blood all over him. I brush it away frantically with my palms, pints of it, gallons of it, and finally his face becomes visible beneath the wet red stickiness, I can see his face at last, and it is mine, oh God it is my face....*

Jackman woke up: sat up in bed, panting as though he had run a great distance, sweat streaming off him and slick beneath his arms; his mouth tasted cottony, abrasively dry. He blinked in the darkness, rubbed at his eyes, wiped his face with part of the sheet. Then, as his breathing became normal, he realized that he was alone in the bed. He glanced automatically toward the bathroom door, but it was open and the light was off inside. Tracy must have gone downstairs for something—a snack maybe, a glass of milk or juice.

The luminous hands on the nightstand clock read 11:45, which meant he had been asleep no more than an hour and a half. He listened to the old house creak and groan and remembered that as a child he had thought it was talking to him, but he could never quite understand what it was saying. Now he knew its voice was that of the Old Man: those glossy, ghostly orations from the past.

He leaned back against the headboard and closed his eyes, but he was not going to be able to get back to sleep right away. Dream remnants still clung to the corners of his mind, like freshly spun spiderwebs. He had had these dreams before, but never all in the same night, one after the other as though they were part of a distorted montage of his life: half-truths and incomplete historical events, filled out with bizarre symbolism so that you could not always separate reality from pure nightmare. Or real fears from those manufactured by the superego. The dream game, an intellectual puzzle that usually required a shrink as opponent or teammate, depending on *his* bent.

—What is it that's really bothering you, Mr. Jackman?

—I don't know that anything really is.

—Of course you do. Part of it is your father, and part of it is the state of the world generally and this country specifically, and part of it is an intermix of Meg and Alicia and Tracy.

—And part of it is me?

—Exactly. Part of it is you.

But he would not see a shrink, because he *could* not.

He found himself thinking, by extension, of Alicia; the dream had implanted her too firmly in his mind for easy rejection. He could see her clearly: small, fragile, colt-brown eyes, sun-colored hair, mouth turned into a perpetual half-pout. And he could hear her voice as it had sounded the last time he saw her— her demands that he marry her; her false vows to marry Alan Pennix if he didn't because she thought it would hurt him if he believed he would lose her to a political opponent; then, when that ploy failed, her threat to kill herself because she could not live without him.

But she had not loved him; she had loved only herself. She was flighty, self-centered, unpredictable, and in most ways an emotional cripple. She lived in a Washington world of parties and affairs and behind-the-scenes political intrigues—a bright soap opera world where all the feelings were intense and all the defeats unbearable tragedies. She sustained herself vampirically on the passions of others, but she was incapable of giving anything in return. Not unlike Meg. Not unlike too many people he knew.

Continuing the relationship with her had been impossible, and the night he had told her so was the night she had threatened to take her life. He had not given the threat serious consideration, and yet when she disappeared so suddenly a week later, he had developed the nagging guilt-oriented fear that she had, after all, committed herself to that childishly dramatic act. The fear had grown, would not give him peace, and he had expended a great deal of time and effort in trying to locate her. But she had no close friends and no family—her widowered father, an ex-ambassador to Nicaragua, had died in 1971—and the search had been futile. For all he was able to learn, she might have vanished off the face of the earth.

After two months he had been so emotionally drained and his nerves so frayed that he had become frightened of a breakdown. And so he had gone into a private hospital in Virginia for two weeks of rest. Quietly, so as not to alert his political opponents who would have found ways to use it against him, or those faithful constituents who equated such visits with serious mental health problems. He had not told Meg (she would have been horrified), or anyone else. Instead he had carefully fabricated a fishing trip in the Canadian wilds, and the truth had not leaked out.

While he was in the hospital he had not been able to discuss Alicia, or the Old Man, or the dreams, or anything else of a personal nature with the resident doctors. He was only able to bring himself to plead overwork and constant pressures as the reasons for his presence there. The simple fact was, there had been no one in his life to whom he could talk, and he no longer had the capacity to bear his soul to *anyone*, least of all to a stranger. Despite John Donne's famous line, he was an island unto himself (one of the reasons, perhaps, why he had always felt a oneness with Jackman Island); he played the David Jackman Game within the boundaries of self.

Those two weeks had calmed him, eased his mind and conscience; for a long while after he came back to Washington—all through his difficult campaign for reelection, into this year—he had not been plagued by guilt and his sleep had been dream-free. In the past few months, however, despite almost daily doses of Librium and having given up smoking and coffee, he had begun to regress. And there was fear in him again....

Jackman's mouth was very dry. He forced his mind away from these painful considerations and thought of joining Tracy in the kitchen for something to drink. Which was where she was, because now he could hear her rattling dishes down there. He got out of bed and put on his trousers and shoes. His shirt was not there: Tracy must have used it for a makeshift housecoat.

While he was dressing he looked out the window and along the rear of the house. The fog had come in thickly, a low furry ground fog that undulated and curled around trees and the barn and the long retaining wall. In places you could not see the earth at all. The moon, high above the evergreens, barely discernible from the window, painted the sky and landscape a shiny silver and made the mist seem almost luminescent. The whole effect was eerie, unreal, but to Jackman comforting in its familiarity.

When he had his belt fastened he started to turn from the window, and something—movement—caught his eye and drew him back. It had come, or seemed to have come, from his left, between this house and Jonas' cottage. He stared out again, but nothing moved now except the floating carpet of fog. His breath misted the glass and he wiped it clear again with a palm, still did not see any further motion. A deer, maybe. Or his imagination again.

He went across the room, extended his arm toward the knob on the closed door.

Someone screamed.

Down in the kitchen someone screamed.

Tracy screamed down in the kitchen.

It brought him up short with his hand on the knob, froze him there for an instant because people did not scream in this house. Laughter, yes. Tears, yes. But no one had screamed here since it was built and no one should be screaming here now; this was the island, no one screamed on the island.

"David! David, *David!*"

He opened the door and began to run.

□ □ □

When he reached the bottom of the stairs, caught the newel post and swung around toward the archway, he saw Tracy come running into the parlor from the center corridor. He stretched out a hand as he passed through the arch, flipped the light switch on the wall; bright illumination flooded the room from the twin chandeliers, made him blink and then squint. They came together near the couch, and she put her palms flat against his chest as though she was not quite able to stand without aid. Her eyes were wide, her face darkly flushed; his shirt, the only thing she wore, was unbuttoned half-way down and her breasts heaved with the labor of her breathing.

"For God's sake," he said, "what is it, what happened?"

"There was someone... at the kitchen window."

"What! Are you sure?"

"I saw him, David, I was putting the orange juice away in the fridge and when I glanced over he was there. Looking in, with his face pressed to the glass."

"Did he try to get inside?"

"No. He was just standing there looking at me, smiling at me. His eyes were big as eggs, they didn't seem to have any pupils—"

Like Little Orphan Annie, he thought incongruously. He felt lightheaded; what she was telling him sounded as surreal as his dreams.

"—wild eyes, the kind you see on somebody who's heavy into dope. He was on something, David, I'd swear to it."

"All right, just take it easy."

"He stood there when I screamed," Tracy said, "and stood there when I shouted for you. Then he was gone. I looked out and saw him running toward the cottage, kind of bounding the way an animal runs."

"Animal?"

"I don't know, an animal or a person in one of those slow-motion TV commercials, you know what I mean."

Surrealism. "What did he look like?"

"Young, twenties somewhere. He wore a beard."

"You didn't see anyone else?"

"Isn't one enough? God, I knew there was somebody on the island—I *told* you...."

He shook his head: a reflex movement. I was so sure there was nobody here, he thought. Then he thought: Old Mr. Bugbear—and he said again, "All right, calm down. There's no point in making more out of this than necessary. We don't know who he is or what he wants."

"I don't *want* to know. I saw him, you didn't."

"We're in no immediate danger. He didn't try to come inside, you said that yourself."

"Not this time. But what's to stop a next time?"

"I'd better go out and see if I can find him."

"David...."

"Got to be done," he said, and stepped around her and went out of the parlor, down the hallway and onto the rear porch. Foul-weather oilskins hung on pegs beside the door. He put one on, mostly just to cover his naked torso. Then,

from the wall cabinet, he took down one of the flashlights they had used earlier.

Tracy had followed him; she said, "You'd better take some kind of weapon,"
in a shaky voice. "A knife or something."

"Why? He didn't have a weapon, did he?"

"Not that I could see—"

"Then there's no reason to assume he's armed."

"No? Are you forgetting those missing guns?"

A tic jumped along his jaw. "Lock the door when I go out," he said. "I'll come
back in through the front with my key."

Jackman opened the back door and went out before she could say anything
further, paused as she slammed it after him. The lock clicked. He felt oddly
detached, angry at the violation of the island's sanctity, a little confused. He
knew Tracy wanted to leave immediately, take the boat and head in to Weymouth Village, but he was not ready to give in to that, not just yet. The idea
of running away was still distasteful—and from what would they be running?
A young bearded man who may or may not be on dope; an apparition in the
night, a Peeping Tom, a trespasser who had shown no indication of malice
toward either of them. He had never been afraid of or antagonistic toward
young people, as so many of his generation seemed to be these days; he had
always managed a certain sympathetic rapport with the frustrations and
ideals, if not always the methods, of the subculture. And this was his island,
damn it; his was the position of authority here.

But he could not exercise that authority unless he found the intruder; and
he realized that he would not find him unless the man wanted to be found.
The island was too large, the night too full of deep shadows and clever hiding
places. All of which meant, then, that he might be left with no choice except
to give in to Tracy's apprehension and take them back to the mainland. It
would be foolish to do anything else. If he were alone here, perhaps—but not
with Tracy as his responsibility.

He put the flash on and stepped away through the eddying ground fog: it
came up nearly to his knees, so thick that he had the sensation at first of wad-
ing in gray liquid. The night's chill penetrated the oilskin, put goosebumps on
his skin, numbed his bare ankles and insteps where they were exposed
between trouser legs and shoe tops. The moonlight added a frosty violet tint
to the sky, whitened the trees and the buildings, provided him with clear visibility.

He went around the northern corner of the house and halfway down toward
Jonas' cottage. There, he stopped and looked across the front of the house, over
to Eider Neck, along the rim of the bay, back to the beach where thin fog-crust-
ed waves licked phosphorescently at the shale chunks and cobblestones. Stillness, save for the faint sibilance of the ocean. Everything frozen in stark relief,
moon-drenched, carpeted in shiny mist.

Walking again, he swung the flash slowly from left to right. Threads of fog
capered in the beam like will-o'-the-wisps. When he reached the front corner

of the cottage, he stopped again and listened and heard nothing but the sea; even the wind was silent now. He walked around the edge of the porch at a measured pace, along its railed front—and came to another halt, abruptly this time. The hackles went up on the back of his neck; his groin knotted. He turned his head fully toward the cottage entrance.

There was something up there, sitting in front of the door.

And something smeared across the door and part of the wall beside it.

Jackman put the light up, held it still. His stomach jerked and bile pumped into the back of his throat. And he just stood staring with a kind of sick fascination.

What was sitting in front of the door was the blood-spattered head of a fawn, the eyes huge and terrified and reflecting the light like disks of polished milk-glass. The fawn had been a male: its severed genitals were visible where they had been stuffed into one side of its open mouth.

What was smeared on the door and wall was blood, the fawn's blood, and it formed both a crude cabalistic sign totally alien to him and the letters of a word. The word was:

LUCIFER!

Another five seconds went by while Jackman stared; then he made a sound of anguish and disgust and wrenched the light and his gaze away. Chills raced along his back and the bile taste was stronger. For the first time he felt real anxiety, the beginnings of genuine terror.

He turned and fled straight back to the house, onto the front porch. Fumbled his key into the lock, went inside, shut the door and leaned back against it. Icy sweat rolled down from his armpits and along his side. Don't panic, he thought. There's no cause for panic.

Footsteps overhead, hurrying along the upstairs hall to the head of the stairs. Tracy called warily, "David?"

"I'm here," he said. His voice was calmer than he had expected it would be.

"You didn't find him, did you?"

"No." He went up the stairs, arranging his face into a mask so that none of what he had seen and what he had felt would show through. When he got to the landing he saw that she was already dressed; her face was pale now.

She said, "I can't stay here any longer, David; I can't handle this kind of situation. I need people around me tonight, lots of them."

"You're right," he said. "You've been right all along. We'll take the boat."

"Now?"

"Soon as we gather up our things."

In the bedroom, while he shed the oilskins and put on his shirt and socks and jacket, she closed and fastened the catches on their bags. Then they went downstairs and out onto the porch, walked rapidly across the lawn and onto the path that skirted the beach—Tracy as though she were prepared to break into a run at any second, Jackman holding himself and his strides in careful check. No one pursued them. No one revealed himself.

He was sweating when they reached the boathouse door. Beside him, Tracy breathed heavily and stood looking back over her shoulder; the house and the cottage, draped in fog, had dull-white sheens, as if they had been dusted with talcum. And then he got the door open and they stepped inside.

Only to stop again, abruptly—staring.

Tracy said, "Oh my *God!*"

The outer doors were wide open: the boat was gone.

# PART TWO

Saturday, May 23
THE ISLAND

*What wouldst thou, waylayer, from me?*
*Thou lightning-shrouded one! Unknown one!*
*Speak, what wilt thou....*
                              —NIETZSCHE, *Thus Spake Zarathustra*

They sat together in the dark kitchen, at the long antique-finished cobbler's bench which served as a table, backs to one wall so that they could watch the hallway arch and the window over the sink. When they had come back from the boathouse forty minutes ago, Jackman had put on the low-wattage hallway lights but no others; that illumination combined with the pale moonglow filtering past the window curtains to soften the edges of the night shadows. The refrigerator hummed steadily to itself and the sink tap dripped every few seconds. Otherwise there were no sounds: the house, too, seemed to be listening and waiting.

After a time the grandfather clock in the parlor struck one o'clock. The single note echoed through the darkness, left a ghostly aftersound that Jackman thought he could hear for at least half a minute. He shifted slightly in his chair, eyes avoiding the butcher knives and flashlights they had gathered on the table. The feeling of surrealism was back with him again, stronger now, wrapped in a thin layer of fear. He still had himself under control, but it was mostly external—a facade of calm, his political face, as if this were another of the crises he met and handled with aplomb in Washington. Inwardly, he was trembling and unable as yet to cope with the situation.

He looked at Tracy beside him, sitting stiffly, eyes staring straight ahead, and knew that she blamed him for what was happening here: he had been so complacently sure that evil could not touch Jackman Island, that the danger signs could be explained away normally; if he had agreed to leave with her earlier, they would be safe in Weymouth Village now. Unless the boat had been stolen while they were up on the cliffs; but even if that were the case, she would still think it his fault for having brought her here in the first place.

That burden of culpability—warranted or not—had joined with the fear to build a wall between them. The real test of a relationship was a crisis: if there was anything at all solid between two people, they would grow more aware of each other, grow closer together; if there was not any foundation, then they would realize that fact and it would be over. Just like that—finished.

So it was finished for them, beyond any doubt. And he was not surprised. Subconsciously, perhaps, the arrangement had begun some time ago to dissolve for him. It would explain his annoyance at certain things she said, certain of her character traits; and it would explain why, facing her now, he had no feeling of intimacy, no feeling at all beyond concern for their mutual safety. He was looking at a familiar stranger—and it was like being alone.

And yet, ironically, the fear also bound them together: a stronger and more basic emotion than any of those which had united them during the months of their affair.

When she seemed to feel him watching her and turned her head, her eyes looked like wells of ink in the gloom. Her lips, thin and tight, glistened blackly where she had moistened them with her tongue. She said, "I can't take much more of this, David. My nerves are raw already."

"Get up and move around a little," he said.

"Damn you, we have to do something!"

"I know that."

"There's got to be some other way off this island—"

"No. I told you at the boathouse there wasn't."

"What about a rubber raft or a rowboat?"

"There's nothing. And even if there was, the currents are unpredictable this far out from the mainland; we'd probably be carried out to sea."

"So we couldn't swim to one of the other islands."

He shook his head. "That water is like ice all year round."

She fisted her hands on the table and was silent for a time. Then: "Why don't *they* do something, for God's sake? They stole the boat, they've trapped us here, why don't they show themselves and get it over with?"

"They're playing games with us," he said.

"What?"

"Games. Cat and mouse."

"Why? Who are they? What do they want?"

"I have no idea," he lied.

The refrigerator made a clicking noise and stopped humming to itself. Tracy's head snapped toward it, swiveled back to Jackman; she wet her lips again. "That thing up on the cliffs—it was some kind of sacrificial altar, wasn't it? That's the only explanation for the squirrel that makes any sense."

He had not told her about the fawn's head, or the blood on the door and wall of Jonas' cottage and what it spelled out. "Maybe," he said. "We can't be sure."

"David, let's dispense with the bullshit, okay? You think that thing is a sacrificial altar, don't you?"

"Yes."

"Then that bearded freak at the window could be a devil cultist, isn't that right? There could be a whole goddamn coven or whatever it is they call themselves on this island right now."

*Lucifer!* And a fawn's head with its genitals stuffed inside its mouth. And the disemboweled squirrel. And the altar. He did not say anything, listening to the sink tap drip and then drip again seven seconds later.

"Well?" she said.

"It's just kids," he said carefully. "High on drugs, playing thrill games."

"You think that would make them any less dangerous?"

"Killing animals is one thing; killing people is another."

"Yes? Well what about people like Manson and Starkweather?"

He was silent.

"And what about all those kids who were taught how to kill in Vietnam?" Tracy said. "Taught how to use drugs and how to hate and how to lose their perception of right and wrong. Some of them had to turn on to all that horror, the law of averages says that, and now they're right back here in this country. Maybe devil worship is their big orgasm. Maybe they get off on human as well as animal sacrifices. What the hell, David, all the big respectable owners of this democracy, all the war profiteers, got off for ten years on the dead bodies of tens of thousands of Americans and Vietnamese. This is a sick fucking world sometimes, or are you too busy fostering your own image, like most of your asshole political peers, to worry about what's really going on?"

*...kneeling beside the boy in Saigon, brushing away the blood, searching for his face beneath the blood, and his face is mine....*

He stood abruptly and went over to the sink and ran water into his cupped hands. Splashed his face as if cleansing it. She was right in this, too—and she had not needed the fawn's head and the bloody message in order to interpret the kind of nightmare they might be facing here. His comments to her replayed in his mind and sounded fatuous and condescending now; their relationship was over, yes, but that was no reason to begin treating her as a mental inferior, as a hysterical stereotype who needed false reassurances.

Turning, he looked across at the table, saw her as a silhouette sitting motionless behind it. "Maybe I deserved that," he said.

"And maybe you didn't." She drew an audible breath, heavy and tense. "The point is, it could be any kind of sick weirdo out there—and what's to stop him or them from killing us? They've got guns, they took your father's guns."

He came back to stand in front of the table. "We still don't *know* who and what they are, but there's no use lying anymore to myself or to you: we've got to assume they mean us harm. Which means the only way to survive is to play this game better than they play it, outthink them, outmaneuver them."

"Then we've got to decide what we're going to do right now."

Jackman said, "All right, we—"

And the door chimes went off.

Behind the table Tracy made a startled noise and her body jerked and she came up onto her feet as though in reaction to an electric shock. Jackman half spun and stared into the lighted hallway. The fear crawled down through him and seemed to center in his genitals. Pulse thudded in his ears; there was a metallic taste in his mouth.

Tracy said, "God, David...."

The chimes rang again, a sweet clear echoing melody—but as chilling in that moment as a music box playing in a sealed crypt.

He swept a flashlight and a butcher knife off the table. What sort of tactic was this? A subtle form of torture, like a drop of water on an exposed nerve? Or a diversion to take them to the front door so that access could be gained through the rear? Most likely the former, in which case whoever had pushed the door button would be gone by now, hidden again, watching. Countermove to the rear porch, then, just to be sure.

He stepped over beside Tracy, caught her arm with his free hand. "Stay with me," he said sotto voce.

When she nodded he led her out onto the enclosed porch and then motioned her to the wall on the unwindowed side of the door. He took a place next to the window. Outside it was quiet, not a murmur of sound. From inside, the same: the chimes had not gone off again. He leaned his head toward the frame of glass.

In that same instant it exploded inward, spraying gleaming black fragments; something long and slender hurtled past Jackman's head.

He lunged backward, releasing both the knife and the flashlight and bringing his hands up, turning his head downward, closing his eyes—all of it instinctive. But there were needle-pricks of pain on his left cheekbone, under the right eye, above the right corner of his mouth. Dimly he heard Tracy stifle a cry, the shards falling like crystalline raindrops, the thud of whatever had smashed the window as it struck the inner wall and then dropped clattering to the floor.

He blinked his eyes open, and they were undamaged, he could see all right. The cuts began to sting, and when he touched his cheeks he felt the tear-stream wetness of blood, the gritty sharpness of tiny glass particles. He took the handkerchief out of his back pocket and dabbed and brushed gingerly at his face. His hands were trembling.

Tracy was talking to him, he realized, asking in an urgent whisper if he were badly cut. "No," he said, "I'm okay," and pivoted and looked through the frame of the window, past jagged edges of glass like unevenly serrated teeth in an open mouth. Breaths of cold air burned against the cuts, chilled the sweat on his forehead. In the silvery moonlight outside, the mist crept sinuously along the ground, concealing most of the stone fence, enwrapping the lower boles of the two apple trees as though in furry gray moss. For all he could see, it seemed now to have the night to itself.

Jackman picked up the knife and the flashlight, gave the latter to Tracy and put the weapon through his belt on the right side. Then he thought of the object which had been hurled through the window, and went over to the inner wall and knelt. Groped along the floor until his fingers touched it—but as soon as they did, he pulled the hand back. "Christ," he said softly.

Tracy said "What is it?" and dropped down beside him and clicked on the light.

It was not as bad as he had expected from the feel of it, but it was bad enough: a jagged piece of bone, probably from the slaughtered fawn, with bits of gristled meat clinging to it. There was something else clinging to it as well—a crumpled sheet of ruled paper, fastened on with a rubber band.

"They killed another animal," Tracy said sickly.

He nodded. Don't look at the paper, he thought. You don't want to know what's on it; Tracy doesn't want to know.

She looked at him as though reading his thoughts. He held her gaze for several seconds and then, because they both knew looking at the paper was unavoidable and inevitable, he swallowed bile and lifted the bone between thumb and forefinger. Took the sheet off of it, spread the paper open on the floor as Tracy lowered the flash.

The same cabalistic symbol, and letters fingerpainted in crimson:

YOUR BLOOD NEXT FOR THE CUP OF LUCIFER.

□ □ □

In the kitchen again Jackman soaked the handkerchief in cold tap water and used it to staunch the last flow of blood from the glass cuts. The feeling of surrealism had been jarred out of him: his thoughts were clear, analytical, as he sifted through possible moves, possible alternatives. The fear remained, but there was no way you could rid yourself of fear until you eliminated or deactivated its source; the problem was keeping it at a manageable level.

And the secret to that lay in continuing to think of all this as a game. A game not at all capricious, not at all created for the thrill of itself alone. A game not unlike those once held in the Coliseum in Rome for the amusement of the decadent masses, in which survival—thumbs up!—was the only purpose; in which the weaker would be destroyed—thumbs down! Every bit this kind of senseless and repulsive game, yes, but a *game* nonetheless. And the Old Man had taught him all there was to know about game-playing....

When he came away from the sink Tracy said, "How much longer do you think we have?"

"No way to tell. They might keep on toying with us all night, or they might have already tired of it. Ty, the only option we've got that makes any sense is to get out of here, away into the woods. Now."

She stared at him in the pale stream of moonlight from the window. "You want us to go out there where they are?"

"It's twice as dangerous if we stay here."

"I don't understand that."

"We're vulnerable here."

"We'd be vulnerable out there."

"Not in the same way. Outside, at least we'd have places to hide, room to maneuver: we can make offensive moves as well as defensive ones. In here we're trapped, they know exactly where we are."

"Yes, but—"

From without, at the front of the house, there were sudden clanking sounds, dull and metallic and not quite identifiable.

Tracy said, "What was that?"

He shook his head, turned past her to look cautiously through the window. Moonlight and shadow. But he heard the sounds again, more distantly this time. Front lawn? Somewhere out there.

They were not repeated a third time.

At length Jackman said, "More scare tactics, maybe. Another turn of the screw. And this is only the beginning." He took her shoulders tightly in both hands, felt the ropelike tension in her muscles and tendons. "Ty, believe me— we've got to get out of here."

"I don't know...."

He said, "There is a way off the island, if we can find it."

"What way?"

"*Their* boat. Christ knows what they did with the cruiser—set it adrift with the bilge plugs open, maybe—but whatever they used to come to the island has to be around the bay here, or at the cove on the east shore."

Tracy's throat worked heavily. "But *how* can we get out, David? They're right outside, they could shoot us down or run us down before we're able to get away...."

"We'll create a diversion."

"What kind of diversion?"

"Give me a minute; I'll think of something."

"Then which way do we leave? Back or front?"

"Neither."

She said, "One of the windows?"

"No. There are outside storm doors on the south side of the house. We'll go down to the basement through the pantry, then up through those doors and into the trees beyond the barn."

"Then?"

"Cross-island to the cove," Jackman said. "It's the most probable spot for them to have landed; coming in, they couldn't have known the buildings here were deserted. And that way we make sure we're completely clear of them."

"But if that's where their boat is, they might realize we'd go there."

"Doesn't matter. I know this island; I can find my way over every inch of it, dark or light. No way they can get to the cove before we do—there's a short-cut. If we can keep them off our backtrail, we should have at least twenty minutes."

Tracy was silent for a moment, but he sensed that she was with him now; the rising inflection in her voice was that of hope. She confirmed it finally by saying, "All right, David. Do we leave right away?"

"As soon as possible."

"What do we take with us?"

He considered that briefly. "One flashlight each. One knife each. I've got a pair of binoculars in my room upstairs that are made for night use as well as day. And we should have more clothing on than these light jackets and sweaters."

"We could wear those oilskins on the porch."

"Good. They'll make us more difficult to see even in the moonlight."

"How about food?"

"Some, maybe. Just in case. But nothing heavy or bulky. Only things that will fit in our pockets and not hamper movement."

"I'll take care of that."

He nodded, and without either of them saying anything else he went into the hallway and across the parlor. As he climbed the stairs to the upper floor, Jackman thought that they were interacting well enough now, functioning with the necessary teamwork to carry out the plan he had made. He was glad it was Tracy and not Meg, because Meg would have been totally helpless, she would have gone to pieces long ago.

And how about me? he thought then. Are *my* nerves going to hold up? Not bad now, because he was keeping his mind focused on the opening gambits of this Most Dangerous Game—but what if those gambits failed and the game became more intricate, dragged on and on?

*One thing you've got to remember, son: make your moves one at a time, and be careful of looking too far ahead. More games are lost by overcalculation, worrying too much about what's coming up later on, and not paying enough attention to the next move on the board.*

He blanked his mind, entered his old room and felt his way across to the tier of shelving on the opposite wall. And in the same moment he found the binoculars, he also found the diversion they would need to get out of the house: his old reel-to-reel tape recorder.

He stood for a dozen seconds, thinking it through. Then he uncased the glasses and looped the carry strap over his head, bent in front of the recorder and removed its top speaker cover. Enough moonshine penetrated the drawn curtains to show him that there was a tape on the two plastic reels, that the microphone was intact in its little compartment. The machine had not been used in a long time, years, and as he drew out the electrical cord and knelt to plug into the wall socket, he prayed that it was still operative.

When he straightened again and touched the ON switch, the time meter light glowed and the recorder made a soft humming sound.

Jackman released the breath he had been holding and rewound the tape, pressed the button for RECORD. The tape began to run, erasing whatever had been on it, but he did not speak into the microphone. He looked at the radium dial of his watch and timed a full five revolutions of the second hand. Then, finally, he said in his normal voice, "This is David Jackman, the owner of this island. I don't know who you are or what you want, but unless you get off my property right now I warn you there'll be serious charges pressed against you. Technically all you've done so far is to commit acts of vandalism and malicious mischief, but that note you wrote us could be considered a direct threat if I choose to interpret it that way. I expect friends on the island in the morning, several of them, and if you're still here by then you'll leave me no alternative except to have you hunted down and arrested...."

He went on in the same vein for another two and a half minutes. Then he unplugged the microphone, rewound the tape again, shut off the recorder, packed it together, and stepped over to the window on the south wall. Below and toward the rear, he could see the dark shape of the storm doors. The moon-drenched ground between the house and the trees beyond the barn was deserted. He came back to the recorder, caught it up, and carried it out of the room.

In the foyer downstairs he put the machine on the antique table, then dragged the table to the right of the door and two feet behind it. Just as he finished, Tracy came hurrying in from the parlor, wearing one of the oils and holding a second draped over her arm. The deep pockets of the slickers bulged, not too fully, with foodstuff and the knives and flashlights.

She said, "What took you so long? I've been ready to jump out of my skin, waiting down here alone."

"Did you see or hear anything outside?"

"Those clanking sounds again. That's all."

Jackman opened the recorder, stood its speaker cover to one side. He said, "This is part of that diversion we're going to need."

She frowned. "Did you record something while you were upstairs?"

"A three-minute speech with a five-minute silence ahead of it," he said. "Those are the five minutes we'll need to get down to the basement and make ready."

"I hope that thing has good loud volume."

"It does."

He found that he had to move the table back another foot in order for the plug to reach the nearest outlet. He did not turn on the machine, just left it where it sat. To Tracy he said, "What I need now is some heavy twine, at least a hundred and fifty feet of it."

"What for?"

"I'll show you when we find the twine."

They went down to the kitchen again, Jackman putting on the second oilskin, and then rummaged through the cupboards and the drawers in the drainboard cabinets. He began to think they were taking too much time, that they should have been out of here by now—but that was the fear working inside him. He had to keep reminding himself not to play recklessly, not to let panic govern any of his actions.

Tracy found the twine, a large ball of it, in a utility drawer. He took it from her and motioned her to follow, and when they came into the foyer once more he skirted the table, unwound an end of the string, and tied it securely around the front doorknob. Unlocked the door, and turned the knob until the latch clicked. Eased the door inward fractionally and then backed off, paying out twine.

And the clanking sounds came again, very loud, very close off to the side of the veranda.

Jackman stiffened, saw Tracy raise a fist to her mouth as though to lock in a cry. Clank. Clank. Silence. Clank—

All at once, he identified the sounds, knew their source. He said "Jesus Christ," and felt a prickly cold settle across the back of his neck.

"David?"

"Gasoline cans," he said.

"What?"

"From the barn, Jonas keeps an extra ration of gasoline in there." He hesitated; then: "Maybe they've got it in their heads to set fire to the house."

Sharp intake of breath. "No," but it was a plea instead of a negative.

Clank.

Clank.

Fear and urgency prodded Jackman into motion. He moved closer to Tracy, gave her the ball of string. "Go back into the pantry and unwind this along the way. Hurry. I'll join you in a minute."

He watched her back away through the parlor, unraveling the twine. When she disappeared into the center corridor, he entered the parlor himself and looked out through the nearest of the south windows. Stillness. He came back into the foyer, considered opening the front door, decided it was too much of a risk, and listened.

Silence.

He switched on the tape recorder, pushed the PLAY button, and turned the volume up as far as it would go. The machine hummed noisily; its lights glowed like tiny yellow eyes in the darkness. He pivoted away from it and moved silently back along the slack path of the twine, making sure there was nothing on which it could hang up once he pulled it taut.

When he came into the pantry, Tracy had already opened the basement door; she stood holding what was left of the string ball. He took it from her and put it on the floor just beyond the sill of the basement door.

Their was a sudden frenzied knocking on the back door—sounds that echoed madly in the stillness.

Tracy's fingers dug into his arm and he felt the bite of her nails. He did not say anything, did not hesitate; he pushed her through the door and followed after her and pulled it to behind him without latching it. Took the flashlight out of his slicker, clicked it on, aimed it down the stairs as they descended.

The basement was damp and cold and had the faint moldlike odor of any underground place long shut-up, long unvisited. The walls and floor were of concrete. Part of the facing wall was covered with hand-built wooden niches, pegged instead of nailed together, for the storage of the fine wines the Old Man had been fond of serving to his summer guests; only a few bottles filled them now. There were also two old casks on a wooden platform—so old that they had been wine-stained to a uniform black color—which a vintner had supplied in payment for some small favor. On another wall were shelves constructed to hold canned goods; all they held now was dust. Cobwebs hung like moss from the low wooden ceiling, spanned some of the supporting timbers in lacy gray patterns.

Jackman pointed the flash across to the far end, where the basement had been widened into a kind of annex that extended beyond the south wall of the house. Another set of wooden steps led up from there to the outer storm doors.

They went over to the annex, and he climbed the steps to the doors: two wooden halves that opened outward from the middle. Now that they were no longer used, heavy iron bars fitted through iron brackets held them locked against the gale-force winds that sometimes buffeted the island during the winter months. Jackman removed the bars, carefully, and carried them down and laid them on the annex floor.

Looking again at his watch, he said, "Seventy seconds. I'll do the twine."

"Should I go up the steps?"

"Yes. But don't touch the doors yet."

He ran back to the pantry stairs and went up and pushed the door open far enough to pick up the twine. Forty seconds. Carefully, he began to take up the slack, reeling it in like a fishline. Twenty seconds. He could feel himself sweating, beads of it breaking and running down off his forehead, stinging against the glass cuts on his cheeks; he half-expected to smell smoke, hear the crackle of flames, at any second.

Fifteen seconds. Ten. And the twine tightened, became taut: the front door was open. Jackman looped the twine around the knob of the basement door, to keep it stretched, and took the steps going down again three at a time.

*"This is David Jackman, the owner of this island. I don't know who you are or what you want...."*

When he came up the annex steps beside Tracy, he said against her ear, "We'll give it a full minute, maybe a minute and a half. It'll take us less than ninety seconds to get from here into the trees."

"You'd better go out first when the time comes," she said. "You know exactly where to go."

"All right."

*"...you're still here by then you'll leave me no alternative but to have you hunted down and arrested. This game you've been playing is senseless and childish, you must realize that. We're not afraid of you...."*

"One minute," Jackman said. "Thirty seconds to go."

He moved around her, one step higher, and put the palms of both hands against the door halves. Stared at the sweep hand on his watch.

*"...what you expect to gain by all this? Kicks, thrills—is that it? Does hiding in the dark like animals, terrifying people, give you some sort of warped pleasure...."*

One minute and thirty seconds.

"Now!"

He shoved the doors apart, pushed them back against their hinge stops so that they would stay open. Raised his body up and out between the halves and swung his gaze from left to right. Moonlit grass, the dark distant sweep of trees, the inner hump of Eider Neck, a long wedge of the front lawn: empty, all of it empty, but light that did not come from flash beams flickering around the corner, out front, out of his vision—and he levered himself off the top step and came out running.

He heard Tracy scramble out behind him, heard his own recorded voice eerily hammering away at the night from the front entrance; he wanted to turn his head, to look for pursuit, but he knew that would slow him and so he kept his eyes on the trees, head ducked down, shoulders hunched, you would never hear the shot that killed you, and then Tracy was beside him, running with him, reaching for and clasping his hand, and he increased the length of his strides, or thought he did, but the trees did not seem to come any closer. Blood pulsed in his ears and his breath sprayed between clamped teeth, he felt as though they were running like squirrels in a cage wheel, disemboweled squirrels, decapitated fawn, "...*warning you, I'll see you prosecuted to the fullest extent of the law if you do not....*" stumbling, sweating, and finally, finally the woods loomed near, almost there, no shot, no sounds behind them—we're going to make it—and the elongated shadows cast by the first of the evergreens reached out and they rushed into them, blended with them, panting.

"...*only going to say this one last time. I won't toler—*"

Jackman heard his voice cut off in mid-word, but the tape would not have run out yet and that meant one of them had turned off the recorder. He had to look back then, like Lot's wife: back and down across the expanse of open ground.

No one there, no one had seen them.

But from this angle he could make out the source of the flickers of light at the front of the house: fire, all right, but not the house—a cross, they had constructed a wooden cross on the lawn and then set it ablaze. It stood there burning within swirls of fog that looked, in the high shimmering glow of the flames, like mists of fresh blood....

□ □ □

Jackman led the way deeper into the woods, skirting a fernbrake and then a small clearing dotted with deadfalls and seedling spruce. A third of the way around the clearing he sensed rather than saw the place where the path began, and picked it up almost immediately.

When the trail began to run in a narrow zigzag through forestland so dense that only patches of the moonlit sky were visible through the canopy of boughs overhead, he stopped abruptly and leaned against one of the pine boles. He drew Tracy in against him, holding tightly to her hand. "We can take time to catch a second wind," he said. "We've got a good jump on them."

She nodded and rubbed at the sheen of sweat and mist on her face. Seconds passed. Then: "How far to the cove?"

"Another third of a mile."

"Can we risk using one of the flashlights now?"

"We'll have to for maximum speed."

"David...."

He looked down into her face.

Hesitation. Finally she said, "Nothing, there's nothing to say," and he knew she had seen and was thinking about the burning cross. And she was right: there was nothing to say.

They had rested long enough, he thought. He put on his flash, angled the beam downward, and they took to the path again, walking rapidly instead of running now because of the jutting lower branches that were a constant danger to the eyes. The upper boughs swayed gently, almost rhythmically, as if to the beat of inaudible music. Fingerlike wisps of fog caressed their legs and lower bodies with damp intimacy.

In the distance Jackman could hear the hissing sound of the rote; the tide was at flood and the ocean restless despite the mild weather, the lack of any but a soft breeze. The open sea beyond the southern cliffs would be treacherous, impossible to navigate, which meant that they would have to take the boat around to the north and across to Little Shad Island and then back in to the mainland; you had to be careful off that side of the island or you would rip the belly out of your craft on one of the ledges—

*If* they had landed at the cove in the first place; been cautious and escaped the ledges and brought their boat in there instead of at the bay.

*If* there was a boat at the cove, and *if* it was one that did not require a key to start the engine, and *if* there had not been a guard posted....

The evergreens thinned after they had gone a quarter mile, and the path led through a field of brown grass riddled with a network of narrow passages built by meadow voles, then up across a ridge of flattish rock and gnarled old birch, and finally down into more pines and spruce. From the east the sound of the rote was much louder now, and the pungent smell of seawater became greater than that of the forest. Jackman remembered that the path hooked around and came out of the woods on the western rim of the cove's wide, rocky beach. But you could leave the trail where it started to loop and continue straight ahead and exit at the trees on the northern lip of the beach, where there was a short multi-ribbed shelf of granite rock. Beyond the shelf was a natural stone dock, maybe sixty yards from the trees; anyone coming into the cove would see that dock and would not look any further for a place to moor his boat—there wasn't any other place nearly as safe or as accessible.

He shut off the flash as they came on a rise in the terrain—on the far side the land sloped sharply downward and then flattened out to the waterline— and said to Tracy, "We can't chance using the light the rest of the way. Once we top this rise, anyone at the cove might be able to see it through the trees."

"I thought you said they couldn't get there before us."

"They can't. But there's the possibility of a sentry."

Pause. "What do we do if there is one?"

"I'm not sure," he said.

"Overpower him?"

"Maybe. Something like that."

"Kill him if necessary? Could you do that, David?"

"If it means saving *our* lives, yes," Jackman said, and did not know if that was the truth or false bravado. How does a man know if he is capable of killing another man until he is put to the test? How does a man know *anything* about himself until something happens to force knowledge on him? Intellectually and spiritually you might consider yourself courageous, capable of dealing with any crisis; but physically or instinctually you might turn out to be a coward. Or vice versa. Dei judicium.

What am I? he thought.

"There won't be a sentry," he said, and shivered inside his slicker. He had not noticed it coming cross-island, but the night had grown very cold: the breath of wind against his face and hands had lost its late-spring softness and become instead hard and chill, as sometimes happened in the black, empty hours between midnight and dawn.

"I hope not," she said, "Jesus," and he looked at her but could not see her face beneath the hood of her oilskin.

Neither of us knows what I am, he thought, and maybe neither of us wants to find out.

They climbed to the high ground, picking their way cautiously in the darkness, guided only by dapples and thin shafts of moonlight and Jackman's recollection of the path's course. The sound of their steps was cushioned by the damp humus underfoot, but now and then one of them would accidentally snap off a dry twig with some part of their body and the crack of it would echo through the silent woods. It would not carry far, though, and even if it did there were enough night sounds—falling cones, the scurrying of rodents and deer—so that it would seem natural and normal to anyone listening.

When they got to the place where the trail hooked toward the rear of the stone beach, Jackman took Tracy's hand and pulled her straight ahead through a tangle of ferns and bayberry shrubs. She followed without question or hesitation. After fifty yards he heard the slap-hiss of waves breaking over the rock shelf, and after another twenty he could see, through the trees ahead, torn patterns of fog drifting low across the shoreline.

Near the last verge of pine, he had a clear view straight out to sea. He could not make out the cove yet, any of the beach or the stone dock, because of the density of vegetation on their right. Out past the breakwater the mist was thicker, a long fluffy blanket that obscured part of the horizon. Above it, stars burned coldly, and the moon stared down like a whitish cyclopean eye; below it, a silver-tipped tier of combers rolled shoreward. The shelf and its hirsute coating of black algae glistened wetly with spray and tide pools.

Jackman stopped and said against Tracy's ear, "The footing gets a little precarious ahead, where you've got to go to see the cove. Maybe you'd better wait here."

"All right," reluctantly. "But not long."

"Not long," he said, and left her and went ahead until the earth beneath his feet gave way to slippery rock. Then he angled to his right and ducked past a cluster of wild cranberry bushes, came out at the inner edge of the shelf. The smooth rock was ten feet high here, too high to see over, and he moved around it vigilantly toward the beach. His foot slipped once on the slick surface and he went down hard to one knee, almost lost the flashlight but recovered in time and knelt there for a moment biting his lip against the pain in his kneecap. Chill spray from a breaking wave spattered the left side of his face, and its salt taste reminded him, oddly, of tears.

He pushed himself erect again and moved out to the beginning of the cobblestone beach, keeping his body humped over and pressed in close to the shelf. From there, then, he could look down across the beach to where the combers ran in, to where the natural dock jutted wet and mist-streaked from the inner wall of the shelf.

There was nothing there: no boat, no guard, nothing.

He swallowed thickly and scanned the beach and the rest of the cove. Emptiness. Lowering himself onto one knee, not the one he had fallen on, he raised the binoculars off his chest and adjusted the focus and swept the area again, slowly. But there was no place to hide a boat, no place to moor one within the cove or on either side of it out past the breakwater.

Jackman stood and turned back the way he had come, into the woods, to where he had left Tracy. She had hidden herself behind a tree, and when she saw him she came out and searched his face.

"It's not there, is it?"

"No," he said.

"Then it's at the bay somewhere."

"Yeah. Eider Neck, maybe."

"So we've got to go back where *they* are."

"They won't find us, Ty."

"Suppose we can't find the boat?"

"We'll find it," he said.

Silence. And then she said, "I knew all along it wasn't going to be here," in a voice that was flat, controlled, but with an unmistakable undercurrent of despair. "I knew it wasn't going to be anywhere near that easy for us."

He said nothing. But he thought: Yes—so did I.

And for the first time, the very first time, he understood that they might lose this game: he stood face to face with his own mortality.

□ □ □

The open meadowland south of Eider Neck seemed to shimmer liquidly in the night wind, mist-fringed and shining as though frosted under the lunar glow from above. Seaward, a marshy area seventy or eighty yards wide at its deepest inland point stretched between the outer edge of the Neck to the wall of trees in which Jackman and Tracy now stood—a distance of some two hundred yards along the slightly convex shoreline. Except for part of the barn and the tip of the house roof, the island buildings were hidden behind the humpbacked peninsula. The sky in that direction was untinged by artificial light of any kind.

Jackman swept the area with the binoculars, did not see anything out of the ordinary. "We'll go straight across the meadow," he whispered, "and onto the

Neck. Before we start looking for their boat, we've got to get an idea of how things look around the house."

"All right."

He took her hand and they moved rapidly out of the trees, slicker bottoms flapping against their legs like rubber wings. When they got to the foot of the Eider Neck slope, Jackman slowed and dropped onto his hands and knees, tugging Tracy down beside him. He gestured for her to wait there and then crawled up the sharp incline, past shale and granite outcroppings. Near the top he slipped the binocular strap over his head and clenched the glasses in one hand, and flattened out onto his stomach and inched up to a point just below the top, where he could see the bay and the whole of the cove behind it.

Propping himself up on his forearms, he steadied the glasses at his eyes. The beach and the greensward over by Jonas' cottage and the lawn before the house were deserted; the wooden cross stood smouldering—one of the charred arms had collapsed. Darkness shrouded all the windows in the house, filled the foyer beyond the still-open front door.

Jackman pushed himself backward, rolled over and skidded down to where Tracy was on heels and one palm. He told her what he had seen, and what he had not seen. "Maybe they're in the house," he said, "or out looking for us."

"Or with their boat," Tracy said.

"We'll take it slow and careful."

"Where do we look first?"

"Out at the end of the Neck. In the marsh."

"Where else can it be, if not there?"

"On the far side of the headland across the bay. There's a shallow inlet there where you could moor a small boat."

"No other place?"

"I don't think so."

"This is your goddamn island; don't you *know?*"

Inside the cowllike hood of her slicker, her face had the look of damp white clay, the eyes like dark holes deeply gouged out by the fingers of an angry sculptor. He knew she was fatigued from all the running and walking they had done, from the constant tension and fear; knew it because even though he was in good physical condition—he played handball whenever he could, jogged whenever he could—he felt the same way himself. No matter how good a shape you were in, you were never prepared for a situation like this: not physically and not mentally. His thoughts had a faint fuzziness at the edges now, the kind of fuzziness you experienced after having the one drink too many. You could still function well enough, but you could not quite trust your judgments or your emotional responses.

With a steadiness that even to him sounded forced, he said, "Jonas has lived out here for nearly forty years, and according to him the bay and the east cove are the only two places you can land a boat. So it's not probable that it could be anywhere else. But I suppose it's possible; just about anything is possible, we both know that all too well."

She looked away from him, scrubbed at her face, looked back. More calmly, then, she said, "I'm sorry, David. Nerves. I'm scared shitless."

"We both are," he said, and caught her hand and helped her to her feet. "Let's just move one square at a time, all right?"

"All right."

They went seaward along the side of the Neck, into the perimeter of the marshland. The earth there was covered with night-grotesque forms: gnarled and stunted pines, flowering shad, bayberry and wild cranberry shrubs, thick patches of catalpa grass and high brown reeds. The croaking of frogs and the occasional screeching of gulls and egrets penetrated fog massed like thin layers of whipped cream or swirling sinuously in changing designs along the shore and out over the water. Their steps made liquid squishing sounds in the boggy ground.

It took them three or five or ten minutes to reach the tip of the peninsula; Jackman was not sure because his sense of time-perception seemed to be malfunctioning. But time did not mean anything now, except in relation to the coming dawn, and that was still at least three hours away.

They uncovered several duck nests and startled a small animal that was probably a muskrat, but they did not uncover any sign of a boat.

They crouched beside a sassafras bush, inside a misty swath of reeds. Water lapped over their ankles, and the footing beneath it was thick mud and slippery rock. Jackman tried to work spit through his dry mouth, but the saliva glands were desiccated. All the moisture in his body seemed to be leaking out through his pores: he felt as though he were marinating in sweat. Much worse than that, the visceral tension was beginning to take its toll; his nerves had tightened to the danger point.

He drew several deep, silent breaths and stared out over the marsh. They had gone over no more than a sixth of it, but it was dotted toward the center with sinkholes and patches of mud as treacherous as quicksand. If the boat were hidden anywhere on this side of the Neck, it would have to have been brought in either in the vicinity of where they now were—in which case they should already have found it—or down near the line of evergreens, a less likely mooring or hiding place.

Jackman swiveled his gaze to the Neck's outer reaches. The land there peaked into a tiny promontory, the base of which was strewn with seaweed-draped boulders and tide-covered mudflats; on the promontory and the rest of the higher ground atop the peninsula, projections and knobs of rock jutted up through the grass like warts and blemishes. There was nowhere at the tip, or near it on this side, where a boat could have been secreted. The only possible place was over on the bay side, just in from the breakwater, where a plot of tall sedges grew close to the sloping side.

The juxtaposition of the rocks at the foot of the point made it too difficult and too dangerous to go around that way. So he would have to head up across the promontory and then down in order to check the plot of sedges, and that meant crawling most of the way to avoid silhouetting himself against the sky.

He whispered all of this to Tracy. She did not want to be left alone again, that was obvious in the way she looked at him, the way her fingers clutched at his arm. But when he said, "It won't take long either way; you'll be able to see me most of the time from here," she nodded jerkily, held his arm a moment longer and then released it.

Jackman straightened and went around the bush, sliding his shoes gingerly through the water and the grasping mud.

When he had waded through a shock of catalpa grass he was on a hummock of dry, solid turf that connected with the side of the Neck. He could move more rapidly then, and he ran bent over across the hummock, onto the slope, up it toward where one of the larger knobs of rock canted skyward at the crest.

He had taken half a dozen steps when the man came out from below and behind the rock knob.

Jackman stopped as suddenly as if he had walked into a wall. He stared incredulously, and his stomach spasmed and turned over; he was unable to move, to react—suspended for a moment in time and space. The man was big, young, naked to the waist. On his chest, gleaming black in the moonlight, was the same cabalistic sign that had been drawn in blood on the cottage door, on the note attached to the fawn's bone. He held a rifle in both hands, but he stood as motionless as Jackman, matching his stare.

Fifty yards away to the right, a second armed and half-naked man appeared on top of the Neck.

It took a cry from Tracy below to release Jackman from paralysis. Panic climbed in him, shrieking mutely. He spun and stumbled downslope, across the hummock; water sprayed up around his ankles as his feet slashed through it and into the muck beneath. Tracy was running too: he could see her plunging away into the marsh. He fought his way through reeds and shrubs, altering his course toward hers, cutting around a stunt pine, avoiding at the last second a pool of muddy water that marked a boghole. Hammering pulse created a rage of sound in his ears; there was pain in his chest, pain in his groin where muscles had knotted.

He did not want to look back, he did not want to see how close the two men were behind him, but it was impossible to resist the need. And when he finally did pivot his head, he saw them still on the slope—coming down it to the marshland at a pace that seemed surprisingly unhurried, the rifles still held across their bodies rather than butted up at their shoulders in shooting position.

He twisted his head to the front again, and Tracy was just disappearing into a cloud of mist that appeared to cling hammocklike between two shad trees spaced thirty yards apart. A moment later he heard a crashing noise, a splash, the muffled plaint of her voice. He bulled through a chest-high swatch of reeds, came out in a wide clump of thistle; thorns stung at his legs below the hem of the oilskin.

When he neared the layer of fog he could still hear Tracy thrashing around somewhere within it. He swept through with his arms flailing and puffs of the mist rising like smoke, his eyes searching down low to the ground. He located her almost instantly: she was on her knees at the edge of a sinkhole, struggling to rise, her back to him. As soon as she heard him coming up behind her she lunged to her feet, staggered, fell again whimpering. He reached her, caught her arm, and she fought him blindly, frantically, nails flashing, until he said, "It's me, Ty, it's me!" and then she sagged into him, and he was able to hoist her upright. He pulled her forward and onto firmer ground, his legs churning awkwardly in the mud as he circled around trees and shrubs blurred by fog and by his own sweat-filmed eyes.

And while they ran, a sense of unreality bordering on farce came over him. An image of the two of them running danced through his mind: they must look ridiculous, stripped of all dignity. If only his fellows in Washington could see him now! Jackman the fool. Reductio ad absurdum. Jesus....

Ahead, the land dipped and opened into a wide backwater pool, heavily verged with sedges and swamp grass. He hesitated at the edge of it. The shortest way to the concealing trees beyond was straight across the pool, and it looked shallow enough, safe enough to wade through without becoming mired—and acting on impulse, then, he took Tracy into the silt-heavy water.

It came up over their knees at first and the footing was good; but when they reached the center, mud slid away beneath his shoes and he went under, brackish water spilling into his open mouth, Tracy's hand sliding out of his: she had gone under too. He kicked up, broke surface and saw her floundering beside him, coughing. He caught hold of her, steadied her against him, and together they swam a few strokes clumsily. When he put his feet down again, the mud supported his weight, and he straightened himself and Tracy up in the waist-deep water and then plowed forward until it was shallow enough to allow them to run again.

The marsh growth was thinner on the opposite side, the earth less swampy. They sprinted through it toward the trees looming blackly ahead, and he knew they were going to get into them all right, get away without being caught. Looked back instinctively to confirm this and saw no sign of the two men in the foggy marsh behind them.

Then they were into the woods, and he cut a diagonal course to the left, inland, not slowing, half-dragging Tracy now because he could tell that her strength was nearly gone. His thoughts had begun to jumble, turn sluggish, but he understood the need to find sanctuary as soon as possible—a place to hide, to rest, to regain control. The fort? Yes, the circle of rocks where he and Dale had pretended to be New World Indians or adventurous explorers, where they had once played a grand hiding game for an entire day in retaliation for what they had considered an unjust punishment, and the Old Man and Charlie Pepper had not been able to find them. Loop through the forest behind the house, out to the point on the north shore and into the rock fort where these men could not find them either.

He understood something else, too: that the two men on the Neck could have caught them, could have used the rifles to wound them. And why hadn't they? Because they felt they were in control of this game, and ending it too soon, like ending any game too soon, would have lessened the ecstasy of a final triumph—the checkmate, the last out, the deathstroke?

Sweet Jesus God....

□ □ □

Sunrise.

Across a section of the rocky point on the north shore, and through a thin copse of trees, the sun appeared poised on the edge of the sea, glinting redly. The sky around it was streaked in diluted crimson, like bloody fingermarks. Early-morning sounds filled the cool air: the singing of land birds, the squawking of the ever-present gulls, the faint buzzing of bees and sand flies. Small black crabs skittered over the rocks; the sea glittered with reflections of light from the new sun.

On the westward, inner edge of the point, a rock overhang jutted out from a steep incline topped by pine and a single weathered oak. Beneath the overhang, sweeping out from it on the inland side, a cluster of craggy boulders and humps of granite six to eight feet high formed four-fifths of a rough circle; the other fifth was open to the sea but could not be seen from anywhere except directly out on the tip of the point. Within that circle was a small pocket: the fort of Jackman's youth.

He and Tracy sat there side by side on a bed of smooth pebbles and strips of seaweed, butted against one of the boulders. There was just enough room in the narrow enclosure for them to stretch their legs out full length. Her eyes were closed, and she seemed to be sleeping; but his eyes were wide, fixed. He sat rigidly with his hands gripping his knees beneath the open flaps of his slicker.

He was calm now and had been for some time, but it was a terrifying kind of calm; there was a primal scream buried just beneath the surface of it. His body ached, and he wanted desperately to sleep—sleep not only renewed strength, it solidified your grip on sanity. But he had not been able to close his eyes for more than a few minutes since they had come to the fort. For the first hour they had held each other, not speaking because there was nothing to say in the dying hours of the night. After awhile, exhausted, she had drifted off into a fitful slumber; and he had simply sat there, watching the sky, waiting for dawn, hanging onto the calm and trying to force his thoughts to remain clear and systematic.

In the past few minutes a sense of overwhelming helplessness had taken hold of him. Every tactic, every potential move, seemed futile.

The boat. If it was in that plot of sedges on the inner curve of Eider Neck—and the presence of the two men there indicated that it probably was—there was no way to get to it, no way to avoid or neutralize the long-range threat of the rifles. There was still a remote possibility that the boat was hidden on the headland that formed the northwestern boundary of the bay; but the terrain

there was too heavily wooded to be easily defensible. They were expert gamesmen too, they had proved that during the night: they would have planned
their own strategy with intelligence and craft, like a military mission. (And
*could* they be former army or marine personnel, as Tracy had half-suggested?)

A signal for help. They had nothing with which to signal a passing lobster
or pleasure boat, or to alert anyone on the nearest inhabited island. Nothing,
that was, except fire—and a fire big enough to command investigation had to
be built either on the cliffs or here on the point, and then tended constantly
to keep it burning bright enough to be seen at a distance; but it would also
attract the attention of the opponents, bring them running to snuff it out and
tell them just where he and Tracy were. Then there was the danger of sparks
carrying on the shifting winds and igniting the forestland. He had seen a small
island on fire once, and the rapidity with which it had been consumed was
astonishing: burning trees sailing through the air like massive hurled faggots
to torch off other trees, fire traveling along the interlocking root structure
beneath the surface of the earth, feeding on the inflammable sap of the pines
and spruce. This entire island could turn into a raging inferno in a matter of
hours—and while that would certainly drive the opponents away in their
boat, it would also trap him and Tracy. There was nowhere they could go to
escape it except into the caves at the foot of the cliffs, and they could only
remain there as long as the tide was at ebb. If they were not found and rescued
before flood tide, they would drown.

Mount some sort of offensive. They were two people armed with knives; the
enemy was at least two and perhaps more, armed with handguns and rifles. A
direct confrontation would be suicidal. Set some sort of traps? But what kind?
Where? He had no tools and no time to dig pitfalls or fashion vine-triggered
missiles or snares, no assurance even if he had that they would work. Jonas and
the Old Man had taught him a little woodsman's lore, and he knew the island
better than the opponents could ever know it; but what good was any of that
except as a help in avoiding capture? It would not give them the upper hand,
and it would not get them off the island.

Wait and hide and pray they would not be found. Jonas and his wife might
come out on Tuesday when he didn't bring the cruiser back, but then again
they might simply think he had decided to stay on and wait days or even a
week before they considered something to be wrong and came to investigate.
And even if they did show up, there was nothing to stop the enemy from
killing them outright or capturing them and making them part of whatever
blood rites were planned for him and Tracy. They had only the small amount
of food she had taken from the kitchen and pantry last night, some of which
had probably been lost or rendered inedible by submergence in the backwater
pool in the marsh; and their chances of getting into the house for more were
realistically zero. They could eat pine nuts and green berries, but without fresh
water—and there was virtually none on the island this time of year except
that piped into the house and cottage from an underground cistern—they
could not last more than five or six days.

What would the Old Man, that Grand Master of Gamesmen, have done in a situation like this? Jackman thought. In 1960, when he had apparently been defeated for reelection with 78 percent of the precincts reporting, he had said, "I will not concede defeat. I will not concede defeat until all the votes are in and I am behind, and even then I will demand a recount." And one of his aides, in Jackman's hearing, had said immediately to another aide, "And if the recount fails, he'll ask for another one and use every dime he's got to fix the results." That was the Old Man, all right: never give up, never say die, ruthlessly competitive to the very end because any game can be won no matter how enormous the odds—even one like this.

If you can stay in it, he thought. If you can keep from breaking down.

Beside him Tracy stirred and made a soft moaning sound. Then, suddenly and violently, her eyes popped open and she jerked away from the boulder and onto her knees, staring at him disconnectedly and with shining terror. He said her name, said it again, and awareness seeped into her and cleared her vision and dulled the terror. She sank back on one hip and lifted her head and breathed tremulously. Her face was pocked with scratches, pimpled red with insect bites, and the skin under her eyes and across her cheekbones had a puckered, waxy look; strands of hair, matted with dried mud, lay flat against her forehead and fell stiffly from inside the pulled-back hood of her slicker. She looked ten years older than she was, and he knew his own appearance was as bad or worse.

Compassion rose in him, and he touched her hand. She pulled it away from him, but impersonally, as if she could not bear to be touched by anyone. She put her spine against the boulder again and hugged herself, staring up at the coralline sky.

He said tentatively, "How do you feel?"

"Wonderful. Lovely. How do you think I feel?"

"Frightened," he said. "Like me."

"How reassuring for both of us."

"I'm just facing facts, Ty."

"So am I. And it's hopeless: we're dead."

"No...."

"Dead, sitting here dead. Why didn't they kill us last night? They could have; they could have caught us in that marsh. At least it would be over now and we wouldn't have to keep on waiting for it to happen. That's worse than dying, David—the waiting for something you know is inevitable."

"It's not inevitable. We've still got a chance."

"What chance? We didn't find the boat, did we."

"It's got to be in that patch of sedges I told you about."

"Suppose it is. How do we get to it?"

"I'm not sure we can."

"Then we can't get off the island. And we can't fight them. What else is there?"

"Faith," he said.

"In what? God? Miracles?"

"In ourselves, in our ability to find a way to survive. There has to *be* a way, Ty; there's always a way to do anything, even what seems to be the impossible."

"Thank you, Reverend Billy Graham."

That made him angry for a reason he could not identify—and with the anger came the realization that through all that had happened last night, all the running and searching and hiding, he had not once felt the emotion of rage. He concentrated on it, and found it surprisingly good, assertive, a stabilizer for the brittle calm; it even helped to dissipate some of the feeling of helplessness, to give strength and credence to what had been little more than empty palliatives for Tracy's and his own fear. There *did* have to be a way. Somewhere in all those postulated negatives, there was a positive action and a positive result, he just had not found it yet.

"All right," he said, putting derision into his voice, "it's hopeless, we're going to die, we're already dead. Then we might as well walk out of here right now and go back to the house and give ourselves over to them. Is that what you want? Give yourself up like a lamb for slaughter? Or do you want to fight for your life? Maybe you'll fail, maybe you will die, but does it make any sense not to fight at all?"

She looked at him for a long moment, as if startled by his vehemence, and then turned her head aside. In a soft dull voice she said, "What do you want to do? Just sit in here, hiding? They'd find us eventually, you know that."

He did not answer. Instead he stood up and peered over the boulder, satisfied himself of the absence of movement among the trees that flanked the point on both inland sides. There was very little breeze: the pine boughs barely stirred. The sun had climbed higher off the eastern horizon, modulating the sky's flush into a soft gold sheen, filling the woods with dusky shafts and patches of its light. The night chill was already fading from the air; in another hour it would be warm, and by midday the temperature would be in the high seventies.

When he turned back, Tracy was watching him. He opened the snaps on his oilskin, shrugged it off, then sat down again with it spread over his lap. He said, "The first thing we have to do is take inventory of what's left after that dunking in the marsh."

He began emptying the slicker pockets, and after a moment, silently, she took hers off and followed suit. They put everything on the pebbles between them, and what they had were the two kitchen knives, one flashlight—the other one had been lost; a key-open tin of Spam, a sealed package of cheddar cheese, two oranges, an apple that was no good because it had gotten sliced open by one of the knives and then been soaked in swamp water, a small sodden inesculent box of raisins, two bars of bitter chocolate; and the mud-caked binoculars that still hung from around his neck. He tried the flashlight, holding the round glass end against his palm, and it worked all right; the batteries had not been water-damaged. One of the binocular lenses had a hairline crack, but when he cleaned both lenses with saliva and then tested them by focusing on the evergreens above, he found that the crack did not impair magnification or clarity.

He picked up the orange and extended it to Tracy, but she shook her head. "I can't eat anything," she said. "I'd just throw it up again, the way my stomach feels."

Jackman nodded—he knew he could not eat anything either—and said, "Okay, we'll save the food for later." He gathered it up and returned it to the pockets of one slicker, along with the flashlight. Then he scooped away pebbles until he exposed damp earth, widened the holes, rolled both oilskins into a bundle and put them into the depression, and covered them over with more of the pebbles.

Tracy said, "What now?"

"I think we ought to go over what we know about those men."

"We don't know anything about them."

"Yes we do. Not much, maybe, but a little. We know to begin with that there are at least two of them—the two that were out on the Neck. The one who showed himself directly in front of me was clean-shaven. I didn't get a good look at the second one, but I had an impression of a beard. How clearly did you see that one?"

"Not very," she said. "I was just starting to run when he showed himself."

"The one you saw at the kitchen window *did* have a beard?"

"Yes. He was no more than five feet away, and he had his face pressed right up to the glass."

"So we're still not sure if there are more than two."

Heavily: "If there are, our chances are that much worse."

"Granted," Jackman said. "But they're going to have to watch the boat, if only from a distance, and they're going to have to watch the house and the cottage; they don't want us getting in to stock up on food and water. One of them could handle all that, but not very well. So if there are only two, I don't think they'd risk a lone hunter to look for us. I doubt if they'd send just one man in any case."

"Why not?"

"Because they can't know the island as well as I do, and they'd have to realize the possibility of an ambush. Whatever else they are, they're not stupid."

"Then all of them are somewhere around the house."

"At this stage of things, yes."

"Then where does that leave us?"

"With some freedom of movement, at least."

"What good is freedom of movement?" Tracy said. She pressed the heels of her hands against both temples, as though her head ached harshly. "Their boat is at the bay, they're at the bay, and we can't get to any of them because we don't know where any of them are."

"We should be able to find out whether or not the boat really is in those sedges."

"How?"

"By going out on the bay headland on this side. From there I can use the binoculars. The house and grounds will be visible from there too."

"But we still can't get to it or them—"

"One square at a time, remember?" Jackman said. The anger continued to energize him, provide him with the impetus for positive thinking and direction. "Once we learn exact locations, we can start worrying about what to do next. We can't accomplish anything as long as we're blind."

Her eyes held his. "You really believe there's hope."

"Yes. Damn it, yes."

"I guess that's enough for both of us, then," she said. Her mouth formed a wry, humorless smile. "The good guys always win, right? All they have to do is to hang in there and they'll come out on top."

"No," he said, "not always. But this time."

He stood again, and Tracy did the same in stiff, enervated movements. Watching her, he became conscious again of the aching in his own body: they must have run five miles or better during the night.

He said, "Maybe I'd better go alone to the headland. You'd be safe here and you could rest—"

"No. No way, Senator. I'm strong enough and I can keep fighting if you can, but not if I have to do any more waiting by myself. I'll revert to stereotype and go to pieces like a damned hysterical female unless we stay together."

Jackman understood that: she took strength from him, and perhaps the reverse was true as well. He nodded grimly.

She asked, "How far is it to the headland?"

"Less than a fifth of a mile."

"I can make that all right."

"We'll take our time," he said. "Later, we can come back here and try to sleep. No matter what we find out, there isn't anything we can do about it during the daylight hours. The only advantage we have is the cover of darkness."

□ □ □

The shallow inlet on the headland's outer, northward curve had ten-foot shale banks that rose steeply out of the placid sea. A dense stand of trees bordered it on the north; toward the bay, the evergreens were more thinly spaced, interspersed with birch and an occasional oak. The ground behind the inlet was clear, covered with meadow grass and wildflowers and a long mossy hump of rock which formed a natural stone bench.

The area was deserted.

Jackman and Tracy crossed through the grass from the north. They had taken thirty minutes or better to approach the inlet, creeping within the woods until they had gotten close enough for him to use the binoculars. The fact that neither the boat nor the enemy was there, as he had suspected would be the case, strengthened his conviction that the craft was hidden in those sedges on Eider Neck.

At the edge of the cleared space he raised the glasses again and peered south through the trees, but he could not see much: patches of sun-bright water, of the Neck. They moved forward toward the bay, weaving from tree to tree, keeping their bodies low to the ground. When they neared the side of the headland, the woods gave way to clumps of fern and high grass and sphagnum moss, and finally to bare rock that fell away in jagged inclines to the water. He knelt behind the trunk of a pine, felt Tracy do the same close behind him. From there he had an unobstructed view of the Neck several hundred yards straight across the open bay, of part of the cove where the house was. The configuration of the headland was such that it bellied outward to his left, and the vegetation there obscured the house itself and the other buildings.

He steadied his left arm against the trunk and focused the glasses on Eider Neck, found the tall brown sedges near the breakwater. Thickly matted, motionless in the calm air, they still seemed far away—and he could not find the boat or a break in the reeds where the boat might be.

Tracy said, "Is it there? Can you see it?"

"No. We're too far away; the glasses aren't powerful enough."

Silence.

And a new possibility struck him, sickeningly. Suppose the boat was a small outboard made of fiberglass or aluminum? Once they had landed on the island, they could have *carried* it out of the water and hidden it somewhere, anywhere, inland. Christ!

His nerves began to jangle again; he struggled to hold onto the calm. No, he thought, no, the boat has to be in those sedges. The two men had been on the Neck last night; why would they have been waiting there unless it was to guard the boat? It was there, all right: he would not let go of the conviction. It was a foundation, no matter how flimsy, from which they could work. Without that foundation, without knowledge of some of the rules the opponents had made up for this game, there was only blind and impotent groping: defeat.

Jackman moved the binoculars slowly over the Neck, pausing at each of the outcroppings and knobs of rock where a guard might conceal himself. He saw no one, no movement. Abruptly he straightened and caught Tracy's hand, and they went laterally to the left and out to where the headland bellied, through the trees there until he had a full view of the closed boathouse, the beach, the three buildings. Again he swung the glasses in a slow arc, left to right, right to left. Stillness. Except for the charred cross standing obscenely on the lawn, the faint reddish smears visible on the front of the cottage, everything appeared just as it had on their arrival yesterday afternoon.

"Anything?" Tracy said.

"No."

"So we haven't gained a thing coming out here," emptily.

"We've got the whole day ahead of us," he said. "There's no reason why we can't stay here, watching, instead of going back to the fort. One of them has to show himself sooner or later."

"All right," and she sank down onto the pine needles and crossed her arms on her knees and laid her head on them.

Jackman sat beside her and lifted the glasses once more to his eyes....

⊔ □ ◻

Chains of seconds.

Chains of minutes.

One hour, two hours, three hours.

The blue of the water, the green and brown of the trees, the white of the cobble beach, the yellow of the sunlight—all of it photograph-still. But once in a while the images and the colors blurred together, soft focus, dissolving—

His body spasmed and his head came up and he shook it rapidly, blinking to clear his vision: he had nearly fallen asleep again. He was lying on his stomach, propped up on his forearms; he shifted position until he was sitting on his right hip, and rubbed at the gritty mucus that filmed both eyes. He had already dozed off twice, once for what might have been several minutes. The air was warm, the cushion of pine needles soft beneath his body, and lassitude had seeped into every space of him.

The hands on his watch indicated that it was twenty past one. Lifting the binoculars for the fiftieth or the hundredth time, he moved them through what had by now become an habitual ninety-degree arc, from the cottage around to the tip of Eider Neck. And for the fiftieth or the hundredth time, he saw the same familiar sights and the same desertion.

Two hours or so earlier, he had thought he discerned movement at one of the house's upstairs front windows. But his perception of it as he panned with the glasses had been so brief, so indistinct at the corner of sight that it was virtually subliminal; and when he had snapped the binoculars back and held them on the window, there was nothing to see. Still, it had been the one in his old room: they could have been taking turns sleeping in there. That would at least partly explain why he had seen no indication of anyone in the past three hours. Spending the day inside the house, watching, feeding vicariously on the frustrations and fears of their quarry; waiting for nightfall, maybe, before they came out again. Creatures of the night, worshipers of Darkness, shadow predators.

But were they really that confident of winning with a minimum of struggle? That unconcerned with the danger of outside intervention? Young men who had lived through the horrors of war, who had adopted a different type of horror as their irreligion, might well be both of these things. Or was there more to it than that—something about the rules of this game that he did not quite understand as yet...?

"You'd better let me take the glasses for a while, David," Tracy's dulled voice said behind him. "You look ready to pass out."

It startled him, jerked his head around: the last time he had checked on her, she had been asleep, curled foetally at the base of a balsam spruce. Now she was sitting up against the bole, watching him. There was color in her cheeks and she appeared rested and alert.

Jackman dry-washed his face, palms scraping audibly across the beard stubble on his cheeks. He did not want to give in to the fatigue, but he would not have a choice pretty soon; he would sleep before long either way, and it would benefit him more if he gave in to it willingly. Tracy could do a far more attentive job of keeping a vigil than he could now.

He said, "Okay, you're right," in a voice that sounded thick, faintly hollow, and took the binoculars from around his neck and gave them to her when she crawled over beside him. Their eyes met, held, shifted apart. She knew he had seen nothing, and he knew she knew it, and there was nothing for either of them to say. He watched her fit the glasses to her eyes, fiddle with the focusing knobs, hold steady in the direction of the house, then begin to scan. When she was looking out toward the end of Eider Neck, without having spoken, he rolled over onto his stomach and put his head in the fold of his arms and closed his eyes.

But sleep did not come immediately, in spite of his exhaustion. Instead his mind drifted, in and out of thought patterns, in and out of nooks and crannies of memory; then, like a roulette ball settling finally into a slot, his consciousness focused on a single memory, forgotten, hidden away, resurrected at this time and place for reasons known only to his psyche: the summer of his fourteenth year, and the girl named Linda Fong who had come into his life then....

Linda Fong is the daughter of the live-in cook the Old Man has hired out of Bangor, and she is one year older than he is—old enough to wear a maid's costume and to help with the cleaning and serving at the parties. She is also a beautiful girl, with huge black eyes, and he is enchanted by her. They become friends, and he shows her the island, shows her the fort and the other special places, and they talk about many things and discover they have many of the same interests and attitudes. She is the happiest person he has ever known, always smiling, and when she laughs, which is often, her eyes sparkle and a dimple appears in her right cheek.

One evening toward the end of summer, the Old Man gives an old-fashioned fish fry. Hoop nets are set out in the bay to catch sculpin and flounder, and there are bonfires along the beach and lanterns hanging from the ornate ground poles, and buffet tables laden with salads and ears of sweet Maine corn and fat tomatoes and home-baked bread and blueberries in sugared cream, and fifty or sixty guests and half a dozen servants and the three-piece band from Milbridge. Linda is supposed to help, but that afternoon he takes her to explore the caves at the bottom of the cliffs and they lose track of time and it is almost dusk before they realize it. They run back through the woods, holding hands—her hand is warm and soft in his and he feels very good even though he is worried about keeping her out so long—and when they reach Eider Neck he sees that most of the guests are already there on the beach. Linda is apprehensive and wants to go directly to her room in the house to change clothes, but he pulls her with him toward the beach because he wants to explain to his father that it is his fault she is late, and because he wants to ask that she be relieved of her duties tonight so she can join him for the fish fry.

When they run in among the guests, hands clasped, activity stops and people stare and begin to murmur, he does not know why, and his father appears looking angry and sends Linda away, harsh-voiced. Then the Old Man takes him aside and asks him what he thinks he's doing, and he says he does not understand, and the Old Man says, "She's Chinese, boy," and he says, "What difference does that make?" and the Old Man says, "It makes all the difference in the world when you come running here holding her hand like she was white," and the next day Jonas takes Linda and her father away from the island and he never sees her again.

But the following week the Old Man invites a congressman, Fred Tremaine, to visit the island for a few days, and when Tremaine arrives he has his daughter with him. Her name is Judy and she is the same age as he is, and pretty—but not as pretty as Linda—and has large breasts and corn-colored hair. During their stay he takes Judy exploring, as he took Linda, but it is not the same, she giggles too much and smokes cigarettes from a package she hides in her purse. On the last night she asks him to take a walk with her and they go into the woods and she maneuvers him into a quiet little glade and before long they are sitting down and she is kissing him, putting his hand on her breast, urging him to open her blouse and take off her bra, and after he has done that she pushes him down on the soft pine needles and touches his erection, rubs it, and says, Take it out, Davey, I want to hold it, and he does that and she grasps it and while he fondles her breasts she masturbates him until he comes into her lace handkerchief—and the next morning, as Judy and her father are preparing to leave for the mainland, the Old Man takes him aside again and says, "Now she's the kind of girl you should be running with, son, she's one of your own...."

Jackman shifted position, and the memory was gone as quickly as it had come. Threads of sleep finally dulled his thoughts, but it was that kind of thin, fitful, oppressive sleep which never quite blocks out awareness. Sounds penetrated—Tracy moving nearby, the song of a blackbird, something scurrying—and then faded to silence, and then returned again in an almost rhythmic cycle. He dreamed, and as always a part of him seemed to stand off at a distance and observe the images flickering back and forth on the screen of his mind.

There was no sequence to the dream or dreams; there was only a disquieting jumble of fragments—a patchwork nightmare. A squirrel sitting on a pine bough, chattering, its belly cut open and blood leaking from the wound. Alicia screaming at him, "I'm going to kill myself, David, I mean it!" and then drawing the sharp blade of a knife across her throat. The Old Man talking, mouth moving at twice the normal speed but with no words coming out. The little Vietnamese boy with the blood all over his face, hiding his face. A half-naked man holding a giant gun, flames leaping and flaring around him and on his chest a symbol of black-magic that glistened red and undulated like a live thing, sensual in its caresses. The Old Man again, mouth still moving too fast, but now his words audible in a kind of Donald Duck chatter: *game plan, great game, man's game, chess game, fair game, all a game game game game....*

The dreams stopped altogether, and there was a void.

And out of the void, a long while later, the face of Jonas and Jonas' gruff Down East voice: "Ayuh, I undertook to sell the *Carrie B* couple months back, Mr. Jackman. Fella from Milbridge offered me a good price, and me gettin too old to go lobsterin much these days, w'a'nt a heft of sense in lettin her sit in drydock most of the year. Fella didn't want my pots and buoys, nor anything else off her, and I ain't got a place here on the Main to store 'em. So put nigh everything in the barn out on the island, hope you don't mind."

Pots and buoys. Boys and pot. Sons and guns, leaps and flares—

Jackman woke up.

He lay for a second, then lifted onto hands and knees, dimly saw slanting rays from the sun tilted westward in a hazy, late-afternoon sky. *Pots and buoys.* The dream still had hold of him, he could still hear Jonas' voice echoing in his mind: a voice from three summers ago, the summer Jonas had sold the lobster boat he'd owned for thirty-five years, the summer of Meg's last visit to the island. And later that same day... later, on the island, he had gone out to the barn and rummaged through the stored goods from the *Carrie B*—a nostalgia trip, a reaching back through the past to touch a tangible part of those cold morning hours before dawn when he and Dale and Jonas had gone out to run the string of lobster traps. *Pots and buoys.* And among them, *sons and guns,* among them, *leaps and flares,* among them—

Flare gun, the emergency flare gun!

Jackman reared up on his knees, did not feel the painful protest in sleep-stiffened joints or the parched soreness in his throat. The dream released him, but there was no feeling of grogginess; instead his thoughts were sharp, and he had a vivid image of the flare pistol as he had seen it—flares, too, half a dozen of them—in a box of miscellaneous goods three years ago. The memory had been buried in his subconscious, and it had taken the random association of his dreams to drag it out; there had been too much strain and too much tension for his conscious mind to have recalled it unaided.

Emotion flooded through him: excitement, fresh hope, resolution. He looked for Tracy, saw her sitting cross-legged beside one of the trees, scanning the cove and Eider Neck with the glasses. When he said her name she turned, shoulders slumped, and moved her head from side to side in a defeated way and started to speak—and then became aware of his expression and frowned questioningly as he came over to her, gripped her arms.

He told her about the flare gun.

She stared at him as if she could not quite believe what he was saying, as if she did not dare to believe it. "David," she said finally, "David, are you *sure?*"

"I'm sure it was there three years ago."

"Three years is a long time—"

"Jonas wouldn't have removed it. He's never bought another boat, and the cruiser had its own emergency pistol."

"But those freaks could have searched the barn, found it—"

"No. No. That collection of guns in my father's study contained a dozen different types of firearm. They would have thought every gun on the island was stored there. They probably searched the cottage, yes; but there wouldn't have been any reason for them to suspect anything was in the barn. It's still there, Ty—and we can get to it. Wherever they are, whatever they're watching for, the barn should be the last place they expect us to go."

She kept on looking at him, and he could see some of the same emotions which filled him slowly seeping into her. "If we can, if the pistol is still there, then what?"

Jackman's mind raced, plotting, calculating: the gamesman in him had been regenerated. "We'll take it to the fort," he said. "There are plenty of boats in this area, pleasure craft, lobster fishermen, trawlers; as soon as we spot one, tonight or tomorrow, we'll fire a flare. They'll respond out of curiosity, if nothing else. When they do we'll swim out and let them pick us up."

"What if *they* see it too?"

"They won't; we'll shoot at a low trajectory. And a flare gun is also a weapon, don't forget that."

Tracy said, "God, maybe... maybe..." and leaned against him, and they sat there hanging onto each other and this new hope in the warmth of the lowering sun.

□ □ □

They came back to the fort a half hour before sunset.

Long shadows stretched through the pine woods and the trees looked black against the variegated backdrop of the sky. The sea had a burnished sheen. A light northerly wind had begun drawing, tinged with coldness, and it fanned their faces as they came out onto the point, slipped around and through, into the small pocket within the rocks.

Jackman sank to his knees and scraped away the pebbles covering the buried slickers. He unrolled the oilskins, took out one of the oranges and the wedge of cheese and a chocolate bar. Peeled the fruit and broke it into halves and gave one to Tracy. The juice soothed away some of the dryness in his throat, and he ate cheese and chocolate ravenously: with hope had come hunger. Tracy had difficulty getting the food down, but she managed to swallow all of it and keep it on her stomach.

Sitting on the headland, they had planned their strategy for tonight. They would wait, first of all, until after dark—but not too long after dark; there was nothing to be gained by holding off until the hours between midnight and dawn, and the waiting would be bad enough without extending it an additional five or six hours. There was no less a risk at three A.M. than there was at ten P.M. Once you were sure of your moves, you had to make them boldly, without hesitation, without worrying about contingencies: another of the Old Man's game-playing maxims.

Then they would circle around to the trees on the slope behind the barn, both of them together because Tracy was determined not to let him go alone,

not wait by herself in the darkness. Come down out of the trees and cross perhaps sixty yards of open ground to the rear wall of the barn. There would be
another full moon, and the sky was cloudless and looked as though it would
remain that way; but even if one of the enemy was stationed on the rear porch
of the house, or at an upstairs window, the barn would block off his view of
the open ground. And once they made their way around to its front, the two
leafy apple trees would act as a screen between the house and the barn, and
provide concealing shadows as well.

After they were inside, Tracy would stand watch at the doors while he located the pistol and the flares; that way, they would have at least some insurance
that when they went out they would not walk into an ambush. If he could
locate the objects immediately, they would have to stay inside the barn no
more than ten minutes, perhaps even as few as five. Then they would come
directly back into the trees and return here to the fort.

It was a simple plan, and it would work; he refused to consider any of the
things that could go wrong. Still, his nerves were thrumming again, and he
seemed to have lost the excitement that had flooded him when he first remembered the flare pistol. He was unable to summon it again, or the anger or any
of the other emotions. These would come later, he told himself, when the time
arrived for them to put the maneuver into action. Meanwhile, there was nothing to do except to keep a tight grip on himself and try not to think—just what
a soldier was taught to do before entering combat in that other mad game of
war.

Tracy shifted beside him, seeking a less uncomfortable position on the bed
of pebbles. She said, "What time is it?"

He glanced at his watch. "Seven-forty."

"Two hours."

"Yes."

"I wish I could sleep it away."

"Maybe you can."

"No way."

"Try closing your eyes."

She said nothing, and after a moment he looked over at her. Her eyes were
closed. She held her hands fisted on her thighs, breathing audibly through her
mouth. In the fading daylight her cheeks looked hollow, the skin of her face
stretched thin and oddly translucent; the bone structure seemed so prominent
that it was like a skull over which thin plastic had been molded to simulate
human features. Jackman turned his head away, tilted it back against the boulder and stared up at the sky.

Time passed—so slowly that he came to imagine the ticking of a faulty clock,
one tick every five or ten seconds. The last of the sunset hues disappeared from
the western horizon—violet and old rose tonight—and the gray-black of encroaching darkness settled down. Cold stars appeared, and light from the
moon that he could not quite see laid a faint whitish glow across the night.
The air cooled more quickly and the wind grew stronger; the sea made whis-

pering sounds, like a thousand muted voices heard from a vast distance.

And all the while gulls wheeled and dived out of sight and appeared again overhead in continuous patterns, their calls querulous and irritable and hungry: the vultures of the sea looking down on him and on Tracy as though resentful of the fact that they were still alive.

□ □ □

10:25.

In the perimeter of the woods behind the barn Jackman rested on one knee and moved the binoculars slowly from side to side. Tracy stood to his left, behind the canted trunk of a dead pine. Both of them wore the black oilskins again, the hoods drawn up to cover their heads.

They had been there for ten minutes, and there had not been anything to see or hear. No lights showed in the house, or anywhere else. Another low ground fog had started to flow in, but it was thinner, wispier than it had been last night. The random tendrils had the look of smoke in the polished-silver shine of the moon.

Jackman dropped the glasses to his chest, straightened up and touched Tracy's arm. "No point in waiting any longer," he murmured. "We'd better get it over with."

She looked at him silently for a moment, as if gathering her courage, and then released a soft sibilant breath. "I guess I'm as ready as I'll ever be," she said.

She stepped behind him and took hold of his slicker, and they went forward cautiously, keeping to the heavier pockets of darkness. When they left the last of the trees they hunched over as one and ran in awkward, shuffling, crablike strides toward the rear barn wall. Wind-blown leaves dotted the open ground and made soft crunching sounds under their feet; hidden twigs snapped twice, sounds that seemed to Jackman as loud as gunshots. He kept his head up and his eyes darting from one direction to another, and it seemed to him that they were running in slow motion, that it was taking an incredibly long time to cross those sixty open yards—the same sensations he had had when they fled the house almost twenty-four hours before. There was feeling in him now, as he had known there would be, but fear and rebuilding tension threatened to dominate; panic scuttled beneath the surface, and his face felt hot and swollen. He had to force his mind to remain blank.

Then, as though in a single enormous stride, they were at the southern corner of the barn. He leaned back against the boarding and took several breaths, took a solid hold on himself before he started forward again.

When they neared the front corner he could see more of the area along the south side of the house, more of the space between the barn and the back of the house. The night seemed unnaturally still—no bird calls, no insect sounds; the sea not whispering in the distance. He stood motionless, straining to hear: something, anything. And a frog croaked somewhere behind them, two crick-

ets serenaded each other in the grass, a mosquito buzzed his left ear, and suddenly he could hear the sea again, too, purling as it always did when the wind
was up. All right. A momentary trick of perception. All right.

He eased his head out around the corner and looked diagonally across the
front of the barn. The rear house door, visible between the trunks of the apple
trees, was closed; shards of glass in the broken porch window gleamed dully.
The upstairs windows were partially obscured by the branches, but he could
see enough of them to tell that they were all like blind black eyes. Gusts of
wind ruffled the leaves and the ferns growing over and along the rock retaining wall, bent the high grass on the lower section of the slope. Moonlight and
shadow—and all of it fixed, empty, silent.

He looked at the barn doors, and they were still latched, as he and Tracy had
left them last evening. It would take them no more than ten seconds to cross
the half-dozen steps to the doors, open them, slip inside.

Jackman made one last reconnaissance of the area, held a breath, and made the
run with Tracy still hanging tightly to his oilskin. His hand shook a little when
he caught onto the latch, but he managed to get it open and himself through the
parted halves without making excess noise. As soon as Tracy followed him in,
he turned and pushed the doors closed to a slit and stood there listening.

To silence, except for the low vibratory hum of the generator.

Sweat trickled into his eyes and he wiped it away with the back of one hand.
The darkness inside the barn was stygian; he could make out nothing except
inchoate masses when he pivoted and let Tracy take his place at the doors. He
lifted the flashlight from his pocket, then the handkerchief he had put in there
with it earlier. When he had wrapped the cloth over the glass he touched the
switch and the filtered light spread out fuzzily, bright enough for him to make
his search but not, if he were careful, bright enough to penetrate the random
chinks in the wall boarding.

He held the flash steady, aiming it straight ahead and angled slightly downward. There were no obstructions in the path to where the lobster traps and
marker buoys and boxes of fishing gear were stacked behind the carriage. The
carriage itself had a supernatural aura in the blurred light, as if he were looking through time to another era.

He started deeper into the barn. The flashlight beam cut away more of the
blackness ahead, letting him see the workbench and the drill press and the piles
of discarded furniture. He went along the left side of the carriage and stepped
around an old hand lawnmower, up to the neat group of lobstering goods.

Beside the stack of curve-topped pots and the squared rows of red-and-white
buoys were two rusting washboards and a coil of potwarp line and half a
dozen rusted snatch blocks and a pile of folded seine nets for catching sardines;
he did not immediately see the carton he remembered from three years ago.
He leaned forward, sweeping the light, and there it was, behind one of the trap
stacks. He knelt beside it, directed the beam inside and rummaged through the
contents.

The flare pistol and the flares were not there.

He felt control begin to slip; each inhalation of air took on a hot-smoke feel in his lungs. They *had* to be there, Jesus they had to! His free hand scrabbled through the carton again, located a tackle box, fumbled it open: it contained tackle and nothing else.

Another carton, he must have overlooked it—and he stood and brought the light over the stacks, probing behind them, on both sides of them. There was no other carton, there was nothing, nothing, and the sweat drenched him now and his face felt swollen again and the primal scream that had underlain his thoughts that morning rose close to the surface. Think! Could Jonas have moved them for some reason, put them somewhere else in here? The workbench. A drawer in the workbench, that made sense, and he turned and started to swing the light around with him

And Tracy cried out.

Shrieked, shrieked in sudden terror.

The stillness seemed to shatter around him like an impacted sheet of ice, slivers of it stinging cold against the back of his neck as the scream reverberated through the dark barn. He wheeled full toward the doors, the light swirling, and the two halves were parted wide now and he saw her silhouetted there in the opening, body turned toward him, struggling wildly because there was an arm around her neck and the half-naked shape of a man behind her, and she screamed again and clawed at the arm, face contorted in a ghastly rictus, and he stared in stunned unbelief as the arm and the shadow heaved her backward off her feet and out through the doors and she was gone, they were gone, and in their place another man-shape appeared briefly and then the doors slammed shut.

*Christ God my God!* and he was lunging along the side of the carriage, and in the night without Tracy shrieked again, half a scream this time that sliced off in mid-octave just as his foot twisted against something, and he lost his balance and sprawled down, pain searing over his upper ribcage, the flashlight jarring loose and spinning tracers of light that brightened as the handkerchief fluttered loose. He lurched up to his knees, to his feet, and saw that the flash had stopped spinning and the beam had steadied into an elongated shaft centered on the old top-coil icebox, and he staggered to where it lay and caught it up and kept on staggering to the doors, not thinking, not able to think, still hearing Tracy's cries, and hit the doors full on with his right shoulder, expecting them to bounce open, but instead he caromed off and spun to one side, down to his knees again, when they bowed outward but did not part. He wagged his head, not comprehending, and gained his feet and hit the doors a second time, and again the latch failed to yield, the doors were *locked,* they had been locked somehow, and he dropped the flash and clawed at them, tearing his nails, screaming himself now, low in his throat, a sound that was not quite human.

Outside, there was only stillness.

□ □ □

When the moans in his throat strangulated into sharp gasping coughs, he stopped clawing at the doors and spun around with his hands spread out against them. At his feet the flashlight still burned, a harsh yellow strip laid across the black floor; a part of his mind registered this and he bent reflexively and picked it up. But then he did nothing except stand there holding the torch, trembling, disoriented, incapable of action or reason.

He said her name, "Tracy," he said, and the one word came out as a coughing sob.

Seconds went by—five, ten—and then his stomach convulsed and he retched emptily and that brought him out of it. Horror surged against the surface of his mind like surf against bare rock.

*Get out of here!*

He began to jerk his gaze and the light back and forth in rapid, frantic motions. Shadows and shapes leaped at him and receded again into walls of darkness. The gamesman in him was totally submerged; he had been reduced to atavism: a trapped animal seeking survival only through escape.

GET OUT OF HERE!

But there were no windows, no other doors, there was no way out except to go through those doors or through the walls, you couldn't walk through solid objects; the shaft of light still swinging back and forth, back and forth, low arc, high arc, the carriage, the stack of lumber, the roofing material, the bench saw, the furniture, the generator, the cordwood, the workbench, the tools hanging inside their painted outlines, the—

Tools.

Ax. Big double-bitted woodsman's ax.

And he put the light back on the wall above the workbench, probing for the ax, the ax should be there, Jonas using it during those summers long ago, using it himself: "Hey, Dad, did you see the way I felled that tree, just like a real lumberjack!" But it wasn't there, the ax was not there, and he ran to the bench and stabbed at the wall with the beam and found hammers, saws, screwdrivers, wrenches, but no ax, not even a hatchet, gone, all gone, and he pivoted away from the bench again, tears and sweat streaming from and into his eyes, half blinding him. He pawed his vision clear, *get out of here!* and ran along that wall, arcing the light, looking for something, anything that would mean a way out, and went past the lobstering gear and across the rows of cordwood and up the south wall, breathing torturedly, the primal scream rising again like bile into the back of his throat.

Nothing, nothing, and he made another circuit, big beast running around and around in a snare, and when he came back along the south wall this time his foot struck one of the plywood sheets and he stopped and shone the flash on the pile of lumber, the pile of lumber—six-foot length of four-by-four that had been left over when the barn was built.

Battering ram.

Immediately he leaned down and hefted the piece of heavy wood and struggled with it to the locked doors. Put the flashlight into the pocket of his slicker, leaving it on, and got a solid two-handed grip on the timber and lunged at the doors. The four-by-four struck off-center on one half, sending echoes of sound through the barn, running splinters into his palms as it recoiled back against his stomach; the doors held. He made another run, and again struck off-center, and the understanding penetrated that he needed the light in order to see his target, the juncture of the two halves where the latch was.

He dropped the length of wood and got the flash out again and located a spindly felt-topped card table among the piled furniture. Carried that over to one side and laid the torch on top of it, positioned it so that the beam held fast on the doors at waist level. Then he stumbled back to the four-by-four and caught it up and made a third run at the doors, aiming at the latch, hitting the joining of the halves a little high. They bowed out, admitting a thin strip of moonlight between them, but still the locking device held them secured.

He made another futile run.

Another.

Another.

His hands were quilled with splinters now, slick with blood, and each time he drove the length of wood against the doors, pain shot up both arms and burst hotly across his chest. He could not get enough air into his lungs; muscles pinched and knotted all through his body; his legs threatened to cave in under him.

Another run.

This time, though the doors still held, there was the squealing sound of metal pulling free of wood.

He staggered back with the four-by-four and put his head down, panting, clinging to the timber with his bloody hands, and ran full speed at the doors, put all his weight behind the thrust. The square end of the wood hit dead center where the latch was, and he felt the other end slam back into his stomach and take away what breath he had been able to draw—

And then he felt it yield.

The doors flew apart, metal screeching, flying outward: a heavy bolt wedged through the padlock hasps that had been fastened to each half.

His momentum carried him through and sent him sprawling atop the four-by-four, then over it to a skidding halt in the wet grass fronting the barn. He tried to rise immediately, but he had no strength left in his arms and he could not breathe. His body flopped, his mouth open wide in silent gasps, as his lungs sought desperately to fill. Pressure built inside his head; he came close to blacking out.

Then both lungs heaved and air spilled in and he began to breathe again so rapidly, so painfully that his body seemed to throb up and down in a caricature of the motions of lovemaking. Strength flowed back into his arms, and he was able to pull himself onto all fours, and all at once he realized where he was and thought, *I did it, I'm out*—and a semblance of sanity returned to him.

He shoved onto his knees and then into a swaying upright position, cleansed his eyes with the back of one blood-smeared hand. He looked to the left, to the right, saw no one, nothing, and focused on the house beyond the screening branches of the apple trees.

The back door was open and there were lights on inside.

No, he thought, oh no, no.

Tracy, he thought.

Run, he thought, they're inside, waiting.

Tracy, he thought.

No. Run, run while you can.

Tracy, Tracy, Tracy....

He groped in the oilskin's left pocket and got the knife out and started spasmodically toward the house. *No, run, into the woods!* and kept on going in a loose shambling walk past the apple trees and around the rock retaining wall, the knife held out in front of him like a short flat spear.

When he reached the open door, the scream tried to break out of him; he fought it back, lurched through and onto the porch. It was empty. The broken window glass glinted in the glare from the naked ceiling bulbs; the bloody animal leg still lay against the inner wall.

Just a game, all a game, only a game.

Run!

*Tracy.*

He went forward into the pantry, soft steps, listening: the house was still, a different kind of stillness from ever before, oppressive and threaded with menace. Into the kitchen, crouching. Lights burned here too, shining fixtures, gleaming linoleum, no sign or feeling of occupancy.

Across to the center corridor. Again he could not seem to take enough air; his breathing came in little choking pants, like the prelude to vomiting. His bladder felt suddenly, achingly bloated and the need to urinate was intense.

Into the center hall. Lightless—but beyond, in the parlor, there was a pale shimmering flicker of illumination. He stopped, heard silence like that in a vacuum: a total absence of sound. Chills capered the length of his body. Don't go in there. Run, Jesus Mary Mother, don't go in there! He tried to make himself back up, make himself turn, but his legs carried him instead to the archway, to where he could look into the parlor.

He could not see the source of the flickering light; it was coming from somewhere along the inner wall, where the fireplace was. He stood for a long moment, shaking, not wanting to go through the archway, knowing he would—Tracy—and then he caught the edge of the wall and propelled himself into the parlor, ten steps inside before he turned and looked at the fireplace.

Candles, six of them, burned atop the mantelpiece; another six flamed along the inner rim of the hearth. Pagan votives on a makeshift altar. And on the rest of the hearth bricks—

Splashes and puddles and streaks of liquid glistening blackly in the wavering light.

Blood.

*Your blood next for the cup of Lucifer....*

Jackman began to shake his head. He stood shaking it faster and faster, until the candle flames became a single pale smear on the darkness. Then, abruptly, he quit that and made a whimpering sound and began backing away along the middle of the room, toward the foyer, and RUN! and he ran—into the foyer, kicked the table going by and sent the tape recorder sliding off it to bang and clatter on the floor. Got the door open and hurled himself through it onto the veranda and missed the top step and skidded down the rest of the stairs to land on one hip at the foot of them. He blinked his eyes free of wetness, started up.

Froze.

Twenty yards away on the lawn, not far from the remains of the charred cross, something stood outlined against the moonlit sky, something fluttered wispily in the cold night wind.

A pole, driven into the turf; and atop it

No

On top of the pole

No

Shining white, shining blood-black

And the fluttering was her hair

Tracy's hair

They they they had cut off her her

He screamed. And kept on screaming as he came up in one motion and ran away from the thing on the lawn, away into darkness that was now both the island and the inclosure of his mind.

# PART THREE

Sunday, May 24:
THE ISLAND

*Whoever battles with monsters had better see that it does not turn him into a monster.
And if you gaze long into an abyss, the abyss will gaze back at you.*
　　　—NIETZSCHE "Aphorisms and Entr'actes," *Beyond Good and Evil*

Blind flight....

Jackman did not know where he was or where he was going, he did not see or feel the tree branches like long-nailed fingers reach for his face and scrape thin furrows in the skin, he did not hear the whimpering explosions of his breath. When something caught his foot and sent him sprawling, he got up immediately and had no awareness of having fallen. Inside his head thoughts swirled in a red-tinged intermix, without coherence or continuity, like bits of flotsam tossing on a nightmare sea.

A stitch in his side impeded his breathing finally, made him slow to a lurching stagger. His hands clawed the air in front of him; then his knees buckled and he fell sideways against a down log, cracked his head with enough force for the pain to register and momentarily blank his mind. He tried to rise, could not. He pulled his knees up to his chest and curled himself and wrapped his arms over his head.

Then he began to tremble, and his body shook with such force that a fantasy thought penetrated: he was going to shake himself apart, limbs and organs and bones would fragment like the atoms in a dropped figurine and there would be nothing left of him but scattered shards. He covered his head more tightly, pressed his knees harder against his chest. But he could not stop the quaking

And he had a sudden sensation of falling, of diminishing in size and turning over and over inside himself and then fracturing, arm coming off and sailing away, a leg, his genitals, his head—and the head shrieked soundlessly and disappeared into a crimson tide that dissolved instantly into black.

Black.

When he came out of it, or seemed to come out of it, he was no longer trembling and his head felt clear—until he sat up and looked around him. Drooping evergreen boughs, thick trunks hung with moss, lacy webs of luminous mist... but all of it was distorted, grotesque, like a piece of forest seen through the bottom of a dark glass bowl.

*Twas brillig, and the slithy toves/Did gyre and gimbel in the wabe....*
Delirium.
Oh my God, don't let me break down!
*All mimsy were the borogroves....*
He shut his eyes, but when he opened them again the distortion remained. And he remembered sitting with Dale during one of those long-ago summers, alone together in Dale's room, all the lights out, telling ghost stories, and Dale saying, "Have you ever thought what it might be like if you got locked up in one of your dreams? I mean, if you couldn't escape the dreamworld by waking up, and you had to spend the rest of your life walking around in it, trying to avoid the things that live there in the shadows?"

Cold encased his body; moisture leaked out of his pores and seemed to crystallize rather than flow wetly. He jammed the heels of his hands against his temples, twisted his head within them. But the warped boughs appeared to droop lower, swaying at odd menacing angles in a wind that did not whisper or sigh but made a sound in his ears like the crinkling of cellophane. Limbs seemed to reach malevolently, like bony fingers. Or claws. Or jaws.

*Beware the Jabberwock, my son! The jaws that bite, the claws that catch!*
He flung himself onto his stomach, hands digging at the soft damp needle humus. But as soon as he closed his eyes this time, he was back in Saigon and the plastique bomb had just exploded. He ran up the smoky, sweltering street, shouting and screaming on all sides, people lying shattered, and saw the boy with blood all over him and knelt beside him and began to brush away the blood pumping bright sticky red, and when the blood was cleared off, the face he saw belonged to Tracy—

He popped his eyes open again. Looked up.
Tracy's head floated above him on a red-smeared cloud, mouth open wide and accusing, strands of midnight hair fanned out in the crinkling-cellophane wind and glowing with a bluish radiance.

A cry burst out of him and he crawled away behind a tree and buried his head in his arms. Tracy, I'm sorry, I'm sorry! The name of the game is horror, and I don't know how to play. They're going to get *my* head too, *my* blood for the cup of Lucifer....

The ground beneath him seemed to begin undulating, as though he were being rocked in a giant cradle. Voices screamed in the night around him: the burbling of Jabberwocks, the wailing of monsters. He could smell the sour urine odor of Death.

Don't let me come apart, don't let me break down....
And slowly, as if in response to his plea, the voices grew still and the sound of the wind faded to quiet; he had the sensation again of drifting within himself. Darkness pressed down on him—empty darkness, free of menace and terror—and he reached out for it desperately and welcomed it with the bruised planes of his mind.

Void.

□ □ □

He awoke to birdsong and warm pale sunlight.

When he opened his eyes and sat up blinking, the sudden movement unleashed a wash of pain so intense in both temples it was like being struck with a blunt object. He clutched his head and leaned over with his face between his knees. Colors swam behind his eyes—blues and reds and sharp hot pulses of yellow and orange. His mouth was dry and bitter with the taste of old bile. Thoughts danced in and out of his consciousness, vague and amorphous, and he could not seem to grasp any of them.

He sat for a long while holding his head. Gradually the bright colors receded and the pain receded, and the thoughts settled into half-formed, thinly cohesive patterns. He remembered most of what had happened the night before—the barn, Tracy's capture, his escape, the blood and the candles at the fireplace—but the only memory which was vivid in every detail was the pole driven into the front lawn and what had been mounted on top of it.

His stomach convulsed, and he rolled over onto hands and knees and vomited a thin sour liquid. Kept on vomiting dryly until the effort left him weak and panting.

There was a flushed burning feel to his face as he crawled away from the odor. He thought of water, and the thought crusted the vomit residue in his mouth and made his throat close up painfully. Sitting again, he became aware of the surrounding trees, the patches of morning sunlight, a baby spruce growing out of a rotted, moss-shawled stump, a bed of delicate-looking lady ferns, a flicker knocking for grubs on a burl-swollen spruce trunk. Normal, all of it. No more of the grotesque distortion of the night.

I didn't break down, he thought.

Did I?

No. No!

When he finally gained his feet, cramped muscles made both legs as wobbly as dry sticks. He staggered once, caught onto the gray bole of a tree to keep himself from falling. Vertigo seized him: the high pine and spruce boughs, the soft blue sky above them, began to spin languidly, like a merry-go-round running at quarter speed. He squeezed his eyes shut, clinging to the tree, and kept them shut even after the dizziness passed.

Where am I? he thought.

Got to find out where I am. Let go of the tree. Walk, look for landmarks.

Jackman released the spruce bole, palms scraping over the grainy bark—and for the first time he became conscious of a sharp stinging pain in both of them and on the inside of the fingers. He shoved away and stood unsteadily with his feet planted wide apart. When he was sure he was not going to fall he turned the hands over and looked down at them and saw that they were torn and tessellated with splinters, coated with dried blood. He shuddered, put them out of sight along his sides, and took a step, another, a third: he had equilibrium again.

Walking, shuffling his feet, he looked around him. Nothing but a maze of trees and undergrowth; nothing to give him his bearings. Except the sun? Where was the sun? He stopped and craned his head back and peered up through the tops of the trees, located a small gold wedge of it. Pretty high. Must be nearly ten o'clock. He thought of his watch and glanced down at his wrist, but it was covered by black rubber. Slicker. Still wearing the oilskin. He had not realized that before either. Brain functioning like an engine on half of its cylinders, missing beats, stalling, blocking out perception. But it would repair itself—wouldn't it? He pushed back the sleeve and looked at his watch, but the crystal was broken; the hands were frozen at 11:35.

When he raised his head again, a filtered refraction of light made him blink. The sun. He had almost forgotten about the sun. He pivoted to face it fully. East. East was the cove, cross-island. Which direction did he want to go? *Where* did he want to go? He tried to swallow, but his throat was still closed off. Water. But the only water was at the house—

The fort. One orange left. Or was there? Yes, one orange, the juice of one orange. The fort, then: he wanted to go to the fort.

Jackman turned his body a quadrant to the left, facing north, and started walking again. Broke an irregular trail through the forest, stopping now and then to rest or when he remembered to make certain the sun remained at his right shoulder. The air grew warm, brought perspiration out of him again, but it did not occur to him to take off the slicker.

Once he thought: I don't feel as afraid as I did yesterday and last night, I don't feel the same horror. Is that because I—? Then the engine stuttered, stalled momentarily, and when it began working again the thought was gone.

He walked in a timeless state through patchworks of light and shadow. The sun climbed inexorably and thin drifting clouds veined the blue of the sky. A small brown doe appeared some distance ahead of him, came to a dead stop and keened the air and then darted away. Butterflies performed aerial acrobatics in the random beams of sunshine. There was the staccato hammering of a flicker, the singing of purple finches, the scolding chatter of chipmunks. The strong spicy scent of bayberry mingled with that of the evergreens and the faint brackish essence of the sea. But Jackman saw and heard and smelled these things without differentiation; his awareness was limited to the positioning of his body with relation to the sun and the search for familiar landmarks, for one of the island paths.

When he finally came on a landmark, he almost passed it before recognizing it for what it was. It was off on his left—a dark maze of lichen-spotted spruce and birch trunks, dead lower branches jutting like gray spikes, interlocking to form a wall barring human passage. The high branches of the trees crowded together to create a canopy which the sunlight could not penetrate; the floor there was thick with damp needle humus, void of undergrowth.

Jackman halted and looked into the dense shade, and knew then that he was on the island's northwestern side, walking away from the house and the bay toward the northshore point. There was no other large section of dead and dying spruce, destroyed by dwarf mistletoe and other parasites, anywhere on the island. The fort would be at a slight angle to the east, then. The path, too, that he and Tracy had taken yesterday to the headland.

Tracy—

Keep on walking, off to the right now. Intersect the path and then go down it to the fort. And his legs moved and carried him in that direction.

□ □ □

The orange was warm and damp and slick, and his fingers spasmed as he tried to peel it. He was sitting in the hot sun inside the fort, back rigid against the rock under the overhang, legs drawn up, elbows pressed in tight to his sides, holding the orange in both hands up close to his face. Dryness furred his tongue, lay like a thin sifting of sand across the roof of his mouth; he kept trying to swallow, anticipating the sweetness of the citrus juice, but the muscles in his throat would not dilate.

He dropped the orange twice before he managed to tear loose a piece of the skin. Then he peeled it with elaborate caution, stripping away all of the white pith before he broke it into sections and lifted one to his mouth. The juice burned acidly, dissolved some of the aridness and trickled down as he tilted his head to finally penetrate the blockage in his throat. When he had sucked out the last drop of moisture, he spat the pulp to one side and repeated the process a section at a time until he had finished half the orange.

He stared at the remaining half. He wanted it badly, but the thought came that he ought to save it for later. But what would he wrap it in? The slicker was filthy, and the rest of his clothes—

What about the rest of his clothes? It occurred to him then to take the oilskin off, and he did that awkwardly and laid it across the hole scooped out of the pebbles. A sharp odor drifted up from his crotch, and when he looked down there he saw that the front of his trousers was stained and damp—one more thing he had failed to notice before. Urine. He had wet himself during the night.

That struck him funny and he burst out laughing. Some blow to the morale of the American public if they ever found out. Esteemed senator pees his pants. Wouldn't *they* be pissed off! Oh wouldn't they! Lost control of his bladder and lost control of his life and lost control of....

And it was no longer funny. The laughter chopped off, and he put his chin on his chest and peered down the front of his sweater. Two buttons missing. He opened the ones that were left and took the sweater off, and the shirt underneath was wrinkled and sour with sweat and the residue of stagnant seawater. One tail hung out of his trousers like a flap of dead gray skin, and he lifted that in his free hand and examined it. Too soiled. Contaminate the orange half if he wrapped it in that. Don't have anything, then. Nothing at all.

He stared once more at the peeled half, and his mouth began to go dry again, and the sun was very hot—and he watched passively as his fingers broke it into even quarters and raised one and pushed it between his lips. He seemed able then to see inside himself, inside his mouth: blunt white teeth grinding down and shredding the segments, sweet juice flowing backward and down the long dark blistered cavern into the hollow below. Fascinating. Worth watching a second time. And his fingers and teeth responded, and the juice ran, soothed, and then there was nothing left but pulp and pith. Pulp and pith and piss, he thought. Piss and pith and pulp. So much for the problem of the orange.

Now what?

Did it matter? They'd find him sooner or later, and when they did they would cut off his head like they cut off Tracy's. Or something worse. Was there something worse?

*One, two! One, two! And through and through the vorpal blade went snicker-snack!*

Oh yes, not much doubt about it now: the island and the game belonged to the Jabberwocks....

The sun's heat was making him drowsy, a little sick. Too hot here in the open. Sunstroke. Bake his brain like bread dough in an oven. Shouldn't be sitting here at all. Should get up and go—

Where?

Round and round, round and round.

Sleep, he thought. Sleep?

He examined that prospect with critical detachment. Good, a good stratagem. Sleep was a panacea for most ills, anybody could tell you that. When you didn't feel right in mind and body, you slept. Healing sleep.

But not here. Some place dark and cool, hidden, where they couldn't find him with their vorpal blade. The woods? Not secure enough, not dark enough.

The caves.

Of course—the caves.

He looked up at the coppery glare of the sun. One o'clock, maybe one-thirty. The tide would start to ebb around three; he could get down into the biggest of the caves then, and he could stay in there until well after midnight. Cool, damp, dark, safe.

Standing, he stared over the top of one boulder. Nothing in the trees but trees. He started out through the seaward opening, and then stopped. The slicker. Take the slicker along, going to need it tonight for the cold. Sweater too. And the tin of Spam and the last chocolate bar; have to eat eventually.

When he put the food into one of the oilskin's pockets, he discovered that it had been empty. The other one too. He could not remember having lost the flashlight and the knife, but he no longer had them. No longer had the binoculars either, for Christ's sake. Gone, all gone.

He rolled the sweater into a cylindrical shape and stuffed it inside one of the sleeves and folded the oils over his right arm. Stepped out onto the point, came around along the cobbles, and went up again into the forest.

□ □ □

There was a strong northeast wind blowing across the cliff flat, making flut-tery sounds among the blueberry shrubs, creating a humming counterpoint to the hiss of the rote. The sun was westering now, hazed by pale cloud drifts: close to four o'clock. It had taken him nearly three hours to come less than two miles, and he had had to pull himself from tree to tree on the last long rise; but he had not fallen a single time. Pyrrhic victory, and not much of a one at that. Just a single completed move on the gameboard. Win a battle, lose the war. Mix the mixed-up metaphors.

Sleep, he thought, got to sleep.

He moved to the edge of the woods, cast furtive looks in both directions along the flat. Deserted. On his left he had a glimpse of the stone altar, wrenched his head away. He stumbled out onto the flat, the slicker trailing from his right hand, then checked himself and forced his weakening legs to carry him heel-and-toe toward the edge of the cliff.

The way down to the caves was well over to the west, through a long nar-row cut spotted with blue-green algae. When he got to there and stood on the edge and looked down to where waves lifted thin sheets of spray over a jum-ble of rocks exposed by the tide, vertigo overcame him again, and he had to sit down hard on his buttocks to keep himself from tumbling over. The dizziness vanished almost immediately, but instead of getting up again he used his hands to push his body forward until his legs were dangling down inside the cut.

Long way to the bottom, much longer than he remembered it; but it had been twenty years since his last visit to the caves, and he had been young and agile then. Have to use both hands: put the slicker on, button it up. He took the rolled-up sweater out of the sleeve, got into that first and then donned the oilskin.

When he was ready he eased himself down, back braced into the hollow, fin-gers clutching at crevices in the rough rock walls. Directly below was a wide flat-topped shelf covered with rubbery brown rockweed, and just above it the cut showed the black-brown presence of barnacles. He lifted his hands at that point and got his feet planted on the shelf and lowered to palms and knees. A small green crab scuttled out in front of him, pivoted and snapped its claws menacingly. Jackman stared at it, not moving: mute confrontation. The crab retreated finally, went down along the side of the shelf and out of sight.

He crawled ten feet and then turned his body, hanging onto the slippery sea-weed, and swung his legs over and found purchase on a narrow jutting ledge. Across the ledge and a short step downward were a staggered row of three rounded outcroppings diminishing in height by four feet each, like a crude staircase. Rockweed and sea lettuce matted the rocks and made the footing treacherous; but he got down them with no difficulty, no damage except a fresh cut in one palm from the shell of a mussel.

One last stratified shelf shawled in red-brown Irish moss, a tide pool in a pocket on its outer lip teeming with sea urchins and anemones. Spray stung his face, clung glistening in tiny beads to the oilskin as he dropped onto the shelf, stepped off it onto a slender strip that fronted the first and highest of the caves.

There were three of them, the other two set side by side in a deep cleft twenty-five feet farther down, where laminarias swayed in the pounding wash of surf between the jumble of exposed rocks at the cliff base. Those two were shallow, with mouths so low you had to enter them on all fours. This one was much larger, extending some fifty feet into the cliff wall, wide enough near its deepest perimeter for a man to stand stooped over or to lie stretched out full length.

A milky translucent moon jellyfish flowed over the rock at the opening to the cave like a sentry barring admittance. Jackman kicked at it, sent it sliding away, and then hunched his shoulders and bent at the waist and went inside. A crab scurried past his foot; an anemone attached to the base of the wall waved faintly luminescent tentacles. Fifteen feet in, the rock was coated with coarse sand and cobbles and deposits of kelp and flotsam, and the light became murky and there was the thick dank raw-salt odor peculiar to seawater caves. Cool in there, too—almost cold: he had forgotten just how chill it could be. And it would get colder still after the sun went down.

Too late to worry about that now. The hell with that.

Sleep.

After forty feet there was no light at all except for the pale sphere of the cave mouth. Jackman stopped there and swung his foot loosely over the floor. More kelp, more chunks of shale and granite; he scraped out a cleared space, a bed for himself. Jonas had taught him that there was nothing to fear in these caves except perhaps the green crabs, but they would not bother you if you were motionless; the sting of the moon jellies was not poisonous, not even a mild irritant.

Fatigue drove him to his knees. His arm felt heavy as he raised it to pull the slicker's hood over his head. He let himself collapse onto his side, got a forearm under his chin; his eyes closed and instantly warm darkness seeped in to blanket his mind. The last things he heard were the constant thrashing of the surf, the hollow whispering of the wind, the faint dripping of water from the ceiling and on the walls, on the walls....

*I dreamt I dwelt in marble halls, and each damp thing that creeps and crawls went wobble-wobble on the walls....*

The Jabberwock stood ten feet tall and had flaming red eyes and a scaly corpus on which a black-magic symbol had been painted; its hands bore long gleaming yellow claws, and one of them clenched a sword with the head of an ax at the tip, bright-stained and dripping. It loomed over him, swinging the vorpal blade in a malevolent arc, its manxome mouth open and fangs like saffron-colored daggers spotted with bits of gristled meat forming an obscene leer.

"Your head," the Jabberwock said, "for the blood of the frumious Bandersnatch."

And he began to laugh. Even though his body cringed away, eyes fixed on the seesawing blade, he could not control himself and the laughter spilled out of his throat and rang madly in the stillness. The Jabberwock swung the vorpal blade up, swung it down—snicker-snack!—and Jackman's head rolled across the stone floor, still laughing wildly, and bounced against the wall and came to rest aslant.

"Wobble-wobble," he said. "Wobble-wobble."

The blade made clanking sounds, like chains dragging, as the Jabberwock lowered it heavily at its feet and began to back away. Growling sounds, burbling sounds, came from its open mouth.

Jackman watched his body get up and come forward and reach down and pick up his head, fit it carefully on the severed stem of his neck.

The Jabberwock darted behind a pillar, hiding.

"Come out, come out, wherever you are," he said, and ran to the pillar—but the creature was gone, there was nothing there except a puddle of fresh blood. He knelt and touched the blood with his fingers, and it turned to water, turned to dust, and the wind came and blew the dust away.

He started walking, looking for the Jabberwock. It was there; where was it? Come out, come out!

Something came out, but it was not the Jabberwock. It was Meg, and she was wearing a lavender evening gown.

Frowning, he said, "What are you doing here?"

"What are *you* doing here?" Meg said, and laughed shrilly.

"Stop it, stop that."

"You're such a fool, David. You've always been such a fool."

"Is that so?"

"Yes. I won't be sorry when you're dead."

"Do you hate me that much?"

"I don't hate you. I don't feel anything for you."

"You don't feel anything, period."

"I suppose you think you do."

"Yes. I loved you once, I tried to make it work—"

"That's all you've ever done, *try* to make things work," she said. "Try to make our marriage work, try to make your political career work, try to make your life work. The only thing you ever really *made* work was that film of yours in college. If you had chosen filmmaking over politics, you'd have been a doer instead of a tryer, David."

"I tried to stand up to the Old Man—"

"Tried. There, you see what I mean?"

"Damn it, *you* wanted me to go into politics as much as he did. If I had had your support...."

"...you would have done just exactly what you did do," Meg said. "You couldn't stand up to me any more than you could to him. You fool, we manipulated you and you let it happen. People have been manipulating you all your life. You're like the camera in *I, Camera, Eye*—useless by yourself; you need someone to activate you, focus you, so you can open your shutter-eyes and see and record...."

"I don't want to hear any more of this," he said. "I have to find the Jabberwock."

The sound of her laughter echoed hollowly as he walked away.

He turned a corner, and sitting on one of the walls was the Old Man. Dressed in a black business suit with a narrow-striped tie, but on top of his head was perched a red, white and blue Uncle Sam hat. The forefinger of his right hand probed gently, exploratorily, at one nostril, and he held a curved clay pipe in a corner of his mouth.

"Survival is a game, just like everything else," the Old Man said. "If you want to survive, you've got to keep thinking of it that way. Start planning strategy: move and countermove."

"The Jabberwock cut off my head," Jackman said, "and I put it back on. But I can't do that with Tracy's head. She's dead for all time."

"What's done is done. What does it matter if you lose a pawn as long as the king remains untouched."

"You son of a bitch, she was a human being!"

"Pawn," the Old Man said obstinately. "They're all pawns, just pieces on the board."

"But I'm not, is that it?"

"You are if you want to be."

"Meaning what?"

"Meaning that it's all up to you."

"But this isn't even a *game* anymore—"

"Of course it is," the Old Man said, and raised a hand. "Everything is a game, and this above all—" There was a clicking in his voice, like that of a switch being thrown, and he broke off. Then: "Of course it is," he said, and raised a hand. "Everything is a game, and this above all—" Click. "Of course it is," he said, and raised a hand. "Everything is a game, and this above all—" Click. "Of course it is...."

Jackman hurried down a long corridor. There was somebody standing at the far end, in front of a dark archway, and when he approached he saw that it was his brother Dale.

"Hello, Dale," he said. "Have you seen the Jabberwock?"

Dale did not answer him; instead he walked over by one of the walls. Jackman could see into the dark archway by then, and there were a lot of people in there. They began to file out one by one: Charlie Pepper. Richard Nixon. Alan Pennix. Senator Lawton. Linda Fong. His mother. A crippled Vietnam veteran. Jonas. Miss Bigelow. James Turner. Fred Tremaine. Gerald Ford. Alicia. A May Day demonstrator. Walter Cronkite. Judy Tremaine. J. Edgar Hoover. The three-piece band from Milbridge. Lyndon Johnson. A dozen more. None of these said anything to him or looked at him either.

All of them formed a tight circle, arms around each other's shoulders, and put their heads together, whispering—and the Jabberwock jumped out of a dark niche and whirled the vorpal sword in a long sweeping arc and cut off all their heads, sent their heads rolling and rattling like marbles on the damp marble walls. Then, burbling, the creature capered away again and the clanking of the ax blade diminished into silence.

Jackman went over to the collapsed and headless bodies, peered down at them. And one sprang up, startling him because it was not headless after all; the Jabberwock had missed one, and the one it had missed was the only black one, Charlie Pepper.

"I'm glad it didn't get you, Charlie," he said.

"Ain't no Jabberwock goin to hurt a smart old nigger like me," Charlie Pepper said. "Don't seem like it hurt you neither, boy—at least not bad as it could've."

He giggled. "Cut off my head, but I put it back on."

"You got it back on straight?"

"I don't know," he said. "Is it straight?"

"Close, maybe; then again, maybe not. You goin to have to get it fastened down tight. Elsewise, your eyes goin to see crooked and you goin to stumble, and then it'll fall right off again. Maybe for good."

"All right. Charlie, you think I can find the Jabberwock and take the vorpal blade away and lop off *its* head?" But Charlie Pepper had vanished.

He sat down on one of the walls, and a damp thing wobbled there, and he was suddenly very cold. His neck throbbed where the sword had sliced through it. He raised his hands to his head, probed it with his fingers. Was it on straight?

Pretty close, anyway.

Pretty close.

□ □ □

He was sitting up against the jagged wall of the cave, shivering, staring into the darkness. Surf ran hissingly, close to the entrance, and the wind whistled and carried droplets of spray like a fine mist; the rote had a restless booming cadence. Faint furry gray at the cave mouth. Night. And cold—damp, numbing. The skin on his exposed face and hands felt brittle, as if it had been frozen over with thin crusts of ice.

He did not remember waking or lifting his body into the seated position; he was simply awake and sitting there. His temples ached, and dryness had closed his throat again, and there was a crick in his neck caused by his sleeping posture, and sharp pain fluctuated under his breastbone in a bodily protest against hunger. He imagined he could hear his cold stiffened joints creaking audibly every time he moved.

Thoughts seemed far away, dulled. Not many details on the morning, the afternoon, the fort, the trek here to the cliffs, the climb downward over the rocks; all like things you had done a long, long time ago, only dimly recalled and with uncertain accuracy. Once, at the age of twelve, he had had an appendectomy, and when he had come out of the anaesthesia his mind had felt like this: drugged, muted, aware but not quite aware. Not unpleasant, but not pleasant either. Things drifting around and around that you wanted to catch hold of—speculations, memories, stratagems—but they darted away like tadpoles in a murky pool when you reached out for them.

Concentrate. Food. Tin of Spam, chocolate bar: he slid his hand into the slicker pocket to make sure they were still there. But he knew as he did so that he would not be able to force anything down his constricted throat. Should not have eaten the whole orange this afternoon. If he could not get fresh water— and it seemed certain he could not—what else was there that contained liquid? Berries? Were there any blueberries or strawberries on those shrubs and patches on the flat? Yes, but they would be green now, inedible. Didn't ripen until late June. Anything else? Nothing else.

Feeling. What did he feel? Cold. Pain. Fear? Grief or guilt for Tracy and what had happened to her? Any emotion? Only the numbness of his body; at this moment, only that.

Time. Late now. The tide was starting to come in, he could judge that by the sound of the surf, the windblown moisture. After midnight, maybe. Better get out of here, get out of the damp cold, climb up the rocks before the breakers came in heavy enough to slick them dangerously. First matter of attention, this. First things first, first moves first.

And he gained his feet, leaning on the wall, and stood for a moment working kinks out of his arms and legs; then he made his way laboriously along the moist rock, through the deposits of kelp, and out through the cave mouth. Foam slithered against the side of the flattish shelf to his left, which meant the other two caves were submerged now; one of the breakers splashed up high and drenched him. The sea was dark, mist-free, choppy—short steep whitecaps riding the tops of long swells. No moon tonight? He looked up, and there were thick black-rimmed clouds scudding rapidly to the west. The pull of the wind out here was strong, cutting, and the air was permeated with the metallic smell of ozone. Gulls wheeled in nervous dogfight patterns.

Summer squall building, he thought.

Then he thought: Squall—rain. Rain.

He *could* get fresh water after all.

But first he had to get up to the flat, and quickly; he couldn't be climbing on these rocks when it broke. How much longer? Not long, clouds massing at a good clip. Half an hour, maybe less.

He tipped his head back and stared up the cliff face, and it looked impossibly high, it looked as if it extended far enough into the sky to touch the running clouds. Don't think about that; you've scaled it dozens of times before, you got down here tonight and you can get back up again. Find a handhold on the near shelf—and he did that and pulled his body atop it. Like pulling up the dead blackfish he and Jonas had discovered floating in the sea one morning when they went out to run the lobster traps, all bloated and stone-heavy.

Spray licked at the nape of his neck where the slicker's hood had fallen back.

He half-turned to press thighs and stomach against the first of the stepping stones, feet planting solidly, fingers groping for new purchase. Heave up! And he was on the outcropping and reaching out for the second one. Firm grip with both hands. Heave up! Third outcropping. Heave up!

He knelt there for a moment, rasping in his lungs like a file on wood. Don't look down, don't look up. The ledge next, watch out for those loose bunches of seaweed, watch out for barnacles and mussels. He hooked into a crevice on the ledge, lifted, but his foot slipped and for a dizzying moment he seemed to hang there, legs flailing, his other hand grabbing desperately for a second handhold. Got it—got the toe of his shoe wedged into another fissure in the rock and steadied himself and then hoisted prone on the ledge and lay still until the strain in his arms lessened.

Worst part of the climb coming up. Slippery rockweed on that wide flat shelf; the long cut that you had to go up the same way you came down, facing away, back braced and making inching progress with hips and heels and hands. Used to do it with no trouble at all except once in a while a cut or a scrape. And what happened to the boy I was then? Where did he go, when did I lose him?

Stand up—slow, lean against the cliff wall. Fingers scuttling like crabs over the rockweed, nails scraping, chipping; tug, and puffy ropes of it came free. He flung them away, found a rocky projection that he could curl his hand around, tested it. Solid. Other hand now, and a water-filled cup deep enough and wide enough to allow a palmhold with fingers splayed. Elbows locked, muscles taut, knees struggling for leverage... just a little more, pull!... and his body wiggled onto the shelf and slid across the slick weed matting to the center.

Rest a moment again. Then a slow bellyslide to the bottom of the cut: sea wracks like a waxed floor under his body, little effort necessary. Careful now, careful. Over onto his right hip, onto his buttocks, arms lifting back above his head, hands probing for the bare rock beyond the line where the barnacles had welded themselves rough and sharp-edged. Anchored hold, legs tenting, heels digging in. Now hoist up again; unfold at the waist. Shooting pains in both forearms—and one heel skidded loose, went out at an angle; but the other one held fast and he arched back hard into the cut and wedged there while he got the one leg pulled in and then jacked down into the base pocket.

Sixty feet below, the angry surf hammered against the rocks.

He kept his eyes straight ahead, looking out toward the nesting islets offshore, as he brought his hands down to armpit level and located other crannies and knobs. Thighs spread slightly, knees flexed, and—squirm, twist, pull, shove up. Two feet, maybe. Rest. Different holds, make sure they're firm. Again. Two more feet. Rest. Different holds. Again—

Slipped, body slipping and scraping downward.

He jammed his wrists, jammed his thighs and shoulders against the rock. Heard the oilskin rip on a barnacle or horny projection. Momentum ceased, but he had lost three or four feet. Agony in his palms, feeling of suffocation. But only fifteen feet left, and the last six or seven of that more easily accessible because the cut bellied deeper into the cliff wall, and you could turn around at that point and pretty much crawl out. Almost there. Almost there.

Holds, shove and pull, rest. Holds, shove and pull, rest. Holds, shove and pull, rest. And his hips and sides felt the inward turn of the rock, and he gave one last push, and he was sitting tilted forward in the depression. Rest. Then one leg pulling up and in, bracing, and buttocks gyrating upward; he turned on his side, looked up, and he could see the edge of the flat and the black tops of trees in the distance, the roiling swarm of clouds obliterating the night sky. And then he dragged himself up the rest of the way on his side in one hauling, scrabbling movement, threw his body out of the cut and lay spread-eagled, breath wheezing through his nostrils, on the wet grass of the flat.

The staggered, drumming beat of his heart was so loud that he was unable to hear the rote or the wind. He did not move, waiting for the feeling of suffocation to abate, for his muscles to unknot. The wind stung his cheeks, wailing emptily across the open space, and under its driving force the sea purled in a turbulent rhythm; the smell of ozone was sharper. The squall would hit the island any minute now.

And he shouldn't be out here either when it did, exposed; if the blow got strong enough, it could pitch a man right off the edge. Into the trees, he thought. Catch as much of the rainwater in his hands as he could and drink his fill and then wait out the squall in some kind of shelter: one of the rock formations, a burrow under a deadfall. After that—

After that was after that.

Heart gentling, constriction easing in his throat. Get up now. And he drew himself into a hump at the middle, got his head and shoulders up until he was kneeling, and then made it to his feet. Swayed. Lifted one hand to his eyes to rub away salty wetness. Blinked and looked over toward the woods.

And one of them was standing there.

Just standing there beside a blueberry bush, naked to the waist, cradling a rifle against the dark symbol on the bare skin of his chest.

Jackman's mouth hinged open and he stared in dumb fascination, heard himself make a moaning sound. Reality shimmered, dissolved dreamily. He took a faltering step to his right, a second, then swung his body and started to run—and ran six steps before he saw the second one coming toward him at an angle from where the stone altar stood, carrying something long and flat.

Ax!

No, he said, oh God no!

But it wasn't an ax, it was a board....

He looked back frantically, and the first one had started to advance, they were converging on him and he had nowhere to run, the cliff was at his flank and he did not have enough time to go back down through the cut. I'm dreaming this too, he thought, but knew that he was not, not this time, and he tried to run straight ahead, and they drifted over to cut him off. He changed direction in midstride, panic raking at him, and ran shambling at the second one; nerve-endings screamed, it felt as though he were moving at a retarded speed.

Then everything seemed to slow down, to happen with incredible precision: his arms opened out and his head lowered and he reached out for the one with the board, but that one stepped aside agilely and Jackman stumbled and lost his balance and started to fall, and it took a long, long time for him to strike the ground, jarring on his knees, on his elbows, and then to roll over gagging and stare up with bulging eyes—and the Jabberwock was looming over him, vorpal board held high over its right shoulder. He cried out, saw the board come forward and down in a graceful slanting arc toward the side of his head, and thought to bring an arm up to protect himself, and began to raise the arm against the manxome thrust—

Snicker-snack!

Too late.

# PART FOUR

Monday, May 25:
THE ISLAND

*With tight-strung bow a wick'd hunter I became—*
*Its quivering tension*
*Bespeaks the hunter's powerful dimension—*
*Beware and flee: this arrow's dangerous aim*
*Is like none other: this is not a game!*
　　　　　　　—NIETZSCHE, "Postlude" to *Beyond Good and Evil*

Pitch blackness, the faint hollow drumming of rain.

Odor of fermented apples.

Thudding pain along the left side of his head.

Thirst.

Cold hard surface under him; cramps in both legs, a tingling sensation in his right arm. He groaned, moved over onto his stomach, and the tingling increased: he had been lying on the arm. He lifted a shaky hand and touched the pain. Pulpy, but there was not any blood that he could feel.

First thought: Still got my head—didn't cut off my head after all.

He pushed up slowly to all fours. Giddiness, nausea. Fever chills capered between his shoulder blades, and his face felt hot and swollen again, caked with salt freeze. Damp all over, clothes sticking clammily to his skin. In a detached way he wondered if he could be coming down with pneumonia.

Pulling back on his knees, he rested the weight of his buttocks against his upthrust heels. Loose tension to his muscles, like ropes too often knotted and stretched. Breathing shallow and irregular. Sea-pulse in both temples now, as well as in the pulpy region over his left ear. Torn and splintered palms stinging, throbbing, where they rested flat against his thighs.

Any strength left? Enough—always seemed to be just enough. He extended both arms, groped through the darkness. Fingertips touched a rough vertical surface at an angle to his right. Leaning that way, he ran his knuckles along it. Wall. Fieldstone wall. He crawled closer, got a shoulder pressed to it, and used it as a fulcrum to hoist himself weakly erect.

Lying, kneeling, standing—up and down continually for the past... what? Thirty-six hours? In and out of consciousness, in and out of pain. But this time his nerves were almost quiet and his mind seemed to be remarkably uncluttered, lucid, as if the blow delivered on the cliffs had driven all the hazy confusion straight out of his head.

And he realized he was afraid again.

He concentrated on the fear, and it was not nearly as stark or crippling as before and during his entrapment in the barn, immediately after his discovery of Tracy's severed head. Just an undercurrent, rippling: watery reflections of death and horror. But rippling there too were rage and hatred and something else too murky to perceive. Feeling—he had regained the capacity to *feel*.

Irrelevant right now. Survival was the only thing that mattered.

The apple smell was overpowering.

Apples, he thought—and knew abruptly where he was. The only place on the island where apples were stored was the fruit cellar under Jonas' cottage. Jonas had a small pot still set up there in which he manufactured a few gallons of applejack each year for his own private use. Claimed he made the best applejack in the state of Maine. Down East white lightning, the Old Man always said, and everyone would laugh.

Why had they put him here?

Why was he still alive?

Because they're in no hurry, he thought; because they feed on terror as much as on blood. They want me conscious when the time comes, like Tracy must have been.

But the explanation did not satisfy him. Something wrong with it. More to it than that—or less to it than that. They—

He could not pursue it, not yet.

Survival. Escape.

Visualize the cellar. Narrow, fairly long. Stairs leading down from the kitchen in the middle of the inner wall. Shelving on the left, crates of apples. Wood-and-copper cooker and mash box and fermentation barrel on that side, in the juncture with the outer wall; water heater there too, and an oil furnace, and a maze of copper and steel and galvanized tin piping. Firewood stacked against the outer wall, and high above, where the wood siding of the cottage joined the fieldstone foundation, a large window hinged so that you could swing it inward. He seemed to remember a small standing freezer along the right-hand wall, but nothing else that might be there.

The door. Sure to be locked. Unless one of them was sitting up there in the kitchen, waiting for him to try coming out, waiting to take him some place then where the candles would burn on a pagan altar—

No.

The window. Storm shutters riveted to the outside wall: would they have thought to close and lock them? Easy for him to get out if they hadn't—too easy. And those shutters were made of heavy wood reinforced with iron bands, fitted with iron lockbolts that snapped into rings top and bottom; forty years of gale-force winds had been unable to break them open once they were locked down.

There was no other way out of the cellar.

The undercurrent of fear grew stronger; his genitals tightened into a ligature. Stay calm, don't lose control again. Check out the window and the door: find out for certain the way things stand.

Orientation. Which part of the cellar was he in? Bare stone wall here. He extended his arms again and shuffle-stepped to his left. Three paces, four—and he came up against something hard at waist level, bumping it with his hip; above it, his hands still slid over empty stone. He turned into the object, reached down to touch it, found its top smooth and flat and cold. The standing freezer. Right-hand wall, then; stairs diagonally to his left, outer wall to his right.

He hesitated. Light in the freezer?

His fingers found the edge of the lid, pulled it up. A rush of icy air, but no light. He lowered the lid again.

There were half a dozen large-wattage bulbs in sockets on the ceiling joists, a switch on the wall beside the door. But getting there would take time, and he didn't need light to examine the window or find a weapon. Those things first and foremost.

He reversed direction, and when he came to the corner he turned his body to face the rear wall and eased along there, arms raised and hands exploring the wood siding just above the level of his forehead. After half a dozen paces his fingers touched the frame of the window. When he found the catch at the bottom, he flipped it loose and pulled back slowly, and the window hinged inward with a faint creaking sound. He drew it open as far as it would go, and the voice of the squall increased in volume—but he felt none of the wind, none of the rain.

Even before his fingers bent against unresisting wood and iron banding, he knew the storm shutters had been secured outside.

He put his back to the wall, teeth clenched, and moved further to his right. Almost immediately his hand touched a solid but yielding object—pine log— and felt it loosen and begin to slide away before he could catch hold of it. It tumbled down, thumping, like something rolling down a short flight of stairs, and then banged into the cement floor and was still. After-echoes faded through the blackness. He held his breath, listening.

No sounds from inside the cottage; no sounds at all except the steady, distant rhythm of wind slapping and hurling rain at the clapboards, at the pitched sides of the roof.

He lowered both hands, carefully, and probed the stack of firewood. Got a firm grip on another of the cut logs and brought it in against his chest. Three feet long, maybe eight inches in diameter. Good.

Now—the door.

The staircase would be fifty feet or so directly in front of him, he judged, and the floor across to it should be clear. He could go around to the stairs by way of the walls, use them to brace his body; but if he could not walk without support, now was the time to find it out. Step away from the fieldstones. Legs jellied, not much feeling in either foot. Shuffle forward in a straight line, heel and toe, sodden shoes making thin liquid noises; both arms stretched out in front of him, hands and the piece of firewood transcribing small, tentative arcs. Must be almost there now—

One toe stubbed against something, then the ankle, and his legs gave way at once, and he sprawled out sideways over the obstacle, came down hard on it and on a second one like it. Slender strips of wood dug into his thigh, his upper right arm; the firewood skidded away. The heel of his hand dislodged several small round things, sent them bouncing and rolling away. Apples. Apple crates. He dragged himself off to one side and crouched on the floor, head raised, listening again.

The cottage above remained silent.

He did not try to stand again: too much pain, old and new, sharp and dull. Instead he crawled around the crates, brushing away spilled apples, hunting for the cordwood. Found it, clutched it. Kept on crawling until he came up against the bottom runner of the staircase.

He looked up to where the door was, but the heavy black let him see nothing at all. No strip of light beneath the door, then, but that did not have to mean anything. One of them could still be up there in the kitchen, sitting in the dark, patient. Creatures of the darkness, like vampires, like Jabberwocks....

Up the stairs on his knees, a runner at a time, hanging onto the railing. He made small bumping sounds that he could not avoid, but clamped lips and teeth to muffle the audible rasp of his breath. When he reached the narrow landing he sat there on one hip and put his ear to the panel. Unbroken stillness. He laid the pine log across his right shoulder, cocking it, and got his left hand up and wrapped around the doorknob. Turned it counterclockwise, half a rotation. The latch did not click, did not release; the knob bound against its lock.

Jackman tugged once, gently, to see whether or not the door was fitted tightly into the jamb, and when it did not yield he released the knob and let his hand fall bonelessly into his lap.

Break it down? Not much chance: the panels were thick, the latch securely fastened. Noise factor, too; he did not know if one of them was close enough to hear some or all of whatever he did in here. Pick the lock? He had no knowledge of how to pick locks, and no tools besides.

Scratch off the door along with the window. Scratch off the only two exits from the cellar.

Escapeproof locked room....

□ □ □

Time.

Seconds running, sliding away.

It might be hours before they decided to come for him, and it might only be minutes. He could not waste any more time sitting here frustrated; all he was doing was waiting for death. Think. Work out a plan. Keep himself together.

Options. He could stay up here on the landing or hide under the stairs and try to overpower them with the firewood when they showed themselves. But the landing was too small for maneuverability, and the door opened into the kitchen, and he was too weak and battered to be effective in a fight, and they were far too cunning not to anticipate some kind of attack and take precautions against it. Was there anything he had forgotten about or that Jonas had added since the last time he had been in here? Anything he could use as a more powerful weapon, as a possible means of escape?

He struggled onto his feet, using the railing and the firewood for leverage. Fumbled along the wall, felt out the plastic casing of the light switch. Flipped the toggle up.

Nothing happened.

Up and down again, and a third time. Empty clicks. Bastards had taken out the bulbs, or thrown the main on the fusebox, or cut the goddamn wiring. He turned away and leaned on the railing and stared down into the heavy darkness.

Matches, he thought.

Firewood for the cooker, you had to have matches to touch it off. And he seemed to recall that Jonas kept candles down here in case of generator failure. There had to be matches, then; Jonas didn't smoke, he had no particular reason to carry matches or a lighter on his person. The shelving. They ought to be on the shelving near the still.

He went down the stairs, supporting most of his weight on the railing. When he reached the floor he dropped onto his knees again because he did not want to risk another fall, pushed forward among the scattered apples to the first of the crates. They were set three abreast, and he moved laterally along them to his left, toward the shelving and the wall. Beyond the last crate in the row was a narrow space large enough for him to pass into: aisleway that Jonas had left clear so he could get to the shelves. Jackman reached out and his fingers contacted a vertical board, then filled mason canning jars on one of the shelves.

He became sharply aware of the arid burning in his mouth and throat, the cracked surfaces of his lips. Liquid—Jonas' applejack? Better not: that stuff was like bottled fire, and in his condition, on a tender empty stomach, even a little would do more damage than good. He had to keep his thoughts clear if he was going to have any chance at all.

Straightening up, he probed higher. More jars, nothing but jars here. The next tier, knee-walking. Larger jars and quart bottles, some empty, some full. Another tier. Lower shelves vacant, dusty. Upper ones: galvanized tin fittings, asbestos sheeting, pieces of copper tubing, a dented pail, a tray of sheet metal nails, a small tackhammer. He weighed the tackhammer for a moment, put it back. Too small, too light to be of any use as a weapon.

Jackman crawled further and his hand brushed over a coiled length of something thick and rubbery on the floor. Hose. He started to push it aside, stopped with his hand on it. Water. Christ, you needed water to run a still too; there was a faucet down here. But where? The hose was not attached to it—just lying there in a coil. Can't remember, but it had to be close by, close to the still.

Matches.

Primary objective was matches. With light he could find the faucet quickly;

with light he could stand up, move around, search the cellar. Forget about water for now.

He shoved at the hose, felt it slide less than six inches and then bunch up against a solid obstruction. A leaning, fingertip examination told him it was a network of piping, and beyond it, the cool metal side of the oil furnace. Near the corner now; the tier of shelves on his left would be the last one. No matches here, then there weren't any matches at all.

Bottom shelf. Empty. Next one. Empty. Next one. Six-ounce cans of something, a small wood-handled tool with a flat squarish blade. Putty knife. Not very sharp, not very useful, but he caught it up anyway, on impulse, and put it into the pocket of his slicker. Next shelf, stretched up on his knees. Empty.

He would have to stand to get to the ones at the top. He hooked his fingers onto one of the horizontal boards and tugged down, testing the tier's sturdiness. Wobbly. If he tried to use it as a fulcrum, he might bring the whole thing crashing down on top of him. He fumbled over the piping, got his hand through it and onto the top edge of the furnace, and used that to bring himself upright.

When he had his balance he turned back to the shelves and swept a palm gently across the one at chest height. Five-pound sack of sugar. A funnel. An earthenware jug. An open box filled with smooth, waxy cylinders—candles. But there was nothing else on the shelf.

Next one above, fingers searching with desperation now. Empty, only dust

And then his hand closed over something in the left-hand corner, felt the rough sandpaper strip along both sides. Matchbox, kitchen matches. He grabbed it, almost blundered it away in his haste, hung on and dragged it down and held it to his chest. Rattling inside: nearly full. He slid it open and took out one of the sticks, reclosed it. Had to will his hands steady as he pressed the tip against the rough strip, scraped it, scraped it a second time.

Light flared, half-blinded him, and then settled into a wavering flame. Blinking, he held the match out in front of him, saw the labyrinth of piping and copper coils, the boxy shape of the furnace, the water heater behind it and the still arrangement a few feet away to the right. Apple crates behind him, floor unoccupied at the front of the cooker and across to where the firewood was stacked.

The matchlight flickered, began to die hotly against his thumb. He shook it out, dropped it, got another one from the box and struck that. This time he used the light to locate the candles, take one out. When he had the wick burning steadily, he put the matchbox into his slicker pocket and stepped toward the pot boiler, around it. The candle flame cast a weird, fluttery glow on the darkness, created mobile shadows—and let him see the faucet jutting out of the fieldstone wall adjacent to the water heater.

Jackman went to the faucet, sank down beside it. The burning thirst in his mouth and throat was so intense that he could not move his tongue. Turn the T-handle slowly, don't want more than a trickle, don't want any more noise; hold the candle out of the way. There—and the valve released and the water came spilling out.

He twisted and ducked his head under the tap, let the icy liquid splash over his face, pour into his mouth. The first cascade seemed to back up against the blockage in his throat; then the muscles relaxed, and he was able to swallow, gagging, gasping audibly in spite of himself. Spasmodic gulps until the dryness was gone, until his stomach convulsed. Enough: you could drink yourself sick when you were this dehydrated. He forced his mouth shut, turned the handle to stop the flow.

The water energized him, gave him a fresh surge of strength; he was able to get up again without aid. He held the candle down low enough so that he could see the floor, oblivious to the hot dripping of wax, and went to his left, hunched over. Quarter cord of the firewood, a small pile of kindling; but no hatchet or other wood-splitting tool. Bare wall under the window and around to where the freezer stood—the right-angled area he had covered blindly earlier.

He crossed beyond the freezer. In the upper cellar corner and along the wall beneath the stairs were drums of oil for the furnace, more five-pound sacks of sugar, two large bags of potatoes. He came back to the foot of the stairs and went around the apple crates to the shelving. Down the aisleway, looking now in the shimmery candlelight at the stored things he had identified by feel. Random objects that he'd missed in the darkness, but nothing usable in any way.

Full circuit, search completed; nothing overlooked. And he was still trapped, still helpless. No way out. Sacrificial sheep penned up and awaiting slaughter.

Standing in the shadows by the pot still, he ran splayed fingers over his face. No choice now except to try battering at the door and keep on battering at it until it opened or, much more probably, they came for him. Impotent rage and hatred became as strong as the fear; he was not going to give up, they would have to knock him out again or drag him off kicking and fighting.

He started to turn, bringing the candle around, and then stopped abruptly. He was facing in toward the corner, and something had caught his attention, started an urgent tickling at the back of his mind. Arm at full extension, he rocked the candle flame from side to side. Focus on the half-born perception. The furnace? Simple oil-burner, frame made of galvanized sheet metal. Gravity feed—

And he had it: not the furnace, the thick round length of cold-air duct pipe that extended up from its top into a box flashing between two of the ceiling joists.

His heart beat faster, skipping tempo. He stepped around the still, moved in as close to the furnace as he could get. The pipe had to be twenty inches in diameter, and that meant the opening covered by the flashing overhead was the same. Big enough for a man his size to fit through; no obstructions in the duct box set through the floor—just a floor register in the room directly above, and you could push that out of the way with one hand.

Christ, sweet Christ, if he could dismantle that pipe....

Hope and urgency mingled inside him, providing stimulus. He shoved lightly against the duct. Sturdy, but it had a snap joint in the middle, no caulking compound or nails. Have to get up on top of the furnace in order to break it loose. Then pry the flashing free, nothing but sheet-metal nails holding it to the ceiling.

He paused to listen. The rain seemed to be slackening now, and you could no longer hear the wind slapping at the sides and eaves of the cottage. Except for an occasional creaking, nothing stirred anywhere in the rooms above.

*Was* there anybody up there?

Going to be noisy work, dismantling the duct pipe. But he had made noise already, and nobody had come to investigate; he had heard nothing to indicate occupancy. Have to go on the assumption that he was alone. No choice in the matter.

He would need tools to pry the flashing loose: the putty knife he had taken off the shelf, the tackhammer he had left there. He came back along the aisle-way, and when he located the hammer he put it into the same pocket with the putty knife. As he turned again, the toe of his shoe nudged one of the apple crates—and it occurred to him that he would need something to stand on once he had cleared the duct opening. The top of the furnace was not high enough to let him reach all the way through the duct to move the register out of the way. And he would have to do that before there was anything for him to grab onto, any leverage to pull himself up.

He went over close to the furnace, bent, turned the candle to let melted wax drip onto the floor, and anchored it upright in the puddle. Got another candle out of the box, lit it, put it down nearby. They did not give off much combined light, but there was enough to throw the furnace and the duct pipe into dusky relief. Farther up, between the ceiling joists, the box flashing was concealed in heavy shadow.

Jackman squatted in front of an apple crate, tilted it, scraped apples out. Repeated the process with a second crate and then carried both of them around to the far side of the still. One at a time, he lifted them and slid them under the asbestos-wrapped hot-air piping and across the furnace top, out of the way. Now he had to get back there, between the water heater and the mash box and the back of the boiler. Copper coils, tubing, tin pipe, steel pipe—all interlocking and jumbling together like components in a Rube Goldberg invention. Wedge in past and through the piping, lean in, find purchase on the furnace edge. He banged his shin against a steel fitting, scraped the pulpy side of his head on one of the hot-air pipes, and clamped his teeth against the deep bites of pain.

Crouching slightly, he levered forward and up. Got a knee on top of the furnace, lunged and caught onto the base of the duct pipe and pulled the other leg up so that he was kneeling there head down, prayer fashion. He raised up alongside the duct, wrapped an arm around it and clung there while he groped for the hammer and putty knife, took them out and laid them inside the nearest of the two crates.

Off with the oils now: too bulky, restricting movement. He unbuttoned the slicker, shrugged out of it awkwardly, tossed it behind him and heard it flutter down in back of the still. Slid his knees around so that he was facing the duct pipe, hugged it with both arms and began to shove forward, pull back, in hard steady thrusts. The snap joint squeaked, bellied forth and back, loosened. Dry smell of dust. Jackman shoved again, wrenched back again, and when he felt the joint begin to separate he braced his weight against his heels and tugged less forcefully while still maintaining tension.

The pipe broke apart into two sections, screeching tinnily.

Dust sifted down, got into his nose and throat and made him cough. The ends of the two pieces of duct rested one on top of the other, off-center, canted up and down at opposing angles. He took his hands away and left the lengths like that and cocked his head, ears flared.

Stillness.

He reached up and ran his fingers across the nailed lips of the box flashing. Five nails in each, and all four lips solidly fitted to the wood crosspieces of the ceiling. He took the hammer and putty knife in his left hand, looped his right forearm over the hot-air run, bent one knee until his shoe was flat under him. Stood up, extending carefully, and found that he could stand fully erect; the top of his head just touched one of the joists.

Jackman transferred the putty knife to his right hand, felt out the flashing lip on the near side, and forced the squared blade between it and the ceiling. Worked it up and down, widening a tiny space as the nails began fractionally to loosen. But the blade was too thin, too pliable, to do any more than that, and he switched the knife for the hammer and jimmied the claw end into the slit as far as it would go. Then he rocked it up, snapped it down hard.

Tearing sounds; one corner of the flashing popped free, and a nail dropped out and bounced metallically on the furnace top. The two pieces of duct pipe grated against each other as the upper section slipped outward. He nudged it with his thigh until he succeeded in dislodging it so that it hung free from where it was nailed into the flashing, no longer touching the lower section.

He moved the hammer claw over, wedged it tightly into the breach. Yanked downward again. The second lip came free, and the broken joint end jerked up and glanced off the hot-air run, and two more nails clattered at his feet. The section hung there now at a faintly vibratory angle.

Sweat stung the cuts and abrasions on the insides of his hands, and after he stooped to lay the hammer and the putty knife down, he dried them on the damp front of his sweater. Then he got a double hold on the flashing and twisted it up and down, side to side—facial muscles contorting into a wince at each thin squeal from the pulling nails. The left side gave first, and when it did the rest of the nails tore out one after the other, like the ripping of stitches, until the flashing and the section of duct came down severed in his hands.

He lowered it immediately, half-squatted to lay it on the furnace top and push it away toward the wall. When he rose up again, there was a sharp binding in his chest: breathing too rapid, too deep—starting to hyperventilate. He relaxed his jaws, opened his mouth and stood motionless, staring upward; the opening of the duct box was just visible in the guttering glow from the candles. No sounds filtered down through it from above, and there was only the faintest suggestion of gray light marking the position of the floor register.

While he waited for his respiration to shallow, he stretched both arms up and felt inside the opening. Smooth, dust-rimed metal; no barrier against passage. He raised onto his toes, but as he'd expected, he could not reach high enough to touch the register.

Bending again, he drew the first crate over and upended it, positioned it flush against the upthrust section of duct. Second crate bottom-up on top of it, angled slightly so that there was an open wedge on the lower crate to serve as a step. He raised his body, pressed down with his hands on the makeshift platform to satisfy himself that it was sturdy. All right—but he would have to keep his weight dead center to avoid slippage.

He put his right foot on the wedge-step, using the broken pipe and the hot-air run for balance. Brought his left knee up and anchored it on the second crate and then joined it with his right knee. Keeping one hand on the hot-air piping, he straightened from the waist and dug the fingers on his other hand into the joist alongside the duct opening.

Now the rough part: getting his feet under him. Draw the left knee up against his chest, toe scraping the crate slats, sliding forward until the leg was flat-footed. The crates wobbled under him, and he froze, sweat streaming down into his eyes. Inch forward then until the platform felt firm again. Position his head so that it was directly beneath the opening. And here we go, slow, slow, weight on the left foot, tendons protesting in arms and thighs and stomach; bring the right leg forward, toe skidding, heel coming down; both feet set... crates shifting again, slide the left foot back until they stabilized... and he felt his hair brush against one of the metal sides as his head pushed into the duct box.

He was not quite standing upright, but he would have to get his left arm inside before his shoulders. He took it away from the hot-air run, neck-bracing himself at the edge of the opening, and brought it up past his face and locked the elbow. The tips of his fingers pressed against the rough metal squares of the register, stiffened until he felt it shift and rise slightly inside the floor hole, and then relaxed again. Still holding onto the joist with his other hand, he straightened up full-length and pushed his shoulders inside the duct.

Going to be a tight fit....

He spread the fingers against the grille, thumb back as far as he could extend it. Then, increasing pressure, he heaved up—and the register lifted out of the floor, and he was balancing it like a tray. The weight of it drove splinters of pain down his arm and into his armpit; dust burned in his nostrils, and he held his mouth clenched shut to keep from coughing and upsetting his precarious stance as he brought his arm and the register forward.

When he felt and heard the edge of the grille scrape against the floorboards, he eased his fingers back a square at a time and then shoved slowly, painstakingly. A third of the register cleared the opening, a half—

And it bound up on something.

Rug, he thought, goddamn rug. He got his fingers around the near edge and tilted it and shoved again. It would not move.

He wanted to scream with frustration, fought down the urge and pulled the register back, turned it diagonally and pushed again. It moved six inches, caught. You son of a bitch, you bastard thing—! He tilted it again, worked it across the edge of the floor opening to the far side, and started to push with violent jabs, and stopped himself in time and pushed steadily instead.

The register's right corner hung up again—but when he spun it around to the left it grated freely across bare wood. One last relentless effort, and he had it completely clear of the opening.

His left arm began to go numb from the strain, and he had to bring it back down past his face and take it out of the duct and let it hang loose at his side. He stood panting, drenched in oily, clammy wetness. I don't have enough strength left to pull myself out, he thought. All this way, all this struggle, and I can't get myself the hell up there.

Then he thought, angrily: Bullshit, that's defeatist bullshit. You can make it because you've *got* to make it.

Wait, rest awhile. Don't try it prematurely. Only going to have one chance; once you kick free of the crates, you'll be committed: make it up or come crashing down and maybe break something.

Jackman flexed the fingers on the left hand, relaxed the grip of his right on the joist. Listen. Silence, except for the dry scratchiness of his breath. The jellied feel was back in his legs, some of the same numbness that was in his left arm, but he knew he did not dare move his feet on the crates. He began to count seconds silently to himself, still flexing the fingers. One minute. Two minutes. Three minutes.

I can't stand like this much longer....

There was a tingling in his left arm now, and he was able to lift it from his side; the numbness evaporated into a series of dull throbbing aches. He put all his concentration on the arm, told himself he could feel strength seeping through it again and refused to believe that this was a lie. Strength in his right arm too, better take it down from the joist, better get it up inside the duct. Right arm first, that's the way to do it. Right arm up there tight on the floor, then the left.

He could make it now, if he was going to make it at all.

And he lowered the right arm and ducked down and brought it and the left arm inside the duct box, raised his body again. He could just get both forearms out of the opening above, palms flat on the floor on opposite sides. Then he shut his eyes, filled his lungs. Tensed.

Now.

He lunged upward off the crates, muscles contracting in his arms, legs kicking. There was a moment of loose suspension as his head came out of the floor hole; his calves scraped against the bottom of the duct box. Agony in his left shoulder and armpit, the arm going numb again, and he heaved frantically, flinging the arm outward along the floor; his fingers touched rough fiber—the

rug—and dug into it, caught a handful of it just as he felt himself beginning
to slide down. The rug did not give, it was weighted by heavy furniture, and
it held him steady long enough so that he could twist to the right and get his
ribcage jammed against the edge, right forearm skidding across bare wood and
onto the rug, that hand gripping it and pulling with it, and he was canted on
his stomach for a second, and the next second it was his hip, and then he was
half lying and half sitting on the rug with just his ankles stretched over the
opening: out of the duct, out of the escapeproof locked cellar.

Out.

□ □ □

There was the pale gray oblong of a window in the rear wall, and just
enough light coming through it to let him see the blurred outlines of a vanity
table, a cedar chest, the corner of a headboard. Bedroom. Thin gusts of wind
tugged at the weather stripping around the window, rattled a shutter somewhere at the front of the cottage. The other sounds were those of any old structure settling emptily in the cold hours of early morning.

His left arm was numb again, and he had to push awkwardly with the heel
of his right hand to move himself backward with agonizing slowness until one
shoulder butted against mattress and box springs. And he just sat there,
wheezing hoarsely, because he knew he could not get up yet; even the desire
for self-preservation could not make him get up yet. The effort in climbing out
of the duct had been supreme, and it had wrung the last remnants of energy
from him like droplets of water from a crumbling sponge.

And yet he felt totally controlled sitting there, as if with a kind of deliver-
ance—as if the struggle to get free of the cellar had been an ultimate escape
and horror could not touch him any longer. The undercurrent of fear was still
with him, but it was submerged deeply in weariness and an existentialistic resignation: he was not responding to it. He had been consumed, driven by terror for so long that he seemed to have developed a reactionary immunity to it,
the way the body does to poisons administered in sustained, nonlethal doses.

He found himself thinking of Tracy as he waited. His feelings about her were
a dull jumble in which only sorrow and pain were recognizable. If he had not
brought her here to the island, she would still be alive. But if life and the universe were wholly ordered, if man was a wholly rational animal, there would
be no wars and no apocalypses and he would not be where he was now. *If.* If
you never crossed a street or walked a sidewalk, you could never be run down
by a car. If you lived in a hermitage on a mountaintop, you would not suffer
from any of the evils of civilization. Where was the blame in anything that
happened to you or to someone else in the normal course of existence? Where
was the guilt? No man could be held accountable for circumstances beyond his
control, for the whims of fate or a supposedly benevolent deity.

Rationalizations? Maybe. Maybe not.

I didn't know her, he thought. All the hours together, all the physical intimacies, and at the end of it we were still strangers. No love, nothing but sex and filmmaking. Interlude. A face in the night—the long night of a lifetime. What sense, what result except a crushing of self, in passively mourning the unjust deaths of strangers? All the strangers, like Alicia and the little boy in Saigon? *I'm sorry you're dead, I wish with all my heart that it didn't have to happen to you when it did, but it happens to all of us sooner or later. All of us. Sooner or later.*

The tightness in his chest lessened as the wheezing ceased, and the tingling sensation started up the left arm from wrist to shoulder. The fingers remained numb; when he lifted the arm experimentally, they hung like thick strips of flayed meat. He dropped them back onto the rug. More light seemed to be coming in through the window now, and he saw that the panes were misty. Close to dawn. Of what day? Sunday, Monday? He had little perception of time, but except in terms of when the final moves would take place, time had ceased to matter.

Final moves, he thought.

Games.

And the realization came to him that throughout the ordeal in the cellar and the duct box, he had not once thought in terms of game-playing. Why? Every facet of his adult life had been translated into those terms, every action and reaction, every consideration; he had even managed to think of this nightmare as a game, foe against foe, move and countermove. But it was not a game—oh no, and it never had been a game.

Perhaps *nothing* was a game; perhaps the Old Man's philosophical legacy, like the Old Man's life, had been deceitful and fraudulent. And perhaps he had understood this subconsciously and had begun to reject game-playing, begun to exorcise finally and irrevocably, by extension, the Old Man himself.

That was an interesting insight, and he dwelt on it. The Old Man had dominated him during his lifetime, even dominated him from the grave; he had let himself be molded into the image of Thomas R. Jackman, so that in a spiritual sense the Old Man could live on one more generation in the son he had sired. Cheap, venal hunger for immortality. But hadn't the Old Man's entire life been predicated on a cheap, venal hunger for immortality? Hadn't that been the one true and absolute goal toward which he directed all his games— to leave an indelible mark on the pages of history?

Only he had failed, he had *lost:* he was already being forgotten, as liars and frauds—unless their sins were far greater and far more evil than his—were always eventually forgotten. Before long his mark would fade altogether, and his name would be nothing more than a meaningless word in political science books and moldering copies of *The Congressional Record.* The ultimate result of his game-playing had been death, nothing more, because if life was a game, then death was the final outcome for all the players. You won the game of life by accepting its rules and living according to them; if you tried to cheat by dividing it up into private games of your own, with your own rules, you were a loser from the beginning.

Ironic how the change points in your life sometimes came about, how maybe they came about too late. And he *was* undergoing a metamorphosis, no mistake about that. He was in few ways the same David Jackman who had arrived on the island on Friday afternoon. Fear and horror and adversity and insight were the catalysts; you never saw yourself so clearly as when you were battling for the preservation of self.

Meg, Dale, the Old Man: he understood them all fully for the first time because he understood himself for the first time. Understood that the preoccupation with games which the Old Man had instilled in him had, more than anything else, been responsible for his slow and inexorable downhill slide toward a nervous breakdown and a personal destruction just as terrible in its own way as the one he faced here and now.

But before he could complete the rejection of the Old Man and of game-playing, and begin to reassess himself and his life, he had to survive; and survival meant winning this last deadly nongame.

He examined his feeling of resignation and found no apathy in it. He wanted to live, and he had not lost any of the rage and hatred, and he had the constant presence of pain as an added motivation. Friday night he had told Tracy that he could kill another human being if it meant saving his own life, and had not known then if he was speaking the truth; now he knew that he had been, knew too that he would do it without hesitation or compunction if it came down to that.

No more running and no more hiding, he thought.

Time to take a stand.

*Always take the offensive whenever you can, David. Play with a certain amount of calculated recklessness, force your opponents off-guard; that's how you create vulnerability and that's how you win your games.* The Old Man had been right about that, so right. For all his charlatanism, Thomas R. Jackman had developed game-playing to a pseudoscience: if you wanted to win, you followed his advice to the letter.

So this one, this last one, is for you, Old Man, Jackman thought. The Final Moves of the Final Game, played in your honor, dedicated to your corrupt memory. You taught me how, you gave me the tools, and if I come out of it alive and intact I'll owe it all to you—and damn your soul for making me what I am.

His left hand began to tingle, then throb; he could feel the nap of the rug with the fingers. There were twinges in both legs, and a cramp in his right calf made him draw that leg up to flex it out. He sensed that he had enough strength finally to get up, and swung over against the bed, and got himself into a seated position on the quilt-covered mattress. The first time he tried to stand, the movement touched off a furious pounding in both temples, and a wave of dizziness forced him down again abruptly. He waited a minute or so, edged over to where a low nightstand sat beside the headboard, and leaned on that and tried again. The pounding was tolerable this time, the giddiness only transitory: he stayed upright, spreading his feet and stiffening his knees to keep them from buckling.

He was not ready yet to walk unaided, and he pressed in against the wall, and then took mincing steps around the nightstand and made it over to the window. The squall had moved inland to blow itself out, and it was no longer raining; the sky was a graying black, with a hint of a rose-colored flush above the tops of the trees eastward, and stars winked palely among tattered-lace clouds. In the half-light he could see drops of rain and dew glistening like tiny prisms on the fronds of a bed of lady ferns beneath the window. Gentling wind gusts provided the only movement.

As he stood there looking out, something nudged his mind, made him frown. Something wrong, something he was overlooking. Discordancy: he had felt it all along without being more than peripherally aware of it. But what? Moves? Rules?

His subconscious refused to give it up.

He put his back to the wall, and he was looking then at the closed sliding doors of a walk-in closet across the room. He took a step, wavered slightly and stopped, and took another: it was like walking on stilts, clumsy and teetering. But he got to the closet without falling, slid one of the doors open quietly, and looked inside.

Neat hanging rows of coats, dresses, shirts, slacks. He thought briefly of exchanging his own damp clothing for some of Jonas'—but Jonas was a small, wizened man, and none of his things would even come close to fitting. Still, the wet wool of the sweater chafed at his arms, and the clamminess of his shirt sent periodic chills along his back. Better to get out of those at least. There was a thick, folded blanket on the upper closet shelf, and he took that down and then stripped off the sweater and the shirt and draped the blanket shawl-like around his shoulders, tied the ends into a double knot.

The closet contained nothing else of any use to him; he started out of the bedroom, hesitated, and went into the adjoining bathroom. The medicine cabinet yielded a bottle of aspirin and a package of cold tablets. He took out four of the aspirin and two of the tablets, clenched them in his palm, and came out and made his way up the hallway to the kitchen, supporting himself now and then on the walls.

The kitchen was large and old-fashioned—propane stove, porcelain sink set into a thick varnished-wood drainboard—and it had one window that looked out toward the main house, curtained in white chintz. He opened drawers until he found a long, thin carving knife; then he bent against the drainboard and peered out through the glass between the curtains.

In the distance the house had a hazy, gray appearance, insubstantial and weathered, as though it were little more than an abandoned shell. If there were any lights on inside, he could not see them from this angle, and there was no outward glow on the waning darkness front or back. Most of the facing lawn was visible: they had taken down the charred cross, and they had removed the pole and its grisly crown. He did not let himself think of what they might have done with Tracy's head, or with her body.

When he was satisfied that the surrounding grounds were deserted, he drew back and opened one of the overhead cupboards and took down a glass. Ran a stream of cold water into it until it was full, swallowed the aspirin and the cold tablets one at a time. Forced himself to drink the rest of the water in small sips.

Hunger pangs made his stomach churn with faint nausea. How long since he had eaten anything? Didn't matter; he had to get something down now, something to help shore up his flagging strength. He put the glass on the drainboard and crossed in an old man's gait to the icebox. As he started to open it he thought of the light that might go on inside, and released the handle and stepped around instead to its side. He had to move it out slightly from the wall in order to expose the electrical cord and then hook the cord around his shoe and tug until the plug pulled free of the wall socket.

The icebox was only a quarter full: Jonas and his wife had probably taken perishables and a few other things with them to the mainland. But there was a small cantaloupe, and a container of homemade tomato juice, and a carton of eggs. Jackman took those out and put them on the drainboard, poured tomato juice into the glass and broke two eggs into it and blended the mixture with the knife blade. Then he sliced the cantaloupe in half, and one of the halves into slender sections, scraping out the seed pulp.

The juice went down all right, and stayed down, but he gagged on the first small swallow of cantaloupe. Had to spit it out into the sink to keep himself from vomiting. Wait awhile, he hold himself—and caught up the knife and took it with him into the hallway.

At the far end, to the right, was a utility porch with a washing machine and a dryer and a cement laundry tray on a wooden stand. Venetian blinds were partially drawn over the one window, but enough light filtered through to fade the darkness into gray-sheened shadows. He stepped to the back door and tested the knob. Locked. So they must have jimmied the lock on the front door and brought him in through there. When they came again, that would be the entrance they'd use—and that was where he would have to set himself up in ambush.

An idea came to him. There were storage cupboards on the wall and the side end of the porch, and two white-painted cabinets standing beneath them; he went there and opened each of the cupboards in turn. Detergents, a pile of rags. He bent to the cabinet on the left, and inside were an assortment of plumbing supplies, cans of touch-up paint and pipe dope and all-purpose oil, a plastic quart bottle of liquid drain-cleaner—

Drain-cleaner.

Jackman picked up the bottle, turned it over in his hands, but it was too dark for him to read any of the label. He set it on top of the second cabinet, opened the doors on that one. Wrenches, screwdrivers, a hammer, jars of assorted screws and fasteners, a hacksaw, a soldering iron, spools of wire solder. And what he had set out looking for: a spool of narrow-gauge, resilient copper wire.

Carrying the wire and the bottle of drain-cleaner, he returned to the kitchen and looked out again through the window at the main house. Dawn was breaking now, and the reddish tinge was brighter on the sky; the wind was dying. Nothing stirred anywhere that he could see.

He picked up one of the slices of cantaloupe, and this time he was able to swallow tiny bites without choking, without his stomach jumping. While he ate he read the label on the quart bottle, holding it up to catch the window light. As he had guessed, one of the ingredients was potassium hydroxide. All right.

When he had finished two of the slices and drunk a little more tomato juice, he hunted through the cupboards until he discovered a widemouthed canning jar. He unscrewed the cap on the drain-cleaner and filled the jar to within an inch of the lip. Then, balancing the jar in one hand and the knife and the spool of wire in the other, he walked up the hall to the vestibule.

It was bare of furnishings, but on the right was the closed door of a coat closet. He reversed direction and entered the parlor that opened off to the south, just long enough to set the jar down on the nearest flat surface: Jonas' trestle desk. In the vestibule again he tried the front door, and it opened silently under his hand; he widened a narrow crack and put his eye to it and looked out. No one coming. And the fawn's head was gone from the porch, although he could see the dried smears of its blood at the door's edge.

He shut it again, moved over to the closet door and opened it all the way back so that the knob touched the wall. On the floor inside was a metal shoe rack fastened firmly to the back wall with screws. Jackman knelt in front of it on one knee, then unraveled two feet of the copper wire and looped the end around a crossbar near the bottom of the rack, six inches off the floor. Twisted the wire together in tight coils until it was secure, and he could not jerk it loose.

His legs felt wobbly again when he stood up, and he had to rest a shoulder against the jamb. Too much walking and too much added exertion; the nourishment he had taken had bolstered him a little, but he was still functioning on bare reserves. Not much more to do, he told himself. Get it done and then you can sit down and rest and begin the wait.

He pushed away from the jamb and backed up slowly, unwinding the wire. When he was standing in the entrance to the parlor, he checked the angle of the stretched length. Too far out from the door if he anchored it to something inside the parlor—more than five feet—because of the width of the outer partition separating the parlor from the vestibule. Where he wanted it was just beyond the full inward swing of the front door, maybe three feet.

Have to move out a piece of furniture, he thought; push it against the partition. No other way to do it.

Jackman turned to face into the parlor and scanned the room hurriedly. The horsehair sofa was too bulky, the straight-backed chairs too lightweight, the china cabinet too stolid. The desk? Yes: it was sturdy without being too heavy to move, and it was the closest object—he would not have to transport it far.

He put the knife and the spool of wire on the floor in the hall, out of the way. Entered the parlor and crossed to the curtained window in the side wall opposite the entranceway. The grounds outside were still deserted. He came back to the desk, transferred the jar to an end table, and cleared the polished top of blotter, inkwell, and a clutter of loose papers and miscellany. At the far side, then, he pressed the heels of his torn palms against the edge and thrust forward.

The carved wooden feet scraped loudly across the floor, but that could not be avoided. He gritted his teeth and kept on shoving, trying to ignore the muscle protest in arms and shoulders; the desk skidded out along the wall, into the entranceway. The knots in the blanket unwound and it slipped back off his shoulders, fell to the floor; he paid no attention. Got the desk turned and maneuvered it through into the vestibule and then, finally, a minute later, had it set solidly into the angle formed by the partition and the front wall.

Immediately he stumbled over to pick up the knife and the wire, came back with them, laid the knife on the desktop, and dropped to one knee again. Passed the spool around the pegged support piece just above the near foot, pulled the length taut, bound it with a dozen over-and-under loops. It seemed too close to the front door now. He struggled up and stepped over the wire and eased the door open, looked out. Solitude, bathed in a deepening reddish glow. Have to risk opening the door all the way, but do it fast—and he swung it in past his body, clinging to the knob. The edge rubbed against the wire.

Shut the door, return to the desk, drag it toward him eight inches. Into the parlor. The jar of drain-cleaner, one of the straight-backed chairs; put the chair into the entranceway beside the desk, the jar down next to the knife.

And he was ready.

He caught up the blanket, wiped wetness from his face and eyes with it, redraped his torso, and lowered himself exhaustedly onto the chair, legs sprawled out in front of him. You can come any time now, he thought. Any time. Any time.

He waited.

□ □ □

And waited.

And kept on waiting.

Light came into the vestibule from the two parlor windows, herding shadows down the hallway. The cottage was still. The air in there lost some of its coldness, became almost comfortable as the rising sun warmed the clapboards. Lassitude settled over him, and that and the effects of the cold capsules made him drowsy, blanked his mind for short periods so that he had to fight against torpor by constantly shifting position on the chair. His tailbone ached, his head ached, his hands ached—but all in a dull, tolerable way that did nothing to help keep him alert.

He got up once to stare out through the far window, saw nothing more or less than he had earlier. Came back and sat and waited. Got up again when his eyes drooped shut and had another futile look outside. Debated going to the kitchen for more tomato juice, decided against it, and sat down. And waited, waited, waited.

*Goddamn* it, why didn't they come?

The physical exertion of his preparations, then the lassitude, had blunted the nagging feeling of discordancy; but now it was bothering him again, gaining magnitude. It lay in his subconscious like a series of coded messages awaiting decyphering. Not unlike dreams, he thought then. Dreams, too, were coded messages. The Jabberwock dream in the cave....

He stood once more, paced back to the parlor window. Concentrate. Messages. There was bright sunshine on the empty grounds, bright sunshine reflecting splinters of light off the glass panes on the house's near side wall, bright sunshine giving the blue waters of the bay a mercurial sheen. Midmorning now.

Messages.

Dreams.

Something overlooked, something wrong.

Discordancy—

*Why hadn't they killed him as quickly as they had killed Tracy? Why had they left him alone in the dark cellar for so long? If they wanted to prolong the agony and the terror, why not have bound him, put him in a room with them and physically or at least mentally tortured him, let him watch them prepare for a blood rite while they watched* him?

The sudden inpouring of questions, the breakthrough, the connection between conscious and subconscious turned him rigid and set his scalp to tingling. And immediately there were other questions, a chain of them: keys with which to decode the messages.

How had the Chris-Craft been stolen?

Why were the boathouse doors closed on Saturday morning?

How had they known he and Tracy would be on Eider Neck Friday night?

Why had they let Tracy and him escape through the marsh?

Why hadn't there been any axes and hatchets in the barn when he and Tracy went after the flare pistol?

How had they known he would be at the caves last night?

How had they known about the caves in the first place?

And as the messages decoded, as the answers became clear, Jackman felt a coldness settle like a hand between his shoulder blades. He reached into his trouser pockets, took everything out and stared at it. Two dimes and a quarter. Comb. Wallet. Key ring: keys for the house here, the house in Washington, his office, his car, his safe-deposit box. But that was all. That was *all*.

Proof.

When he had put the items away again, he stood looking blindly out of the window. He imagined a game board, the intricate design of a game board, all the pieces spread out along it; he saw the whole of the board, end to end, side to side, square to square—and each of the pieces took on form and clarity, each of the moves become recognizable. He studied it with his mental eye, fascinated, horrified. He had misinterpreted the rules all along: not just the moves, but the basic rules of the game.

Oh Jesus! he thought. Oh Jesus, Jesus, Jesus! Oh sweet Mary Mother of God!

He knew where their boat was.

He knew where the Jabberwocks were.

He knew exactly how he could win this Final Game.

Emotion swelled inside him, waves of it lifting, lifting, and when it crested the flood sent him hurrying back into the vestibule. His eyes glittered when he stared at the knife and the jar, over at the length of stretched copper wire. *Wrong move.* The strategy was not passive offense, it was aggressive offense. Take the game to them. Attack. Become the hunter instead of the hunted.

So the first moves toward checkmate, then, were ones calculated to confuse them and then separate them. Use one of the hidden game props they themselves had provided and used so successfully; turn the tables, hoist them on their own petard, divide them and conquer them—each of those clichés was applicable.

The lassitude was gone; he felt strong again, stronger than he had ever felt in his life. The rage and hatred were controlled, calculated, now. He threw off the blanket, took up the knife and the jar of drain cleaner from the desk, and ran down the hallway into the kitchen.

The same cupboard in which he had found the jar yielded a ring top and lid. He tightened those down to seal in the liquid. Opened drawers, found a cache of empty five-pound sugar sacks and put the jar and the knife, handle down, inside one of them.

He paused just long enough to swallow the last of the tomato juice; then he retraced his steps up the hallway to where a closed door on the right opened into a small sitting room. There was a shade drawn over the window in the facing wall, and he crossed to there and raised it. Outside were a hundred sun-lit yards of grass, and beyond them the shadowed line of forest stretching from the headland to the interior of the island.

Jackman unlocked the window, lifted the sash, climbed over it, and used the cottage to screen the path of his staggered run for the trees.

□ □ □

Dappled with silvery highlights, the sea licked placidly at the shale banks of the inlet on the headland's outer rim. Far out on the northeast, past Little Shad Island, a sailboat sat becalmed; it looked from this distance like a white handkerchief mounted on a stark blue background. Gulls dived in long elegant sweeps, cleaved the water neatly, and came up again trailing shimmery beads of spray.

Jackman stood resting for a moment beside the natural rock bench near the edge, watching the gulls with eyes bright and resolute. Once into the woods he had slowed his pace to a rapid walk, to conserve energy, and his legs had held up amazingly well. Except for the asthmatic nonrhythm of his breathing, he did not feel weakened or otherwise affected by the trek across the headland.

He sat down on the rock, laid the sugar sack carefully beside him. And then he leaned forward and unlaced his shoes and took them off, took his socks off.

Unbuckled his belt and unzipped his fly and stripped out of trousers and underpants.

He took the belt from its trouser loops, wrapped all the clothing and the pair of shoes into a tight bundle, and secured it with the belt. Standing, he brought his arm back and hurled the bundle discus-fashion into the sea. It made a heavy, audible splash when it struck, bobbed for a moment in the ripples, finally sank as the clothing became waterlogged. The surface smoothed again.

First and most important move completed.

Jackman looked down at his nakedness, and the thought came to him that he had reduced himself to primitivism. Naked savage, naked hunter. But the game itself was atavistic, and he was merely playing within its parameters, equalizing advantage. Naked, he had gained a momentary freedom—imperatively as well as symbolically.

Turning, he caught up the sugar sack and went back into the cool shade of the woods.

□ □ □

The sun was directly overhead when he crept forward at the top of the rear slope, equidistant between the house and Jonas' cottage, and lowered himself onto a grassy ledge dotted with wood asters. From there he could see over the cottage roof to the greensward across which he had run earlier, out along the full bayside curve of the headland. Most of the cove was visible straight ahead. All of it was empty, as motionless and vaguely illusory as a hologram. The high-noon stillness was acute; even the cries of the gulls seemed muted, like sounds emanating from somewhere outside the microcosm that the island had become.

He rested his chin on one forearm and eased himself into a more comfortable position, being careful of his exposed genitals. Rubbed the scratched and bruised soles of his feet against his ankles to clean them of pine needles and other bits and pieces of the forest floor. The sugar sack was within easy reach of his right hand; the tip of the carving knife protruded through the open end like a sharp metal tongue. For the first time he felt warm from head to foot: the day's heat had dried away the last lingering traces of dampness and chill. But his forehead and cheekbones were still feverish—the cold capsules and the aspirin seemed to have helped only a little—and he thought again, with clinical detachment, that he might have walking pneumonia.

The hell with it. The threat of pneumonia at this stage of things was meaningless. Unless it prevented him from functioning, and there did not seem to be any immediate danger of that.

He stared down toward the cottage. Nothing altered the fixed tableau. Once, after ten or fifteen minutes, there was a rustling in the undergrowth behind him; startled, he pulled the knife out of the sack and twisted over and sat up on one hip. A small gray squirrel darted out alongside a rotted stump and raced up the trunk of a spruce and disappeared among the boughs. Quiet resettled.

He let himself relax, rolled over onto his stomach again and resumed his vigil.

When the man appeared and then came to a standstill at the front corner of the house, it was with such stealth that he seemed almost to have been there all along.

Jackman tensed but remained rigidly immobile. About time, sonny, he thought.

The sun glinted off the barrel of the rifle the man was holding at present-arms, put a glossy shine on the red-brown marks of the symbol painted on his bare chest. His hair was sandy, cropped short—the same color as his beard—and he might have been any age from twenty to thirty; he did not look as big in perspective as he had on Eider Neck, or last night on the cliffs, but then nothing looked the same as it had at those times. He stood for half a minute, moving his head in a slow 180-degree arc, and then he came out farther into the open space between the house and the cottage. No one followed him: he was alone.

Okay, Jackman thought. Okay.

The bearded man walked toward the front of the cottage, pausing now and then as though to listen. When he reached the end of the porch and started across to the steps, he vanished from sight.

Jackman held his position and kept his gaze steady on the cottage. Minutes trudged away in the silence. The glare of the sunlight seemed to intensify so that everything took on a lacquered, white-gold look, oddly surreal now; the sea shimmered with molten reflections.

And the bearded man appeared again, beyond the far front corner, moving in the same watchful fashion—but limping slightly now—at an angle toward the headland. Trip on the copper wire inside the door, did you, sonny? Too bad you didn't knock yourself senseless, you son of a bitch.

Wolfishly, Jackman's lips flattened in against his teeth. His eyes followed the man's progress across the rim of the beach, saw him stop once and turn a full slow circle. The deliberateness of his actions was that of a trained soldier. At the first of the trees on the long slope above the beach, he halted again and transcribed another small walking circle. Then he entered the woods, blended into the tree shadows.

When Jackman could no longer see him he got up with the sack and went off in the opposite direction, laterally to the southwest.

□ □ □

He made his run to the south wall of the house across exactly the same section of sloping ground that he and Tracy had covered in their rush for freedom the first night.

From behind the bole of a spruce he had studied the windows in that wall for several minutes before stepping out into the open, and he had seen no indication of a watcher; now, as he ran in a half-hobbled stride caused by the impact of his naked feet on grass-hidden rocks, he kept his head up and scanned the blind glass panes. Still no sign of anyone looking out. He came up at the wall just to the left of the storm doors, propped a shoulder against the clapboard siding, and listened. In the vacuumlike stillness, he thought, you ought to be able to hear sounds a long way off; he heard nothing.

They had closed the storm doors—he remembered that he had left them hinged open when he and Tracy burst out of the basement. He went over and caught the metal handle on one, tugged up. They hadn't bothered to replace the iron locking bars: the door half rose instantly under his hand. Exhaling through his nostrils, he dragged the door all the way up slowly to keep the hinges from squeaking, and laid it back. Sunlight cut into the gloom below, illuminated part of the wooden stairs. He paused to listen again—silence— and then stepped into the opening and started down, pulling the door half closed above him as he went.

When he was standing on the cold concrete floor, he waited to let his eyes adjust to the heavy black. Sunspots danced at the periphery of his vision, fused into wavy distortional lines like those on an oscilloscope, then faded and vanished altogether. The darkness was absolute, and that meant the door to the pantry at the far end was closed. Otherwise, he would have been able to see some sort of light over there.

He felt his way forward until he was out of the annex. Vague shapes began to take form here and there, none directly in front of him. He recalled no obstructions in the path across to the inside staircase, but he had learned a wise lesson in Jonas' fruit cellar. Instead of trying to walk and maybe knocking over some unexpected object, he got down on his knees and began to crawl, holding the top of the sugar sack between his teeth. He had become very adept at crawling the past few days, he thought bitterly.

The cold floor, the dampness of the basement, robbed his body of sun-warmth and started him shivering again. His knees made faint slithery sounds on the smooth concrete. The outline of the steps loomed in front of him, and he got his right hand around the bottom of the railing support, took the sack in his left. Once he was on his feet again, he removed the knife from the sack, tightened his fingers around the handle, and rested that fist on the railing. Then he began the climb.

The third runner creaked sharply when he put his weight on it. He drew his foot back, froze.

The house did not lose any of its hush.

Jackman moved over to the side, located with his toes the end of the second runner where it was nailed to the frame, and tried again. No creak this time. He mounted the remaining treads in the same spots, soundlessly. Stood then on the narrow landing in front of the pantry door.

With the hand holding the knife he touched the knob, rotated it. There was a muffled click, and the door opened into the pantry on oiled hinges. Tensing, he used the knife point to push it perpendicular to the jamb. Retreated a half step instead of going forward and through into the pantry, and dipped into a slight crouch.

The shadowed larder was empty.

What he could see of the kitchen beyond was empty.

But he held his position, throat working dryly. A soft creaking came from somewhere in the center of the house. Natural grumbling of old timbers? Or someone moving around? He had no way of telling, not from here. And the sound was not repeated.

Step forward, into the doorway. Instinct told him the kitchen was as deserted as it appeared—but not the house. No, not the house. Inside the pantry he squatted and took the jar out of the sugar sack, gripped it between his right arm and chest, unscrewed the cap and lid carefully with his left hand and laid them on top of the sack. Cupped his palm under the bottom of the jar, fingers and thumb splayed upward around the heavy glass. Rising, he crossed to within one pace of the kitchen entrance.

Littered remnants of several lunches and dinners on the cobbler's-bench table: plates, glasses, utensils, an empty milk carton toppled on its side, orange peelings and apple cores and melon rinds. Rays of sunlight filtered in through the curtained window over the sink, extended dustily into the center corridor.

He entered the kitchen, walking on the balls of his feet, and went across it and stopped again just inside the right curve of the hallway arch. The air in there had a stifling warmth: they must have the furnace turned up to seventy or more. Like spiders, he thought. Flourishing on heat like a nest of spiders. There was silence in the hall, silence everywhere. He craned his head forward and began to ease it through the arch so that he could look up the length of the passage.

*Bong!*

*Bong!*

The sudden sounds erupted with the concussive volume of cannon shots, shredding the quiet and buffeting his sensitized eardrums like physical blows. He started violently and in reflex snapped his head and body back, and the movement jerked his left arm up and out. Drain liquid sloshed over the mouth of the jar, splattered on the floor behind him. In automatic reaction he tightened his fingers and dug his nails into the glass to keep it balanced, to steady it; a droplet burned on one of the cuts in that palm. The surge of his heart swelled veins in both temples and set them to thudding. Clock, his mind said, goddamn bastard grandfather clock striking two P.M. He leaned shakily on the wall as the last echoes fled away, as the hush resettled to what seemed like an even deeper aphonic level than before.

The palm cut continued to burn hellishly, numbingly, as more liquid flowed down along the sides of the jar. He stood away from the wall and went over to the drainboard and took a dish towel off its cupboard hook. Put the knife and the jar down, not taking his eyes off the archway, and scrubbed at his palm and kept scrubbing at it until the fire diminished and the numbness disappeared. Then he dried the jar, set it once more into his cupped fingers, picked up the knife, and returned to the right curve of the arch.

From that angle he had to put his head only part way out before he could see the whole of the corridor. The bathroom, library and study doors were closed. Sunshine streaming into the parlor and through its hall entrance a few yards distant—but no other light of any kind—created in the duskiness a pale illuminated cube from floor to ceiling across the width of the hall; dust motes floated languidly inside.

Still moving on the balls of his feet, Jackman went to the opposite wall and sidestepped upward along its base. Part of the parlor came into view: sideboards, chairs, a third of the leather couch that faced the fireplace. Empty. He took three more steps, to the rim of the cube of sunlight.

Overhead and toward the front, a board creaked.

Again.

Jackman held himself still, not breathing. The creaking came a third time, and there was a short series of barely audible thumps. Heavy footsteps: the other man. He tried to place the exact origin of the sounds, thought they might have come from one of the forward rooms on the north side. His old room, or Dale's next to it. He waited, head tilted up, but he was listening to silence again.

He padded slowly across to the near edge of the entranceway. With each step, more of the parlor appeared before him, and when he reached the edge and slid his back against it, one foot inside and one foot in the hall, he could see all of the room and through into the near half of the foyer. Unoccupied. And cheerless despite the sunlight, a part of him noticed—as though the violation of its genteel sanctity had destroyed all the summer memories and stilled forever the party laughter and the strains of music and the ghostly echo of the Old Man's voice.

He went the length of the parlor, glancing once toward the fireplace: the candles, burned down to blobs of yellowish wax, still remained on the mantelpiece and on the hearth, and the splashes and smears of dried blood still defaced the bricks like a madman's graffiti. But these things held no terror for him anymore; they only deepened his rage. When he took his eyes away from them, they no longer existed in the spaces of his mind.

A pace inside the foyer, he halted and looked over at the staircase. And a board creaked again above and beyond the top of the stairs, and he heard the same short series of heavy steps, louder now. He started to back away, then stood motionless when they ceased abruptly. Bedsprings protested as a weight dropped inertly and settled on them.

Quiet.

My room, all right, Jackman thought. My bed. Nice irony in that. Must have gone over to the window to look for the other one, and now he's come back to sit or lie and wait. Does he have the door open? If he's got the door open, he can see out into the hall from the bed.

Strategy. Up the stairs, take the chance the door is closed? No—the damned runners are liable to creak as loudly as those floorboards, and if the door *isn't* shut, there's no way to get to him without being seen first. Have to make him come out of there, then; make him come downstairs. Not too much time before the other one returns, it has to be fast. Knock something over, make some sort of noise? No good. That would only alert him, bring him down armed and prepared and blow the only advantage I've got. Has to be another way. But what? What?

He turned into the parlor again, stared searchingly around the room. Sweat rolled down his cheeks and dripped from his chin onto the sparse hairs on his chest; he did not bother to brush any of it away. His eyes quit their roaming, and he realized his gaze was fixed on one of the windows on the outside wall, on the bright flood of sunlight there.

Sunlight. Hot. Sweltering in here because of the sun and because—

The furnace.

But was there enough time before the bearded one came back? Calculated gamble; there was a risk factor in any move he made now. What you had to do was to choose the gambit that offered the least potential line of resistance in order to achieve optimum results. Wasn't that right, Old Man? Wasn't that the way you taught it to me?

There was only one thermostat in the house, and it regulated an even temperature throughout the upstairs and downstairs. It was here in the parlor, on the opposite wall by the center corridor. Jackman crossed to it, keeping his steps slow and measured. Set at seventy, as he'd guessed. He moved the dial full to the right, returned to the front wall and flattened himself there two strides from the foyer entrance.

One thing was certain: even if you thrived on heat, and even if you opened all the windows in one room, it would not take long before you started to suffocate when the day was this warm and the furnace was turned all the way up to ninety degrees.

□ □ □

After five minutes, the heat became uncomfortable.

After ten minutes, it became nearly intolerable.

Perspiration oiled Jackman's body, distorted his vision, fled in runnels down his naked torso and legs to create widening patches of wetness on the floor. Nausea kicked again in his stomach; his head drummed, felt light and giddy. The surfaces of his hands were slippery on the knife handle, on the mason jar, and he lowered three times to his haunches to dry the palms on an edge of the nearest rug.

At first the only sound from overhead had been a squeaking of springs as the man up there shifted position on the bed. Then his footfalls had thudded again, heavier, impatient or irritable or both, and there had been the scrape of the window sash being raised. Now, and for the past three or four minutes— utter silence.

Jackman kept expecting the front door to open, the other, bearded man to come stalking inside. It was like waiting for a slow-burning fuse to touch off a powder magazine: sooner or later, you knew it had to happen, and the longer it took, the more sure you were that it would be in the next second. Or the next. Or the next.

Waves of heat shimmered in the room, so thick and so intense they were palpable. Temperature had to be up into the eighties now. Breathing became painful, and his sinuses seemed to clog and swell. Dryness coated his mouth; dripping sweat filled the ridged cracks in both lips and needled there like bee stings. He squatted a fourth time to rub first one palm, then the other over the rough nap of the rug.

When he straightened, the footsteps began again.

This time they didn't stop within the confines of the room. This time they stumped away from the front of the house, into the upstairs hallway—and there was no caution or suspicion in the quick, hard beat of them; there was only annoyance and discomfort. He was coming down, and he was not thinking about anything except the heat.

A rush of adrenaline made Jackman's heart beat conclusively. He pushed back until he felt his buttocks flatten hard against the wall, raised the jar to neck height and held it out away from his body. The cords in his neck bulged like steel rods. Keep coming, keep coming! And the man was on the stairs, hurrying down the stairs with the same lack of suspicion, and Jackman heard him descend the last of the treads and pivot on the foyer floor, heard the congested plaint of his breath; then the Jabberwock started through into the parlor—quick perception of stubbled cheeks and dark hair, the faded image of the symbol on a bare chest, the butt of a handgun above his belt—and Jackman stepped out from the wall and hurled the contents of the jar, hurled the jar, straight into that hard young malignant face.

There was an instant of shocked comprehension before the drain-cleaner splashed into the staring eyes; the jar glanced off the man's chin, dropped away to one side. The sound of its impact with the floor was lost in a guttural scream. He flung his hands up to his face and reeled drunkenly into the parlor and struck an edge of the end table beside the sofa and knocked the lamp there to the floor, came staggering away in a graceless pirouette—all the while tearing animal-like at his wounded eyes.

Jackman went after him and hit him in the small of the back with a lowered shoulder and sent him hurtling forward and into the bar in the far corner. One of the stools spun away and the other clattered into the outer wall, and the man dropped one hand blindly as he started to fall and caught the back edge of the bar, and his weight heaved it backward and then pulled it over and down across his legs as he jarred into the floor. Bottles and glasses shattered, bounced, rolled. The combined explosions of noise rattled the panes in the near window, reverberated hollowly on the heat-thick air.

The man struggled to unpin his legs, seemed then to remember the gun in his belt and groped for it. But Jackman was down on one knee beside him by then, and he got his own hand on the weapon just as the other's fingers touched the butt, wrenched it free. Jabberwock made a frightened keening cry and swung wildly with both arms, like a groggy prizefighter; his eyes were swollen to sightless slits, streaked with tears and drain-cleaner, the skin around them blistered and flaming.

Pent-up hatred seethed through Jackman, twisted his mouth into a grimace. He started to raise the knife—plunge it down into that writhing chest, kill him, kill the Jabberwock. But the moaning cries grated in his ears, and he could smell the sour odor of the man's fear and pain, and the hand trembled and the muscles in his arm refused to unlock: he could not do it, he could not. Meaningless and cold-blooded act now. Aboriginal savagery, man reduced to his lowest common denominator. When you stripped away the veneer of civilization, this was what you saw and this was what you were.

Jackman flung the knife viciously at the wall, sliding back away from more blind frantic swings, and took the gun by its barrel and slammed the butt into the side of the man's head. Grunt of pain, body spasms stilling into twitches; the arms dropped leadenly, and the cries became strangulated whimpers. Jackman tasted brassiness mingled with bile, steeled himself and drove the gun butt down a second time. The twitches and spasms ceased altogether. And the upturned face, in repose, was eyeless—the face of a man out of the Dark Ages whose eyes had been plucked from their sockets and the wounds cauterized with a white-hot iron.

He lurched to his feet, looking away, and dry-retched. Then he stumbled into the foyer and paused beside the door to regain control of his breathing, to search for sounds from outside. There were none. He cracked the door, peered out at the beach, across the veranda at the headland and the front of Jonas' cottage. Sun-washed desertion. Momentary relief pulled a sigh from him; he closed the door and ran back across the parlor.

The waves of heat battered at his body, and he veered to the thermostat and spun the dial back to sixty. Leave it up the way it had been and eventually the furnace would blow. Then he knelt again beside the unconscious man, not looking at the distended face, and began to fumble through the pockets of the Levi's he was wearing.

Luck was riding with Jackman now: he found what looked like a boat key on a metal ring.

Now he could get off the island. *Now* at long bloody last. Checkmate—almost.

Standing, clenching the key in moist fingers, he hesitated. Take the pants too? Time, time. But he would need to wear something when he came in to Weymouth Village, and this one was about his own size; they would fit all right. He made his decision: set the gun and the key down and opened the belt with both hands, opened the Levi's and unzipped them. Glanced furtively over his shoulder, still expecting the front door to burst inward at any second, and then tugged the jeans over the shoes and got them off. Stood up quickly and stepped into them, fastened the button at the top but left the belt ends hanging. Then, gun in one hand, key in the other, he ran once more into the foyer. Listened, eased the door open.

Stillness.

Luck holding, holding.

Jackman retained a breath, threw the door wide and came out running.

Down the porch steps, across the lawn, onto the path that skirted the edge of the cobble beach. His bare feet slapped against the packed earth; the hard glare of the sun dried the oily sweat on his back and face. He swiveled his gaze from the tip of the headland around to the cottage, saw nothing except an unbroken wall of trees, a motionless sweep of grass.

His destination was the dock; he raced out along it, came up hard against the closed boathouse door and fumbled at the knob. Turned it and pulled the door open and stepped inside, closed the door behind him. He stood for a moment in the semidarkness, blinking.

When his eyes adjusted he saw the Jabberwock's boat—a fifteen-foot inboard-outboard—tied to the left-hand walk.

But it was not alone in there: the Chris-Craft, undamaged, was moored opposite.

Jackman was not surprised; he had expected to find both boats. So damned obvious all along, like the purloined letter in the Poe story. He swung down into the inboard-outboard, fitted the key into the dashboard ignition. It was the right one; it slid easily into the slot, and when he turned it the lights in the gasoline gauge and the tachometer came on.

He left the key in the ignition, climbed out onto the walkway, and went to where the long hooked pole lay near the outer doors. Tucked the Jabberwock's gun into the waistband of the Levi's, bent to pick up the pole. Started to turn toward the outer doors.

And the dockside door burst open suddenly and the bearded one, rifle balanced in the crook of one arm, stood framed against the brassy rectangle of sunlight.

□ □ □

There was an instant of frozen shock, and the thought came to Jackman that the bearded man must have been up in the perimeter of the trees, must have seen him make his run from the house; but even while he was thinking that, the momentary paralysis left him and a fresh surge of fury made his reaction immediate and instinctive. He was beyond capitulation, beyond retreat; the gamesman in him was wholly geared to attacking.

He took a firmer grip on the pole, sliding his right hand back on the shaft, planting his left foot, the one pointing toward the Jabberwock. When the bearded man saw him moving he started to snap the rifle out and up, to bring the weapon to bear. Jackman put all his weight on the left foot, pivoted forward.

And hurled the pole like a trackman throwing a javelin.

The bearded man was still partially blinded by the sudden change from glaring light to semigloom, and he did not seem to see the pole until after it left Jackman's hand and came flying toward him; he dodged sharply to his right, half turning, staggering off-balance. The pole just missed his head, sailed past him and out through the open door, clattered on the dock and then skidded off into the bay.

Jackman had started running as soon as he released the pole, fumbling the handgun out of his waistband; but he had no intention of firing it, he had never fired a gun in his life, he thought of it only as a club. He came in on the bearded man before the other could regain his equilibrium, and his wrist and the side of the pistol cracked across the Jabberwock's neck, spun him backward and hard into the wall beside the door. The bearded man made a growling noise, twisted and slashed out with the rifle barrel, and the front sights gouged into Jackman's ribs.

Flare of agony: he gasped and a red mist wheeled behind his eyes. He groped for the rifle and managed to catch hold of it with his free hand and get a fisted grip on the barrel, turning his body on blind impulse away from the muzzle. But the bearded man was stronger, unhurt, and he ripped the rifle free and the sudden movement laid the barrel up on his shoulder, baseball fashion, Jabberwock at the Bat, and he tensed to swing it as he or the one in the house had swung the board last night on the cliffs.

In defensive fury, wielding the handgun, Jackman plunged into him, and there was a moist slapping sound when their chests came together. The rifle barrel cleaved air harmlessly past Jackman's shoulder, but then struck a glancing blow on his right forearm; the pistol slipped out of sweat slick fingers, bounced on the walkway behind them. Jackman heaved up in reflex, under the rifle, and the impact tore it loose, sent it clattering after the pistol; small dull echoes fled through the enclosure.

Jabberwock's fingers dug into the muscles across Jackman's back, wrenched him around. They staggered sideways into the doorway, scraped off the jamb and reeled out onto the dock like a pair of stumble-footed dancers. Jackman kicked at an ankle, felt the heel of his foot strike bone: the bearded man grunted and lurched hard forward, off-balance again. Jackman's sole slid across the edge of the dock, into empty space, and he felt himself toppling over backward, falling with a sickening sensation of weightlessness—and both of them, locked together, plunged down into the crystallike surface of the bay.

Sheets of water mushroomed up around them, consumed them and poured into Jackman's open mouth, into his nose; the icy shock of it constricted his lungs. They tumbled over in a kind of aquatic somersault so that the bearded man was above when the roll ended and their momentum ceased. Through the swirls of white froth, Jackman could see the staring eyes and the distorted face close to his own, as ghastly in the murky light as that of a sea creature. Arms like tentacles slithered over his bare torso, fingers scratched and fumbled at his throat.

He thrashed frantically, parrying, trying to get his legs under him so that he could lunge upward; but weakness and the absence of oxygen made the movements sluggish. Pressure built to a roaring inside his head, seemed to expand it until it felt enormous, ready to burst. Panic assailed him again for the first time since his escape from the fruit cellar.

Air!

One of the grasping hands caught his jaw, hung on with nails gouging. He twisted his neck in a forward quadrant, broke the grip and felt his cheek touch the inside of the bearded man's forearm. Flailed up with his elbow, and there was a solid impact—got him across the breastbone—and the man rolled aside. Desperation gave Jackman the power to pull his legs in, kick them out scissoring, and claw himself upward at an angle like someone climbing a ladder. Fingertips grazed his ankle, slid away—

*Air!*

—and his head broke surface and he shook it and opened his mouth and made a sucking, gasping noise. His chest heaved and then there was a burning pain and his lungs inflated, deflated with a spitting whoosh, inflated again. Salt blurred his vision, but he could see that he had come up directly in front of one of the dock pilings, near where the hooked pole—too light and porous to sink—bobbed on the disturbed surface. He looked wildly toward the beach: too far away, he could not swim fast enough to get clear. Looked back and saw the pole, the pole, and threw out an arm and his fingers closed around it below the metal hook.

Three feet to his left, Jabberwock's head surfaced. And the upper half of the man's body hurtled out of the water in almost the same motion, seal-like, eclipsing the sun at the apex of his lunge.

Jackman had just enough time to drag the pole diagonally across the front of his body, lean back and get the metal hook up like a spearhead before his face.

The bearded man saw the pole and the hook at the last second, tried to wrench away from it—too late. The knobby upper end of the hook caught him just above the bridge of the nose with an audible cracking thud.

Jabberwock went rigid, became a sudden inert weight, and his body drove Jackman under again, drove the pole out of his grasp and down and away from him. He had managed to retain a breath, to get his mouth clamped shut so that no water spilled in; he twisted aside from the weight, pulled his legs under him—and felt the soles of his feet scrape over the rocky bottom just before he kicked upward and through into daylight again. Shallow water, shallow enough for him to stand. And thank God for that: he did not have enough strength left to swim more than a few strokes.

Panting thickly, anchoring the balls of both feet to keep his head clear of the water, Jackman stared over at where the bearded man had gone under. A moment later Jabberwock's naked back appeared in a loose, face-down float. The head did not lift or turn; the body did not move.

Jackman waited—but no one could hold his breath that long, or float with that stillness if he was conscious. Finally he took half a dozen bobbing steps to the other man and slapped weakly at the head with his palm: It wobbled, did not come up. He hoisted it out of the water by the hair, turned it, and the eyes were closed, the mouth contorted into a rictus of pain. There was a pulpy-looking indentation above the nose, where the hook end had struck; ruptured blood vessels beneath the skin stained it with spreading blue-black color.

Dead, Jackman thought. Or was he? Didn't the eyes of a dead man come open and his features go slack?

He rolled the bearded man onto his back, lifted one of the limp arms and felt for a pulse. It was there, faint and irregular. Concussion, then—maybe a skull fracture. It would be a long while before he came around again.

Checkmate.

Tension drained out of Jackman, left him limp and a little dizzy. The Final Game was over now, indisputably finished. *O frabjous day! Callooh, callay....*

□ □ □

He was kneeling on the sun-hot cobbles of the beach, head hanging down, and there was little strength left in his arms. When he raised his head he saw the Jabberwock lying on his back in a nest of seaweed at the water's edge. Jackman vaguely remembered thinking that he couldn't leave the bearded man out in the bay to drown, and then grabbing a handful of the sandy hair, but he could not recall anything about the swim in to the beach. Lost time, timeless time.

He knelt there for a while longer, until he was sure he could move without collapsing. Then he crawled to the bearded man and turned him over with hands that were alternately steady and paroxysmal, opened his belt and pulled it out of the trouser loops. Kneed the body prone again, dragged the arms back and belted them together.

When he searched the pockets he did not find anything at all.

Jackman managed to stand with effort, made his way across the beach and across the path to the nearest of the ornate iron lantern poles jutting out of the lawn. He leaned against it, staring up at the house. The sun's rays dried him, lay across his back like a healing hand; strength flowed back into him slowly. He heard the screaming of seabirds with an acute suddenness that made him realize he had not been hearing anything at all for several minutes.

And something seemed to make a soft creaking sound a long way off, and he turned his head but could not locate the sound. There was not a breath of wind, and the sun-glare was so intense that it created mirages and false shadows. Nothing that could have made the creaking sound. Trick of the mind—?

Soft creaks, he thought.

Yes.

He started walking again, up the slope to the veranda, up the steps to the front door. It stood ajar; he pushed it wide and entered the foyer. It was still oppressively hot in there, but the palpable waves of heat were gone. Through the parlor arch he could see the still form of the first Jabberwock lying in exactly the same position as before, half pinned under the toppled bar.

Jackman turned for the stairs, mounted them deliberately, looked into his old room. Then he pushed open the door to Dale's room, the door to one of the guest rooms. The door to the master bedroom was already standing wide; he went up to it and stared inside.

And kept on staring, leaning against the jamb.

"Hello, Ty," he said, and watched Tracy—the third Jabberwock—get up off the antique four-poster and stand stiffly facing him.

□ □ □

She wore a pair of slacks and a scoop-neck blouse, and her hair was freshly washed, freshly brushed. Artfully applied makeup covered the healing scratches on her cheeks. She looked young and soft—except for her face. It was an emotionless mask, full of age, and the eyes were as empty as abandoned, half-finished houses.

Jackman felt nothing at all, looking at her. No surprise, because he had known for hours that she was alive and might still be on the island; because the soft creaks he had seemed to hear outside were in reality echoes in his memory: those he'd heard when he came up naked through the basement earlier, soft creaks at the center of the house when the Jabberwock's steps had been heavy in Jackman's old room. Nor was there any of the rage, the hatred that he had focused on the other two. He was bereft of emotion; the fight with the one at the boathouse had left him hollow, at least for a while. And maybe that was something to be grateful for.

"I've been waiting for you," Tracy said, and her voice was as empty as her eyes. "It was obvious you'd guessed the truth when the transmitters stopped working properly, and I thought you might come after what happened downstairs. When you didn't, I went down and opened the door and saw the whole thing at the boathouse; I knew you'd come then."

"Why didn't you run and hide?"

"Why should I? I might as well face you now as later."

He came into the room and leaned heavily against the dresser. A feeling of detachment had begun to seep through him. "Transmitters," he said. "Let's see: a crystal-controlled voice transmitter, and some sort of homing bleeper. Sophisticated, long-range, waterproofed. Right? I've read enough reports on electronic surveillance; I should have tumbled long before I did."

She was silent.

"Where were they hidden?" he said.

"You didn't find them?"

"No. I might have if I'd looked for them, but just knowing they existed was enough."

"The voice transmitter was in your belt buckle," she said tonelessly. "The other one was in a shoe heel."

He nodded. "The outfit you gave me before we left Washington."

"Yes. So that was how you guessed the truth—the bugs."

"Partly. It was the only explanation for those two always knowing where we were and where I was—Eider Neck, the barn, the cliffs last night. And it was the only way they could have known about the caves: I had to have told them myself, through conversation with you."

"What else gave it away?"

"The Chris-Craft being stolen, for one. It's not nearly as simple to cross ignition wires on a boat as it is on a car. So it followed they might have had a key, and the only way they could have gotten one was if you'd taken *my* key while I was sleeping Friday night and passed it over. I knew that was the answer when I checked my pockets this morning and didn't find the boat key.

"Then there were the missing axes and hatchets in the barn when we went for the flare pistol. Those things were there Friday night; I saw them hanging on the wall. But all the knives and cleavers had been left here, in the kitchen, so they couldn't have been worried I'd use an ax or a hatchet as a weapon. Which left one answer: I wasn't supposed to escape the barn easily or too soon, because all of you needed time to stage the fake murder and set up the fake severed head and the animal blood.

"I was expected to believe you'd been killed quickly, but when they got me last night all they did was lock me in the cottage cellar. Didn't make sense unless they had no intention of murdering me at all, unless they figured to accomplish their real purpose by leaving me alone there."

He stopped speaking; the words were thick and bitter on his tongue, and he felt he had been talking as if by rote. But he was thinking of the Jabberwock dream, and the subconscious message that Jabberwocks were nothing more than the creations, like things that went wobble-wobble on the walls of the mind, of a nineteenth-century fantasy writer—mythical creatures living in mythical lands and presenting illusory menaces. Of Charlie Pepper, who had taught him about old Mr. Bugbear, and that there was never any reason to be afraid of what you don't know or what you don't understand or what you only think might be. And of the Old Man, from whom he had learned all there was to know about game-playing.

He did not tell her any of these things, because she would not have understood.

She stood motionless, and after a time she gave a short, mirthless little laugh. "Funny," she said. "I thought it was such an airtight scenario—the best thing I'd ever written."

"Oh it was good, clever," he said. "A game that wasn't a game that was a game. A murder that wasn't a murder, a head that wasn't a head. Illusion, misdirection, moves within moves. Careful manipulation too: let me make all the decisions, anticipate my reactions, guide me through the prescribed moves."

She was silent again.

"What I want to know now is who produced it? Not those other two; they're pawns, set pieces like you and all the rest of it."

Imperceptible shrug. "Alan Pennix."

That did not surprise him; nothing anyone did or said would surprise him for a long time. He said only, "Why?"

"Your politics, for one thing."

"That's not enough, even for a man like Pennix."

"There was a girl—he says he loved her."

"Alicia?"

"Alicia. Trite, isn't it?"

He knew what was coming. "She committed suicide, didn't she?" he said.

"Yes. In a town down south somewhere last September. Just before she did it, she called Pennix and told him; he couldn't talk her out of it. She blamed you."

Jackman winced. But he was no longer able to accept that burden of guilt any more than he had been able to accept guilt when he believed Tracy to be dead. It belonged not to him but to the being that had been Alicia, and to the fates that controlled the universe.

He said, "Why this elaborate plot for revenge? Why not something simple, something out of Nixon's bag of tricks maybe?"

"It didn't start out to be elaborate. But Pennix wanted you to suffer. He knew you had emotional problems; he found out somehow that you'd spent two weeks in a private hospital last year."

"And he thought I could be broken."

"Yes."

"So he hired you to get next to me, to set something up."

"Yes."

"Did you really need six months to find a way?"

A shadow passed across her face, vanished again. "There were other opportunities," she said. "But he didn't like any of them. He's a patient man."

And a venal one, Jackman thought. Just like the Old Man.

He said, "Why you?"

"I was balling him—I still am, if that matters—and he bared his soul to me one night. That's all."

"How much did he pay you?"

"I didn't do it for money."

"Then it was just a game to you, is that it?"

"Does that disgust you?"

Yes, he thought. All games disgust me now. "Isn't there anything that touches you, Ty?" he said. "Isn't there anything you care about?"

The shadow came again. "Would you believe me if I said I cared about you as much as I could ever care about anyone? That it was partly my doing Pennix didn't act on any of those other opportunities? That I almost didn't go through with it this weekend, and that I'm not so sorry it turned out the way it has?"

Jackman stared at her.

"No," she said, "I didn't suppose you would. But then, it doesn't matter, does it? It's too late now." Her mouth tightened. "All right, you want to know why I did it? I did it because I live for just one thing, the only thing worth living for. Orgasm. I told you that Friday night. And this was the biggest turn-on of my life; it was something to get off on for *months,* do you understand? Unrelieved ecstasy."

He turned abruptly away from the dresser, went to the doorway on legs that felt swollen and heavy.

Behind him she said, "What are you going to do when you get back to the mainland?" but not as if she really cared.

"To you? Nothing. I don't want revenge; that's for fools like Pennix. All I want is for you to get everything cleaned up out here before Jonas comes back tomorrow—the blood, the props, all of it. That's the way it was supposed to work anyway, wasn't it? No telltale signs to corroborate a madman's story. Just the madman and his mad tale."

Silence.

He looked at her for the last time. "Where's the key to the Chris-Craft? It wasn't on either of the other two."

"In your old room. On the desk."

He turned again.

"Good-bye, David," she said.

Jackman went out without answering, leaving her there alone with her words and her thoughts and her emptiness.

# EPILOGUE

Monday Afternoon, May 25:
THE ISLAND

*Out of life's school of war: What does not destroy me, makes me stronger.*
—NIETZSCHE, *Twilight of the Idols*

The stark white glare of the sun had begun to fade slightly when Jackman came outside, and sharp-edged afternoon shadows were gathering in the island forests. Against the too-blue backdrop of the sky, the tree boughs had a sooty, wilted look. The resin smell, the ocean smell, seemed tainted with the overriding odor of dust and heat.

He walked slowly down to the dock. The man on the beach had not moved, and the sun had baked his naked back to a brick-red color. Far off to the south, a speedboat made figure-eight loops on the smooth face of the sea, trailing plumes of spray. The screeching of the gulls grated in his ears, scraped at nerve ends like fingernails drawn across a blackboard.

When he entered the boathouse he saw the rifle and the handgun lying where they had fallen during the struggle earlier. He picked them up, carried them onto the dock, and threw them one by one into the bay. Then he went back inside and used an emergency oar from the Chris-Craft to open the outer doors. Untied the cruiser's bow and stern lines and stepped down behind the wheel.

For a time he sat limp, resting, in the helmsman's chair. He thought briefly of Tracy, but she was as unfathomable to him as a beautifully carved idol from a culture far removed from his own. Forget her. And forget Alicia. The future was all that mattered now; the past was dead and awaiting burial, and so was the David Jackman who had lived it.

Meg? Well, Meg was part of that dead past. A loveless marriage, a marriage of convenience, had no place in a new beginning. When he got home to Washington, to their redbrick Georgian house in Georgetown, he would have to sit her down and tell her he was ending it.

Pennix? Confront him eventually, make it clear to him that any future attempts at mindless vengeance would result in criminal charges and public exposure. And then make him pay for this weekend in the only way it counted: in the political arena.

Himself, his career? He did not know yet whether he would continue in politics, learn to be a better senator as well as a better man—or finish out his term and then attempt twenty years late to pursue the dreams of his college years, the promise of I, *Camera, Eye*. Time would determine the choice, and make it the right one; time would determine everything.

He roused himself at length and started the cruiser's engine. Backed the boat out into the bay and swung it in a tight arc and took it out toward the breakwater at quarter throttle.

When he passed the tip of Eider Neck he looked back at the house, the cottage, the barn—and saw them now through different eyes, in a wholly different perspective. They were no longer the intimate, beckoning monuments of the sweet (but not so sweet) summers of his youth; instead there was about them an atmosphere of subtle decay, of false and grotesque nostalgia, like mausoleums in an old pastoral graveyard. The silhouetted forestland and the long grassy hump of the Neck and the broad flat sea and the ascendant land that marked the cliffs seemed alien to him: he felt no communion with them now, no sense of need or love or joy, no sense of a good high place on which a man could stand and perhaps learn to touch infinity.

This was Jackman Island, nothing more, and the Jackman to which it had belonged from the beginning was the Old Man—in the flesh and in the spirit. It was never mine, he thought; I never possessed any of it. Once, he might have claimed it for his own, but that time was long gone, had been forfeited through weakness and self-delusion. When he had discovered himself, he had lost the island forever: he could never return to it again.

He put his back to it and pointed the cruiser toward the eye of the westering sun.

## THE END

# BILL PRONZINI BIBLIOGRAPHY

**Non-Series Suspense Novels:**

The Stalker (Random House, 1971)

Panic! (Random House, 1972)

A Run in Diamonds (as by Alex Saxon; Pocket Books, 1973)

Snowbound (Putnam's, 1974)

Games (Putnam's, 1976)

Masques (Arbor House, 1981)

Day of the Moon (with Jeffrey Wallmann as by William Jeffrey; Robert Hale, 1983)

The Eye (with John Lutz; Mysterious Press, 1984)

Beyond the Grave (with Marcia Muller; Walker, 1986)

The Lighthouse (with Marcia Muller; St. Martin's, 1987)

With an Extreme Burning (Carroll & Graf, 1994; also published as The Tormentor, Leisure, 2000)

Blue Lonesome (Walker, 1995)

A Wasteland of Strangers (Walker, 1997)

Nothing But the Night (Walker, 1999)

In an Evil Time (Walker, 2001)

Step to the Graveyard Easy (Walker, 2002)

The Alias Man (Walker, 2004)

The Crimes of Jordan Wise (Walker, 2006)

**"Nameless Detective" Novels:**

The Snatch (Random House, 1972)

The Vanished (Random House, 1973)

Undercurrent (Random House, 1973)

Blowback (Random House, 1977)

Twospot (with Colin Wilcox; Putnam's, 1978)

Labyrinth (St. Martin's, 1980)

Hoodwink (St. Martin's, 1981)

Scattershot (St. Martin's, 1982)

Dragonfire (St. Martin's, 1982)

Bindlestiff (St. Martin's, 1983)

Quicksilver (St. Martin's, 1984)

Double (with Marcia Muller; St. Martin's, 1984)

Nighshades (St. Martin's, 1984)

Bones (St. Martin's, 1985)

Deadfall (St. Martin's, 1986)

Shackles (St. Martin's, 1988)

Jackpot (Delacorte, 1990)

Breakdown (Delacorte, 1991)

Quarry (Delacorte, 1992)

Epitaphs (Delacorte, 1992)

Demons (Delacorte, 1993)

Hardcase (Delacorte, 1995)

Sentinels (Carroll & Graf, 1996)

Illusions (Carroll & Graf, 1997)

Boobytrap (Carroll & Graf, 1998)

Crazybone (Carroll & Graf, 2000)

Bleeders (Carroll & Graf, 2002)

Spook (Carroll & Graf, 2003)

Nightcrawlers (Tor/Forge, 2005)

Mourners (Tor/Forge, 2006)

Savages (Tor/Forge, 2007)

Fever (Tor/Forge, 2008 [forthcoming])

Phantoms (Tor/Forge, 2009 [forthcoming])

## Mainstream Novel:

The Cambodia File (with Jack Anderson; Doubleday, 1981)

## Mysteries as by Jack Foxx:

The Jade Figurine (Bobbs-Merrill, 1972)

Dead Run (Bobbs-Merrill, 1975)

Freebooty (Bobbs-Merrill, 1976)

Wildfire (Bobbs-Merrill, 1978)

## Suspense Novels with Barry N. Malzberg:

The Running of Beasts (Putnam's, 1976)

Acts of Mercy (Putnam's, 1977)

Night Screams (Playboy Press, 1979)

Prose Bowl (St. Martin's, 1980)

## Mystery Short-Story Collections:

Casefile: The Best of the "Nameless Detective" Stories (St. Martin's, 1983)

Graveyard Plots (St. Martin's, 1985)

Small Felonies (St. Martin's, 1988)

Stacked Deck (Pulphouse, 1991)

Carmody's Run (Dark Harvest, 1992)

Spadework: "Nameless Detective" Stories (Crippen & Landru, 1996)

Duo (with Marcia Muller; Five-Star, 1998)

Carpenter and Quincannon (Crippen & Landru, 1998)

Sleuths (Five-Star, 1999)

Night Freight (Leisure, 2000)

Oddments (Five-Star, 2000)

More Oddments (Five-Star, 2001)

Scenarios: A "Nameless Detective" Casebook (Five-Star, 2003)

Problems Solved (with Barry N. Malzberg; Crippen & Landru, 2003)

Burgade's Crossing (Five-Star, 2003)

Quincannon's Game (Five-Star, 2005)

## Western Novels:

Duel at Gold Buttes (with Jeffrey Wallman as by William Jeffrey; Tower, 1981)

Border Fever (with Jeffrey Wallman as by William Jeffrey; Leisure, 1983)

The Gallows Land (Walker, 1983)

Starvation Camp (Doubleday, 1984)

Quincannon (Walker, 1985)

The Last Days of Horse-Shy Halloran (M. Evans, 1987)

The Hangings (Walker, 1989)

Firewind (M. Evans, 1989)

## Western Short-Story Collections:

The Best Western Stories of Bill Pronzini (Ohio University Press, 1990)

All the Long Years: Western Stories (Five-Star, 2001)

Coyote and Quarter-Moon (Five-Star, 2006)

Crucifixion River (with Marcia Muller; Five-Star, 2007)

## Science Fiction Collection:

On Account of Darkness and Other SF Stories (with Barry N. Malzberg; Five-Star, 2004)

**Non-Fiction Books:**

Gun in Cheek
(Coward McCann, 1982)

1001 Midnights: The Aficionado's
Guide to Mystery and Detective
Fiction (with Marcia Muller;
Arbor House, 1986)

Son of a Gun in Cheek
(Mysterious Press, 1987)

Sixgun in Cheek
(Crossover Press, 1997)